I Never Said I Was Conor

Waking Up In Howth

Ian R Forman

Published by New Generation Publishing in 2021

Copyright © Ian R Forman 2021

First Edition

The author asserts the moral right under the Copyright, Designs and Patents Act 1988 to be identified as the author of this work.

All Rights reserved. No part of this publication may be reproduced, stored in a retrieval system or transmitted, in any form or by any means without the prior consent of the author, nor be otherwise circulated in any form of binding or cover other than that in which it is published and without a similar condition being imposed on the subsequent purchaser.

Paperback ISBN: 978-1-80031-455-9
Hardback ISBN: 978-1-80031-454-2
Ebook ISBN: 978-1-80031-453-5

www.newgeneration-publishing.com

New Generation Publishing

Chapter 1

I was slowly becoming aware, though I wasn't yet ready to open my eyes. I often played this game when I awoke alone, in some strange bed. I always knew when I wasn't in my own bed, but which city and which hotel? I liked to lie motionless for a few moments, eyes closed but ears and mind alert to any tell-tale background noises. I would slowly begin to remember the events of the evening before and step by step recover full consciousness. Only when I think I know where I am, do I open my eyes. If the room is still in darkness I would reach for the light switch. If the switch wasn't where I expected it to be, I would close my eyes again and think some more. This way, I seldom got out of bed in a strange room!

Right now, I knew that I was lying uncomfortably on a hard surface. I could hear seagulls 'screeching' angrily and water lapping gently. I could feel light drizzle falling on my face and a cool sea breeze chilling the tips of my ears. The dull traffic noise seemed to hypnotise my brain.

I knew I was out in the open and I knew I was in Howth!

I opened my eyes. I think the rain must have woken me, as I wasn't really wet -through yet. The kids had already given up on kicking football and moved on to do some mischief elsewhere.

I opened my i-Phone to check the time, five-fifteen. Shit! I must have slept for quite a while. No harm done though, luckily, I still had about half an hour to get back to the Marine Hotel, in Sutton Cross. Good job the rain woke me up when it did!

Best to get back to the car quickly, I thought, as I stood up, and lifting my light grey rain-jacket from the bench, I slipped it over my head. The feather-weight jacket had been a useful but uncomfortable pillow for the last hour or so. I felt really good, no ill effects from the migraine, and no feeling of drowsiness from the Co-Codamol tablet, which I had taken earlier. The extended nap had worked wonders. As I looked around, I couldn't put my finger on it, everything seemed the same but somehow different. I even thought that the front door of the yacht club had been re-painted primrose from dark blue. I thought about walking over to see if the paint was still wet, but no time to waste, need to get back to my car.

The car park seemed smaller than earlier and the cars looked different. I did not recognise some of the models parked there. No sign of my Hyundai Santa Fe. No more than fifteen or twenty cars parked there and none of them was mine! I walked around the car park several times with an ever-increasing sense of panic!

Car definitely not there! Maybe I didn't park it there, perhaps over at one of the spaces at the top of the east pier. Started walking, gradually increasing my pace until I was finally jogging. No, not there either!

Ok, don't panic, stay cool, sit down and think!

Although the drizzle had stopped by now, I didn't want to sit on the nearby damp park bench so I stood behind it and bending forwards, I rested both of my hands on the back support. I bowed my head forward, to try to block out the world and I let out a long slow gasp. I stood there with my eyes closed for several seconds. I started to pant, it felt as though my heart was bursting out of my chest. I was starting to shiver but my hands were 'clammy' and I could feel a trickle of cold sweat running down my back.

I took a good look around me. I felt very uncomfortable. The tied-up small colourful sailing boats were still bobbing up and down on the agitated water. I took several loud deep breaths. I needed to get my heart to stop pounding!

Not many people around and I didn't recognize anyone, but this was not unusual as more than forty years had passed since I first left Howth.

I must have appeared to be panic stricken because some of the people walking by stopped and stared at me. Two of them turned and took a step towards me, with concern written all over their weather-beaten faces. The older of the two, a well-built man about six-foot tall, with a mop of greying hair and clean shaven, stood right in front of me. He looked a little younger than me, maybe sixty or so. The second man was a little shorter and looked to be in his mid-thirties. He had a head of jet-black shoulder length hair, which still appeared to be wet from the earlier shower. Neither of them seemed to bother with either rain coats or hats, both wore matching blue denim jackets and jeans. They seemed to know each other well, could maybe be father and son? The younger man stood hesitantly slightly behind his 'dad'. 'Dad' looked straight at me, but not at all in a threatening way.

"Are you ok, are you lost?" he asked quietly.

"No, not at all," I blurted out, "but I can't seem to find my car, and I've looked everywhere. I think it must have been stolen."

"Very unusual for cars to get stolen these days, they're so easily tracked, did you leave any valuables inside?"

"Well yes, two sets of fairly new golf clubs, but they were locked in the boot. Guess that's the end of our planned golf for Monday now," I tried to sound relaxed.

"Also, I stupidly left my rucksack on the back seat. It has our passports and our return ferry tickets to Holyhead in the front pocket. It also has my i-Pad inside. My wife will be really pissed off with me for being so careless."

"Oh dear, where do you think you parked your car," asked the 'son'.

"I thought I'd parked it over there in the main car park," I responded, as I lifted my left arm and pointed back along the promenade.

"Ok, let's not panic yet," said 'Dad', "we know this area well, would you like us to help you find it, Mr ??"

"Forman, Ian Forman," I replied.

"Well-known name around here, is Forman, with or without an 'e'," asked the 'son'.

"Without," I smiled.

"Well, I'm Paddy and this is my son Jamie," said dad, as he held out his hand.

"Pleased to meet you both, and yes, if it's not too much trouble, I think I could use your help even though I also know the area quite well, or at least I think I do."

I walked around the bench to shake their hands, nice reassuring handshakes from both Paddy and Jamie, neither of them felt the need to squeeze my hand so tightly as to send a bolt of pain through my arthritic fingers, thank God. We all headed off to where I thought I had parked.

"What type of car is it?" asked Jamie, as we walked quickly along the concrete promenade.

I somehow felt a little better now, but knew that would all change as soon as I called my wife Mary. If the car has been stolen, at least it's insured and we can always hire a car in the meantime. I was trying hard to calm myself down!

"It's a silver Hyundai, a Santa Fe, with an English registration," I said quickly.

"Santa Fe, did you say, can't say I know that make, do you know it Jamie?"

"No, I'm afraid I don't know it either, mustn't be available in Ireland yet," replied Jamie.

I began to now think, that there was definitely something very odd about both Paddy and Jamie because I had seen an identical silver Santa Fe, as I drove from Sutton Cross to Howth and I think I also saw another one on the car ferry from Holyhead to Dublin, earlier that day.

I decided however to 'keep stum' as we approached the car park.

We checked every car in the car park, no sign of my car!

"Ian, I think you had better report the matter to the police, do you know where the police station is?" asked Paddy.

"I first better call my wife to give her the bad news, we are supposed to be going to my older brother's seventieth birthday 'bash' tonight, she will be in a right panic but I suppose we can get a taxi to the party in Malahide tonight and sort out a rental car tomorrow. Hopefully my insurance company will cover the cost," I replied, "and yes, I should know where the police station is, I used to live right next to it, many years ago," I added.

"Ok then, we will leave you to it, and good luck with explaining it all to your wife," said Jamie with a wink.

I thanked them and off they wandered back towards the east pier. So, they had really gone out of their way to try to help me find my car!

I opened my mobile and scrolled down to Mary Forman, mobile.

Clicked on her name, no response!

Then I noticed that I had no signal, oh shit, just what I needed!

I considered running after Paddy and Jamie to borrow a phone, but they had already gone out of sight. Thought it best to make my way to the police station, I'm sure they will allow me to make a phone call.

With a great sense of urgency, I walked quickly along the promenade and a few minutes later I walked up Carey's Steps.

The huge austere grey police station still stood imposingly, right at the crossroads of Main Street and 'The Back Road'. I had often wondered why such a large police building was needed for such a tiny village like Howth, but I was grateful for its presence right now. I thought how I'd lived not one hundred and fifty yards from its outer walls for twenty-four years and had never gone through the front door. I couldn't believe that I felt a bit nervous and for a moment considered walking the couple of hundred yards past the station and knock on my cousin Tishy's door instead, but knew I had to report the theft asap. I would call on Tishy and Ronnie afterwards, perhaps Ronnie would offer me a lift back to the hotel. Although we hadn't really kept in touch, Ronnie and Tishy were always welcoming when I visited, wished I could remember their children's names, so I could ask about them. Wished now that I had called on them when I last visited Howth about two years ago, must be close to six years since I last dropped in unannounced on them, I hadn't heard otherwise so I assumed everyone was still ok.

Anyway, that was for later, I was now through the door of the police station and standing in front of a high wooden counter which was 'L' shaped and filled almost one whole side of the room. Behind the counter was an opening with a door ajar about forty-five degrees, opened inwards. No one in sight but I could hear voices coming from inside the room. I pushed the plunger on the circular bell and was startled by the very loud 'ding' that echoed around the empty room. A large but friendly looking man, in a navy-blue police uniform and a matching peaked cap, came through the door and looked straight into my eyes. He didn't really look 'stern enough' to be a policeman, looked more like a friendly social worker.

"Good-day to you sir, and what can I do for you? If you don't mind me saying so, you look like you need help," he said, with a heavy Kerry accent.

"I've come to report my car missing, looked everywhere, it must have been stolen. But first I need to call my wife, she will be expecting me back at the Marine hotel about now and I'm unable to get a signal on my mobile," I blurted out.

I looked at my mobile again, still no network available!

"Oh dear, you'd better contact your wife before we do anything else, you can use that phone over there on the end of the desk. Do you have her phone number with you?" he asked.

"I don't remember it but I have her mobile number plumbed into my mobile," I smiled.

I looked up Mary's mobile number on my contacts and dialed it using the police phone. Nothing! The line seemed dead. Then I remembered I needed to put the prefix for international and then for the UK.

I dialed the full number, trying my best to stay relaxed.....

00 44 7603 ******. Heard a few bleeps and then the message "sorry but this number has not been recognized, please check and try again."

I tried again, same message.

"Sorry officer, I can't think straight, is this phone able to call an English mobile number?"

"Sergeant Murphy at your service, Mr ...."

"Forman, Ian Forman," I said, as patiently as I could.

I thought that my blood pressure must have been 'off the scale' by then, I took a couple of deep breaths.

Sergeant Murphy raised his eyebrows in surprise as he confirmed that he thought that his phone was in perfect working order.

"Perhaps your wife is having the same problem with her mobile as you are having," he said, trying to be helpful.

I could again feel my heart pounding in my chest and Sergeant Murphy must have seen I was in distress, as he asked me to come behind the counter and to take a seat in the back office.

I 'plonked' down on a large brown leather armchair, which almost embarrassingly gave out a 'wheeze' as I sank into it. The only other officer in the room, a youngster who looked no more than seventeen or eighteen years of age, but was probably twenty–five or thirty, stood up from his chair, where he had been sitting behind a badly scratched green steel desk, typing something into his laptop.

"Garda Moore," said Sergeant Murphy, "please meet Mr. Ian Forman."

Garda Moore was 'impossibly' tall, especially for an Irishman. He looked more like a Dutchman, very thin but standing at least six feet four inches tall, in his 'size thirteen' black boots. I stood up to shake hands with him. He seemed to take just two strides to reach my chair.

"Pleasure to meet you Mr. Forman, are you from around here or are you just visiting?" enquired Garda Moore.

Garda Moore had a friendly face but with a strong square jaw. He had his policeman's uniform on, but without the cap. His short reddish curly hair, which probably never needed combing, framed his pale fresh complexion. He spoke quietly in a gentle Howth accent, very recognisable.

"We will get to that in a minute Mick, we first need to quickly contact Mr Forman's wife, she might be starting to get worried about where Mr Forman is," said the sergeant, quietly taking charge of the situation.

"Where did you say you were staying Mr Forman? You mentioned the

Marine .."

"Yes, it's the Marine Hotel, in Sutton, room 402," I replied, as I fumbled for and eventually pulled the hotel room key card from my wallet and handed it to him.

He picked up his phone and started to dial the phone number which was printed on the card.

Chapter 2

"What did you say your wife's name was again, Mr Forman?" asked the sergeant.

"It's Mary, Mary Forman. We booked in this morning for five nights," I replied.

I could hear the phone ringing and then a girl's voice 'sing'.

"Good afternoon, Marine Hotel, Felicity speaking, can I help you?"

"Yes, I'm sure you can," said the sergeant as he glanced reassuringly at me.

"This is Sergeant Murphy from Howth Garda station, can you please check to see if you can locate Mrs Mary Forman? She's staying there with her husband in room 402," asked the sergeant, as he glanced at the key card.

"Oh dear," exclaimed the receptionist, "is anything wrong sergeant?"

"No, not at all, please see if you can locate her while I hold on, and just tell her that her husband is on the phone," said the sergeant in a controlled, steady, and authoritative voice.

"Ok, I'll try her room number first, you did say room 402, didn't you, please hold on."

The sergeant said nothing but instead nodded his head to confirm, as if the receptionist could see him.

It seemed like an eternity passed before Felicity came back on the phone.

"I'm sorry but a Mrs O'Keefe answered the phone in room 402, she is staying there with her young daughter Helen, for just one night. I checked the register and it's correct. I took a while to get back to you because I also checked the bookings for all our rooms. I'm afraid that we don't appear to have a Mr and Mrs Forman booked in. Is it possible they booked in under another name, or at another hotel maybe?"

The receptionist was trying her best to be helpful.

"No, it's definitely the Marine and it's definitely room 402, I have the key card here in my hand," said the sergeant slowly and clearly, whilst trying to disguise his obvious impatience.

He glanced at me with his eyebrows raised.

"Why the hell would we book in under a different name, and how on earth is there someone else in our room, she has really cocked up big time," I shouted out loud, in frustration.

I looked at the clock on the station wall in front of me, Christ it's already after six o'clock!

"You seem to have a problem Felicity," said the sergeant, "have you any way to make a general announcement, has anyone come to you asking about her husband or is anyone waiting in reception?"

The sergeant's rapid-fire questioning seemed to throw the receptionist into a panic.

"No, no one has and there's nobody hanging about in reception. What does she look like?" Felicity asked, in a quivering voice.

"Ok, let's not waste any more time, we'll be with you in less than ten minutes," said the sergeant, as he slammed his phone down.

"C'mon Mr Forman, I'm giving you a lift to your hotel. Mick, will you take care of the shop for a few minutes. I will jot down the details about the stolen car when we get to the hotel and after we locate Mrs Forman," said the sergeant, as he grabbed the keys of his squad car.

It probably took just six or seven minutes to get to the Marine but it seemed like hours. The sergeant drove like he was in a stock car race and despite his attempts at small talk, I did not feel like engaging in any conversation.

He parked right in front of the main door, in front of the NO PARKING sign and in one movement was out of the car. We slammed the car doors shut as we took off.

Felicity was waiting for us, just inside the door. She was standing beside a short, plump and balding man of about forty, who was dressed in a dark-grey wrinkled suit, which had seen better days. Felicity was just what I imagined, in her mid-twenties, long blond tied back hair and a worried, but not unattractive, oval face. She was dressed in a dark-grey trouser suit, which unlike her manager's, was immaculately laundered.

The man introduced himself and held out his hand to shake ours.

"Hello, I'm Pete Walsh, I'm the general manager here, what seems to be the problem sergeant?"

"We're trying to locate Mr Forman's wife Mary," said Sergeant Murphy in that, now familiar, controlled manner of his. "We know they are staying in room 402, look I have the room key-card here."

"That's very strange sergeant, can I take a look at that card?" asked the manager.

"I can see that this is a key card to room 402 at this hotel, but it's not like our other key cards, where did you get it from?" asked the manager, in a puzzled manner.

He went behind the counter and took a blank key card from under the counter and showed it to us. We all looked at the key card in complete silence.

The card was different. It was red and white rather than green and white!

"Is Bernadette still here?" I asked hurriedly. "We checked in with her earlier this afternoon, she gave us two keys, my wife Mary has the other one," I said in a raised voice.

The manager looked at Felicity, who shrugged her shoulders, before turning back to Sergeant Murphy and slowly stating, matter-of-factly:

"We do not have anyone called Bernadette working here and like my colleague Felicity said, we do not have a Mr and Mrs Forman checked in here. I have gone through the records myself, you must be mistaken Mr Forman. Would you care to look at the register yourself?" he asked, as he turned the computer screen around to face us.

I could hardly read the names on the screen, my mind was in a 'whirl' and my eyes just couldn't focus. Sergeant Murphy scoured the screen for what seemed an eternity, then looked at the previous day's entries and then back to today's page. He looked at me with a puzzled look and shrugged his shoulders. He then scrolled back to Thursday and started reading out the names of everyone listed, right through to the present time.

I felt weak and sick to my stomach, I stumbled the few steps to the huge bottle- green upholstered armchair in the corner next to the front door and collapsed in despair.

What the hell was going on? Was this a nightmare?

I forced myself to pinch the back of my left hand …….. I'm afraid I didn't wake up!

Had I gone mad? Had I gone senile?

Had the water, which I got in the pub earlier, been spiked?

Sergeant Murphy tried his best to take control of the situation.

"Why don't we see if Mr Forman's key-card opens room 402," he said encouragingly.

Felicity went back to her reception duties and we quickly walked up the badly worn red and green carpeted stairs and along the corridor until we were outside room 402.

The manager knocked on the door, and stood back expectantly.

"Who's there?" came a woman's voice from the other side of the white painted door.

"Hi, Mrs O'Keefe, this is Pete Walsh, the general manager. Can we have a word please?" he asked, in a polite, apologetic tone.

We heard the door being unlocked. Mrs O'Keefe opened the door slowly, leaving the security chain in place. She peered at us through the gap, quickly closed the door and then opened it again.

"What's the problem?" she asked in a high-pitched quizzical tone.

"Would you mind if we came inside for a moment or two, Mrs O'Keefe?" asked Sergeant Murphy. "There is no problem, we just want to talk to you for a moment."

Mrs O'Keefe did not reply, she just turned and walked inside and sat down on the edge of one of the two single beds. We all entered the room slowly and the manager closed the door behind us. The bed looked as though she had been lying on it just before we knocked, perhaps she had been taking a nap but more likely she had been reading the Saturday Independent, which was strewn on the green carpet, between the two single beds.

Mrs O'Keefe suddenly looked panicked, her carefully made up face, a picture of alarm. A self-assured woman, probably in her mid-thirties, dressed in a designer mauve trouser suit with white mid height sandals. With her blond hair brushed back off her forehead, she appeared dressed to go out to dinner. She looked straight into the sergeant's eyes, with their faces level, just inches apart.

"Oh my God, it's Helen isn't it, what's happened to her, what has she done, is she ok?" Mrs O' Keefe was clearly distraught.

Sergeant Murphy quickly placed his right hand on Mrs O'Keefe's shoulder as he explained to her that he was not there to talk about her daughter Helen.

"Where is Helen, by the way?" asked the sergeant.

Mrs O'Keefe then hurriedly told us that Helen should be back soon from her short swim in the indoor pool.

Without giving any information away or explaining that we were actually trying to locate my wife Mary, Sergeant Murphy 'chatted' to Mrs O' Keefe and established that she and her daughter Helen had driven up from Kildare that morning and had checked into the Marine Hotel at about lunchtime. They spent the afternoon relaxing, and now planned to take a taxi to go to the traditional Irish dinner and entertainment evening at the Abbey Tavern, in Howth. The conversation was restricted to just Mrs O'Keefe and the sergeant, neither the manager nor I asked anything, which might have disrupted the flow.

I had stopped listening anyway, my mind in a state of total confusion, my legs weak. We took our leave of Mrs O'Keefe. I can't recall if any of us bothered to thank her or to apologise for the intrusion.

After he closed the bedroom door behind us, Sergeant Murphy tried my room key-card in the door. It didn't open the door and we were all startled when Mrs O'Keefe suddenly opened the door again.

Down in reception, Sergeant Murphy led me back to the green armchair and almost pushed me into it. He asked the manager to bring me a glass of water. I slowly drank the water. My eyes could no longer focus. I was aware that there were several people laughing and joking as they checked in at reception, but I could not make out a word of what they were saying or laughing about, everything seemed just like background noise.

Sergeant Murphy thanked Mr Walsh as he guided me out through the hotel doors. The Garda car was still parked where we had left it. We both sat down in the car and pulled our doors shut.

We sat there in silence for a minute or so.

"Maybe she took a taxi to her sister Ann's flat." I was now clutching at straws.

"Does Mary's sister live nearby?" asked Sergeant Murphy, trying to sound interested and enthusiastic, but not very convincingly.

"Yes, it's just a couple of miles from here, on Baldoyle Road," I replied.

"Do you know the exact address?" asked Sergeant Murphy.

I explained that I did not have the address but I knew exactly where the flat was. We always visited Ann when we came to Ireland, she is Mary's only sister. I told Sergeant Murphy more about Ann as we drove. I told him that she was six or seven years older than Mary and that she lived alone, her husband had died several years previously.

We soon pulled up in the small car park. There was nowhere to park, but no problem, Sergeant Murphy parked right outside the main door. I explained to Sergeant Murphy that it would be better if I went in alone, Ann would panic if she saw a policeman standing outside the apartment block. She would recognise me in the camera and then I would give the sergeant 'the nod'.

I pushed the white buzzer for apartment No 6, took a step back and waited, shifting my weight from one foot to the other but being careful to keep my eyes fixed on the overhead camera. After quite a lengthy wait, Ann finally answered.

"Hello, can I help you?" Ann asked, in what seemed to me to be a slightly nervous tone.

"Hi Ann, is Mary there?" I asked, doing my best to appear relaxed and calm.

"Sorry, who is this?" she asked. "I think you might have the wrong address."

"It's me Ann, it's Ian. I know we said we would call on you tomorrow but I wondered if Mary is with you?" I asked, in a slightly panicky way.

Ann got cut off. I pressed the buzzer again, waited a minute or so, no response. I pressed it again and this time a man answered.

"Yes, can I help you?" asked a man, a little impatiently.

I recognised Tom's voice straight away. Tom had been Ann's boyfriend for quite a few years now, we had spent a couple of holidays together in Tenerife and both he and Ann had visited us together, in Buckingham, UK, several times. It was reassuring to hear Tom's voice.

"Hi Tom, it's me, Ian. Sorry to disturb you, but I'm trying to track down Mary, I think she's trying to lose me," I said, in what I hoped sounded like a light-hearted way.

"You must have the wrong address, I don't know who you are but there is no one called Mary here," said Tom.

"Tom, please don't muck about, I'm really very worried now. My car has been stolen and we are supposed to be at my brother Peter's party very soon. I've no idea where Mary is, I've looked everywhere and she is not answering her mobile. Please let me in and I will explain. I left her at the Marine Hotel earlier today and haven't seen her since," I said pleadingly.

"Look, whoever you are, we can't help you, there's no one called Mary here. You've got the wrong address. Good night," said Tom sternly and he hung up.

I pressed the buzzer again, no answer. I walked back to the car, opened the door and 'plonked' down in the passenger seat.

"They're hiding something. They won't let me in," I said, as I looked straight ahead out of the windscreen.

"Who won't let you in, is Ann not there?" asked Sergeant Murphy.

"Yes, she's there ok, she's with her boyfriend Tom, but there is something strange going on. They pretended not to know me, I told them I didn't think it was funny but they just hung up. I don't know if Mary is there or not, I think Ann and Tom know something but they don't want to tell me," I said slowly, without looking at Sergeant Murphy.

"Ok, let me have a word with them, they will soon realise this is not a joke. Please wait here till I come back," said Sergeant Murphy, as he got out of the car.

"Apartment six," I shouted after him.

I watched him, as he stood in the porch, in front of the double glass door. I saw him press the buzzer and stand back. I could see him speaking but he was too far away from me to hear the conversation. I then saw him take something from his pocket and hold it up to the camera, I guess it was his ID badge.

Sergeant Murphy then disappeared inside, looking back to make sure the glass doors closed behind him. He saw me looking straight at him and gave me the 'thumbs up'.

He was gone only for a couple of minutes but just as I was about to follow him, he appeared at the car door. He got in, without saying a word and started the engine.

"Well".... I said, in an expectant tone.

"Mary is definitely not there, Ann hasn't spoken to her for several weeks," explained Sergeant Murphy.

"Best we go back to the station and make some phone calls. I have already called Garda Moore, to give him an update," added Sergeant Murphy.

Chapter 3

Back at the police station the atmosphere had changed from friendly to business-like. Sergeant Murphy went behind the counter and motioned for me to stand right in front of the counter, facing him. His face took on a serious and almost angry expression. Garda Moore sensed the mood and quickly retreated into the back room.

"Ok Mr Forman, or whoever you are, just what is going on here?" he stated slowly and sternly through clenched teeth.

"That's exactly what I'm trying to understand, what the hell is going on here?" I replied in a whisper.

"Ok, let's start at the beginning" said the sergeant as he took a blank police report form from under the counter.

"What is your full name and address?" he asked in a bored tone.

"As I said earlier, my name is Ian Raymond Forman, without an 'e'."

I continued to answer all of the sergeant's questions in a slow deliberate manner, to allow him enough time to write everything down.

I explained that I lived with my wife Mary in a town called Buckingham, in the UK, giving him my post code, my home and mobile phone numbers and my e-mail address. I told him that I was born and brought up in Howth and that Mary was from Clontarf, near Dublin City. We had emigrated just after we were married in July 1973.

"So, have you been living in Buckingham since 1973 then?" he asked.

"No, it's a long story which I won't bore you with now, but we lived in Canada for a couple of years and then in Belgium for another ten years." I replied.

"Ok, don't bore me then, but what are you doing here in Howth now?" he asked.

I explained that Mary and I were back for a few days to go to my brother's seventieth birthday party, which was being held at Oscar Taylors in Malahide that night. All my relations would be there, my younger brother Patrick had even travelled from Chicago, with his wife Susan, to attend.

"Oscar Taylors you say, at what time?" he asked.

"The party has probably already begun. I'm sure Mary and the others will be wondering where I am. They'll probably think I'm drinking somewhere and have lost track of time!" I replied.

Sergeant Murphy left me standing at the counter on my own and walked quickly into the back room, closing the door behind him. I rested my two elbows on the counter top and sunk my worried face into my trembling sweaty palms. When would this nightmare end? Would it have a happy ending? How could it have a happy ending now?

The sergeant returned several minutes later, this time accompanied by

Garda Moore. They both stood behind the counter, Garda Moore with a puzzled look on his face and Sergeant Murphy with a smirk on his face.

"Look Mr 'whoever you are', why don't you stop bullshitting us, tell us who you are and why you are wasting our time?" asked the sergeant. "We are busy people and don't have time to waste on jokers, so start talking sense or get out of here before I arrest you for wasting police time!" he added in a raised voice.

"I'm not wasting your time, I've explained everything, why can't you help me?" I exclaimed. "I'm beginning to think I've gone insane"

"That's just what we are thinking. You want us to find your non-existing wife Mary, your so-called sister-in-law has never heard of you, you did not check into the Marine Hotel this morning and we've checked and there is no such car model as a Hyundai Santa Fe. To top it all off, I have just spoken on the phone to Peter Forman, who I personally know quite well and who you claim is your brother. For your information, he is right now enjoying a birthday dinner with his family at home, not as you claim, partying at Oscar Taylor's. Also surprise surprise, he does not have a brother called Ian Forman. In fact, he was very upset that someone was now standing in front of me claiming to be his brother Ian!"

My head felt light, I could feel myself slumping against the counter and my legs turned to jelly. Sergeant Murphy was smiling but Garda Moore looked concerned and ran from behind the counter to catch me before I hit the floor. I was half-carried into the back office and I collapsed onto the large red leather armchair. Silence descended on the room as Sergeant Murphy handed me a large blue mug of scalding hot white tea. I tried to take a sip. It was 'poisoned' with sugar but it was what I needed.

Sergeant Murphy broke the silence.

"You don't happen to have any photo ID on you, by any chance," he asked.

I opened my wallet and handed him my HSBC credit and debit cards, my membership card for my golf club and my MK Dons football season membership card.

He studied them for several seconds and then asked..

"Have you anything with a photo on it, driving licence perhaps?"

"No, I'm afraid not, my passport is in my rucksack, which I left in my stolen car and I don't yet have a photo driving licence," I replied sheepishly.

"Do you have any cash with you Mr Forman," he asked.

I handed the sergeant my wallet and invited him to take a look at whatever he wanted to. He pulled out several Euro bank-notes, I must have had a few hundred in total. I sipped on my tea as Sergeant Murphy seemed to spend a long time examining the bank notes, which I couldn't understand since they were not at all unusual, except maybe for the fifty Euro bank-note.

"Where did you get this 'funny money' from?" asked Sergeant Murphy.

I could tell from his tone that he wasn't expecting an answer, so I didn't respond.

"Look, I'm sorry if I came on a little strong earlier, I can see you are upset and perhaps confused. Would it be ok with you if I call a local doctor and ask him to come over," said Sergeant Murphy in a gentle tone, that surprised me.

I put my face in my hands and took a deep breath. I needed to get out of here now!

"I need some air", I uttered quietly, as I stood up straight.

"Ok, take a few minutes outside, do you want me to go with you?" asked Sergeant Murphy.

"No, I'll be fine," I replied. "Why don't you call the doctor and I'll be back in a few minutes."

Out on the road, I took off as quickly as I could. I ran up Main Street at my fastest 'pensioner pace', not stopping until I was sure they wouldn't know which way I went. I passed the graveyard, turned left and quickly ran down the crumbling concrete steps. I continued to walk briskly down Abbey Street. At least now I was free to think, I wasn't being bombarded with questions from idiots, who probably thought I was mad. Or were they perhaps part of some weird unexplainable conspiracy?

What to do now?

Who could I call on?

I stopped and leaned back against the wall of McGuirks golf shop. I scrolled through the contact list on my phone. Surely there must be someone who knows me and is not part of this stupid conspiracy. I came upon the name 'Barbara Ivory'. My Niece Barbara is married to Graham and I knew Graham worked some nights behind the bar in O'Connell's pub at the top of the east pier. The pub was only a couple of minutes-walk away. There was no way that Graham could be part of any sinister plot, I knew he was a straight-talking friendly guy who I got on very well with. I hoped he was at work and wasn't at my brother Peter's seventieth birthday party. I was very apprehensive as I walked into the crowded pub and dragged myself up onto the last remaining bar stool. I ignored the men who sat on either side of me, I didn't even acknowledge their greetings. Graham approached me with a broad smile. He reminded me of the Irish professional golfer Shane Lowry, same full beard and same burly build.

"What can I get you sir?" he asked politely.

Not even a flicker of recognition in his expression!

"Hi Graham, how are Barbara and the kids?" I asked.

"Oh, they are fine thanks, and how are you keepin' yourself?" he asked.

"Well not too great Graham," I whispered.

"Nothing that a good pint or two won't put right, I hope," he joked. "Now what can I get you?"

"Graham, do you really not know who I am. I'm Ian, for Christ sake," I said.

"Sorry I can't remember you, Ian who?" he asked defensively.

"I'm Ian Forman, Barbara's uncle. Don't tell me you are part of this, I can't take any more Graham! Stop feckin' about, this stupid game is driving me insane."

Graham could see I was upset so he quickly filled a half-pint glass with tap water and placed it in front of me.

"Here, get that into you, I'll be back in a minute," he said as he walked away.

I sat on the barstool staring straight at the glass of water. I wasn't thirsty, I wasn't anything. Yes, maybe I was something, I was stark raving mad!

Graham eventually returned and asked me if I was feeling any better. He asked me if I would like a small Jameson whiskey, "on the house, of course."

"Graham, I need help, I know I need help, I'm really frightened," I pleaded.

"How can I help you," he offered immediately.

"Well you could start by not pretending you don't know me, it's driving me mad"

"Look, I don't know how you know me but I certainly don't know you. I just called Barbara and she said she doesn't have an uncle Ian," said Graham.

"Oh my God, can I speak to Barbara on the phone Graham, please, please?"

Graham looked at me thoughtfully. He was obviously trying to pick his words carefully. I could see he was becoming seriously bothered by our conversation.

"I'm not sure who you are or what your game is, but Barbara told me that her dad Peter used to have a brother called Ian, but she said that Ian died long before she was born. She joked that you must have climbed out of your grave in the Abbey Graveyard," said Graham in a 'mocking tone'.

"Why don't you stick your Jameson where the sun don't shine," I exclaimed, as I slid off the barstool and left the pub. I could hear howls of laughter as I let the door slam behind me.

I never felt so angry or confused. I told myself to stop panicking. There must be a simple explanation for all this, and if anyone could get to the bottom of it, I could. Yes, after all, I was a trained mechanical engineer. Wasn't I always taught to 'think in a straight line'. Didn't I enjoy trying to find solutions to novel problems and it didn't get more 'novel' than this situation. Yes, just like most problems, all that this problem needs is some logical thinking.

Ok, let's start by disproving Graham's statement that Ian Forman was buried in the Abbey Graveyard, simple and straightforward enough! Why had he said such a thing? He must be in on the conspiracy, but what was the purpose of all this deception?

I approached the graveyard iron gates with a sense of purpose. This was one un-truth which I could easily expose. I couldn't wait to go back to Graham and 'bring the whole house of cards down'. The gates were locked and the street lights barely lit up the first few treacherous crumbly steps. I turned on the light on my i-Phone. Putting the phone in my pocket for the moment, I climbed over the spiked gates. I thought that if anyone saw me now, they would call for a doctor or more likely the police! The light from my i-Phone was pretty hopeless and I stumbled several times but never fell over, until I eventually stood in front of the family grave. I glanced back to the locked gates some two hundred yards up the steps and imagined I could see someone looking down on me. I knew the grave so well, I always visited it on return trips to my childhood home. In fact, hadn't I just visited it earlier this afternoon, before I got that migraine and then fell asleep on that bench. I had even taken a photograph of the headstone, to remind me of the 'spooky' coincidence about the dates my two brothers had died.

I stood a little closer and shone the light from my I-Phone on the headstone. As I slowly read the inscriptions, I tried to take it all in. I dropped my phone and sank to my knees. I fumbled on the gravel and picking up my phone, I illuminated the inscription once more. I forced myself to read aloud…..

Cherished Memories

Of

A dear son and brother tragically drowned
IAN FORMAN
Died 12th July 1961 Aged 12 Years

A loving grandmother, mother and daughter
JEAN BAYLIS
Died 4th June 2000 Aged 54 Years

A dear husband, father and grandfather
PETER FORMAN
Died 25th July 2001 Aged 77 Years

Our loving mother and grandmother

GEORGINA FLORENCE FORMAN
Died 19th May 2011 Aged 85 Years

Their dear son, sadly missed
LOUIS FORMAN
Died 12th May 2005 Aged 55 Years

Still kneeling, I dropped my phone and putting my head in my hands I tried to scream but I didn't hear any sound. I lay down on the grave, in the foetal position and wept uncontrollably. After several minutes I tried to stand up but my legs couldn't hold me. I sat on the gravel and tried to clear my mind.

I know that I didn't drown as a child.
I know that I'm not buried here.
I know that my sister Jean is dead but she isn't buried here.
I know that my dad died in an accident when he was only 56 years old.
I know that my brother Robert is buried here, I was at his funeral.

The details about my mother and my brother Louis are correct however.

Is this what it is like to go mad?

How can any of this be true?

I picked up my phone and opened up my photos. Within seconds I had the photo of the headstone, which I had taken earlier that day, on the screen. It was exactly as I remembered everything. Photos don't lie! My brothers Louis and Robert had each died of different natural causes when they were both just fifty-five years old. The photo proved that they were both buried in this grave. What everyone, not just me, thought spooky was that Robert, who was seven years younger than Louis, died seven years after Louis on the same date, May 12th. I remember telling my wife Mary that I would hire a doctor to 'shadow me' each May 12th from then on. I then confirmed that my dad had not lived until he was seventy-seven, he died in an accident when only fifty-six.

I shone the light on the headstone again, what was going on?

I tried to stay calm and think straight but my heart was pounding.

Why had someone gone to the trouble of changing the headstone and inscribing lies all over it? Why? Why?

None of this makes any sense! I can now see why Barbara and Graham think that I died when I was twelve, except that I know that I didn't.

Ok, ok, there must be a simple explanation for this. I know that I am thinking clearly, I know who I am and where I come from, so why does nobody know me?

I tried to consider all possible explanations for my situation ...
- Everybody is trying to convince me that I am insane, but why?
- I really am insane. I'm told insane people don't realise that they are.

- Perhaps I'm dead and don't exist anymore. Am I a ghost?
- Am I in some strange afterlife, where nothing has to make sense anyway?
- Have I been talking to ghosts since I woke up on that bench?
- Could there have been two Ian Formans?
- Is this all a dream, a terrible nightmare?

I just couldn't figure it all out. I didn't really think that some people were trying to drive me mad. Neither did I think that I was really insane, but then I wouldn't, would I? Could I be someone else whose brainwaves have crossed with some departed soul and become jumbled up. If I wasn't really Ian Forman, and I was starting to believe that I may not be, then who was I and where were all my vivid recollections coming from?

I deduced that the two most likely explanations were that I was either having a very realistic and prolonged nightmare or alternatively that I am dead and already in some afterlife.

But I feel hungry and thirsty, would a ghost feel thirst?

How come I have Ian Forman's phone and credit cards?

How come I know everybody?

How come I know my way around Howth?

Just one conclusion left …. I'm stark raving mad!

Whatever the explanation, I still don't know what to do now. If I'm really buried in this grave then I can't be kneeling here reading the inscription.

I tried to read the headstone inscription again but my phone battery had died, no light.

I lay down on my back, stretching out on the grave, my head close to the headstone. My gravel bed was more than a little uncomfortable but I suddenly felt completely at ease. I tried to visualise myself lying under the ground, deep in the earth, next to the dead child Ian Forman, side by side, sharing the same wooden coffin. I folded my arms across my chest and I visualised myself as a deceased twelve-year-old child. Nothing made sense but I was at peace. Perhaps if I could fall asleep right here, I would never wake up or if I do wake up, I will be back on that park bench and everything since will have just been a dreadful nightmare.

I lay there very still, my arms crossed and I looked up at the heavens. If this is what the afterlife is like, I don't want any part of it!

I started to feel the cold penetrate my bones but still I didn't stir. I closed my eyes and thought about Mary, what must she be thinking right now? Is she missing me as much as I am missing her? I hope she is at peace, wherever she is! What about our son John and our daughter Annette? What about our four gorgeous grandchildren? Are they real? Did I imagine them all, I hope not, but where are they now? I need them!

Chapter 4

I was awakened by something brushing against my right foot and by a loud voice in my ear.

"Are you ok there? Are you awake?"

I opened my eyes straight away, not trying to wake up gradually this time. Sergeant Murphy was leaning over me, with a troubled, concerned look on his face.

"I told Garda Moore that we shouldn't have let you go outside last night but he reassured me that you would be back for your wallet," he said apologetically.

I attempted to roll over to try to stand up but I was so stiff and my back ached so much I just moaned and lay down on my back again.

"For how long have you been lying there, can you get up?" he asked.

"I don't know, what time is it now?" I replied.

"It almost seven am, have you been here all night? I got a call a few minutes ago that there was someone desecrating a grave here. Didn't expect to find you here. What the hell are you doing?" he asked, "are you ok?"

"I'm not desecrating anyone's grave, I'm trying to connect with my real self," I replied without thinking.

Sergeant Murphy looked sympathetically down at me. He asked me to lie still and not to try to move. He then took off his jacket and placed it over me. He then placed his cap under my head. I could hear him call an ambulance and soon the paramedics had me on a stretcher and minutes later we were speeding off in an ambulance. Sergeant Murphy accompanied me in the ambulance to, what I learned later was, Beaumont Hospital, in Dublin.

A&E at Beaumont Hospital is typical of any other big city hospital. Sick and injured patients impatiently sitting around in the reception area, totally bored and feeling unwelcome. Someone asked me if they could call somebody to sit with me.

"Yes, could you please call my wife Mary. Tell her I'm ok but I need her to come here to be with me, as soon as she can."

I couldn't remember her mobile number. I searched my pockets but my phone wasn't to be found. I must have left it at the side of the grave, or perhaps Sergeant Murphy or one of the paramedics had it. A thorough search didn't uncover it. I closed my eyes in despair. Sergeant Murphy said he would return to the graveyard to try to locate my phone and would let me know how he got on. Before he left, I overheard him talk to one of the doctors. I learned later that it was Doctor Gail Mulligan. He quickly briefed her about what had happened to me and about my state of confusion. He tried to speak very low but I could hear him. They talked about me as though I wasn't present in the room. He warned her against leaving me alone, stressing that he didn't think I was a danger to myself or others but that I needed 'checking out'.

As soon as Sergeant Murphy left, with a promise to return, I was back on my feet and walking around the reception area. I thanked the two paramedics, whose names I couldn't remember, as they said goodbye to me. I could easily have walked straight out the front double-doors. So much for not leaving me alone! But where would I go? I had no money, shit, didn't even have my wallet! Still, I expect Sergeant Murphy will return everything to me when he comes back with my mobile phone.

I sat down on the end of a row of red plastic chairs. What was I waiting for?

Would they really be able to contact Mary and get her to come? Well not until they have her phone number, they won't!

A stern looking middle aged lady, with greying wild hair and no makeup on her face appeared, 'from nowhere' and handed me a one-page double sided form and a ballpoint pen. The only professional aspect about her was her immaculately laundered light blue uniform.

"Complete this form as best you can" she said, without a please or thank you. "When you are finished hand it back to anyone on the reception desk opposite."

I looked at the form. Where do I start? What do I now write for my name and address? Oh Jesus, I can't put the name of someone everyone thinks is dead!

I decided to just 'tell it like it is'. I gave my full name, my correct address in Buckingham, my next of kin as Mary, with mobile phone number unknown. I gave my e-mail address plus my home and mobile phone numbers. Over the page, I was expected to write the reason for my visit to the hospital and whether I had ever visited for treatment on a previous date.

Should I just leave it blank? I decided to write in block capitals ..

'I HAVE NO IDEA WHY I'M HERE. I WAS BROUGHT HERE IN AN AMBULANCE BY SERGEANT MURPHY, WHY DON'T YOU ASK HIM!

I handed my completed form to the same 'grumpy' receptionist and immediately returned to my chair. I watched her as she read through the first page and then watched her expression as she turned the page over and read what I had written on the back. She glanced up at me and our eyes met for a few seconds. Not even a flicker of a smile crossed her face. She looked back at the form and placing it on the desk she made a phone call and spoke very quietly to someone. She glanced over at me as she hung up. Minutes later, a tall thin balding man, in a white coat, approached me.

"Hello Mr Forman, I'm Doctor Staelens, I'm one of the Registrars here. What can I do for you?"

"I wish I knew doctor! I need help but I don't know where to start," I softly replied.

"The paramedics reported that you were brought here suffering from suspected exposure and in a state of confusion," he said.

Doctor Staelens had a friendly round face. He had a perpetual smile on his face which stayed there even as he spoke. From his name and familiar accent, I guessed he was from Flanders in Belgium.

"I don't think I'm suffering from any physical ailment," I responded, "but nobody seems to know me, or at least that's what they say. I know I shouldn't say it to a doctor, Doctor Staelens, but I think I may be temporarily insane."

"Why do you say temporarily?" he asked.

I knew from the tone that he was not expecting an answer! What a stupid question for him to ask, I thought! Doctor Staelens then invited me to follow him into a vacant cubicle and without drawing the privacy curtain, he gave me a quick medical examination. When he finished, he informed me that my blood pressure, heart rate, temperature and breathing were all normal.

"Mr Forman," he said formally, "I really cannot find anything physically wrong with you. Is that why you suggested we ask this, what is his name, oh yes, Sergeant Murphy, why he called for an ambulance?"

"To be honest that was a bit tongue-in-cheek," I confessed.

"Well as for as I am concerned, Mr Forman, you are free to leave. Sergeant Murphy did not say why he arranged for you to be brought here, and we haven't heard from him since. Is there any reason why I shouldn't call someone to pick you up and take you home, or would you prefer to make your own way home?"

"If only I could doctor," I mumbled, "but nobody knows me, I don't know where I live, I've no mobile phone, no money, no wallet, no identity. No sanity!"

"I read that your home address is in England but have you friends or relations here in Ireland, Mr. Forman. Could someone come to pick you up?" he asked enthusiastically.

I provided the doctor with the names of my brothers and sisters and he said he would come back as soon as he 'tracked someone down'. I decided not to mention Mary, since I knew he would have no luck there. I sat on the hard, wooden chair in the corner of the cubicle, bent forward with my head in my hands. What will 'the helpful doctor' come up with, I wondered? I was there a good fifteen minutes and was beginning to think that he had forgotten about me, when Doctor Staelens returned. He was accompanied by a lady in a white coat with the obligatory stethoscope draped around her neck.

"This is Doctor Gail Mulligan, I believe you may have met her already," he said.

We 'fist bumped' and I smiled. She explained that she was one of the A&E Consultants and that Doctor Staelens had asked her to talk to me. She was tiny, probably less than five feet tall. She looked to be only about thirty years old, with short 'mousy brown' hair but with a knowledgeable 'know it all' attractive smile.

I 'took to her' straight away. They both stood in front of me as Doctor Staelens explained that he had managed to contact a Fiona Forman and a Peter Forman.

"Great", I exclaimed, and jumped up from my chair.

"Well, there is a problem Mr. Forman," he continued. "I realise that you told me that Fiona is your younger sister and that Peter is your older brother but they both said that they do not have a brother named Ian."

I slumped back in my chair. Why did I expect a different outcome? I know that I am insane! Who can help me? Who the hell am I? Is there someone out there looking for me now? Did I get a bump on the head? Has the ghost of a twelve-year-old child called Ian Forman somehow taken over my brain? Questions..questions.. someone must have the answers!

Doctor Mulligan interrupted my irrational morbid thoughts.

"Mr. Forman, I have spoken to Sergeant Murphy and he has briefed me about your recent unusual experiences. The good news is that he has found your mobile phone and he will bring it in later, together with your wallet. He will be here in a couple of hours or so. I told him that we will keep you here overnight to run some tests on you," she stated very matter-of-factly. "Is that all right with you Mr Forman?" she asked sympathetically.

I answered meekly that since I had nowhere else to go and no means to get there, that this was fine.

A jolly large hospital male porter wheeled me to my isolation ward and asked me if I needed anything. I resisted the temptation to reply that, like the scarecrow in the Wizard of Oz, I could do with a new brain. I almost smiled as I thought about asking the wizard for help, but what was there to smile about?

I had only just settled into my comfortable hospital bed when Doctor Mulligan came and sat down on the brown plastic chair on my left.

"Mr Forman, I am here to help you," she started. "You mentioned that you are feeling a little confused at the moment and both Doctor Staelens and I are minded to agree with you for now. Would you be ok to undergo some tests?"

"What sort of tests?" I asked defensively.

"Perhaps we should start with a friendly chat and see where that gets us, what do you think?" she smiled.

"Ok, what do you want to talk about?" I asked.

"How about you tell me where and when you started to feel confused. Is this something new or have you felt like this before?" she asked.

"No, I have never felt anything like this before, never, never ever!"

"What do you think happened to you, then?" she asked gently.

I closed my eyes, trying to gather my thoughts. I took a deep breath and then went on to tell Doctor Mulligan how my wife Mary and I had travelled over to Dublin, from Hollyhead, on the 'fast ferry' Jonathan Swift the day before. We checked into the Marine Hotel and then while Mary was having her hair done in a nearby salon, I drove out to Howth, my childhood home.

"Sorry to interrupt you Mr Forman, but did you feel alright as you left Mary?" she asked.

"Yes, I felt great. We were looking forward to going to my brother's seventieth birthday party that night in Malahide," I replied.

"And did you both go to the party Mr Forman?" she asked, innocently.

"Oh Jesus Christ, I never got that far. Everything changed when I got to Howth!" I exclaimed loudly.

"Ok, Mr Forman let's stay calm if we can. What exactly changed and when?" she asked quietly.

I sat back in my chair and slowly related the details about my first visit to the graveyard and afterwards that I booked Sunday lunch for Mary and I at the seafood restaurant Crabby Jo's on the West Pier. Shortly afterwards, I started to feel a migraine attack coming on.

"How could you tell that a migraine attack was imminent?" she asked in a 'medical tone'.

I explained that ever since I was a teenager, I get one or two migraine attacks a year, often at the beginning of a holiday, or after a period of stressful activity. Both of my eyes suddenly become blurry and I have to take a tablet to prevent a dreadful disabling headache following ten minutes or so later. Many years ago, at the onset of an attack, a friend offered me a couple of Co-Codomol tablets and they turned out to be a miracle cure. After taking even just one tablet, within about twenty minutes, my eyesight becomes clear and the headache never develops," I explained.

"That's very interesting, Mr Forman, but you know you shouldn't take Codeine regularly." They can become addictive, you need to be careful," advised Doctor Mulligan.

"I hardly think that two or three tablets a year will lead to an addiction, doctor," I replied somewhat cynically.

Doctor Mulligan smiled and nodded her head.

"So, did you have some tablets with you?" she asked.

"Yes, I always carry them with me. I took just one tablet with a glass of water and sat down on a park bench to wait until my eyes cleared. I must have been exhausted, which does tend to happen after I take Co-Codomol, because I fell asleep for half an hour or more," I answered.

"Then what happened, Mr Forman. Had you got a headache when you woke up?"

"No, I felt great, no blurred vision and no headache." I replied.

"So, you felt great and no confused mind?" she asked. "Then what?"

I suddenly froze, I couldn't answer for several seconds.

"That's when everything changed," I blurted out. "From the time I woke up nothing made sense. My car was stolen, I couldn't find Mary, nobody knew me, I visited my own grave, I think I must have gone insane."

"Are you sure you took just one tablet, have you still got some of those tablets with you now?" she asked.

I wondered if she was 'onto something'.

"I'm certain it was just one, two tend to make me a little drowsy these days," I replied. "Do you think there was something wrong with the tablet doctor?"

'Well it's a possibility, I will have the tablets checked out later in the lab," she nodded.

"Ok, so continue. When you woke up you felt different. Did you realise straight away that you were confused?" she asked.

"No, I didn't feel different. I was exactly the same as before, minus the blurred eyes," I replied.

"So, when did things change then Mr Forman, when did you realise something was wrong?"

"That's just it, doctor, I didn't change at all," I replied, "but everybody else plus many other things changed!"

I saw Doctor Mulligan frown and it suddenly 'sank in' just how stupid I must have sounded to her.

"So, do you still think that you are Mr Ian Forman who is married to Mary and that you live in the UK?" she asked rather sceptically.

"I don't think I am, doctor, I know I am. Our son John is married with a ten-year old son. He lives in North London and is a doctor in a London hospital. Our daughter Annette is married to Phil. They have a son and two daughters. She is a primary school teacher."

"Have you tried to contact either of them since you started to feel 'different'?" she asked.

"No, I haven't, and now I don't have my phone," I replied sheepishly.

Why didn't I think of that earlier? I suppose I didn't want to alarm or bother them.

"It should be easy enough to get hold of your son, if you tell me at which hospital does John works, I will try to contact him? Would you like me to try?"

"Yes, that would be fantastic," I enthused, but don't tell him too much for now. Don't tell him that I can't find his mother. I would rather try to explain everything to him myself."

"I need to check on another patient first but then I will contact John, I should be back in half an hour or so. Will you be ok here on your own?"

"Well where else could I go?" I whispered, "but thank you for your help doctor."

I lay back on my bed and closed my eyes. I felt that I was making progress. Surely John will be able to confirm everything and get to the bottom of this sick joke or conspiracy or whatever it was. But how am I going to start the conversation with John? Where will I start? Hey, he must already know where his mother is, surely, she has contacted him to tell him that I have 'gone missing'! I think I will start the conversation by just saying 'hello' and then let him speak. Oh, I can't wait for the doctor to return. What's keeping her anyway? She must be gone at least an hour.

Eventually Doctor Mulligan returned, accompanied by Doctor Staelens. Doctor Mulligan sat down beside my bed and Doctor Staelens stood next to her. I felt really excited but didn't like their concerned expressions!

"Where's your phone doctor?" I asked, "I thought that you were going to allow me to talk to my son."

"Mr Forman, I spoke with several managers at the hospital you mentioned and I'm afraid none of them know a John Forman. They insisted that he is definitely not employed there. I then 'googled' his name but I couldn't find any John Forman who is a doctor at any London hospital. I haven't yet tried to locate your daughter, but if you give me her home address and the name of the school she works at, I could try. Do you want me to try?"

I couldn't speak for several minutes. I knew exactly where John worked, Mary and I had visited him there several times. I tried to hide my devastation and gave the Doctor the contact details for our daughter Annette. She left saying that she would be 'back in a while' but that Doctor Staelens would sit with me and have a chat when she was gone.

Doctor Staelens wanted to know all about my medical history, especially if I had any previous 'issues' with my memory or my brain. I told him that I had meningitis, with which I was seriously ill when I was a one-year old child and about the encephalitis, for which I was hospitalised in 2015.

I told him that when I was a one-year old toddler I caught meningitis. I went on to explain that many years later, I was told by my mother that I was 'on death's door' with the brain infection and that I was one of the first people in Ireland to be given a new 'miracle drug'. My mother said that she was told, at the time, that the new drug was my last hope. Doctor Staelens asked me what year this was and when I told him it was 1950, he said that the drug might have been penicillin, which was first used to treat bacterial infections during the forties. Anyway, I told him that it obviously worked, whatever it was.

I then explained that I was treated for encephalitis in Stoke Mandeville hospital in England, in the summer of 2015. I never did find out if it was a bacterial or a viral infection, as my doctor son John 'insisted very strongly' that the doctors treat me for both, rather than waiting until the tests revealed the cause. Ten days passed before I was well enough to return home but many more weeks before I was anywhere back to 'normal'. During that first week in hospital I was really frightened that I could not remember anything that was said to me, for more than a few seconds. The problem was that I knew that something was seriously wrong. I suspected the worst when I woke up in an isolation ward with two separate intravenous tubes attached to my arm. I definitely owe my life to the doctors and nurses at Stoke Mandeville but I really believe that had my wife Mary not acted as quickly as she did that Sunday morning, when I kept falling over, I would have had a very different outcome. I am convinced that her insistence on prompt medical attention and the forceful speedy intervention of our son John, prevented permanent brain damage.

Doctor Mulligan returned just before I had finished recounting my experience at Stoke Mandeville but she didn't seem interested to know any more. Doctor Staelens stood up and invited Doctor Mulligan to sit down beside me again. She reached out and took hold of my left hand, which started to tremble violently.

"Mr Forman, I have tried everything but have been unable to contact your daughter. I have asked for help from the local police in the UK and they still have to come back to me but so far no luck," said Doctor Mulligan.

She spoke as if she was reading it from an invisible report. No expressions.

I should have been getting used to this but I couldn't help myself, I was filled with terror. Why can't they find John or Annette?

Chapter 5

I buried my face in my pillow and started to sob uncontrollably. I felt a tender comforting hand on my shoulder. After several minutes I was composed enough to turn around to face the world again. Doctor Mulligan said that she would like to arrange further testing to try to establish what my problem was. She asked if I was well enough to face an MRI scan. She explained that she could see that I was mentally upset and confused and that a brain scan would show if there was a physical cause for my condition. She added that if I agreed, she could expedite the scan and hoped that it could happen within a few hours.

"So, you think that I might have a brain tumour then?" I asked

"Probably not," she answered, "but it would be best to eliminate it, right at the beginning."

Having confirmed once more that I would be ok to be left alone for a while, I lay back in bed and tried to control my heart beat. I had just refused to take a sedative, I was always able to mentally 'step back' from the brink of a panic attack by clearing my mind and thinking about past calm pleasurable moments. I closed my eyes and attempted to imagine that I was walking along the promenade between Los Americas and Los Cristianos. Mary and I strolling along together, side by side, in the sunshine, on the Spanish island of Tenerife. We had to eat the "99" ice creams a little quicker than we would have liked to make sure they didn't melt before we finished eating them. We were not in any hurry, just ambling along. I loved listening to the waves breaking on the loose stones and the rhythmic grating noise as the stones tumbled over each other as the wave retreated, a noisy but a 'nice' noise. I counted how many steps I took before the next wave broke, always the same, so dependable. I was happy to just walk along and listen, just 'taking it all in' and 'savouring' every passing moment. The past didn't matter, the future didn't matter either, the present was simply everything. When the ice creams were finished, Mary took my hand and guided me towards the looming handbag and shoe shop. Mary has hundreds of handbags and even more pairs of shoes for every imaginable occasion, but she reminded me, more than once, that a woman can never have enough of either! She didn't mind that I waited outside the shop, leaning over the stone wall, staring out at the surfers falling over and picking themselves up, time and time again. If I could swim, I think I would like to go surfing, experienced surfers really must be 'in the moment', waiting for the next perfect wave. Eventually my peace would be disturbed by Mary calling to me to come and look at the most gorgeous pair of shoes and matching handbag she had ever seen. So comfortable and so handy to have! It was always a bargain, which she simply couldn't resist. Well nobody could, could they? She suggested that we had better pay for them now and pick them up on the way back to the hotel, otherwise she was sure that some other woman would soon come along and snap them up, even though she didn't need them as much as Mary did! We must have saved thousands of pounds picking up so many bargains over the years! After 'securing' our purchase, as always, I resisted Mary's attempts to get me to buy a new pair of shorts or a pair of leather sandals for myself.

I heard someone enter my room. I opened my eyes. I knew that I hadn't really succeeded in 'switching off' and letting my mind go elsewhere. I was trying hard but you can't simply force it! My mind was not going anywhere! I lay on my back staring at the ceiling but not really seeing it. Doctor Staelens looked down at me and told me that I would be taken down for my scan in about thirty minutes and asked if I felt any better. I lied that I felt a lot better now and thanked him.

When I got back to my room from the noisy scan, I saw that my leather wallet, which Mary had last year bought for me in Tenerife and my mobile phone were on my bedside table. I thanked Jack, the hospital porter, and asked him if he could get me a cheese sandwich and a cup of tea. I must be feeling better! I must remember to thank Sergeant Murphy when I next bump into him.

I went through my wallet and thankfully everything was still there. I turned on my phone, but still no life in the battery. When the tall, pale, skinny young nurse brought me my tea and sandwich I asked her if she could find me a charger for my mobile phone. She looked at my i-Phone, frowned and said she would see what she could do, when she had a few spare minutes.

I finished my sandwich and lay back down on my bed, expecting the nurse to return at any minute. I couldn't wait to charge the battery and then pull up my library of photos which would soon prove that I really was, who I said I was!

Hours seemed to pass before Doctor Staelens returned, accompanied by a very tall smiling lady dressed in a full-length white coat. I guess she was about middle aged, although her short grey hair made her look older.

"Hello again, Mr Forman," said Doctor Staelens, "it was great to hear that you were well enough to have something to eat and drink. Can I get you something else?"

Before I could answer, Doctor Staelens continued ..

"Can I introduce you to my colleague Mrs O'Brien. Mrs O'Brien is a renowned psychiatrist who splits her time between our hospital here and her main place of work, which is a nearby hospital called The Phoenix Centre."

I suddenly felt very guarded. I had never spoken to a 'trick cyclist' before and I had never heard of The Phoenix Centre. I smiled back at her but said nothing. I will let her lead the conversation.

"Hello Mr Forman, please don't be alarmed by Doctor Staelen's introduction. I'm just here to see if I can help you in any way," she said in a refined Dublin accent.

I still said nothing.

"I have very good news for you, Mr Forman. You will be pleased to hear that your scan did not show up any abnormalities. Your brain looks fit and healthy, no sign of a tumour or any sign of trauma to your skull. Your blood tests confirmed that you are currently not and have not recently been a substance abuser. You are not running a temperature and you say that you are not in pain or have an upset stomach. In short Mr Forman we cannot find anything medically wrong with you," she folded her arms across her chest as she finished.

"So why am I lying here then, Mrs O'Brien?" I asked politely.

Mrs O'Brien said that there was no need for me to be in bed and suggested that I get dressed and that we have a chat in a comfortable quiet room nearby. I removed my hospital pyjamas and put on the same clothes that I had been wearing since I got on that car-ferry, it seems like months ago.

I shifted uncomfortably as I sat on an armless hard wooden chair in this claustrophobic dimly lit room. Mrs O'Brien sat opposite me behind a solid wooden desk with a notebook and pen in front of her. Alongside her sat Doctor Staelens.

"Thank you for agreeing to have a chat with us, Mr Forman. I have gone through your notes and I have spoken to some of the people that you have already spent time with since you arrived in Dublin, on Saturday. We would like to try to help you in any way we can," said Mrs O'Brien, in a formal tone.

I thanked both of them and repeated that I know I am definitely suffering some type of identity confusion, which I can't figure out.

"Why don't you start by telling us who you are, where you live and a little about your family," she asked.

"Do you want the long or the short version?" I asked.

"Neither I, nor Doctor Staelens, are in any great hurry, Mr Forman. Just talk to us about yourself and we will probably ask questions as we proceed. Would you mind if I record our conversation, just to help me afterwards make sense of my notes."

I sat back and started to relate my life story. I talked for about twenty minutes after which they knew where I was born and brought up. They knew all about my parents, brothers and sisters, wife Mary and our son John and daughter Annette. They were now aware that we had moved to Canada just after we married and that we stayed there for a couple of years. A job promotion for me, led us to move to Belgium, where we lived for almost ten years before I was transferred to the UK. We now lived in Buckingham, which is not that far from London.

I explained that Mary and I had travelled from Holyhead to Dublin on the car ferry to go to my brother Peter's seventieth birthday party. I told them that shortly afterwards things started to go wrong.

"What exactly went wrong Mr Forman, when and how?" asked Mrs O'Brien.

I repeated everything that had happened to me since I woke up last Saturday on that park bench in Howth. I left absolutely nothing out, even though I knew that when she heard the full story that that she would surely conclude that I had 'lost my mind'.

"So, Mrs O'Brien, what exactly is wrong with me? Can you help me?" I pleaded.

"So where are Mary, John and Annette now?" she asked. "I have heard that you have been unable to speak to any of them."

"I wish I knew Doctor, it's not for the want of trying," I replied.

"Are you really convinced that your name is Ian Forman, even though I have been told that you saw that name on a gravestone in a cemetery in Howth," she asked.

"I know, I know, I know," I repeated.

"Hold on a minute doctor," I exclaimed, as I opened my wallet and took out the collection of cards it contained.

Mrs O'Brien and Doctor Staelens scrutinised my HSBC credit and debit cards, my membership card for my golf club and my season card for the MK Dons football club, which is located in Milton Keynes, near Buckingham. They then closely examined all of the Euro banknotes.

"Splendid, splendid," exclaimed Mrs O'Brien. Doctor Staelens, would you mind contacting Mr Forman's golf club and his football club, the phone numbers are printed on the cards. In the meantime, Mr Forman and I will drop down to the hospital lobby and see if Mr Forman can access his bank. Perhaps he can obtain some cash to spend in the canteen," added Mrs O'Brien.

I was happy to be out of the stuffy room and to be free to wander around the hospital, even if I was accompanied by Mrs O'Brien. I felt that very soon I would be making progress with my identity crisis. Unfortunately, neither of my bank cards were recognised, both were rejected by the automatic machine, even before I typed in my PIN number. Mrs O'Brien shrugged her shoulders and she didn't seem to be in the least bit surprised. Back in the 'interview room' we met up again with Doctor Staelens. He handed me both of my membership cards and explained that neither of them was valid. He said that he had spoken to 'people' at both clubs and they were insistent and certain that I was not a member of the golf club and neither was I a season ticket holder of the football club.

"Mr Forman, the membership numbers printed on the cards simply don't exist, they both said that you must have bought them from a crooked tout," said Doctor Staelens somewhat cynically.

"Mr Forman, what's even more worrying are these bank notes. They look like genuine foreign Euro notes but they have Ireland printed on them. You know that Ireland doesn't use the Euro, so why are you trying to pass them on, surely you know that they are of no use!" added Mrs O'Brien.

"What are you talking about now Mrs O'Brien?" I screamed. "I got these bank notes from my local post office in Buckingham just a few days ago!"

"I'm afraid, Mr Forman, that I have to report this to the Gardai. You are in possession of false bank cards and counterfeit money. I cannot deal with this," she said slowly, as her face took on a grave expression.

"You can do what the feck you want Mrs O'Brien, and thanks for all your help," I replied. "Hey, what about my mobile phone? One of your nurses took it away to see if she could find a charger. It has lots of family photos on it. Photos of Mary, John, Annette, my grandchildren, some of my brothers and sisters and lots of our friends."

Mrs O'Brien took my i-Phone out of her coat pocket and handed it to me without saying a word. I tried to turn it on but the battery was still dead.

"It's another mystery Mr Forman. No one at the hospital has a charger which fits into the slot. The slot seems to have been tampered with so we are unable to charge your phone. I would have liked to look at your photo albums but 'conveniently' someone has made this impossible," said Mrs O'Brien.

"Your sarcasm is very disturbing Mrs O'Brien and not what I would expect from an experienced professional doctor," I said, without trying to hide my anger.

"I apologise for my comments Mr Forman," she replied immediately. "I hope I haven't upset you. We really are doing our utmost to try to help you but we don't think you are making it easy for us. We don't think that you are being fully open and honest. It's as if you are deliberately trying to mislead us."

"I'm not trying to feckin' mislead you, everything I have told you is true. Do you want me to make up a more believable story, is that what you want?" I responded in a very controlled tone of voice.

I didn't want them to think I was becoming aggressive. Perhaps they were trying to goad me so they could sedate me. I need to stay calm at all times!

"Mrs O'Brien and Doctor Staelens, I really appreciate your help. I know that you are professional enough to want to find out what's wrong with me. But we won't get anywhere if you don't believe me. If you think that everything I have said, is nothing but lies, we won't get to the bottom of my problem. Please believe me, you are my only hope." I pleaded.

They looked at each other and then both stared straight at me. Mrs

O'Brien spoke ..

"Mr Forman, I apologise if we have upset you. We believe that you are fully convinced that you think that you really are Mr Ian Forman, married to Mary and that you have two children. We do not think that you are deliberately trying to mislead us, but we needed to ask you. The problem is Mr Forman, that most of what you have told us about yourself and your family is simply not true."

Mrs O'Brien suggested that we all take a few minutes break. She left the room saying that she would request some tea and biscuits. She left Doctor Staelens and me staring at each other across the desk. I could see that he was as awkward as I was. Neither of us wanted to speak without Mrs O'Brien being present. Those five or so minutes of silence and 'thumb twiddling' seemed like hours. Eventually Mrs O'Brien returned and smiled at me as she took up her seat. She asked me to again confirm that I really thought that I was Mr Ian Forman. Christ this was like a police grilling! She asked where I would go if they decided to discharge me from the hospital right away. I explained that I would probably go back to the police station in Howth and ask them to find one of my relations.

"But they would likely bring you back here, Mr Forman," said Doctor Staelens. "We could go around in circles for ever!"

I reminded them that I only had those few hundred Euros, I had nowhere else to go, nobody that I knew seemed to want to know me. I had to accept that I had been abandoned by everyone.

"Do you now think that you are deluded, Mr Forman?" asked Mrs O'Brien.

I answered that I didn't think I was deluded but I just didn't know what to think.

"Mr Forman, we do not want you to walk out of here right now, we think you need help and we can try to arrange for it at a more appropriate institution," said Mrs O'Brien.

So, she eventually arrived at the conclusion which I feared from the beginning. They are convinced that I am mentally disturbed and need treatment. Mrs O'Brien repeated that she had a duty to confiscate my counterfeit money and the forged bank cards and to hand them over to the Gardai. She was very apologetic about this but said that she had no choice. She explained that she concluded that I was delusional since I still really believed that I was someone who had died many years ago. Since I wasn't who I said I was, she said she would also ask the Gardai to go through their missing persons records and ask them to request the police in England to do the same. She added that my case was so unusual that the Gardai might want to take photos of me to put on social media or even on TV. She warned me to be prepared for this because someone, somewhere must be missing me and know who I am. She said the Gardai will find my family, eventually.

Mrs O'Brien outlined what would happen next. She would arrange for me to be admitted to a hospital called the Phoenix Care Centre, which is located in Grangegorman Campus in Dublin. I would be a guest of the Department of Health. Since I did not seem to have any health insurance and I couldn't show a current national insurance card she explained that the state would cover all the costs until my true identity was established. I would be held there, forcibly if absolutely necessary, for assessment, until further notice.

I nodded to show I understood but said nothing. Christ they are going to lock me up and throw away the key!

Much later that afternoon, I was told to pack my things and prepare to be transferred to The Phoenix Centre. Pack my things? That's a joke. I've only got what I was now standing in. The trip to the hospital took less than half an hour. I sat behind the silent driver as we trundled through the Dublin streets in the white transit minibus, which I had noticed had Patient Transportation Bus, written on the side. Mrs O'Brien was seated beside me, she said she wanted to make sure that I settled in as smoothly as possible. She mentioned that she didn't normally travel with her patients but that I was no ordinary patient. I was beginning to like Mrs O'Brien!

The driver dropped us off in front of the main door and Mrs O'Brien and I approached the reception desk. The receptionist recognised her immediately.

"Good afternoon Mrs O'Brien," she announced. "Your guest's room is ready as you requested."

The receptionist didn't even look at me, let alone speak to me. Mrs O'Brien walked in front of me as we made our way up the staircase. I wondered if the receptionist noticed that I wasn't carrying a suitcase, but I doubt it. She seemed oblivious to me entirely. I entered my new 'private room' which I was already thinking of as my 'private prison'. It was 'comfortable enough' with its own ensuite bathroom. I hated the lack of a window anywhere, not even in the ensuite. A hospital worker suddenly appeared in the room. He nodded silently at Mrs O'Brien and introduced himself to me, as Nurse Jones. I detected a Welch accent. He explained that I was a guest in a secure seclusion room in the Oak Ward of the care centre. He said his immediate responsibility was to make me feel comfortable and take care of any catering needs I had. He picked up the room menu from my bedside table and asked me if I would like anything to eat and drink. He was 'business like" rather than friendly and I think he was a little wary of me, even though he was close to six-foot tall, well-built and young enough to be my son. I ordered a peri-peri chicken wrap and a mug of black coffee. Nurse Jones left me alone in my room with Mrs O'Brien, saying he would be back soon. I thought it odd that he left the room door ajar. Mrs O'Brien asked me, twice or three times, if I was ok and if I liked my room.

"Thank you, Mrs O'Brien for helping me," I said. "What's going to happen now and how long will I be here for?"

She sat down on one of the two bedside chairs and I sat at the end of the single bed, which was covered in a 'crispy' plain royal blue duvet. She told me that I was to undergo a thorough assessment of my condition and as soon as it was established what was causing my confusion an 'Individual Care Plan' would be prepared.

"So, for how long will I be kept locked up here?" Mrs O'Brien.

"Mr Forman, you are not being kept here locked up. You are here on the invitation of the director of this 'world famous' hospital. If you had anywhere else to go, or the means to get there, you would be welcome to leave at any time. Please confirm that you are happy to stay here as long as it takes for us to find and fix whatever it is that is causing your distress," she answered firmly.

I once more found myself apologising and confirming that I appreciated everyone's help.

"Anyway, perhaps the Gardai will, in the meantime, succeed in establishing your real identity and you will soon be heading home."

I 'bit my tongue' and kept silent! Jesus, how many times do I have to say that I know who I am. It's everyone else that is confused!

Mrs O'Brien sat chatting to me until Nurse Jones reappeared with my meal. After he left, she stood up to leave me alone to eat. She said that I needed to get some sleep. She would return early the next morning with some fresh clothes. She explained that she was going to raid her husband Brendan's wardrobe. She said he was about the same size as me. She added that he was one of those men who had lots and lots of different clothes, all selected and bought by her, but who just put on whatever clothes were closest to him in the wardrobe.

"He won't even miss his own clothes, he probably wouldn't even recognise them on you if you were standing in front of him," she said, with a chuckle.

I liked that she had a sense of humour. Mrs O'Brien pointed out the call button, which was attached to my bedside table, beside the reading lamp.

"Don't be shy to press the button if you need anything, Mr Forman. Nurse Jones is at your service and he keeps saying how much he loves his job."

I heard her turn the key in the lock on the outside of the door as she left. I waited a couple of minutes before I tried the door. Yes, it was locked. So much for me being here of my own free will!

I devoured the chicken wrap and drank the cold coffee. The tomato pasta was delicious and quite satisfying. I felt quite tired.

Chapter 6

I washed my hands and face and pored myself a glass of water from the tap. There was no notice to warn that it was not drinking water and it tasted fine. Oh, what a risk taker I am!

Not bothering to undress, I lay on the top of the duvet and closed my eyes. My empty plate and mug were on the table beside me. Should I press the button to get them collected by Nurse Jones or will I leave them there till morning? I decided not to bother Nurse Jones and just hope that he wouldn't come in later and wake me from my sleep.

I couldn't sleep. I kept needing to wipe the tears from my eyes as I thought that I may never see my wife Mary, my children and my grandchildren again. I must have eventually fallen asleep but wished I hadn't. I had a very frightening nightmare. In the dream, I rang the doorbell of our house in Buckingham. Mary answered. My children and grandchildren were crowding behind her. They were laughing out loud at me. They laughed even more hysterically when I told them who I was. Suddenly a very familiar man suddenly appeared behind Mary. It was me!

I awoke in a sweat. I sat bolt upright, shaking and still very frightened. I lay back down again and tried to breathe deeply. When I composed myself sufficiently, I got up and turned the light on. I drank some more water and splashed cold water over my face. I looked at the large cheap white wall clock. Three fifteen. Everything was quiet, it must be early morning.

I turned off the light and lay back down.

I awoke again to the sound of a loud knock on a door and a key turning in a lock. Was I dreaming again? I sat up as my room door opened slowly and I was momentarily filled with dread. The light from the corridor outside my room was bright enough for me to recognise Mrs O'Brien as she entered, accompanied by a man I didn't know. I think she must have noticed that I was still half-asleep and looking somewhat bewildered.

"Good morning, Mr Forman," she said cheerfully. "Sorry to wake you up so suddenly, remember me? I'm Mrs O'Brien," she said as she switched the light on and closed the door behind her.

I looked at the clock, eight twenty. It must be morning.

"This is Mr Simon Cox," she announced. "Mr Cox will be working with me as part of a team of people who will be responsible for your care while you are at The Phoenix Care Centre."

Mr Cox held out his hand to shake mine. I stood up from the bed and took a step backwards to look at him properly. He was only slightly taller than me, approximately the same weight. I guessed he was in his late forties or early fifties. He was clean shaven, with very little expression on his face. He had, as some people might say, a very forgettable face.

I clenched my right fist and held my arm out in front of me.

"Hello Mr Cox," I said. "I heard that doctors prefer to 'fist bump' now rather than shake hands."

We "fist bumped' and he welcomed me to The Phoenix Care Centre, where he hoped I would settle in quickly. Still not even the hint of a welcoming smile on his face. He told me that he was a senior psychologist, attached to the PCC. He explained that he worked regularly with Mrs O'Brien, who was a senior psychiatrist, and who was also attached to the PCC.

Mrs O'Brien then handed me a small green rucksack. She suggested that I take a shower and change into these fresh, second hand clothes. They would 'leave me to it' and return in about half an hour and have a chat about what comes next. They closed the door behind them. I didn't hear the door being locked but I didn't try to open it. Perhaps they are still waiting outside waiting to see if I will try to come out of my room. I didn't.

When they returned, both of them were smiling. So, Mr Cox's face didn't crack when he smiled after all!

"My God, you look just like my husband, Mr Forman," she exclaimed.

I thanked her for the 'loan' of the clothes, which fitted nicely. I said I would return them as soon as I could buy some new ones. She told me to ask Nurse Jones to have my own clothes laundered in the meantime.

I sat at the bottom of the bed and they pulled up the bedside chairs close to me. Mrs O'Brien then said that she hoped that I had had a good night's sleep and started to outline the coming action. I was in a seclusion room in the Oak Ward of the PCC. It had been opened in 2013 to provide specialist mental health services to patients residing in Dublin, who had already been deemed to require mental support. She explained that I was an unusual 'patient', if patient is the right word, because I had not been officially diagnosed as suffering from mental illness. She didn't know what was causing my confusion and whether it might just be a temporary situation. She was confident that they would soon find out was the problem was, she stressed that I was definitely in the right place. If it is eventually established that I was suffering from ill health, a diagnosis and a 'proper' care plan would be put together by a Multidisciplinary Team (MDT). Since my symptoms were unique for the Care Centre and because she was already involved, she said that she had offered to remain on this 'fascinating' case. The members had already been chosen to be Mr Cox, and a psychiatric nurse named Danny Boyd, who I would meet later that day. Standard practice meant that I should also be assigned a Key Worker, whose job it would be to co-ordinate the delivery of my individual care and treatment plan. She herself had volunteered to be my Key Worker and she would liaise with the MDT and also my family. What family, I thought?

"So, what exactly are you planning to do with me here that you were not able to do in Beaumont Hospital," I asked.

"We need to determine definitively if you are suffering from any form of mental illness and if so, what it is exactly. Only then can we come up with an agreed care plan," answered Mrs O'Brien.

"But I thought that is what you have been trying to do since we first met, what's different now?" I was persistent.

"Well, so far we have not been examining you in the recommended prescribed systematic way. We have, in truth, been jumping from 'Billy to Jack'. We now need to proceed step by step, so that when we are finished you will have a diagnosis and an agreed care plan," replied Mrs O'Brien.

"So how exactly do you go about doing that," I asked sceptically.

"Well, let's just see how it goes, shall we? I would like to start by 'talking you through' the main points you should know about schizophrenia. One possibility is that you may be suffering from this brain condition, so we need to dig deeper. When I have finished speaking and have answered all of your questions, I will leave you some booklets to read later. The more you know about the condition, the better. Do you understand Mr Forman?"

"Yes perfectly," I answered meekly.

Mrs O'Brien 'put on her serious face' and continued..

"First of all, please understand that it is very difficult to get a one hundred percent certain diagnosis for schizophrenia. The Department of Health advises that it can be diagnosed if:

- *You have experienced one or more of the following symptoms most of the time for a month: delusions, hallucinations, hearing voices, incoherent speech or negative symptoms, such as a flattening of emotions.*
- *Your symptoms have had a significant impact on your ability to work, study or perform daily tasks.*
- *All other possible causes, such as recreational drug use or bipolar disorder have been ruled out.*

"For a month!" I shouted in panic.

"Don't worry about that for now Mr Forman. Let's see how we get on for the next week or so, I'm sure you will want us to do the job properly rather than trying to 'beat the clock'," answered Mrs O'Brien. "Do you understand the procedure Mr Forman?"

"I'm not sure I understand what you mean by a flattening of emotions," I answered.

"Ok, let me read an extract from this yellow booklet here. It puts a little more 'flesh on the bones'," explained Mrs O'Brien, as she fumbled to find the right place in the booklet.

She then read from the booklet word for word:

"Other people might notice symptoms before you do, because the condition means you don't always know what's real. Symptoms include:

- *Delusions, where you 'just know' things that seem unreal to other people.*
- *Hallucinations, where you see, feel, smell or hear things that aren't true.*
- *Muddled thinking and difficulty concentrating.*
- *A feeling that you are being controlled by something outside yourself.*
- *Not feeling up to normal activities like washing, dressing or seeing friends."*

"My God, that's scary stuff. Should I just lie to you so that I pass the test?" I half-jokingly asked.

"I'm sure you wouldn't do that Mr Forman. Please remember that you also need to know what is going on. Remember that, whatever you are suffering from, it is extremely likely that it can be treated successfully," answered Mrs O'Brien.

Mrs O'Brien then handed me three booklets and suggested that I read through them all a few times, until I was sure I understood the condition. She stood up and mentioned that it was almost 10.00am and that Nurse Danny would call in on me shortly. She said that he preferred to be simply called Danny rather than Nurse Danny or even Nurse Boyd. Mrs O'Brien and Doctor Cox both smiled as they stood up and left me alone, again locking the door behind them.

I lay down on my bed and started to read the yellow booklet. A sudden knock on the door and in walked a stranger. He was carrying a white plastic tray with two mugs of coffee and 'mountains' of buttered toast on an oval plate. There was no sugar or milk on the tray, so he knew how I liked my coffee. I moved and sat at the small wooden table. The stranger sat down right opposite me.

"Hello Mr Forman, or can I call you Ian. I'm Danny your appointed psychiatric nurse," he said in an English accent. "Do you mind if I join you for a late breakfast, I'm starving."

I nodded and said good morning. I liked that he called me Ian. But what was an English nurse doing here? Was it because I said that I lived in the UK? Danny didn't look or act like a 'typical' nurse. He was probably in his mid to late fifties but dressed like a teenager from the sixties of seventies. He had long black 'straggly' hair, which he continually kept brushing away from his face. When he first walked in, I had immediately noticed that although he had the standard white coat buttoned up to the neck, that he had a pair of cut-off jeans and a pair of brown 'Jesus Sandals'. He didn't even have a pair of socks on. He didn't look like a nurse, so I discretely pushed the call button. Before starting to eat, I asked Danny where in England, he came from. I decided it would be better to ask, rather than answer questions. Seconds later, to my relief, Mr Cox walked in.

"Good morning again, Mr Forman," he smiled, "I see that you have already met Nurse Boyd. Good morning Danny."

Both Danny and I responded in unison, greeting Mr Cox formally.

"You pushed your button, Mr Forman, can I get you something?" enquired Mr Cox.

I had to think quickly ..

"Oh, did I? Must have happened by mistake. Sorry to bring you here for no reason," I replied.

"No problem Mr Forman, but since I'm here now, can I help you with anything?"

I told Mr Cox that I had everything I needed for the moment. He said he would then leave me in the 'more than capable' hands of Danny and left me, no doubt to attend to more 'urgent cases'.

During breakfast Danny told me that he was from a town called Aylesbury in England. He moved to Dublin several years ago. He had answered an advertisement for a trained experienced Psychiatric Nurse who had 'hands-on' experience of 'recreational drugs'. It changed his life when he took the job in The Phoenix. It came with the use of his own large suite, right on the premises. It was an easy decision to move there with his wife. They both loved Dublin, especially the dynamic music scene everywhere. They didn't have the problem of having to buy a house at the Dublin exorbitant prices. They rented out their house in Aylesbury and it more than paid for the rental of their suite, at The Phoenix. He and his wife were having the best time of their lives, Alison was happy in her work at Sixth Car Rental in Dublin Airport and he was loving his job, not really a job at all, he said. So much better than the strict regime he was under in England, working for bosses that cared more about their own careers than they did about their needy patients, he said.

After breakfast Danny offered to show me around the facility. I was surprised that I would be free to wander around but when Danny saw that I was puzzled, he explained that I was not a 'real' patient, at least not yet anyway. All the other patients already had a diagnosis and were there for treatment. I had not yet been formally diagnosed, but I was deemed to be of no potential harm to others or to myself. As long as I was with Danny, I could move about freely. Danny explained that, since I was not yet being treated for any specific condition that he was simply to be my daily companion. But he 'warned' me that when he was with me, he was actually watching my every move and was listening to everything I said and how I expressed myself. He would be looking for any signs of schizophrenic behaviour. He stressed that he was not spying on me but that his job was to keep me company, gain my trust and monitor my behaviour. He was to give a verbal report to Mr Cox and Mrs O'Brien at the end of each day. He promised to be honest with me and would actually tell me in advance what he was going to report later each day. If I ever disagreed with him, we could discuss it openly. Although I loved Danny's honesty, I was not sure if he was supposed to tell me all that, but I was grateful he did. Perhaps now we will start to get somewhere!

I was amazed with the facilities at the Phoenix Care Centre. They had a fully equipped gym, a games room with a full-sized snooker table, table tennis, computer games consoles, and even card tables. There was a large internal walled garden, with a rectangular manicured lawn, a central water fountain feature and mature shrubs and flowers bordering all the walls. Footpaths zigzagged throughout the garden. There were several comfortable looking wooden benches dotted along the walkways. What a relaxing and pleasant environment!

Good as the walled garden was, it paled into insignificance when I was shown into the music room. More a small theatre than a music room. There was a grand piano on the stage and one or more of every musical instrument you could think of, even a drum kit. All neatly placed around the outsides of the stage. It had a very good-looking sound system with speakers on all of the theatre walls. The centre of the room was completely bare, the highly polished light oak wooden laminate floor was well worn. On the left side of the theatre, several long wooden benches were stacked up, no doubt used for concerts or recitals. I saw at least two electric guitars, two acoustic guitars, a banjo and a mandolin, all on individual music stands on the stage. I almost gasped at the sight of it all. No one was in the theatre. When I questioned how they could justify the cost of such a facility, Danny explained that it had all been donated by Bono of U2. Danny looked straight at me when he told me about Bono, he correctly assumed that I knew all about him. Bono had read somewhere that music was good for people suffering from depression and from other mental conditions and he thought he could 'do something'. He was even paying for a full-time music teacher, guitar and piano, to be employed. I read the notice on the door explaining that if anyone wanted to try another instrument to just mention it to the teacher and it would be provided. Free lessons for every instrument could be provided, free of charge.

"What a generous useful donation," I exclaimed.

"Yes, it has made a huge difference here," replied Danny. "We have regular concerts put on by the patients. The concerts can only be attended by staff members and close relations of the patients who participate. No staff members are permitted to participate, it is reserved only for current and past patients. Some of them have become very proficient and a few have gone on to later forge part-time careers from the experience."

"Danny, would I be free to practice guitar here?" I asked. "That would certainly ease the boredom of passing my days of confinement here."

Danny was very interested in knowing more about my guitar playing. He asked how long I had been playing and smiled in surprise when I explained that I only took it up when I retired a few years ago. He told me that he was an average guitar player and that he and his wife performed 'gigs' at local pubs, most weekends. He guided me up on stage and picked up the brand-new Martin acoustic guitar. He tuned it 'by ear' and proceeded to play several songs, most of which I knew and some of which I used to also try to play, but only when no one was listening of course.

"I live for my guitar playing," he shouted over the loud music, "c'mon you have a go," he urged. "Unfortunately, I can't sing in tune but my wife has a fantastic voice and she's an awesome keyboard player. You must come and listen to us some night!"

Danny handed me his guitar. We were alone in the small theatre. Why not 'go for it', I thought! I placed the strap over my head, and strummed a few bars of *Whiskey in the Jar*.

Once my fingers were working properly I 'launched' into playing and singing the Eagles song *Lying Eyes*. I sang the entire song at the top of my voice, it brought back real happy memories. I know I made quite a few mistakes with the chords but Danny just stood beside me, motionless for the entire song. When I had finished, he applauded for ages.

"Blimey!" he exclaimed, "that was bloody marvellous. What brilliant lyrics and how great a tune was that. When did you write that song Ian?"

I laughed at his comments and then asked him if the music teacher would be willing to give me lessons on strumming. I could play most of the chords and could strum to the beat but I had not learned how to pick the strings yet and my strumming pattern was boring. I asked Danny if the teacher was any good.

"Forget about your flippin' strumming pattern Ian," said Danny, "just stick to the song writing."

I smiled again and then asked Danny if he knew how to play any of the other Eagles songs *Peaceful Easy Feeling*, *Hotel California* or their beautiful slow song, *Desperado*.

Danny picked up the Fender Telecaster electric guitar and within a minute or so he had it tuned and ready to go. He played the intro to *Hotel California* brilliantly and with real passion. I joined in and sang every verse, strumming along to his fantastic guitar playing. Ok, we weren't always in time but we didn't do half-badly. When we finished, I went straight into *Peaceful Easy Feeling* but stopped quickly when Danny didn't join in. Danny asked me to start again, and said that although he didn't know the tune, he would try to join in as I went along. I think I made a half-decent job of playing and singing the song, right to the end. Danny had not bothered to join in. I assumed he didn't like the song. I pulled the strap over my head and placed the guitar carefully back in its stand.

Danny put his electric guitar back in its stand and stood back to applaud.

"Thanks Danny but don't overdo it," I replied, a little embarrassed. "You can see why I could do with some guitar lessons. Do you think your guitar teacher could help me?"

"Blimey Ian," replied Danny. "Where did you learn how to write a song like that. It's fantastic. Can you teach it to me, together with that other one you sang earlier, what was it called again?"

"*Lying Eyes*," I replied.

I was now intrigued. We left the theatre and toured the remainder of the facilities. We relaxed for a while in the television room, watching some wildlife documentary about Alaska. Danny however, kept coming back to the songs I had played earlier. He checked the internet on his phone and then turned it off, putting it back in his pocket.

"Ian, neither of those two songs is by the Eagles. In fact, I can't find that they are by anybody! Where did you get them from?"

I smiled at Danny and re-assured him that I had not written either of the songs and that they were definitely Eagles songs. Danny did not 'push' the issue any further, instead he went silent and I could see that his mind was 'working overtime'. We went together for lunch, in the canteen. Compared to the music room, the canteen was not that impressive. It reminded me of the IKEA canteen in their store in Milton Keynes. The self-service food was 'ok enough' though. My ham, egg and chips were excellent in fact, and Danny's chicken salad looked ok. We both drank diet cokes straight from the bottles. Danny had paid the bill but explained that my meal was 'free gratis'.

After lunch we walked back to the walled garden. I asked him how he had got the job at the Phoenix, did he 'know somebody'. Danny explained that several years ago that in 'The Lions Community' the treatment for mental health had changed dramatically. It was finally accepted that the then used drugs for Post-Traumatic Stress Disorder (PTSD), and Clinical Depression were really not that effective and once a patient started taking them it was difficult for them to give them up. Following lengthy clinical trials in the USA and in England, the decision to switch to MDMA for PTSD and to the psychedelic drug psilocybin for depression, was taken.

"But what's that got to do with you working here Danny?" I asked.

"Well Ian, you probably better know MDMA as ecstasy, you might have even tried it," replied Danny, "and psilocybin is the active ingredient in magic mushrooms."

Danny went on to explain that he was very open and honest at his interview and admitted to having taken lots of party drugs in his student past. He personally knew how it felt to take ecstasy along with cannabis, LSD, heroin and some other so-called designer drugs. His interviewers, having satisfied themselves that Danny had been 'clean' for over thirty years, thought that his student experience would be a huge asset for 'observing' their patients and gave him the 'offer of a lifetime', in his words!

"So, is that what will happen to me Danny?" I asked. "Will I be drugged up to my eyeballs, just to keep me calm and happy?"

Danny considered very carefully before he answered:

"Ian, they don't even know yet if you have any mental illness, let alone know what treatment would be suitable, but if you ask my opinion, and perhaps I shouldn't say it, but I can't see that you are suffering from PTSD and you certainly don't act as if you are depressed. You certainly didn't seem depressed when you were 'belting out' those songs, earlier."

"But aren't you supposed to help them determine whether I am schizophrenic?" I asked.

"Yes, I am, and I will," he replied.

I spent the rest of the day relaxing and just 'hanging out' with Danny. When it was finally time for sleep, he brought me back to my room and making sure that I was ok, he said he would see me next morning.

"So, what will tomorrow bring, Danny?" I asked. "Will my assessment start tomorrow?"

"Ian, it has already begun," he replied. "I will be briefing Mr Cox and Mrs O'Brien shortly.

"So, what are you going to tell them Danny?" I asked.

Danny seemed a little awkward answering me. He would tell them that I seemed to be quite relaxed, not at all anxious. He joked that he would tell them that I was a brilliant song writer.

I kicked off my shoes and lay on my bed, I didn't mind that I was again locked into my room. I didn't want to go anywhere anyway! I went over the events of the day in my head. What a strange day, what a strange situation I was in. Why did Danny pretend that he had never heard of those Eagles' songs? Was it to see my reaction? Was it some type of test? I would try to become Danny's friend and see if he could find Mary for me. I knew she was around somewhere, hadn't Sergeant Murphy earlier confirmed that Ann hadn't seen her sister for some time. Where the hell is Mary?

Yes, I will get to know Danny as well as I can, I will find out all about this place. Who knows, maybe he will let me try some 'magic mushrooms' tomorrow. What did he say, something about 'The Lions Community', what's that all about?

Chapter 7

Days and weeks passed. Boring days and even more boring nights. Danny did his best to 'keep me amused'. I played guitar for several hours each day and Danny continued to be great company but when would my treatment start? When would I be free to leave this place and get on with my life, but then again, what life? Every morning and again each afternoon, I would have formal meetings with Mrs O'Brien and Mr Cox. Talk, talk, talk! Nothing but talk, talk, talk! I concluded that neither of them had the faintest clue how to get to the bottom of my condition. They kept telling me that I had no symptoms of depression, that I appeared to be relaxed and that they didn't think I posed a threat to either myself or others. But they still didn't know who I was or where I came from. Both the Irish and the English police had 'drawn a blank' on their missing persons files, but they knew I couldn't be who I claimed to be. They had confirmation that Ian Forman had died when he was just twelve years old and they had actually spoken to Mary, the person I claimed to be my wife, who is married to someone else and has a grown-up son. She has never heard of me. I clearly have some of the symptoms of schizophrenia but in many other ways I don't show such symptoms. They said that we were still in the observation phase but that they were hopeful that Danny might help them unlock the key. For now, I need to be patient, they were confident that everything will become clear as soon as it is established who I actually am.

"Look, I know who I am," I exclaimed. "How about asking one of my brothers or sisters to come and talk to us. Maybe that would get us somewhere, we are getting nowhere at the moment."

"Mr Forman, you are well aware that none of the people, you claim to be related to, admit to knowing you but let me see what I can do," replied Mrs O'Brien.

Several more days passed and now I was starting to worry that I might begin to show signs of depression. If it wasn't for Danny, I think I would have descended into complete darkness. Finally, on one dark rainy morning I was summoned to the reception area. Danny accompanied me down the stairs, he told me that I had visitors.

I started to tremble when I saw the three people seated on the long brown leather padded bench. My brother Peter, his daughter Barbara and my sister Marian, seated side by side, looking straight at me or should I say, straight through me. I walked quickly towards them, with my arms outstretched, but none of them stood up, I wanted to hug them but they seemed frightened of me. Barbara actually recoiled when she saw me approaching. The three of them sat nervously, not even offering to shake hands with me.

Mrs O'Brien stood on their left and Doctor Cox stood on the right. Mrs O'Brien put her hand on my shoulder and without a word being spoken, ushered all of us into meeting room number three, which was at the end of the short corridor. Deathly silence as we walked to the room and took our seats around a long oak coffee table. Mrs O'Brien sat at the head of the table, she obviously planned to carefully manage our meeting. Peter, Barbara and Marian sat on one side of the table, Doctor Cox, Danny and I sat opposite them. I was immediately opposite Peter.

"Good morning everyone and welcome to the Phoenix Care Centre," began Mrs O'Brien. "Ladies and gentlemen thank you for coming here this morning for this very unusual meeting."

Mrs O' Brien then explained that she wanted to try to have a structured discussion so she asked all of us to speak only when she asked us to. She didn't bother with 'introductions' so I presumed that she and Doctor Cox had already had discussions with Peter, Barbara and Marian. She looked over to me and stated slowly …

"Ok, why don't you tell these people who you think you are and also tell us whether you recognise your visitors."

I cleared my throat and took a deep breath.

"I don't think that I am Ian Forman, I know that I am. Ian Raymond Forman in fact." I looked only at Mrs O'Brien as I spoke. "Yes, of course I recognise my brother Peter, my sister Marian and my niece Barbara, who is Peter's daughter," I added, as I looked at each of them in turn.

Still no change of expression from any of my three visitors. They just 'blanked me'. They were clearly under instructions from Mrs O'Brien.

"Would you mind telling us a little about yourself and what you know about your three visitors here?" asked Mrs O'Brien.

I fixed my eyes on Peter first. He seemed to be quite a bit heavier since I last saw him but he looked very fit and healthy. I told everyone that my older brother Peter had recently turned seventy. He had been happily married to Claire since his early twenties and they had four children together, sons Gavin, Alan and Paul and a daughter Barbara, who was sitting there in front of me. Claire had died from cancer about ten years ago, I think, and Peter was lucky to have such supportive children to 'keep him going'. Peter went straight into the family fish business from secondary school and took over the business after our daddy was killed in a car accident, when he was in his mid-fifties. My sister Marian is several years younger than me and is married to Noel Baylis. She has three children who all live nearby. My niece Barbara is married to Graham and they have three children. My wife Mary and I travelled over from England to go to Barbara and Graham's wedding. I remember it was a big lavish affair, held in the Waterside Hotel in Donabate, County Dublin.

I also remember dancing with Barbara at her brother Alan's wedding to Brenda on the Greek island of Zante. I remember the bride and groom arriving at the reception at the beachside hotel, in a small boat. My younger brothers Robert and Mark certainly celebrated for the whole week they were there. My brother Patrick and his wife came all the way over from Chicago to join in. We all had a great time but it was very noticeable that Peter was still desperately missing Claire as were Alan and Barbara. I paused and looked at Barbara, I think I saw a tear come to her eye!

"Ok, thanks for that Ian," interrupted Mrs O'Brien. "Would you please tell everyone a little about yourself."

"You agreed that you wouldn't call him Ian, Mrs O'Brien," said Peter in a slightly angry tone.

"But that's my name, Peter," I said softly.

I spoke as if to strangers. I told them all about Mary and our son John and daughter Annette. I reminded Peter that he was my 'best man' at Mary's and my wedding in the Crofton Airport Hotel in Dublin. I told them that Mary and I had lived in Canada for a couple of years before living in Belgium for almost ten years. We were now living in England. I asked Peter if he remembered Claire and himself visiting us in Buckingham. Mary took Claire shopping in Milton Keynes while Peter and I travelled down to see his team Arsenal take on West Ham, in their brand-new stadium. Their short break had been a sixtieth birthday present from Peter and Claire's children. In case he had forgotten, I reminded Peter that Arsenal lost 0-1, that day. Peter continued to give me a blank stare throughout.

Mrs O'Brien put her right hand up to signal to me to stop talking for now.

"Peter, Marian and Barbara, thank you for listening, without interrupting. From what you told me earlier, this must have been extremely difficult," said Mrs O'Brien. "As agreed, rather than commenting on what Ian has said, Peter you have prepared some questions for him."

"Yes, I certainly have," said Peter, as he sat up straight in his chair. "Just three simple questions which will blow all the nonsense he has said so far, out of the water."

"*Question No 1*: Mr whoever you are, I have been told that you have seen the date July 12th, 1961 engraved on the family headstone in the Old Abbey Graveyard. I know it's a long shot but do you have any recollection about falling into Howth harbour when you were about twelve years old," asked Peter.

My heart leapt. Of-course I could remember that. I tried to recall the whole event and then about how best to explain what had happened.

I spoke slowly and deliberately, trying hard not to dramatize the event, it didn't need dramatizing! I provided as much detail as I could remember:

"When I was twelve years old, a few of my school friends and I, had been fishing for crabs inside the harbour. It must have been during the school holidays as it was in the early afternoon. I think there were just three of us but there might have been four. I can't remember any of their names, isn't that shocking! We had a little game going. My dad had given each of us a galvanised steel bucket and a medium sized 'skeleton' of a whiting or it could have been a haddock, the fish had already been filleted. The family fish business premises were situated about halfway down the West Pier. My uncle James was working with him that day, probably preparing thousands of herrings, which would be smoked and turned into 'kippers' later that night. We each tied the bait to the pieces of string we had with us and walked straight across the pier to the steps which descended right down to the water. Descending the steps, we filled our buckets to about quarter full with sea water and ascending the steps we placed the partly filled buckets on the side of the quay. Although there was a small lobster fishing boat tied up to the harbour wall, right beside the steps, we decided it wouldn't prevent us from catching enough crabs to have our crab race. We each pulled a six-penny piece from our trouser pockets, it was agreed that I would hold the 'pot' in my pocket as it had a button on the flap to keep it closed. The game involved us catching as many crabs as we could, which we would keep alive in our individual steel buckets until we agreed to 'call it a day'. We planned to lift our crabs from our buckets and line them up in a straight line, on the quayside. The crabs would then be 'encouraged' to crawl to the edge of the harbour wall from where they would tumble straight into the water. The person who 'owned' the crab that first fell back into the water would win the 'pot' of three or four sixpenny pieces. We took great care to ensure that all of the crabs returned safely to the water, none of the crabs were hurt during our game. We had played this many times before and we needed the crabs to be fighting fit for the next day's race. Anyway, we had not been long fishing when the accident happened. We were each standing on separate steps with our suspended bait dangling alongside the brown 'bubbly' seaweed, which clung to the harbour wall. Once a crab had taken the bait with its claws, the skilled part began. Don't know if the crabs knew what was coming because they always held onto the seaweed tightly with their legs, even as their claws were closed on the bait. If the bait was pulled up too abruptly, the crab would immediately let go of it and cling to the seaweed. The only way to catch the crab was to gently 'ease' him away from the seaweed whilst keeping the bait at the same level in the water. Only when the crab was free of the seaweed could we pull it from the water. This exercise in patience required us to lean forward, away from the steps, dangling precariously over the water. Don't know how it happened but I lost my balance and tipped into the water. I cannot remember anything else until I was lying on the harbour pier with my daddy kneeling beside me. I'll never forget that look of fear on his face, I'd never seen it before. He later told me that when I had fallen in, one of my friends ran to get help from him while the others just stood there screaming. The screaming was heard by the owner of the fishing boat who, at the time, was on the deck of the boat, repairing his lobster pots. Cyril Doyle quickly arrived with the gaff, which is a long pole with a brass hook on one end. The boat stood maybe three or four feet above the water but was only a foot or two away from the harbour wall. I was told that Cyril was a real hero that day. Apparently there was no sign of me when he looked down in the water, he thinks that I somehow went under the boat and the water disturbance had caused the hull to sway away from the harbour wall, only for the tightening of the restraining ropes to pull it back to touch the harbour wall. Cyril pushed the boat gently away from the harbour wall and blindly slid the gaff underneath the hull, moving it towards the bow and then the stern in a systematic search pattern. He said that he thought that he had 'hooked me' on at least two other occasions but each time the hook slipped free from my clothing. On the third occasion, he managed to get a firm hold on me and pulled me from the water, gasping for breath. I have lost count of the number of people who told me how lucky I was that day. The trauma left me with a paranoid fear of water, I'm still afraid to even get into a kids swimming pool. Yes, I owe my life to Cyril Doyle, one of the quietest and unassuming men I have ever met. I, no doubt, met him many times since that day and he has never mentioned anything about his heroics."

I crossed my arms to indicate that I was finished my re-telling of the events that day and looked at Peter to see his reaction. I could see that he wanted to speak but he was stopped by Mrs O'Brien, who raised her hand to 'stop him in his tracks'.

"Ian, that's a heart-warming story, thank you for telling us about it," said Mrs O'Brien enthusiastically. Are you ready for question number two now, or do you want that comfort break you earlier didn't need?" she asked.

"No, I'm ready for the next question, let's get these questions out of the way," I answered.

Peter took another deep breath and asked ...

"Mr 'God knows who you are', I have also been told that you mentioned that your daddy had died in a car accident in 1980 and that you somehow thought that you might have been partially responsible. Would you mind expanding a little on that?"

"Yes, I'll try. He did die in 1980, I have a photo of the family headstone on my mobile phone. I could show it to you if someone could figure out how to charge my phone," I replied.

I went on to tell them all about what happened. I was working in my office in a seatbelt manufacturing company, which was located in the town of Ieper in Belgium. Yes, the town is also known by its French name Ypres, the tragic centre of much of the carnage of World War One. I remember that the office was 'buzzing' with much excitement as our team of five Industrial Engineers were still making final 'tweaks' to the layout of the production line, on which our latest design of automatic seatbelts for cars, were being assembled. My secretary, Esther called over to me, asking me to pick up my phone, as my wife Mary was on the line. I picked up the phone and my life changed for ever. Mary told me that she had just received a phone call from my brother Peter, she hesitated for several seconds and then said that she could not think of any other way to tell me, she hesitated again...

"Ian, your daddy has just died in a car accident. I'm really sorry."

I could hear Mary crying, which set me off, 'big time'. I couldn't speak, I just handed the phone back to Esther and hurriedly left the office. I needed privacy to gather my thoughts and to, as they say, 'pull myself together'. I must have sat alone in the 'rest room' for a good twenty minutes, before I came back to the office. Everyone in the office was obviously aware of what had happened, but no one spoke. What could they say? I gratefully accepted a lift home from my colleague Tom, I was in no fit state to drive. On arrival home Mary gave me more details about the accident. My daddy was returning from the Dublin fish market, where he had bought the day's fish needs. He had supervised the loading of the boxes of fish onto the company lorry and then set off on the half hour trip back to Howth, in his car. He was accompanied by my brother Mark, who sat in the passenger seat with my brother, Robert, seated in the back. Robert told me later that somewhere on the coast road between the Centre of Dublin and Howth, they were taking a gentle right-hand bend when suddenly a 'Johnston Mooney and O'Brien' bread van was right in front of them, heading straight at them. My daddy swerved to the left to avoid a head on collision, mounted the footpath and crashed straight through a stone wall, the car finishing in someone's garden. Daddy was pronounced dead at the scene but thankfully both of my brothers survived with just cuts and bruises. Mary and I flew from Brussels' Zaventem airport the next day and later attended the funeral. The church was packed. I was really proud of myself that I could 'hold myself together' well enough to take a 'reading'.

"Is that enough about that for now, Mrs O'Brien?" I asked.

"Thanks for that Ian, it must have been a very sad time for you all but especially traumatic for your mother and your young siblings Mark and Fiona. But you mentioned earlier that you were really upset because you thought that you might be somehow responsible, how could that be when you were hundreds of miles away in Belgium?"

"Because just a couple of weeks before the accident, I had personally fitted a pair of the new seatbelts in the front seats of Daddy's car. They were the, then new, 'retractor style' automatic seat belts. I had taken a set of them from our production line and I carried them with me, when Mary and I returned to Ireland for a holiday in early July. I told my daddy that I would replace his old 'fixed seat belts' with this new style and I remember him thanking me. Within just a few minutes about hearing of my daddy's death, all I could think about was that his seatbelt didn't work. Maybe I had fitted it incorrectly, had I killed my daddy?"

I couldn't sleep properly for days. Although I couldn't bear to hear the answer, after the funeral, I finally plucked up the courage to ask my brother Mark about the accident. How had Daddy died when both he and Robert had suffered just cuts and bruises. He told me that Daddy didn't bother to put on his seat belt, he left it permanently fastened behind his back, he didn't like all the fuss with putting it on. He died when the car came to a sudden stop. He was shot forward and his chest was crushed on the steering wheel. Mark could hear Daddy groan in pain for a couple of minutes before he died. Mark said that the sound would be 'with him' forever. I hope Mark didn't notice the sense of relief that must have been 'all over' my face.

When I asked Mark about his own seatbelt, he unbuttoned his shirt and showed me the red mark burned diagonally across his chest. He had his seatbelt on and it had worked.

I hadn't killed my daddy!

I felt elated, felt a great sense of relief, I wanted to tell everyone. I then looked behind me and saw my mother 'in bits'. A great surge of grief engulfed me. How could I have wanted to 'almost celebrate' that although my daddy had died, it wasn't my fault?

Robert's minor injuries, which were caused by being thrown about in the back of the car, were largely ignored. The whole family was devastated. My daddy's sudden death had changed everything for the whole family, and not for the better.

"So yes Mrs O'Brien, for a time I felt that I may have been responsible. Is that enough about that for now?" I asked.

"That's very useful and helpful information Ian, as you will hear later," replied Mrs O'Brien. "Are you ready to go straight to question number three now?"

I nodded and Peter posed his next question:

"Look stranger, you spin a great yearn," Peter said very sarcastically. "I've also heard that you have said that your brother Robert died from a heart attack in May 2012. Could you tell us a little more about how it happened?"

"Christ it's difficult even now talking about these events. Robert had been separated from his wife for some years and was living alone in his apartment on the coast road in Clontarf, Dublin. Sometime in late March or early April 2012 he called me. Mary and I were living in Buckingham, England at the time. He told me he wanted to arrange a memorial service for our mother and our brother Louis. Louis had died on May 12th almost seven years earlier and Mammy's one-year anniversary was coming up on

May 19th. He explained that he would go ahead with organising the service if Mary and I would come over and that he believed our brother Patrick would also make the trip from Chicago. We immediately agreed to go. Robert was clearly 'over the moon' and explained that it would be a great opportunity for the family to get together and celebrate their lives. The memorial service was booked, I think for the day of my mother's anniversary. We had our car ferry tickets booked, we would travel on May 13th.

On May 12th, I received a phone call from Peter. He told me that Robert had died that day, from a suspected heart attack. We did make the trip to Dublin, but not for a memorial service. We attended Robert's funeral service! I still cannot believe that he died on May 12th, the same date as my brother Louis, exactly seven years later. Both aged fifty-five.

Do you need more detail about this Mrs O'Brien or is this ok for now? I am getting very emotional about it all, can we talk about something else now?"

"Of-course we can, and that is more than enough detail for now about Robert," she answered sympathetically.

"How about we change the subject away from talking about your family for a while? You have earlier told us that you and your family live in England. Could you tell us about what it's like living in England? Have you ever thought about returning to Ireland?"

"Yes, we have often thought about coming back, but with our children and grandchildren living nearby it would be a big wrench. We have made England our home and we are very happy there. We visit Ireland regularly, at least once per year, and we have become used to dealing with the Euro and the varying exchange rate with the British Pound."

"So, what was the exchange rate this trip?" interrupted Mr Cox.

"To be honest, I'm not sure. Mary sorts that out for us. I know that the pound has weakened but it's still worth more than the Euro, maybe ten per cent or so, I think," I replied hesitantly.

"So, what do you think about Irish politics Mr Forman? Is it better now than years ago?" asked Mr Cox.

Why was he now suddenly interested in joining in?

"I know practically nothing about Irish politics but I am very happy that there is no longer any terrorism. I always believed that it would be better, and more 'natural' if Ireland was finally united but I don't think it will happen in my lifetime. Too many vested interests in the status quo. You cannot use bombs and bullets to force people to think the way you want them to. Still it's great that the Republic is back on track financially and as long as the British government is prepared to subsidise the North, I think peace will reign."

"Have you recently visited the North, Ian?" asked Doctor Cox.

"No, I haven't had cause to, for many, many, years, but I know that there is no fixed border, that was a big step forward," I replied.

"Can I ask a few quick questions, Mrs. O'Brien?" I was surprised that Peter had interrupted suddenly!

'Why not," she replied. "What harm can it do?"

Peter looked straight at me and appeared to brace himself. I could see the tension in his neck muscles. He was very nervous and his voice trembled as he spoke without referring to my name.

"What was your daddy's nickname, what did his friends and family call him?"

"Bubby," I replied triumphantly.

"What did his friends call him when he wasn't with them?"

"I'm not sure I understand what you mean, how would I know that? Oh! ... I think I know what you mean now. Anytime anyone was speaking about him, rather than to him, they referred to him as: 'The Blind Fella'.

"And why was that?"

"Because from early middle age his eyesight started to deteriorate but he refused to wear glasses. He had to 'squint' anytime he was reading."

"What was Ian's nickname and why was he called that?"

"I was called 'Bones', because I was so thin," I replied matter-of-factly. "As a child, I was 'forced' to drink a pint of milk every day for years."

"What did we call my grandfather, my daddy's daddy that is?"

"We all called him Pop."

"What did my daddy call my mammy?"

"I don't remember him having a special name for Mammy, I think he just called her Flo."

"What was the name of our headmaster at school?"

"I think it was Mr Leavy, in fact it definitely was. His son Alan was in my class and we were good friends."

"I just don't understand how he knows all that," exclaimed Peter out loud, in a very frustrated tone.

Mrs O'Brien nodded and smiled at Peter.

"Ok, have you finished with your questions for now Peter? Are you now ready to answer the same questions that Ian has already answered?"

Peter asked if he could take a break for a few minutes. He said he wanted to stand up for a minute or two and wanted to get a glass of water, before he began.

Chapter 8

Peter returned to the room and sat down. He looked like he was primed and ready to go.

"Do you want me to ask the first question again Peter, or can you still remember it?" asked Mrs O'Brien.

"How could I ever forget July 12th, 1961," began Peter. "My mammy was distraught. She hardly spoke at all. Mammy and Daddy never went out anymore after that and I don't remember ever seeing either of them laughing again. That is until Mark and Fiona arrived. Even though I was only fourteen years of age, I could see that Mammy lost interest in everybody and everything. Little or no conversation with me or anyone else for that matter and no one dare mention Ian or she would be 'off' again. A deep sense of melancholy descended on our home that 'cloaked' our home for many years."

"Why was that?" interrupted Mrs O'Brien.

"Because my brother Ian drowned in Howth harbour that day," answered Peter. "I can still remember my sister Jean coming to find me. I was playing in what was known as the 'sand pit', just a few-minutes-walk, from our house. She came running up to me, red in the face. She told me that something bad had happened and that I was to come home right away. When I arrived home the house was full of people. People, some of whom I didn't even know, were standing around, huddled in little groups. Many were crying and hugging each other."

"Did anyone tell you exactly how it happened Peter?" interrupted Mrs O'Brien again.

"Yes, but not straight away," replied Peter. "Over the following weeks I gradually learned what had happened. 'His' story is correct up to a point. His story about the crab race is what I also remember being told about. Yes, Cyril Doyle did try to 'hook' Ian with the gaff, but each time he thought he had him, Ian slipped away. Eventually Cyril handed the gaff to one of Ian's friends who was still standing on the steps and asked him to push on the hull of the boat, to keep it away from the harbour wall. With that, Cyril slipped off his boots and dropped, feet first, into the water. My daddy had, by then, arrived on the scene and, running down the steps, also dropped into the water. It took a little while for them to find Ian, who I'm told had been under the keel of the boat. I'm afraid that when they brought him to the surface Ian was 'blue in the face'. Despite an onlooker knowing how to resuscitate, his effort failed. Ian was dead! Weeks later my daddy tried to thank Cyril for his attempt to save Ian but Cyril rejected his 'hand of friendship'. Cyril blamed himself for the drowning. He was never the same man again, he told anyone who would listen, that he should have dropped into the water straight away, wished he hadn't tried to use the gaff. He later said that he was convinced that he might even have pushed Ian under the keel of the boat with the gaff. Instead of being praised for his efforts he said he should have been charged with murder!"

"Peter, thank you for re-living that painful experience," said Mrs O'Brien.

She then turned to me:

"Ian, I can see you are deeply upset by Peter's recounting of the events that day. I suggest we take a short break to compose ourselves before we continue with the second question."

A good ten minutes or so later, we were back in our seats. I was still upset but I knew that I hadn't actually drowned that day. I wondered what Peter was going to say about Daddy's car accident.

Peter's account of the car accident was much less dramatic than mine. Peter said that Daddy did indeed swerve to avoid the bread van and his car went through a wall and finished in someone's garden. However fortunately, no one was seriously hurt. Luckily Daddy and Mark had their seat belts on and suffered just cuts and bruises. Robert came out the worst as he was thrown about the back of the car.

"So, Daddy had his seat belt on!" I exclaimed.

Peter turned his head slowly towards me and whispered loudly:

"Although Daddy didn't like wearing his seat belt, fortunately he realised that it was the right thing to do and he eventually got into the habit of fastening it around his waist before each trip."

It suddenly 'dawned on me'. I wasn't around then. I hadn't replaced Daddy's seat belts. I couldn't have! According to Peter, I had died many years before. Daddy mustn't have minded wearing the 'old style' fixed seatbelts!

"I don't think I can take any more of this," I shouted. "What are we achieving? This is getting worse and worse. What are we trying to prove? I don't want to hear any more, it just cannot be true!"

I stood up suddenly and walked around the room a couple of times. I kept looking over at Peter to see his reaction .... None, just a blank stare forward!

"Ian, would you mind sitting down again so we can talk about Robert," pleaded Doctor Cox... he hesitated for a moment and then said:

"Can you tell us about Robert's heart attack Peter? I believe he did suffer a heart attack on the date that Ian here says he died."

Peter tilted his head to the left and turned his eyes to the left and up to the ceiling as he tried to remember...

"I'm not sure about the date but it must have been around that time. It's not at all like this 'deluded imposter' here says he can recall. Robert was lying in bed, fast asleep beside his wife. Suddenly his wife woke up to find him sitting up and groaning in pain. He was clutching his chest, his face contorted with pain. He was very cold but sweating. Fortunately, she realised what was happening and immediately ran to the medicine cupboard in the upstairs bathroom. With much fumbling and swearing she says she managed to open Robert's mouth and put an aspirin under his tongue. She later added, in amusement, that Robert almost bit her finger off as she tried to get him to close his mouth. She then ran down the stairs, and missing the last couple of steps she fell in a heap at the bottom of the stairs. Luckily, the hall was carpeted, so she was able to quickly pull herself to her feet and make the emergency call, for an ambulance. When she returned to the bedroom, she saw that Robert had suffered a cardiac arrest. Her training as a school teacher had included learning CPR, so she managed to get Robert's heart beating again, it could only have been stopped for a matter of seconds. She said that she waited for the ambulance for, what seemed like hours. It even crossed her mind that she might herself suffer a heart attack while she waited. Just in time, the ambulance arrived and she accompanied Robert in the ambulance to Beaumont Hospital."

"Did Robert suffer any permanent damage Peter?" interrupted Mrs O'Brien.

"No. In fact, it probably did him good. He realised that it was a big warning and within twelve months he had lost a couple of stone in weight and had cut down dramatically on the booze. He knew that he had had a very lucky escape. Since the incident, he affectionately only ever refers to his wife as Vinny, after Vinny Jones who he saw performing CPR on a TV advertisement to the beat of the Beegees song *Stayin' Alive*. The nickname stuck, everybody now calls her Vinny. She got used to it and I think loves it. In fact, she encourages it," said Peter with a smirk. "Oh, now I remember. The date 'he' mentioned must be about right. Robert was kept in hospital for several days and despite his protests he was unable to attend the memorial service that he himself had organised for Mammy and Louis," added Peter.

"Oh, I wish that was how I remember it, so Vinny saved the day," I sighed.

I saw Peter looking at his watch and Marian started shifting in her chair, she appeared to be getting agitated. Barbara had still not said anything or hadn't moved since she sat down. Mrs O'Brien thought that Peter, Marian and Barbara were probably thinking that her patient, whatever his name was, was mentally disturbed. She was intrigued with how the discussions had gone but she was no further to understanding just what her patient was suffering from. What should she do now? She felt completely helpless, not knowledgeable enough to deal with anything like this. Was there someone else she could turn to for help or advice? She felt inadequate and embarrassed. She could see that everyone was looking at her, expecting her to come up with answers!

Peter broke the deafening silence.

"Mrs O Brien, Doctor Cox and Nurse ...., sorry I don't know your name, thank you for inviting us here today. I think I can also speak for my sister and daughter, when I say that this is the craziest meeting we have ever attended. I can't say it was enlightening or even entertaining but nevertheless it was interesting. Your patient clearly needs help but I think he knows that himself. Someone has briefed him about certain events concerning our family but very badly on other events. If you are finished with us, we need to leave now. We have a family meeting to attend."

We all stood up. I was in shock, I couldn't speak. Was that it? My family had listened to me and then dismissed me as some type of lunatic! Why didn't Mrs O'Brien tell them they were wrong, I wasn't mad. I walked out of the room first and headed for my room, I didn't look at or say goodbye to anyone. Danny shouted after me to wait for him.

Back in my room I lay down on my bed, staring at the ceiling. Danny had followed me in and sat down beside my bed.

"Danny, am I mad?" I asked. "Just tell me the truth."

I waited for his response but nothing came. I continued asking unanswerable questions ..

"How come nobody knows me? I know who I am, but how can I be someone who died years ago? I now desperately want to meet my brother Robert but I know that he is dead, although Peter says he is still alive. What do you say to your dead brother? Do I get another chance to say sorry to him for the many 'childhood pranks' I played on him, I'm sure some of them must have hurt. I really hate myself! Who am I Danny? Who the hell am I? Am I a ghost? Am I really dead and is this Hell? Are you dead Danny? Would you even know or tell me if you were a ghost? Can a ghost play the guitar?"

I asked Danny if he would mind leaving me alone for the rest of the day. I wanted to be alone. I wasn't hungry, I wasn't thirsty, I wasn't tired, I wasn't anything. I wasn't even me! I told Danny that I would push the call button if I ever needed him again. I wondered if I didn't eat or drink anything from now on, what would happen? Would that put an end to my misery? But surely ghosts can't die. Even if this is all just a dreadful nightmare, surely if I starve myself in the dream I would wake up!

Danny left saying that he would look in on me soon, he said he understood but knew that I would feel much better after I had rested for a while. He told me that I was probably now suffering from mental exhaustion after the meeting and that a short rest would do me good.

"Not mental exhaustion," I shouted after Danny, "more like mental illness."

Chapter 9

Marian sat in the front passenger seat as Peter drove out of the Care Centre car park. Barbara sat silently in the back seat. In his mirror, Peter could see that Barbara was deep in thought. She looked really troubled and he was concerned. He couldn't understand why Mrs O'Brien had asked him and Marian to give a sample for DNA testing. What the feck was she thinking? She couldn't actually be thinking that 'this idiot'' was in any way related to them, could she? Peter turned on his car radio and turned up the volume really high. The Rolling Stones *I Can't Get No Satisfaction* was blaring out as Peter tapped out the beat on the steering wheel. No possibility of conversation!

Marian leaned over and turned off the radio.

"What do we do now Peter?" asked Marian.

"What do you mean 'what do we do', replied Peter. "We do feckin' nothing, that's what we do, feck all"

"Sorry about the bad language Barbara," added Peter as he turned momentarily around to see her reaction.

"But we can't just ignore this Daddy," pleaded Barbara. "This problem won't go away on its own."

"Oh, for Christ's sake, don't you feckin' start," replied Peter. "It's not our problem. We don't run that mental hospital."

Peter turned the radio back on and turned up the volume even louder. Nat King Cole's song *Smile, Though Your Heart Is Breakin'* started playing.

Marian leaned forward again and turned the radio off once more.

"Peter, we have to tell the others," she said. "We have to tell Robert, Mark and Fiona and I think you should also call Patrick in Chicago."

"Tell them what?" answered Peter. "That we have just had a long conversation with our dead brother Ian, who is not now dead but instead is being detained in a mental home. I think they will say that it is us who should be in the feckin' nuthouse. Oh yes, and I'll also tell Robert that this nutcase said that he was already dead, died of a feckin' heart attack years ago."

"You don't have to put it that way," interrupted Barbara.

"Look if you won't tell them Peter, then I will," said Marian in a slightly raised voice.

Peter dropped his daughter Barbara off outside her house. He 'ordered her' not to speak to anyone about what had happened earlier. He was slightly shocked when she responded angrily, telling him that she would tell anybody she wanted to.

"I'm all grown up now Daddy, in case you haven't noticed," she said. "You no longer decide what I say to anyone any more. But why the hell did he say that he had danced with me at the wedding? What a stupid thing to say when he knows full well that I have never met him before. Oh, he gives me the 'creeps', just make sure, Daddy, that you keep him as far away from me as possible."

Peter asked Barbara to close the car door. He reluctantly agreed that he would brief the others but he wanted to control what was and wasn't said. He asked Marian if she would call their brother Patrick in Chicago and ask him if he could be available for a conference call that evening at say eight pm. He agreed that she could tell Patrick that there was a man in a mental home in Dublin who was claiming to be their brother Ian and that he thought they should discuss it and agree what they should do, if anything. Peter said that he would invite Robert, Mark and Fiona to come to the meeting and would just give them 'sketchy' details about what the meeting was to be about. He politely asked Barbara if she would mind not attending the meeting, he thought that it should only involve his brothers and sisters for now. He asked her to please not talk to anyone about it, until after their meeting.

"Ok Daddy," she replied sarcastically, "since you asked so nicely."

Peter dropped Marian off outside the hotel in the centre of Howth called The Forman's Family Hotel. The hotel was owned by the family and Marian was the general manager. The conference call would be held in the board room upstairs.

When Peter got to his home, which was next to the Garda Station, where he lived alone, he decided to act immediately, before he had a chance to change his mind. He called Robert first, asking him if he could attend the meeting. Robert must have assumed that it was to be a business meeting, as he agreed without asking any questions. Fiona didn't ask any questions either, of course she would love to chat to Patrick again, this was going to be easier than he thought! Mark wasn't so easy and Peter thought that Mark suspected something was amiss. Just half an hour after he hung up, Mark arrived at Peter's house.

"'Ok big bro' what are you up to this time?" asked Mark. "What great coup are you planning this time?"

Peter decided to tell Mark all about their experience at the Care Centre. Mark had already heard rumours about this stranger and was intrigued. He wondered why had samples for a DNA analysis been taken. Mark just wouldn't leave Peter alone, he kept asking one question after another. Peter thought it would be better to satisfy Marks curiosity now rather than at the meeting later. Eventually Peter stood up and made two cups of white coffee. Mark took a sip and then said half-jokingly.

"Maybe it is Ian, crossed over from another dimension, maybe from a parallel universe," he laughed.

Peter didn't laugh or even smile.

"Jaysus, I might have known you would come up with some stupid answer," said Peter. "You always believed in all that 'mumbo jumbo'. Don't talk like that tonight or you will piss everybody off!"

When Mark finally left, Peter tuned his radio to 'Easy Listening Radio' and sat back in his beige leather recliner. How will the meeting go tonight, he wondered? We have to try to find answers, we can't just talk about coming back from another dimension. Peter had read about the Many Worlds Theory and although he considered himself to be very open minded, he just didn't believe in it. He took a long hot bath, listening to the soothing music for more than an hour, regularly topping up the bath with hot water. As he lay there, ridiculous thoughts crossed his mind. What would he do if his wife Claire came back from another dimension. Apart from the fact that he would probably die from a heart attack if he saw her alive again, he allowed himself to think about how wonderful it would be again, how happy he would be again, how happy everyone would be again! What would they talk about? Would she already know all about what had happened to him and their children since she died? Would she recognise their grandchildren who hadn't even been born before she had passed away? But how would she find her way home? Their family home had since been sold and he now lived elsewhere! If she was in another dimension, could she still see and follow everything from the dimension she left? Would he have to introduce her to her grandchildren and would they be frightened of her?

He suddenly sat up straight and said out loud.

"Stop this ridiculous thinking, you silly old fart!"

Peter 'pulled himself together' and got dressed. He decided there and then that he would visit Claire's grave tomorrow and tell her all about everything that had happed to him and the family since she passed away. You just never know, he said silently to himself, maybe she is still somehow aware of everything that is happening today. Maybe she is sad that I don't talk to her anymore, even though she knows that I cannot hear her answers. Anyway, why do some people say 'passed over' rather than 'passed away' or that dreadful 'final' word 'died'. He thought that he would only say 'passed over' in future, still leaves the options open, not yet final! He decided he would visit Claire's grave every Sunday from now on and make sure he kept her up to date on absolutely everything! Didn't Christ talk about 'everlasting life'. He also decided he had better visit his daddy and mammy's graves and, for that matter, his sister Jean's and also his brothers Ian's and Louis' graves. Well at least he had something to do every Sunday from now on. Try as much as he could he just couldn't laugh at or dismiss Mark's stupid thought. He wanted it to be at least possible!

He pulled on his navy-blue jacket before he slammed the glass front door behind him.

"Why do I keep doing that?" he said out loud! "I will definitely break that glass some day!"

Peter walked up Church Street and crossing the road at the top of the hill, he leaned over and rested both his elbows on top of the cold hard cemetery stone wall. He could clearly see the black marble headstone of the family grave. It was too far away to read anything on it, even if it had been facing the right way, which it wasn't. He suddenly found himself really emotional. He pulled his white linen handkerchief from his coat pocket and 'secretly' wiped the tears from both his eyes. But why was he crying? Were any of those he still dreadfully missed, really dead or were some, maybe all, still living in another dimension?

Were their souls in heaven or do their souls perhaps 'fly away' with them to their 'new existence', in another universe? Lots of questions but no answers. What are we in fact, he thought? What are we here on Earth for, anyway? Why can't we just accept that life just begins and then ends, why do we expect or even think we deserve something more? Why do we 'need' to believe in life after death? Shouldn't we just be grateful for just the one life!

Peter arrived at the open doors of Forman's Hotel. He looked at his watch, still only 7:40pm. He walked straight in and was greeted by Joan, the receptionist. As usual she didn't even bother to stop filing her nails when he walked in. Although Joan was 'ok enough', he thought that she was getting a little 'full of herself' for a twenty something year old, these days. He had to reluctantly accept however, that at almost five foot nine, well-built but still nicely slim, deep green eyes with long shiny dark hair framing her very attractive face, she was entitled to feel confident and good about herself. Peter was always annoyed that anytime he visited the hotel that she continued to file her red painted nails for several seconds before looking up at him. It seemed to Peter, that she spoke differently to young male guests than to older men, or for that matter to any female guests. She did really act, as they say, as if she was God's gift to men.

Marian, Peter's younger sister suddenly 'appeared' beside him and welcomed him with a nervous laugh. The interruption 'pulled' Peter back into the present. Marian said that everyone except Robert had already arrived and were sitting around the board room table upstairs, expectantly. Peter followed Marian upstairs, they didn't bother to use the lift, not worth it for just three floors. They entered through the open double doors and everyone stood up to greet Peter, with handshakes. The gathering seemed surreal to Peter. Mark was in great form, smiling as always. He appeared to be on his second pint bottle of Guinness but was just sipping it slowly from a half pint tumbler. Fiona and Mark immediately sat down next to each other. Fiona opened up her i-Phone and started to look intently at the screen, she seemed bored and plainly irritated to have been 'summoned' for this family meeting. Her dark coloured hair, pale complexion and oval green-brown eyes reminded Peter of Louis, each time he looked at her.

A stranger would never guess that Mark and Fiona were twins, neither by their looks or by their personality. Even before taking his 'allocated' seat, Peter opened the conversation:

"Marian, you really need to do something with that receptionist of yours."

Mark quickly seized his opportunity:

"Who, do you mean Joan? Well you can leave that to me. I'd really like to do something with her!"

"Mark Forman, you are disgusting, do you ever think of anything else?" Fiona spoke, without even looking up from her phone.

"Welcome everyone, does anyone want a drink before we 'FaceTime' Patrick? We are due to call him in about ten-minutes, it will be 3:00pm in the afternoon in Chicago then. I hope Robert gets here before then."

Everyone declined the offer of drinks. Marian opened up her i-Pad and checked again that the white extension cable connecting the i-Pad to the wall-mounted fifty-five-inch flat screen television was properly pushed home. She was about to take her seat when Robert walked purposely through the open doors. He closed both doors behind him and without saying a word he nodded to the, now silent, assembly. 'Thunder' was written all over his face as he sat down opposite Peter. Marian sat next to him but didn't dare look him straight in the face. Fiona finally turned her mobile phone off, no doubt prompted by the look of disgust she saw on Robert's face. Everyone was seated and ready now, Peter, Marian, Mark, Fiona and Robert. Still five minutes before the phone call to Patrick was due.

Robert got straight to the point:

"Why don't we call Patrick right now, he suggested, more like 'ordered'. I'm sure he will already be sitting there impatiently."

Without replying, Marian dialled Patrick.

The phone rang maybe just two or three times before Patrick picked up. The connection was excellent, clear and uninterrupted. Patrick's smiling face filled the whole television screen. His full head of shiny grey hair and 'hardly wrinkled' full face, set him apart from his other brothers. Only Mark still had a full head of blond hair, but he was much younger.

Standing behind Patrick was his wife Susan, with their two grown up children, son Packy and their daughter Sarah.

"Did you hear about the guy in New York who decided he would surprise his wife on their tenth wedding anniversary by cooking a surprise gourmet North Korean meal for her?" asked Patrick.

Without waiting for an answer, Patrick answered his own question.

"His nine-year-old son spoiled it by letting the cat out of the bag".

Patrick then 'roared out loud' with laughter but stopped abruptly when he saw that no one around the table was even smiling, let alone laughing.

"You guys need to 'lighten up' over there. Do you not get the joke?"

"It's just that you told us the same joke the last time we spoke with you Patrick," responded Fiona. "Hello Susan, Packy and Sarah, it's good to see you all looking so well."

Robert interrupted the friendly family exchange, by asking:

"Peter you said that this was an important meeting which was to be restricted to just brothers and sisters?"

"Yes, I know all that, but the 'Chicago Formans' are all intrigued, they all want to sit in," explained Patrick, again with a smile.

To head off a potential row, Peter 'jumped in'.

"Patrick, none of our extended families has any idea what this is all about either. I think it would be best to keep it that way, until we know 'what's what'. Susan, would you mind terribly if you all leave Patrick on his own, for this discussion. I'm sure he will brief you all, as much as we agree that he can anyway, afterwards."

Susan nodded but didn't say anything. A couple of minutes later Patrick was sitting all alone in his basement 'man cave'.

Peter took a deep breath and looking, in turn, at all the faces around the table he dwelt on Mark's serious face and began to relate everything that had happened and had been said since he had first been contacted by Mrs O'Brien.

His audience remained completely silent, not one question was asked which might interrupt Peter's flow. As the minutes ticked by, Peter became more and more relaxed. He could see that he was holding everyone's attention, they all seemed enthralled with his story. It took him the best part of half an hour to talk about all the events, after which he folded his arms and sat back. He was silently inviting comments and questions.

Robert stood up abruptly, knocking his chair over in the process. The chair tumbled quietly onto the mottled blue, slightly worn, carpet behind him. No one moved or said anything. All eyes were now on Robert's angry face.

"Well I've never heard such a greater load of 'bollocks' in all my life! Peter you are a complete naïve 'gobshite'. Do you really believe that Ian has returned from the dead after more than fifty years?" Robert's question was rhetorical but no one was tempted to answer anyway.

Peter tried to recover the situation by looking at Mark and asking him directly for his comments. Mark took some time to gather his thoughts, trying to find some 'common ground'.

"Well as I see it, there is this sixty-eight-year old man, who has appeared from nowhere. He claims to be our brother Ian and that he never died when he was twelve. Although he appears to know a lot about our family, much of what he has said is completely wrong. For example, we can all see and particularly hear, that Robert is 'far from deceased'."

"Why don't we get rid of this madman by having a simple DNA test performed on him?" asked Patrick.

"I think that has already started," answered Peter. Marian and I gave samples at the Care Home, earlier today.

"One way or the other we need to establish this guy's identity. Robert, do you think he is an imposter who is trying to muscle in on a potential inheritance?" asked Marian.

"Well if he is an imposter, he is making a complete balls of it," suggested Fiona. "Why didn't he do his research on the family history properly and then 'reveal himself' as our long -lost brother with a plausible explanation of where he has been hiding all these years. Why pretend to be the 'risen' Ian?"

Robert was starting to calm down a little now, so decided to ask Peter about what he really thought about it all:

"Peter you have actually met and spoken to Mr X. Of all of us here, you must have the best-informed opinion."

"I don't know Robert, but I think we do need to seriously consider a range of possibilities and decide what we do in each eventuality." Peter was doing his best to sound rational and objective.

"For fecks sake Peter, we all know, by the way you are talking, that you think he really is Ian, risen from the grave. Who is the real delusional one here?" Robert's anger had suddenly returned.

"Ok, so what do we do now then?" asked Patrick in a calm relaxed tone.

"I suggest that we throw him back into the feckin' harbour and see how long it takes him to get out this feckin' time!" shouted Robert.

"Ah, now there's no need to talk like that Robert. Whoever this person is, he is a real person. Ok, he might be a bit disturbed but he is not trying to do us any harm. I don't think we need to do anything, let's wait and see how it pans out," offered Mark.

"Oh, that's a great idea Mark. Yes, let's sit back and let this 'bastard' take a share of the family fortune. Have you any other brilliant ideas?" shouted Robert sarcastically.

"Why don't we all calm down guys," interrupted Patrick. "We can't have a sensible conversation when one of us is trying to shout the other one down. We clearly need a plan of action for what to do, if anything, for now. Fiona, you have stayed calm throughout, what do you think? Not so much who do you think he is, but what do you think we should do about him now?"

"I have no idea who he is, but hopefully the 'authorities' will eventually get to the bottom of it all. At the moment there's really nothing positive we can do, so for now I suggest we avoid contact with him unless the authorities ask for our help. In the meantime, we should do nothing which might appear to give credence to this guy's fantasy story," answered Fiona. "I also think that we shouldn't talk to anyone else about this, even close family."

"I think that's a sensible course of action Fiona," said Peter. "We can reconvene when we hear about any DNA evidence, assuming that it will put an end to all this nonsense."

"Marian, you also spoke to this guy, does he appear mad to you? asked Patrick.

"Well it's hard to tell from just a short conversation, even if the conversation itself was mad," answered Marian. "To be honest he looked a little like us, probably a lot like me in fact!"

"Look we have to stop all this nonsense right now," said Robert quite calmly. Does everyone agree?"

Peter went 'around the table' and asked everyone to repeat the phrase 'I agree', finishing with addressing Patrick over the internet. He couldn't believe that they had actually agreed on something, if only temporarily. He knew that the real test was still to come however.

Robert always had to have the last say so after Peter had thanked everyone and offered to buy everyone in the room a drink he said:

"And Mark, if someone tries to tell you that he really is our long lost brother, for Christ's sake don't jump to the conclusion that he must have been abducted by aliens, kept in an alien zoo and once they had finished their analysis of his brain and body, fed him with false memories and dropped him back here on earth."

Unfortunately, Peter could see that Robert's sarcastic remark put Mark's brain into overdrive, rather than humiliating him. The meeting was brought to a close when Marian, thanked Patrick.

Patrick said goodbye and then said:

"Always remember, you can tune a piano but you can't tuna fish."

Marian immediately cut Patrick off.

No one was 'in the mood' to discuss the matter further over a drink, so they all made their way home, some of them intrigued, all of them confused.

Chapter 10

Marian couldn't wait for the results of the DNA tests, she wanted to know now! Four days had passed and she hadn't heard anything. She phoned Mrs O'Brien and asked if the DNA sample had shed any light on the stranger in her care. She got very suspicious when Mrs O'Brien hesitated to answer.

"Did you discover anything interesting then, Mrs O'Brien?" asked Marian.

"Well we got some unexpected results so we are having the samples checked at a second facility," answered Mrs O'Brien.

"Mrs O'Brien, would it be ok if I drop in to see you for a few minutes now?" asked Marian hopefully.

Although she said that she was really busy and that she only had unverified results, Mrs O'Brien agreed to spare Marian a few minutes, if she could come straight away.

Without informing anyone else, Marian made her way to the Phoenix Centre. She felt a little guilty about her 'secret' meeting with Mrs O'Brien but she was both excited and apprehensive beyond belief. Mrs O'Brien met her in the reception area and Marian was surprised that she was not invited to go to a private room. Instead Mrs O'Brien invited Marian to sit beside her on the leather couch, in the reception area.

"Thanks for seeing me at such short notice Mrs O'Brien," began Marian.

"Look, I did say it's a bit premature because we are still awaiting the confirmation of what we have found," responded Mrs O'Brien.

Mrs O'Brien then came straight out and told Marian that the first results indicate that her patient and Peter are brothers and that she was also his sister.

"All three of you are siblings", she said as she looked straight at Marian. She was searching for a reaction.

"But how could that be?" exclaimed Marian. "Are you sure?"

"Well that's why we are re-running the tests at another independent laboratory," Mrs O'Brien responded. "I am aware that you said that you don't know this person, hence the double-check. We will have the result of the second test later today."

"What do you think it will show Mrs O'Brien?" whispered Marian.

"Well I wouldn't like to speculate, but in all my years working here I have never known there to be a mistake with DNA analysis. But why don't you wait until later tonight. Give me your mobile number and I will call you when I get the second test results," said Mrs O'Brien as she stood up, bringing the conversation to an end.

Marian drove back to the FFF Hotel in Howth and pulled up outside the main doors. She lived in the small bungalow next to the hotel, with her husband Noel. She knew Noel would be at home but she didn't want to talk to him yet so she quickly walked through the open swinging doors and straight into the hotel lounge. Marian had been the manager of the 'Forman's Friendly Family Hotel' for many years. She was the part owner with the bulk of the shares being owned by the family business, 'Forman Enterprises'.

She poured herself a large gin and tonic, didn't bother with the ice and slice, and sat down on the comfy brown leather armchair. She just couldn't make any sense of what she had learned today and had no idea what she should do with the information. Before she took her first sip of her G&T, her mobile rang!

After thanking Mrs O'Brien, she hung up. Confirmation had been received, she was definitely this man's sister. How could it be? It can't be! Who is he? Where has he been all these years? I don't have another older brother!

She downed the drink in one and poured herself another one, this time with ice and slice. She sat sipping and tried to think of what next to do. She would have to call another meeting straight-away, this was now a family issue, which had to be dealt with.

By 6:50pm that evening, Marian, Robert, Peter, Mark and Fiona were sitting around the conference room table in the meeting room of the FFF Hotel. Despite being asked many times that day why Marian had called this meeting, she had refused to give details, saying only that some important family decisions needed to be made and that they should all attend. Just before seven Marian called Patrick. Seconds later that big screen lit up with Patrick's smiling face almost filling the whole screen.

"Hi you guys," said Patrick, "what's going down over there? I didn't expect to hear from you again, so soon."

"Hi Patrick," said Marian. "I called this meeting because we have a couple of very important decisions to make. Decisions which will affect the whole family. Earlier today, I called into the Phoenix Care Centre in Grangegorman. I had a short meeting with Mrs O'Brien."

"Oh, for fecks sake," exploded Robert, as he stood up knocking his chair over. "Didn't we all agree that we would wait until someone got back to us before we did anything. What's the point in discussing and agreeing it and then totally ignoring what was decided by us all?"

Robert quickly 'pulled himself together' however and picking up his chair he sat down and let out a long gasp.

"Isn't that the place they lock up all the mental head-cases?" asked Mark.

"It's an assessment and treatment centre for people who are suffering from mental problems," responded Marian. "Since I got back from there, I have looked up their website. The facility is very impressive and they get great results. You wouldn't believe how many people suffer some form of breakdown or other mental issue at some time in their lives. Until today, I didn't realise how many people can be helped. Most make at least a partial recovery and some make a full recovery."

"Ok, ok, spare us the advertising slogans Marian," thundered Robert. "Why is 'what's his name' being held there? Is he 'nuts' like we all believe?"

"Well I, for one, don't believe he is deranged," said Peter.

"Look, why did you call all of us here Marian?" asked Robert. "As far as I am concerned this is all 'bollocks'. Why don't you just get on with it."

"Well I hope you are all ready for this bombshell," said Marian with a trembling voice. "The DNA evidence shows that I am definitely this man's sister and that Peter is definitely his brother."

"Jaysus, can we trust the DNA evidence?" asked Robert, "they must have got it wrong!"

"No mistake, they checked it again at another lab," replied Marian.

"They must have mixed up the DNA samples, either that or they have been contaminated," said Robert, "we need to get new DNA samples from him and everyone else and get them checked privately. This is a serious matter, a very serious matter. We need to be very sure and certain."

Patrick's face suddenly took on a serious expression and he agreed that they should definitely have more checks done but that they should, for the moment at least, accept the DNA results and try to work out what to do now with their long-lost brother.

Marian told everyone that Mrs O' Brien had told him that they couldn't find anything wrong with their patient and that his psychiatric nurse, Danny Boyd, had been monitoring him for quite a while now and he doesn't think that his patient is suffering from any mental illness that he has ever seen or heard of.

"Who the feck is Danny?" interrupted Robert.

"Danny is our new brother's full-time psychiatric nurse. His job seems to consist of spending lots of time with him and then reporting back regularly to the two consultants who are responsible for making the diagnosis. Their names are Cox and O'Brien," responded Marian calmly.

"Christ! they sound like a firm of solicitors," interrupted Mark.

"Get on with it, Marian," said Robert, in a raised voice.

"I'm trying to, if you'd all only let me," answered Marian. She was brilliant at staying calm under constant bombardment.

"I don't see how they can keep him at the Care Centre, I think they would discharge him now if they could. If he had anywhere to go!"

"So, what then?" asked Patrick. "Where does he go then?"

"Well that's the first decision we have to make," replied Marian. "I think that he is our responsibility. If he really is our long-lost brother, we need to take care of him for a while."

"What do you mean by 'take care of him' and what does 'for a while' really mean?" asked Fiona.

It seemed to Peter that Fiona was already trying to calculate the financial implications of taking care of this mystery man."

"Look, steady on here," said Robert calmly. "We still don't know if this stranger really is a part of our family. I vote we wait until we do proper DNA checks. Maybe Mrs O' Brien is just trying to get rid of this guy."

"Well that brings me nicely to the second decision we have to make," replied Marian.

She continued…

"The Gardai will now become involved. They have been told that this man has some counterfeit money in his possession and that he has already tried to withdraw money from a cash machine using forged credit and debit cards. So far they have not been able to trace him on any of the 'missing persons' files they have been able to access. As soon as they are informed that he is a Forman, part of our family, they will pay us a visit for sure."

"But we haven't done anything wrong, have we?" asked Peter.

"Look this guy is still claiming to be our brother Ian Forman and that it wasn't him who died when he was twelve," said Mark suddenly. "The Gardai will want to know if it was really Ian who we buried that day and if not, then who was it?"

"Jaysus how do we answer that, for Christ's sake?" exclaimed Peter.

Fiona stood up immediately and cleared her throat, she was preparing to make an announcement. She hesitated, looking nervously at everyone in turn and then stated that she had something to say that she had promised her mammy that she would never reveal. She went on to say that when Mammy knew she was very close to passing away, that she told her that her son Ian was actually a twin. Fiona said that she hoped that Mammy would forgive her for revealing her secret, which for some reason, their mammy didn't want anyone else to know.

Peter then stood up, interrupting Fiona. He announced to everyone that their sister Jean had told him, just before she died, that our granny, that is Mammy's mammy had told her, in confidence, that Ian had a twin who had died shortly after he was born, but Mammy didn't want anyone to know. Only one of the twins had survived. Peter than sat down again, to stunned silence for a few moments.

Fiona continued her story by telling everyone that Mammy told her that Ian's twin had only lived for a few days but that he had been baptised and named Conor, after his uncle Conor Finnerty.

Fiona cleared her throat and then said that several months after Mammy's funeral and after she herself had started to get over the loss of Mammy that she decided to investigate Mammy's revelation. She checked on line and found the birth certificate for Conor Forman. All the details were correct, father and mother's name, father's occupation and of course the date of birth. What was really strange and spooky though was that, although she tried, she had been unable to find a death certificate for Conor Forman.

Fiona's voice was breaking up as she spoke about the missing death certificate. She suddenly stopped speaking. Everyone could see that her eyes were 'filling up'. She stood up and walked quickly toward the door and 'flinging' it open, she disappeared out of the room. Marian ran out after her.

"Oh, for Christ's sake," exclaimed Mark. "What was all that about?"

Robert stood up and paced impatiently around the room several times. Peter and Mark both stood up, their arms resting on the backs of their chairs. Patrick's face was a picture of puzzlement. No one spoke for several minutes. Nobody knew what to say! Eventually Patrick stood up and his face disappeared from the screen to show the black back wall of his 'man cave' with the huge tv screen, blank and ignored, hanging there expectantly.

"Sorry guys," he said slowly, "I need to go to the 'washroom'. Back in a few minutes."

"Now what?" asked Mark.

No one answered! A few minutes later Fiona and Marian came back into the room and sat back down on their respective chairs. The three brothers followed suit. All five siblings were seated and silent, waiting for Patrick to come back in view.

Patrick re-appeared moments later and his face filled the screen again.

"Have I missed anything?" he asked.

"No Patrick, you haven't," answered Peter, "but we now need to decide what, if anything, we should do about this new revelation of Fiona's."

"So, do you think Conor is still alive Fiona?" asked Patrick.

"I've no idea Patrick. I didn't try very hard to trace him. In truth I didn't want to know. I couldn't bear the thought of Mammy maybe giving Ian's twin up for adoption," responded Fiona. "I decided not to seek expert help in trying to trace him, I wouldn't know what to do if he was found."

"Well if Mammy did have twins and she gave one away for financial or other reasons, it would explain why she tried to keep it all a secret," offered Marian.

Mark shifted uneasily in his chair, he wanted to say something.

"Fiona do you remember years and years ago when we were just 'nippers', Rose Rorke visiting us and looking over at us twins, asking Mammy if twins ran in the family?" asked Mark.

"No Mark, I don't remember it at all," replied Fiona "What did Mammy say?"

"Well, I vividly remember it," said Mark, "she avoided the question.

Instead of just saying NO, she appeared to be 'flustered' and changed the subject. She asked Rose if her husband Dessie was feeling any better."

"Mark, there is no way you could remember something like that," said Robert, "your mind is playing tricks on you."

Robert stood up slowly and pushing his chair under the table he walked to the end of the table. He wanted to take control of the discussion.

"Look this could really be a blessing in disguise" announced Robert. "If this guy really is our brother Conor it would at least provide some sort of explanation."

"Maybe so," interrupted Patrick, "but it would then raise a load of other questions. Like who raised him, where has he been for the last sixty eight years, why appear now, why is he pretending to be Ian, does he not know who he is, why all the bullshit, what does he really want, is he just making a bad job of lying about who he is, is he perhaps actually testing us?"

"Ok, ok, Patrick 'we get the message'," interrupted Robert.

Robert called for a fifteen-minute break so everyone could have time to think. He promised to call Patrick back.

When the meeting was reconvened, Robert took charge. He said that he did not have any good answers to Patrick's questions but he did have a proposal. He would hire a professional investigator to check out the possible 'Conor connection' but, for now, the only possible way forward was to accept this newcomer as their brother Conor Forman. He said that there was no way that the family could accept his mad claim that he is actually Ian. He proposed that they assume responsibility for Conor and that they 'put him up' in the Voluntary Adult Support Centre called Saint John's at Howth summit, as soon as possible. Patrick was not that familiar with the Centre but he quickly agreed, once Fiona explained all about it. Everyone agreed this was the right thing to do, that the business would pay all costs and hopefully find out more about Conor's past, over the next few weeks. After a further short discussion, it was also agreed that Mark would be charged with setting it all up and with meeting Conor and telling him what had been decided. Fiona reminded everyone that St John's only accepts people who voluntarily want to stay there, if Conor didn't want to stay there, they couldn't force him to do so.

"We feckin' won't give him a choice!" shouted Robert.

Chapter 11

Mark thought that the meeting the previous evening had gone as well as he thought it could have. Why was Robert so good at finding solutions to seemingly impossible problems? Mark was really intrigued and was pleased that he had been trusted with making it all happen. He visited St John's that morning and met with the managing director a Mr Cuthbert. Mark gave Mr Cuthbert just the sketchiest of details about Conor. He told him that his brother was confused and needed plenty of rest and maybe some counselling. He explained that Conor was, at the moment, staying at the Phoenix Care Centre but was not found to be suffering from mental illness and was ready to be discharged. Mr Cuthbert told Mark that there was a room free at the centre and that he would be very welcome to stay there for as long as his brother wanted to, up to a maximum of twelve weeks. Mr Cuthbert handed Mark some brochures about the facility and the costs.

He phoned Mrs O'Brien and thanked her for taking care of his brother and informed her that the family were now willing and able to take over his brother's care from today onwards. He was careful not to talk about his long-lost brother Conor, it would just complicate the matter. He arrived at the Phoenix Care Centre not 'having a clue' about how his upcoming meeting and discussion with his newly unveiled older brother would go. Mrs O'Brien agreed that after Mark had been introduced to his brother that they could spend some time in a private room, alone.

I was walking in the garden with Danny, trying unsuccessfully to talk about politics and religion when Danny's mobile rang. Several minutes later I was sitting in a private room with Danny when Mrs O'Brien walked in, accompanied by my brother Mark. I couldn't believe how fit and well he looked, he was clearly back into bodybuilding. But by now I knew not to go overboard with my greeting. Without standing up, I greeted Mark casually, as if it was no big deal.

"Hello Mark, it's great to see you again, thanks for coming to see me," I said.

Mrs O'Brien smiled at me and then at Mark and, turning back to look straight at me, she told me that Mark had come to discuss my future. Although Danny offered to stay with me, I confirmed that I was happy to have a private conversation with Mark. I couldn't contain my excitement when Mark told me about the DNA result, he now has to accept that we are brothers! I jumped up to shake his hand but Mark remained sitting and suggested that I wait until he had finished explaining everything. I was totally bewildered when Mark told me all about the revelation about my twin brother Conor, and even more so when he said that my brothers and sisters were now convinced that I must be Conor.

"But I'm not Conor, I'm Ian," I whispered.

"You can't be Ian. Ian died and was buried several years before I was born. I'm told that you even saw the gravestone yourself. You must be Conor," Mark said calmly.

"But I've never even heard of Conor before, how can I now suddenly be him? Why am I convinced that I'm Ian? Apparently, I'm not suffering from any mental illness," I said in exasperation.

"Look Conor we don't have all the answers yet but we will get to the bottom of it all, trust me," replied Mark, confidently.

Mark was well prepared for the conversation that followed. He explained that the sooner I stopped claiming to be his brother Ian and instead accept that I was his long-lost brother Conor, the sooner everyone could move on and set about welcoming me back into the family. "But I'm not feckin' Conor," I shouted, as I stood up.

Mark stood up and walked away from the table, I could see that he was very agitated. I sat down again and he did the same.

"Conor you are not making this easy for us. We want to help you. We want to support you but you have to meet us half way. It has already been agreed by everyone that we can offer you a home and support you financially but you have to help us, help you," said Mark.

"I wish that you would stop calling me Conor," I said quietly. "Are you really asking me to live a lie, to pretend to be Conor?"

"Well it's better than pretending to be Ian, for Christ's sake," replied Mark sarcastically.

Mark's remark stunned me. Did he really think I was pretending to be Ian? I was momentarily lost for words.

"Sorry Conor, I don't think that you are really pretending to be Ian, I'm told that you really believe that you are Ian," added Mark sympathetically.

"So, what would happen if I agree to go along with this pretence to be Conor," I asked calmly.

"Look, if you continue to insist that it is a pretence then nothing can happen at all. We are not going to drag you from here 'kicking and screaming' against your will. The only way forward is for you to say you are Conor and to convince everyone that you are him, do you not get it?" said Mark forcefully.

"Ok, ok. I get it, I get it," I replied. "But where am I going to say I have been living and hiding for the last sixty-eight years? How am I now going to explain why I have been pretending to be Ian for the last few months?"

Mark readily admitted that there were lots of issues still to be sorted out before I could be re-habilitated, but they had to start somewhere. They needed to find somewhere for me to live for the next few months, somewhere where I wouldn't be treated as mentally insane but rather as someone who was a bit confused and needed care, love and support. Hopefully during my period of rest, I would start to remember more about my past life. They would recruit a top private investigator to help me rediscover and re-construct my past.

"The most important thing for you to keep in mind Conor, is that you will now be back amongst your welcoming family," said Mark.

I resisted the temptation to tell Mark that he was asking me to accept that I never married Mary and that my children John and Annette were never born and consequently that I had no grandchildren either. I realised however that if I mentioned this, Mark would have simply told me that I had to accept these facts, because they were true!

"But will they simply let me walk out of here Mark?" I asked.

"If you want to leave here and if Mrs O'Brien has evidence that you have somewhere safe to go and have someone to look after you, they have no choice," replied Mark with a broad grin. "They will not keep you here against your will or the will of your family."

I could see that Mark was beginning to think he was getting somewhere. He told me that there were certain formalities that he would have to take care of before I could be moved. He would have to sign some documents confirming that, until further notice, he personally would be fully responsible for my welfare. He also mentioned that the Gardai, were still holding onto my counterfeit money and my forged credit and debit cards, for now. Anyway, the cards were in the name of Ian Forman, so of no use to me. He told me not to worry about this as I hadn't managed to obtain money with the cards and the Gardai had no resources to follow up on anything, these days. He promised that he would arrange for new cards for me.

Mark then told me that the family had booked me into a Voluntary Adult Support Centre. There is a vacancy in St John's in Howth and I had been accepted there. I could stay there as long as I liked, up to a maximum of 12 weeks. I would have a private ensuite bathroom with my own TV but I would be free to come and go whenever I choose and could welcome as many visitors as I pleased, whenever I wanted to. It had an excellent restaurant and everything would be paid for by the family.

"What sort of facility is this Mark? I've never heard of a place where you could just come and go as you please. Is it a hospital or a care home?" I asked.

"It's neither of these Conor, haven't you ever heard of a VASC, a voluntary adult support centre? Anyone can go there to recoup after a personal setback. You must commit to stay for a minimum of two weeks, or should I say, pay for at least two weeks but you must leave after a maximum of twelve weeks, to make room for new guests. However, you can re-apply to return as many times as you want. You go on a waiting list, first come first served. It's run by the National Health Service but it's not free, it costs a lot but it has an excellent reputation for helping guests get back on track with their lives. Nearly everyone ends up staying there at some point in their lives," replied Mark enthusiastically."

"But surely you need to be suffering from something to be referred there?" I asked.

Mark explained that the centre is open to anyone over eighteen years of age, who can afford it. Residents are not ill, there is no medical treatment available, just support, care and also some short information courses aimed at helping people cope. All residents sign themselves in and out. There are a wide range of courses and therapies available, which the resident can opt for, but no drugs are permitted there, not even tobacco or alcohol.

"Ok so if I agree to try it for a while, when would you let me out?" I asked.

"Conor, nobody is going to force you to go there or to stay there. You can leave whenever you want, but I'm not sure where else you could go at the moment. It's your choice but I really hope you accept our offer," replied Mark.

"Mark, I am very grateful for the offer," I announced. "When can I go? I can hardly wait."

Mark was so happy and relieved that he didn't seem to notice the sarcasm in my voice.

He told me everything should be ready within a couple of days or so. He left me with some brochures and pamphlets from St John's and asked me to read them carefully. As he stood up to leave, I asked Mark if I could ask him a serious question…

"Is Robert really alive?"

"Jesus Conor, you really have a lot of catching up to do, of course he is," he replied. "I'm sure you will get to meet him in the next few days."

Meet him in the next few days, I thought! Christ what will I say to him? I think he will scare the life out of me.

After Mark had left, I walked back to reception and asked the receptionist to contact Danny. I told Danny all about my conversation with Mark. He knew about St. John's and said that it had a great reputation, he said I was lucky to find a vacancy so quickly. I showed Danny my collection of brochures and told him I was going to read them in my room, if he was ok with that. I agreed to his suggestion that, after I had finished my reading, we would play some music together. He said that he wanted to spend as much time as possible playing and learning 'new' songs before I disappeared from his life to find new fame as a song writer. I reminded Danny that he could visit me in my new temporary home as often as he liked. He smiled and seemed genuinely happy with the thought of visiting.

"Would we be allowed to play our guitars there? Could my wife Alison come along and help us out with the singing?" he asked excitedly.

"Not sure about that," I responded. "I will have to come back to you as soon as I settle in."

I propped three pillows on top of my duvet, slipped off my shoes and looked at the covers of the three glossy brochures....

- St John's Voluntary Adult Support Centre History, Facilities, Staff, Aims and Guest Comments.
- St John's Voluntary Adult Support Centre Guest Eligibility and Financial Information.
- St John's Voluntary Adult Support Centre Short Courses Available.

I skipped through all three of the booklets quite quickly. Mark had explained the setup quite well. All guests were there voluntarily and attendance at all courses was also voluntary and subject to availability. The charge for staying full board in a single room with an ensuite bathroom was shown but it was in some sort of code. It would cost 1900 Pride per week! What the hell did this mean?

The photos were many and they were clearly aimed at 'selling' the business. The buildings showed the facilities to be a sprawling palace and the rooms looked very well appointed. At full capacity the facility welcomed a maximum of 356 staying guests, no wonder the complex looked huge! In addition to the catering and housekeeping staff the part-time staff included a team of psychologists, psychiatrists, financial advisors, general medical practitioners, religious instructors, politicians, speech therapists, and several other support professionals. There was no one-to-one interaction between staff and guests and the courses, which ranged in duration from just one day to two weeks were designed to help guests overcome a real or perceived worry or condition. The facility could not accept guests who were already diagnosed with a severe mental condition or to be suffering from advanced dementia, there were alternative facilities better suited to treat these conditions. Its goal was to help each guest learn more about their particular problem or issue, in order to help them better cope with whatever might be bothering them. The guests could not drink alcohol or smoke tobacco while on the premises but vaping in open areas was permitted. Anyone found to be taking illegal drugs would be asked to leave the facility immediately. Social media was tolerated but not encouraged. There were probably fifty or more courses to choose from. These included ..

- Meditation and self-hypnosis as a healing tool.
- How to recognise and 'count' your blessings.
- What makes you sad / What makes you happy.
- Getting control of your finances.
- Coping with a busy life.
- Sounder sleeping techniques.
- Controlling your anger / Diffuse anger situations.

- Building self-confidence.
- Dealing with bereavement.
- Managing your anxiety.
- Living with alcoholism / Living with an alcoholic.
- Living with drug addiction / Living with a drug addict.
- Recognising when you are being abusive – stopping it dead.
- Dealing with an abusive partner, relation or friend.
- Embracing people of different sex, race, colour, religion or political persuasion.
- Irish politics - learning from the past.
- World politics – learning from the past.
- Religion in the modern age.

Yes, a very impressive and wide choice of subjects. I could easily understand how so many people could benefit from a short stay at the facility but I still couldn't see how I could be helped. I couldn't find any courses on any of the following ..

- Why do I think that I am someone who is dead?
- Why does everybody think I drowned when I was a twelve-year old child?
- How to find my missing wife, children and grandchildren?
- How to discover who I really am?

I knew that my line of thinking was ridiculous. I just needed a break. I needed to learn how to accept the life I now had and to forget about those stupid false memories. I needed to recapture the memories which must have once resided in Conor Forman's brain. Oh, I wish I believed that I actually was Conor. It would be interesting to learn more about him. Perhaps the mediation and self-hypnosis sessions could help me after all!

Chapter 12

Saying farewell to Mrs O'Brien and Doctor Cox was a relief, but perhaps more so for them than me. They both said that they were really pleased that it had now been established that I was actually Conor Forman and they said that they hoped that I would soon recover all my memories. They asked me to visit them when I was fully recovered, they were intrigued to know all about me. To me, they seemed to be taking credit for 'sorting me out', although we all knew that they had done precisely nothing! Well, ok, perhaps Mrs O'Brien arranged the DNA checks. I later heard from Danny that Mrs O'Brien was actually furious when she heard that my brother Robert had not believed her capable and had privately arranged for further DNA checks.

I was actually a little sad to be leaving Danny. Over the months I had really got to know him well and enjoyed singing and playing music with him. He didn't judge me at all, he was just my friend and companion.

"Your parents really must have had a sense of humour calling you Danny," I said. "I would have thought that with a surname like Boyd that the last Christian name you needed was Danny. You must be sick and tired of people singing a few bars of *Danny Boy* when they first meet you."

"Conor, I'm not the only one with a name change," he answered. "My Christian name is actually Christopher, Chris to my friends and relations. That is until we came to live in Ireland. Then someone started calling me Danny and the name stuck. To be honest I quite like it. It's a good talking point, especially when you are a 'would-be' full time performer like me."

We agreed that we would meet up again 'in the real world' as he called it.

Mark picked me up in his red Tesla and we drove quietly to Howth. I asked him to do a loop of the Howth peninsula before bringing me to St John's. I enjoyed the tour, we found time to drop in and have coffee in the Howth Golf Club. It was just as I remembered it when I was a student member there, all those years ago, or was I? Mark agreed to take me to the graveyard again and he put his left hand on my right elbow as I looked at that inscription again. Yes, Ian Forman must be dead because he is definitely buried in this grave. So, I was never married to Mary and John and Annette really don't exist. Then where have all the great memories come from? But what about the photos on my phone?

Oh Jesus, I wish I could make sense of all this! Nobody had figured out how to charge my mobile phone and Mark didn't want to know. He asked me what I was trying to prove.

"Just forget all that nonsense Conor. You need to get on with becoming my living brother and help all of us try to find out where you have been and who you have been with, for the past sixty-eight years," he pleaded.

"Nobody, but nobody will ever accept that you are my brother Ian, returned from the dead," he added.

I decided not to react to Mark's remarks, I knew that anything I could say would come out wrong.

I signed the register at St. John's, as Conor Forman. It was a strange feeling, almost as if I had accepted that I am Conor and that Ian was dead. But I knew better. I felt a fraud, but which is preferable feeling a fraud or accepting that you are dead? I changed the way I usually signed Forman, don't know why. Mark showed me all around the facilities, introduced me to some of the staff and stayed until I had unpacked the suitcase of clothes he had taken from the boot of his car. As Mark was preparing to leave, I looked at him and asked …

"Mark, who is paying for my stay here? It must be costing a fortune."

"Don't worry about that Conor, it's actually not that expensive, I think it's less than two thousand Pride per week," he answered.

"Mark what the hell is Pride, is that what you call Euro now?" I asked.

Mark stopped walking towards the door, turned around and looked straight at me.

"Conor, is that a serious question? Do you really not know what a Pride is?" he asked.

"Mark there are lots of things I don't seem to know and what I do know, nobody else seems to know. Almost nothing makes any sense to me anymore!" I answered.

Mark walked slowly towards the small wooden desk and sat down heavily on the three- legged wooden stool. He sat facing me, one elbow resting on the desk.

"Conor, would you mind if we had an honest chat for a few minutes? I want to ask you some simple questions and I want you to answer all of them honestly. Don't feel like that you have to tell me what you think I want to hear. I promise to believe everything you tell me and I promise that everything you say will be between you and me. Don't worry about what others might think," he said in a very serious tone.

I sat down on the edge of the bed. Our faces were no more than a few feet apart.

"Mark, I always answer honestly and I actually don't care what others think anyway, so 'fire away' with your questions," I responded.

"Ok thanks. Conor what country do you think you are in now?"

"Ireland, the country I was born in sixty-eight years ago," I answered.

"And what do you think the currency is here?"

"Here, in the Republic of Ireland it's the Euro ever since it joined the Eurozone but in Northern Ireland it's the Pound Sterling just like in the UK," I answered immediately.

"And what year is this?"

"Jesus, what a question, it's 2017 of course."

"Did you ever hear of 'The Lions Community'?" he asked.

"Well, I heard someone mention it recently but I don't know anything about it. Is it something to do with the rugby team 'The British and Irish Lions'? What a great team we have had over the years. The concept of players from England, Scotland, Wales and all of Ireland playing together on the same team was inspired. Gave us some memorable contests against New Zealand, Australia and South Africa," I answered.

"Conor have you ever seen them play?"

"Only on TV. Everyone gets behind them during the test matches. Rather than focussing on the differences between the communities, which is partly due to their different religious and nationalistic persuasions, the matches demonstrate how closely we can all cooperate when we have a common purpose or cause," I answered.

"Conor, when did you last visit Northern Ireland," asked Mark.

"Oh, not since many years ago. It must be ten years or so since I played golf with some friends in Royal County Down. It was good fun but the course was too difficult for me," I smiled. "Mary found it almost impossible to play," I added without thinking.

"Is this your wife Mary?" he asked hesitantly.

"Oh dear, now that I've agreed to be Conor, I shouldn't have mentioned Mary, should I?" I asked.

"Conor, as I said at the beginning, just speak your mind, without fear."

To ease the tension, I stood up to make two coffees from the coffee machine. I expected Mark to take the opportunity to break off and leave me alone, but he didn't.

We sat sipping our coffees, staring at each other. How to break the silence?

"Are you looking forward to meeting Robert soon?" asked Mark. His eyes were staring straight at mine, he didn't blink.

"Of course, I am really looking forward to it, when will this happen anyway?"

"Are you apprehensive, Conor."

I had to stand up and think before I spoke. I knew what Mark was trying to 'trick me' into saying. He wanted to me repeat that I had said that I thought Robert was already dead. But Mark had asked me to 'tell it like it is'.

"Mark, I have to admit that it will be a bit daunting meeting my younger brother Robert, whose funeral I attended years ago," I whispered, with my eyes turned down towards the floor.

"Conor, how long have you been married to Mary for?"

"Conor isn't married to Mary, but I married Mary on July 13th, 1973. I have lots of photos, I think one or two will have you in them, as a child," I answered 'bravely'.

"Conor, I heard you earlier claimed to have two children and four grandchildren, do you still think this is true?" asked Mark.

"Yes, that's correct, Mary and I have two grown up children and four grandchildren, all six of whom live in England," I answered.

"Do you still think that you are my brother Ian, even though you have seen concrete evidence that Ian died when he was twelve?" he asked.

I explained to Mark that I could not help thinking this because that is what my brain was telling me. My memories were very clear, I had no idea what was going on, for a time I thought that I must be a ghost but that I did not believe this now. I told him that I didn't believe that I was ill and although I knew I wasn't this 'missing brother' Conor Forman, I was prepared to go along with this pretence because it seemed to be the only way forward. I told him that I appreciated that he let me speak openly and I apologised if this made everything more difficult for him now.

Mark stood up and paced around the room a few times. He was making me nervous. I didn't know what was coming next! Had I just 'blown' my one chance to be given a home and accepted into the family? Eventually he sat down again and this time he asked me if he could speak openly to me, without fear of me repeating anything he said to anyone else, no matter what happens.

"Conor, one more question before it's my turn to 'open up'," he said a little nervously.

"Have you made any progress on getting someone to charge your mobile phone?"

I told Mark that nobody seemed interested in trying to fix my phone and I now thought that they didn't want to because they might see photos which couldn't be explained.

"Conor, when we are finished speaking today, I will ask you if I could 'secretly' borrow your phone," he asked. "I know someone who could definitely find a way to charge it."

I explained that if it could be done in my presence it would be great, but I didn't want to allow my phone out of my sight, it's my only link to reality.

"Conor, if you ever repeat anything about what I am now about to talk about, I will deny it and say that you are completely deluded," he said gravely. "Do you understand?"

"Mark, I've no idea what you are going to talk about but it cannot be as bizarre as what I have been saying for months. But I assure you that I will only speak about it if you ever ask me to do so," I replied, with as much sincerity as I could muster.

"Conor, have you ever heard of the expressions 'parallel universe or different dimensions'? Perhaps you may even have heard the expression 'Many Worlds Interpretation'?" he asked.

Mark seemed a little embarrassed to have asked me these questions. I told him that I had heard of all three expressions and went on to inform him that I understood that they 'emerged' from the scientific observations on the strange but now proven behaviour of sub-atomic particles. Mark seemed to know a lot more than me about the uncertainty of just about everything. He started by stating that the workings of nature are very strange indeed. Thanks to Einstein, we all know now know that energy and matter are one and the same and that matter can spontaneously appear out of a vacuum. The intricate internal workings of the atom are fully understood by very few people, despite the huge amount of research completed. It has been shown by many repeatable experiments that the 'position' and 'state' of the smallest moving particles can never be known with certainty. The probability of both can be calculated but until the particle is physically 'observed' it is believed to be in several states and positions at the same time. Many scientists believe that once the 'external observation' as it is called, happens, that the particle 'collapses' into the state that you can see but that all the other options also happen and at the same time. In other words, anything that can happen, will happen, and in fact does happen. We see just one outcome but all the other outcomes happen in other dimensions, which are hidden from us. As far as we are concerned there has only been one outcome but this is in conflict with what's observed in particle physics.

"The basic theory has come from renowned scientists and not science fiction writers," added Mark. "The theory proposes that any time we are faced with a decision that has more than one possible choice, say a crossroads, that if you choose one path, another version of you chooses the other direction, in another dimension. Both outcomes actually happen and are real to both versions of you but each is unaware of the other."

"Mark, are you saying that you think that I might be Ian Forman and that I have come from another dimension?" I exclaimed loudly.

"Shush, whispered Mark," as he looked around the room.

"Well, until recently I never believed this was possible. The theory contends that there can never be any form of communication between any of the separate universes. A new universe is said to come into existence each time an outcome is decided or determined. The universe splits in two at that moment with two or more versions existing from that time onwards. If the interpretation is correct there should be billions upon billions of universes out there," said Mark.

"You say that until recently you didn't believe this possible, has something changed your mind?" I asked.

"Well, sort of, maybe, perhaps," replied Mark.

Mark then asked me if I had ever heard of a book called 'The Many Lives Interpretation' by Professor Carlos Prieto. When I answered that I never heard of the book or the author, Mark said that he had read it fairly recently and that it made very interesting reading. He said that he still had the book and that he would drop it in to me later that day. He asked me to wait until I had finished reading it before we discussed it further.

"Conor, do you believe in other dimensions?" asked Mark.

I replied that I was not sure but that I had an open mind about it all. Mark smiled and then said that anybody who is in anyway religious and believes in an 'afterlife' or in Heaven, believes in at least one other dimension. No one believes that their soul finds another home 'up in the sky'. No, they implicitly believe that their soul lives on in some other inaccessible dimension. So, millions of people believe in other dimensions, without thinking about it!

"Mark, are you now saying that I have come back here from Heaven?" I asked, in surprise.

"Conor, I have no idea where you came from but I am broad minded and clever enough to know that I don't know everything about everything. Let's chat after you have read the book," he answered.

"Jesus Mark, that's heavy stuff! You are talking science fiction here," I whispered.

"Conor, on the tiniest particle levels the Many Worlds Interpretation is the one that fits very neatly with scientific observation, so who knows? Is it science fiction or science fact?" replied Mark.

Mark suddenly said that he had to get back to help get everything ready for the party tonight. He said that the family had arranged for a welcoming party for me in the FFF hotel at 7:30pm that evening. He said that everybody would be there. He would be back to collect me to take me to the party and reminded me to get ready to play the part of Conor.

"Don't cock it up, Conor," he half-joked, "no mention of Ian or anything about what we have just discussed, ok?"

"Ok, I promise," I replied.

Chapter 13

It must have been just after 7:30 that evening when Mark and I pulled into the last remaining car parking spot. It had a 'reserved' sign on it. The hotel looked much bigger than I had remembered. On its left stood the function room, where Mary and I had 'partied' so many times before. The Palace Lounge looked to have been completely re-built. Under the huge red neon letters spelling out its name were a pair of glass doors, both fully opened inwards. My sister Fiona stood right in front of the door. She hadn't changed a bit since I last met her, still smiling. Remember, remember, you are Conor and you don't yet know who she is! I whispered to myself.

I was really nervous and couldn't move for a few seconds. I just sat there as Mark got out of the car and walked around to the passenger side of the car. He opened the door and I tried to get out but I couldn't move!

"Why don't you try opening your seat belt, ye feckin' egit," laughed Mark.

I could hardly support myself as I walked towards Fiona. She was dressed in a long sky-blue shimmering 'party dress' with blue high heels. I held out my hand to her as I slowly approached. She ignored my hand and instead put both of her bare arms around my neck. We must have hugged for a good minute or so and I could tell that it was heartfelt. She eventually broke off, stood back and spoke.

"Welcome back to your family, Conor," she said loudly, "I'm your sister Fiona and I have been dying to meet you."

Strange way to put it I thought ... dying to meet me.

"Thanks Fiona," I answered formally. "It's great to finally meet you."

Christ, I almost said that it was great to see her again! I will never pull this pretence off!

Fiona showed me through the open doors, it was pitch dark inside. I looked at Fiona, expecting her to switch on the lights. Just then all the lights came on, momentarily blinding me. A loud cheer went up. A crowd of maybe fifty people was standing inside the door, all clapping loudly. Over the bar hung a large silver and red banner.

WELCOME HOME CONOR

Millions of silver and red balloons hung from the ceiling. Then the speakers crackled and the Peters and Lee song *Welcome Home* started blaring out. It seemed like everyone, except me, joined in with the singing. Over the din, I could hear champagne corks popping. People young and old were slapping me on my back, some of them put their arms around my shoulders. Others were grabbing at both of my hands, trying to shake hands with me. I couldn't take it all in, it was overwhelming! I knew some of the people but there were a few I didn't recognise. Was this welcome all for me? Of course not! It was for the long-lost Conor!

I saw Peter sitting a little subdued on a bar stool in the corner. He was drinking red wine rather than champagne. Then as I looked around the room, lots of children running around, I didn't recognise many of them, I caught sight of Robert. He was standing beside his wife, not more than twenty steps away from me. My heart jumped a beat! I had tried to prepare myself for this expected moment. It's not every day you get to meet your dead brother again, full of life and face to face. Robert was staring straight back at me, with a beaming smile. They were dressed ready to party and certainly looked the part. My attempt to smile must have appeared as an awkward facial contortion. I steadied myself against the bar and tried to breathe slowly. I was afraid to walk over to Robert, I felt I might fall over on the way there. I think Robert must have sensed my difficulty because he walked over to me. He reached out his hand to me and we shook hands, rather formally. I didn't know what to say, wish he would say something! There we were standing at the bar, two brothers but two complete strangers. I was trying to start a conversation with Robert, whose funeral I had attended several years ago. Robert didn't know what to say to his older brother, who he had never seen before and who had been missing for sixty-eight years. We stood looking at each other for what seemed like ages, Robert smiling, me grimacing. Peter's son Paul, who I remembered to pretend I didn't know, came to the rescue by barging in between us and throwing both of his arms around me. He almost knocked Robert over in his haste.

"Welcome home uncle Conor," he exclaimed, "can I buy you a drink? The Guinness isn't that bad now that a few pints have already been poured through the pipes."

I nodded and he jumped in behind the bar and started to pour a couple of pints himself. Robert declined the offer, saying that he would stick with the champagne.

Robert looked great, much trimmer than when I last saw him alive, looking very healthy.

"Well, how have you been keeping?" I asked.

"Conor, can I introduce you to Peter's son Paul, he's Barbara's brother, who I think you have already met," said Robert.

Paul and I shook hands for what seemed like ages, he was exactly as I remembered, Christ it is so hard to pretend that I was meeting him for the first time.

"Not too bad," replied Robert, "but more to the point, how are you?"

"Yeah, how did you get on in the nut house," interrupted Paul. "Bet you're glad to be out of that place!"

My sister Fiona quickly appeared beside us.

"Paul Forman, you just don't have a clue, do you," she sneered. "If you haven't anything nice to say why don't you keep your mouth shut."

"What's not nice about getting out of the nut house Aunty Fiona?" replied Paul. "I'm just making sure that Conor starts to feel at home here."

I 'clinked glasses' with Paul and took a long swig from my pint of Guinness. It tasted great. I was starting to feel a bit more relaxed.

"So where have you been hiding for the last sixty-eight years Conor?" asked Robert. "Can you please tell Fiona where it is and give her directions how to get there.

Hopefully, she won't be able to find her way back!"

"Robert, we agreed that we would leave Conor alone for now," interrupted Peter, before Fiona could 'take the bait'.

"Conor, I would like to welcome you here today. Please ignore all questions until you are 'good and ready' to answer them. We all understand what you have gone through, probably still going through, so just relax. Ask any questions you want to but don't feel like you have to satisfy anybody's idle curiosity right now, especially not Robert's," said Peter.

"Just chill out everyone," replied Robert. "I'm sure Conor is well capable of handling himself."

"Hello again Conor," he said as he raised his glass.

He then turned to face all the 'partygoers', coughed loudly and shouted..

"Ladies, gentlemen and children. I'd like to propose a toast. Could everyone 'charge' their glasses and raise them with me to welcome my brother Conor back into the family.

"To Conor, welcome home, 'prodigal' brother!"

Apart from one or two young children, everyone stood up, raised their glasses and repeated.

"To Conor … welcome home. To Conor … welcome home."

Several white cotton covers were then removed from a long table which ran down one whole side of the room. A lavish seafood buffet was laid out. Lobster, prawns, smoked fish, plaice goujons and lots more. There were plenty of salads and different breads to complement the fish and a selection of different sized paper plates. The cutlery was stainless steel, must have been borrowed from the hotel.

When I had finished snacking on the delicious buffet, Marian came over to me and handed me an i-Pad. I took it and saw my brother Patrick smiling at me on the screen. I smiled when he said something but I couldn't make out a word he was saying over the noise of the crowd. He said some other words and seemed to laugh out loud but again I couldn't hear what he said. I just laughed along with him. Marian then told him that it was too noisy in the room so she would call him back after the crowd had gone. He waved at us as Marian said goodbye and cut him off.

"Conor, in case you haven't guessed it, that was your brother Patrick calling from Chicago," said Marian. "You will get to see him and all his family soon, when he comes over to meet you."

Robert's wife walked up to me in a quiet moment.

"Conor, welcome home," she said. "You don't know me but I am Robert's wife. Everyone calls me Vinny."

"Hello Vinny, I've heard all about you," I said as I shook hands with her. "I believe you are a bit of a hero."

We chatted for several minutes, she apologised that her daughters couldn't be there but she promised that I would meet them very soon. We were still talking when Peter's daughter Barbara interrupted us. At least I didn't have to pretend that I didn't know her!

"Hello uncle Conor," she said. "I'm sorry if I acted a little strange in front of you the last time we met. You really scared me when you said that you had danced with me at my brother Alan's wedding. Why did you say that Conor? You knew very well that we hadn't met before! Why did you say such a thing?"

"Barbara I really don't know why I said it, I didn't mean to scare you," I said. "My brain is still very confused. I have weird and random memories about lots of things. That's why I'm now getting support at St. John's. Can we start afresh, if I promise not to say stupid things again."

"Ok, uncle Conor," said Barbara as we shook hands again.

This marked a major change in my behaviour. I was now fully and unashamedly claiming to be Conor. I had decided to 'bury' Ian. From now on I was going to be Conor to everyone. Everyone that is, except me.

I spent the next hour or so being introduced individually to everyone in the room. It was a strange ritual. People lined up in front of me to be introduced, one by one, by Marian. I knew most of my cousins, nephews and nieces very well, but I had to pretend that I didn't. Tishy and Ronnie made small talk with me, I almost told them that I was close to knocking on their door when I first 'came back from the dead'. There were quite a few people I didn't know, so I concentrated on trying to remember their names. They would all be very impressed to later find how I managed to remember everyone's name after just one short introduction.

The party was in full swing but I had decided to drink very little alcohol, I didn't want to let my real thoughts slip out and I certainly didn't want to talk about my earlier conversation with Mark. I couldn't wait to read the book that Mark promised to loan me later, wonder if he already had it in his car.

It must have been almost twelve o'clock before I noticed most people had drifted off home already. Marian approached me and asked me how I was getting back to St John's. She said I was very welcome to stay overnight in the hotel, she said she could drop me back in the morning. Before I could answer Mark appeared beside us and asked me if I was ready to go 'home'. When Marian looked incredulously at him, he told her that he was ok to drive as he only had drunk three pints of 'Neither'.

It took only a few minutes to drive back to St John's. On route, Mark asked me if I had enjoyed the evening and mentioned that I seemed to have pulled off the impersonation of Conor really well. I thanked him but was surprised that now he openly seemed to have decided that I wasn't Conor after all. When we pulled up outside St John's, he opened the glove box and handed me a brown paper bag.

"Enjoy the book, Mr Forman," he said as we parted. "Don't be tempted to stay up all night reading it but I look forward to discussing it with you, after you have 'digested' it."

Back in my room I removed the book from the paper bag. The thin paperback had a plain light purple cover with the title emblazoned in silver letters.

The Many Lives Interpretation by Professor Carlos Prieto.

I 'thumbed' quickly through the book to the end as I stood in the middle of my room still in my clothes and shoes. Only 164 pages in total. I quickly undressed and slid into bed, not even stopping to brush my teeth. In the Preface, the author explained that he had derived his title from the 'Many Worlds Interpretation' and briefly explained, in just a couple of pages, the theory of other dimensions and parallel universes. I was 'hooked' after reading just these first few pages. I propped myself up and started reading.

I awoke with the sun shining on my face, I had forgotten to pull the curtains last night. The clock beside the TV indicated that it was 11:25am. My book was lying upside down on the floor next to my bed, my reading glasses must have fallen off my nose and landed on the bedroom floor, next to the book. I must have drifted off in the early hours. I immediately reached down for the book and my glasses. There was no bookmark but I soon found the place where I had stopped reading and started reading again. I had missed breakfast but I didn't care, I was still quite full from the buffet last night. After a short time, my concentration was broken by the phone on the bedside table ringing. It was Mark. He asked me what I had for breakfast. I lied that I just had tea and toast, don't know why I lied but I guess I was becoming very good at lying, very good indeed. He asked me what I had thought about the book and when I told him that I was enjoying it so much that I would probably finish the complete book in a few hours. Mark asked if he could pick me up at about 6:30 that evening. He said that we could have dinner in the nearby pub called 'The Summit Inn', where we could talk about the book. I stayed in bed until I had finished reading the book. I was greatly affected by Professor Prieto's words. It was already after five pm when I had finished showering and shaving. I took a slow walk inside the spacious 'hospital like' premises. Several people nodded at me as they strolled around but seemingly strolling with purpose. I walked past several numbered rooms, all of which had wooden doors with large glass panels. I guessed that these must be the session rooms. I took a peek inside a few of the rooms but moved on each time someone from inside looked back at me. Most of the rooms had lots of people sitting on chairs facing the lecturer, while others had only a few seemingly disinterested 'pupils' trying their best to look as if they cared about what was being said. I walked unchallenged through the front doors and then sat alone on a bench just outside reception, on the veranda. I was starving but didn't want to eat now, as Mark was due to pick me up soon. I sat and thought about my life. What was it all about? What is it all about? Why are we here on Earth? Why am I here on Earth now? Are we here just to be observers so that events can happen? But why? What difference would it make if I didn't exist? What difference would it make if nobody existed? How different would the planet be if people had never evolved from that earliest mammal? I thought that if humans had not evolved then there would have been no ancient history, no Romans or Greeks, no Abraham, no Jesus or Buddha, no religion, no religious persecution, no countries, no Hitler, no Beethoven, no Leonardo Da Vinci, no Beatles or Rolling Stones, no Elvis, no singing, no music, no language, no humour, no distress, no hunger, no thirst, no hatred but also sadly, no love. Hard to imagine such a world. Perhaps, without humans, some other animal would have evolved to be as intelligent or even more intelligent than a human being and developed a similar culture. Perhaps create a world which would be fairer and less cruel than the one which we developed. Why did God put us on Earth? If it was only to prepare us for entry to Heaven then why, in his wisdom, didn't he just let our souls join him in Heaven straight away and skip the need for a potentially hazardous preparation on this Earth? I think that if I was the God who loved everyone and everything, I wouldn't have created life that depends mostly on the death of some other life. I would have permitted only love to exist and banished hatred and suffering. What a dream!

    I started to feel chilly, it was already after six pm. I went back to my room, put on my brown leather jacket, picked up my book and waited in reception for Mark to arrive.

Chapter 14

Mark had reserved a table for two in a quiet corner of the restaurant. We had just ordered our prawn cocktail starters and had taken our first sips of our Sauvignon Blanc when Mark smiled and looked straight at me.

"Thanks for joining me for dinner tonight, 'big bro'," he said. "Have you ever been here at the Summit Inn before?"

I told Mark that I had been there many times before with Mary. Mary and I used to go to the music evenings there, with our brother Patrick and his American girlfriend Susan. I was a student at the time but Patrick had an old Renault car and occasionally he seemed to have plenty of money from working as a fisherman.

"So, are you saying that you knew Susan before she and Patrick got married?" asked Mark.

"Yes of course I did, but unfortunately, I didn't have the money to go to their wedding in Chicago," I replied.

"Conor, you believe that you didn't drown when you were twelve so you must have lots of memories about growing up in Howth as a teenager, tell me about some of the most memorable," asked Mark.

I told Mark about my closest friends Kieran, Eamonn, Dermot and Mick and a little about what we got up to in those innocent days. I told him that I helped open and run a 'record hop', we called it 'The Twist Club'. One of the first records the club purchased was *She Loves You* by the Beatles. He asked me did I know where my old friends were now and I told him that Mick tragically drowned in Howth harbour after Mary and I had emigrated and that I knew that Eamonn was now married and living in the Isle of Wight. I lost track of Kieran many years ago but I met Dermot at our brother's Louis funeral. Mark was definitely interested and was clearly intrigued.

"Conor did you ever hear about a guy called Finbar Davis?" asked Mark.

"Yes, I used to hang around with him a bit before Mary and I emigrated." I answered. "What a tragedy it was!"

I relayed to Mark what I had heard about the accident. Just a few months after Mary and I got married and emigrated to Canada in July 1973, I got a phone call from my older brother Peter, who told me that my good friend Finbar (Barry) Davis had died, at the very young age of just twenty-two years. He was one of five crew members aboard the fishing trawler St. Ibar, when she slowly started to sink, off Howth in October 1973. Shortly after the incident I heard one version of what happened that night. Apparently, the trawl net had snagged on the propeller and had brought the boat to a standstill. The skipper, who I was told, was a very good swimmer and an experienced diver, donned his wet suit and jumping overboard into the freezing sea, he tried to free the propeller by cutting away the net. He only partially succeeded but thought he had done enough. Climbing back on board, he started the engine and putting it in reverse, he thought it would clear itself. Unfortunately, the net got even more tangled and the power of the engine pulled the propeller out of the hull, dragging the drive shaft out of its casing. The net, the propeller and the drive shaft all sank to the bottom of the sea. Sea water immediately started to flow into the void and began to fill the bottom of the boat. There was no way to bail out the water so it was decided that the skipper, who was the only crew member with a wet suit, would swim the three or more miles to shore and bring back help. The skipper did manage to swim to shore but by the time he brought back help, it was too late. The would-be rescuers could see that the crew had set fire to the empty wooden fish boxes on the boat deck in an attempt to raise the alarm and to help keep themselves warm. But when all the wooden boxes had been burnt and the fire had gone out, the boat was continuing to slowly sink from the stern. All they could do was to cling on and hope that help would arrive soon. Unfortunately, by the time help arrived, all four crew members had died of exposure. None of them had drowned. For reasons still unknown, despite insistent family requests, I don't think that a public enquiry was held and I am unaware of any written accounts about the events of that tragic night. The story I heard was passed from person to person, I never heard or saw any first-hand evidence. The incident and the 'aftermath' still haunt me to this day and whenever I come back to Howth, I make a pilgrimage to look at the plaque, which was commissioned partly in Barry's and the other crew members memory, on a monument standing on the promenade. Sometimes I lie awake at night, thinking of the terror the men must have felt as they clung on for hour after hour, slowly losing consciousness, knowing their end was approaching.

"Conor, that's more or less the same story I also heard and that plaque you mentioned is still present on that monument," said Mark slowly.

Our identical main meals of black sole, green beans and boiled potatoes arrived, temporarily putting a stop to our conversation, allowing Mark to change the subject.

"Conor, what did you think of the book I lent you," asked Mark. "Did you enjoy reading it?"

"Yes, I really enjoyed reading the *Many Lives Interpretation,* thank you," I replied. "I think it is a very clever title."

"Did you 'get it', did you understand the theory the professor was trying to get across," he asked.

I told Mark that I understood Professor Prieto's theory but that I didn't think that the evidence he presented was really all that convincing. The professor believed strongly in parallel universes and that when someone dies from 'unnatural' causes, say as the result of a violent crime or a tragic accident, that their time on earth has been 'falsely' cut short. He believes that their body was not yet meant to die and that if in one universe they die, that the 'suddenness' of the event causes the universe to split in two and that another version of them lives on, in another universe. He thinks the duplicate version of them lives on elsewhere, until they 'finally' die of natural causes. In one universe the family and friends are bereaved and go to the funeral but in another universe the person somehow avoids death and continues to live on, still surrounded by his friends and family. They all 'move' to a parallel universe, both universes carry on, oblivious of each other.

Mark said that he had an open mind on the subject but that my presence seems to give credence to the professors' ideas. Lots of other scientists have made out cases for parallel universes, mainly using the strange behaviour of matter in the quantum world, but only Professor Prieto has taken it a step further by suggesting that the person who lived on in the new universe can somehow, perhaps only in very rare circumstances, return to their 'old' previous universe, hours, days or even years later.

"Yes Mark, I understand all that," I said, "are you now suggesting you think that is what happened to me?"

"Yes, I am," he responded. "Everything that I have heard you say directly to me and what I heard you have said to others, points to it. I even heard about the new 'old' Eagles songs you wrote. How else can we explain your insistence about your extended family and life in England and elsewhere? How else could you be convinced that your brother Robert is dead and that Daddy died in an accident?" he exclaimed.

I looked open-mouthed at Mark but didn't know what to say. Mark went on to explain that maybe when I drowned in Howth harbour that day, that another version of me was actually saved and lived on, together with all those around me, in a parallel universe. Perhaps I was pulled out of the water still alive in that other universe. Both universes continued to exist and that himself and his twin sister Fiona were born into both universes. As time went on however, the universes diverged, everything that I continued to influence in my 'new' universe was different to the 'old' universe in which I had died and so couldn't influence. In Mark's current universe our daddy didn't die in a car accident because I had been drowned long before I could have fitted those new seatbelts in Daddy's car.

"So, do you think that in the universe I used to live in, that Daddy died in a car accident, but in this universe, that is this universe, he lived to a 'ripe' old age?" I asked.

"Yes, that's a possibility but the strange thing is Conor... how and why did you come back here into my universe, years afterwards?" he asked. "What caused this to happen and why?"

"Maybe we should ask Professor Prieto," I suggested flippantly.

We continued to eat our meals without speaking for a few minutes. I couldn't taste anything. I thought that although Mark's explanation sounded like 'science fiction' it would explain a lot of what had happened to me over the past few months. If he was correct however, it meant that I would never get back with Mary again and I would never be able to speak to my children and grandchildren again. But if Mark really thought that I was 'the returned' Ian, then why was he still calling me Conor and for that matter, where is my 'long lost' twin brother Conor. Mark could see that I was deep in morbid thought so changed the subject again.

"Are you a religious man Conor? Do you believe in God? Do you believe that Jesus was the Son of God?" he asked.

Christ how can he change the subject like that, what's he up to now? I thought.

"I don't know what to think Mark," I replied. "I wish I believed in God but I struggle to really believe. I believe, of course, that Jesus existed and that he was a good, maybe even a great and very influential man. I can't help asking myself however, why someone who knew everything, past present and future, didn't make sure that he was clearly understood and believed by everyone. In addition to performing the recorded miracles, why didn't he, for example, tell us about bacteria and viruses and advise us how to deal with them. He would have had the power to prevent millions, maybe billions of people suffering and dying in pain, from many horrible but now curable diseases. Why would permitting the suffering and death of countless innocent people please Almighty God. I also can't help thinking that if he was truly divine that he could have done a better job of bringing us all together to work for the benefit of everyone and everything on earth. It's a shame he didn't recruit one or more scribes to record every spoken word that he said."

"Well at least you must be very pleased with the 'teachings' of Pope Patrick," smiled Mark.

"Pope Patrick, do you mean Saint Patrick," I asked.

"My God, have you never heard of Pope Patrick," asked Mark incredulously.

I explained that I had never heard of any Pope called Patrick. Mark told me that he was definitely now convinced that I must have been living in an alternative universe.

I continued eating my meal as Mark explained that we could talk about boring politics later but since he himself was a strong fan and supporter of Pope Patrick he had to tell me about him right now. Mark started by telling me that Archbishop Patrick, who hailed from what was known then as Northern Ireland, was greatly affected by the religious and political conflict in Ireland. He became Pope in the late eighties and eventually came to be regarded by many people, as one of the most influential men that ever existed.

I sat in shocked silence as Mark explained how Pope Patrick had, many years previously, turned the Catholic Religion completely on its head. He had given an interview to the well-known Irish talk-show host Terry Donnelly on New-Years Day, in the year 2000, it later famously became known as the 'Heaven isn't only for Christians interview'. He started by apologising for all the harm that had been done in the name of his religion, much in ignorance but unfortunately also too often by evil people with their own greedy vested interests. He said he deplored divisive tragedies such as the Inquisition, the Crusades and also the selling of indulgences, which directly led to Martin Luther and a catastrophic split in Christianity. In a nutshell, Pope Patrick wanted to return Catholicism to its root purpose of helping all those in need and to do it for the benefit of humanity, not for the 'Glory of God'. He said that Jesus neither sought, needed or desired praise and glory. What he wanted was for all the people on earth to love and care for one another and to devote as much of their time, money and effort as they could, to promoting peace and love between all races, colours and genders. Pope Patrick said that he believed that the way to heaven was not by going to mass each day but rather by acting with compassion to everyone throughout one's life. He asked for the original message of Christ to again be the true purpose of Catholicism. He officially gave it a new name, calling it 'Catholicism 2000'. To help get the new message across, a website with that name had since been created, which is managed by the Vatican, and it includes everything you might want to know about the religion, past and present. All the Bibles are included, with advice on the dangers of taking them literally, and even the latest interpretation of the Dead Sea Scrolls and many other religious manuscripts. Life histories of every Pope and what they achieved is available for personal interpretation, as are the known 'facts' about such momentous events as the Inquisition and the Crusades. The Church's view on divisive issues such as divorce, abortion, homosexuality and capital punishment are now clearly set out for anyone wants to know. Helping the poor and disadvantaged wasn't absolutely necessary for entry to Heaven, but it was the key to personal inner peace and contentment here on Earth. It was not necessary to be a 'baptised' Christian to get to Heaven, in fact it wasn't even necessary to believe in any God or even any other 'Higher Being' to please God. God is 'way above' man's petty squabbles for power and influence. He loved everyone, all the time. Pope Patrick believed that God's only wish was that we would simply love and respect each other. He said that Jesus was badly and tragically misquoted by his earliest followers when they insisted that the only way to Heaven was through him. This had the effect of dividing people rather than bringing them together. There is no first-hand evidence that Jesus wanted everyone on Earth to follow any one particular narrow set of beliefs, not even his. All religions or cults, which followed basic love for one another, were equally good and a route to inner peace, which could open a gateway to Heaven. Pope Patrick stated that since it was no longer necessary to believe in every one of the teachings of the Catholic Religion that it was no longer necessary to 'pretend' to believe in every single, 'man-made' doctrine. Pope Patrick then asked his 'team' of nuns, priests, bishops, arch-bishops and cardinals etcetera, to come together to do their utmost to make the sweeping changes needed to help make the world a better, more loving and more inclusive place. They were to begin by each swallowing a large glass of 'humility' and to forget their false sense of self-importance. He asked that the highest priority and the most urgent task was to open up the priesthood to women, who he suggested had been discriminated against by the Catholic Church, throughout history. The second priority was to abolish the requirement for priests to be celibate. Ordination was to be made available for all people, who demonstrated their willingness and ability to perform the task. Only when open to all races, men and women, married, single or divorced and also to gay and transgender people could we start to really follow the teachings of Jesus.

"Oh my God, did they put him in a lunatic asylum?" I interrupted.

"No, they certainly did not. The Pope started a silent, non-violent but non-stoppable, religious and even cultural revolution. Not just amongst Catholics, many of whom had secretly harboured similar views to Pope Patrick, but also amongst people of many other faiths, not just Christians. The silent revolution still continues to this day, in religions and in politics, in nearly every part of the world and all for the better. Most people in Ireland put down the start of the coming together of Northern Ireland and The Republic of Ireland to this moment. I think we will soon have another Saint Patrick," said Mark admiringly.

"Did Terry not ask him if he believed that Jesus was the Son of God?" I asked.

"Yes, he did and Pope Patrick answered that he certainly did. He went on to say however that it was not relevant whether you believed this or not. It was only several hundred years after Jesus' death that at a number of separate Church Councils, several hundred Catholic Church Bishops voted, but only by a majority and not unanimously, to accept that Jesus really was the Son of God."

"I didn't know that there was a vote Mark, I assumed that some Pope had just decided that to be fact," I interrupted.

Mark told me that there is a free App called 'Responsa', which is Latin for 'Answers' which is a bit like Google, U Tube and Wikipedia all rolled into one, for all matters relating to Catholicism 2000. He opened up the App..

"It was at the Council of Chalcedon, in the fifth century, that it was finally agreed by a majority of the voting clergy that Jesus was both 'Fully God and Fully Man', taking his flesh and human nature from the Virgin

Mary," announced Mark.

Mark then added that Pope Patrick mentioned that he was aware that many Catholics still don't really believe this, but so what. He said that it may be possible to force people to say that they 'believe' but that you cannot force their brains to actually really believe," explained Mark.

"My God, what else did he say," I asked.

"He also shocked many by saying that it was not necessary to be baptised to go to heaven, he knew for certain that no Neanderthals had been baptised and he believed that no loving God would prevent even one deserving Neanderthal from entering heaven just because he was born thousands of years before John The Baptist appeared on Earth. Also, why would a loving and caring God exclude billions of deserving Chinese or Indian people eternal happiness, just because they happened to be born in China or India? He couldn't and he wouldn't of course!"

"That must have been shocking for all Catholics, was he called a heretic?"

"Yes, many did want him removed from office but when he 'went on' to speak of the vast expanse of the Universe and the possibility or even likelihood that many more forms of intelligent life could well exist on countless other planets, people understood his message. Heaven was available for everyone, not just for inhabitants of Earth. It was for all deserving beings, human, non-human, even alien. God loved all beings, without judging any of them. Hell was invented by human beings who wanted to frighten people to get them to behave as they thought they should, not by God."

"My God, that's unbelievable, what happened afterwards?" I asked.

"Well, now there are as many women as men priests. The priesthood is open to married couples, even same sex couples. Gays, lesbians and cross gender people are welcomed."

"And what do they do all day?" I asked

"They follow the original teachings of Christ. They help those less fortunate than themselves. They also conduct marriages, funerals and christenings, but hardly anybody goes to mass these days. People still gather at the Church to talk about how they can help others. They no longer go there just to glorify God, but if they want to, they can of course."

"But it sounds like he hinted that everybody goes to heaven no matter what. What did he say about Hell?"

"Well, what he said about Hell really caused a stir. He reminded us that we are all God's children and that God is unlikely to be 'into' punishing any of his children for eternity, whatever the circumstances."

"But who did he say goes to Hell then?" I asked Mark.

"He said that when God created us, he had the power to make us strong enough to resist all temptation, but he chose not to. He gave us free will, knowing full well that our human frailties would lead many of us into trouble at some time during our lives on this Earth. Pope Patrick then stated that he doubts if a loving and forgiving God would create a purpose-built punishment centre for those of His children who He already knew couldn't resist temptation at all times."

"So, if Pope Patrick said that he questions the existence of Hell, what did he say happens to those evil or cruel people who inflict pain and suffering on others, when they die?"

"He said that God gave us the intelligence and compassion to deal with injustice. He suggested that collectively we have the power to deal with evil people here on earth, we shouldn't just sit back and think that it is acceptable to just leave it to God to punish them after they die," answered Mark.

"So, if the Pope said that Hell was not a God made purpose-built punishment centre, did he say that everyone goes to Heaven whatever their behaviour here on Earth is?" I asked.

"Well, here the Pope was not so certain. He explained that since no one has ever come back from Hell to tell us all about it, no one can be certain of anything," answered Mark.

"That sounds like a bit of a fudge to me, Mark," I responded.

"He said that neither he, nor most of the others at the Vatican now really believes that God would punish anyone for eternity, no matter how evil they were during their lifetime. The Catholic Hierarchy now suggest that there is a Heaven for those who deserve it and who would be happy to be there, but that there is probably no Hell," said Mark.

"So, what happened to Hitler's soul then?" I asked.

"The Vatican now propose that undeserving souls don't go anywhere at all. They think it most likely that both their mortal and spiritual lives just cease to exist. They even gave it a name Conor, they call it 'Irritum'. It is the Latin word for nothingness, oblivion, a vacuum. Pope Patrick said that the consensus at the Vatican is that a loving and caring God would welcome all deserving souls to Heaven and simply exclude those who are not. The evil souls are not tortured forever, they are instead simply excluded from paradise, but they will not be in pain as they will be unaware of this, as their souls will be in a state of Irritum," explained Mark.

"Well I suppose that is a 'sort of' Hell," I replied.

"They prefer to call it a state of Irritum, Conor. They don't want to use the word Hell anymore," answered Mark.

"Irritum … Irritum" … I repeated, "sounds more like an upset tummy to me but at least I wouldn't meet Hitler if I do ever make it to Heaven! And we no longer have to fear going to Hell then if we are naughty," I smiled.

"Pope Patrick pleaded that more of us should expose and condemn evil so that the individuals or regimes involved, can be dealt with swiftly but compassionately, in their lifetime, by those of us who are responsible for and capable of applying justice. He wants his priests, nuns and other church 'workers' to devote all of their free time to helping those unfortunate individuals who are victims of deliberate or careless evil actions, of poverty, of natural disasters, of prejudice, of physical or mental cruelty. To put it simply, he asked us all to help everyone in need," said Mark, in a very serious tone.

This was 'heavy stuff', I thought.

"Pope Patrick said that his mission, from now on, was to get as many people as possible, whatever their race, religious persuasion or gender to truly bond as a group dedicated to helping others on this earth. He asked his followers to lead by example," added Mark.

"How about the other world religions, how did they react?" I asked.

"Change is gradually happening there to. There is much less religious friction but still a long way to go. Protestants and Catholics are no longer suspicious of each other, they get along just fine."

"My God Mark, what a brilliant and forward-thinking man," I exclaimed. "He surely will be made a Saint someday."

Mark looked at his watch and said that it was getting late and that he should be getting back home. He looked to me as if he had gotten a lot off his chest and was smiling. He repeated that he was now completely convinced that I was Ian but that he would have to continue to call me Conor. He explained that no one would ever believe I was 'another' Ian, so to be accepted, I had to convince everyone that I must be Conor. He said I didn't need to make up 'stories' about where I had been for the past sixty-eight years. I just need to say that I can't remember. He stressed the importance of me becoming familiar with the current political situation in Ireland and the rest of the world. He suggested that I read as much as I can, from the library books at the centre. He warned against me asking 'stupid' questions which might betray my ignorance of the universe which I now found myself in. He suggested that I start by reading about the Lions Community. As he dropped me back at the front door, Mark asked if I would object to him trying to contact Professor Prieto. I replied that I didn't care one way or the other.

Chapter 15

The library was closed when I got back to the centre. It was already past eleven pm, when I rang the doorbell. The jovial night porter looked at me through the glass door and asked me to hold up my ID Badge to the glass. I'm sure Mick knew me but I guess he had to be 'seen' to be doing his job professionally. I stood under the canopy, shifting from one foot to the other in an effort to try to keep warm. The temperature had dropped significantly, which I suppose was normal for this time of year. Mick unlocked the door and pulling one leaf open, he stood aside to allow me to walk in. Not the most impressive of security men, I thought as I nodded at Mick. He was probably close to seventy years of age, stood only about five foot two tall and probably weighed less than nine and a half stone. His mop of neat grey hair, immaculate navy-blue uniform and his mobile phone strapped to his waist however, gave him an air of importance. He was proud of his job and believed himself to be a vital member of the staff at the centre. At least as important as some of those so-called consultants, who 'didn't know their arse from their elbow'. Everybody knew him and he did his best to get to know everybody, always there to greet people with a welcoming smile and never considering himself to be more important than the customers, not like some of the other staff.

"Evening Mick, thanks for letting me in out of the cold," I said.

"No problem Mr Forman, it's a pleasure," he replied in a friendly tone. "Can I get you something? maybe a sandwich or a glass of milk before you retire to your room."

"No thanks Mick, I just need to get one or two books from the library before I lay my head to rest."

"I'm afraid you will have to wait until the morning Mr Forman, the library re-opens at seven thirty in the morning."

"But don't you have a key Mick? Could you open up for me, I just need five or so quick minutes, reading helps me drop off to sleep you see," I pleaded.

"Are you trying to get me sacked Mr Forman," he replied. "You know that I am not allowed to do that."

"Ok, no prob, I just thought I'd try, but I guess I will have to wait until the morning," I replied with a smile.

I could see that Mick was unhappy that he couldn't help me. He couldn't hide his disappointed expression. I was sorry now that I had asked him to break the rules and I hoped that it wouldn't bother him for too long.

I lay down on my bed, with the bedroom light still shining in my eyes. I knew I wasn't ready to sleep yet, but I closed my eyes to let me think more clearly. What a night that had been! What a transformation by Mark! I no longer felt alone in the world, I had a friend who believed in me and wanted to help. Deep down I had to admit that everything Mark had said about my situation made more and more sense. Of course, I knew that I wasn't Conor Forman, I was Ian Forman but I knew that my brain or my soul or whatever our essence in each different universe is, didn't now inhabit the body of the Ian Forman that was buried in the graveyard. What about the soul of the twelve-year old Ian, has it already gone to Heaven or does it have to wait until I finally die of old age? Do I have two or more souls, maybe some in Heaven but others in Irritum? How does all this work? Even if I accept that I went into another dimension when I both drowned but also didn't drown, how the hell did I arrive back here where I started from? If the professor's theory is correct then I must have died a second time. Did I die suddenly on that park bench from the effects of perhaps a 'dodgy' codeine tablet, when I thought that I had only fallen asleep. Did I fail to wake up in my original universe, and Mary has since had me cremated. Did I then simultaneously 'wake' up in this new universe, the one I left when I was twelve years old but which had since 'moved on', without me? This is all too ridiculous to believe, no sane person would believe that this could happen. If someone told me this story, I would assume that they were mentally disturbed, as anyone would. But what now? If I am to try to make a new life here, I will have to live as Conor Forman. How else could I open a bank account and obtain a valid credit and debit card, how could I even sign a new mobile phone contact, no, not as Ian Forman. My new passport will have to be in the name of Conor Forman, as will my driving license. Oh my God, will I have to do another driving test? I had better start learning the rules of the road again, I hope they are the same as where I came from.

What about my old credit cards and those Irish Euro banknotes. Will the police get involved? I suddenly thought about my mobile phone, should I allow Mark to get it charged up again. If this happened how could I explain away all those family photographs to other people. Those countless photos of Mary and our children and grandchildren on holiday or celebrating birthdays. I even copied our wedding photos into a separate gallery. I decided I had better not let anyone mess with my mobile and I would let Mark deal with any questions from the police. But do I want to make a new life here at sixty-eight years of age? Without Mary what would be the point in living anyway? What possible pleasure would I get out of just existing here, I could never be happy as I wouldn't have my wife, children or grandchildren to live for. Sure, perhaps I might find some moments of pleasure in say watching a movie or a football match, playing my guitar and singing, or even playing a round of golf or a game of snooker but everyone knows that pleasure is temporary and fleeting, while happiness is a state of mind and is long lasting. I used to be very happy but I now know that I will never, ever be happy again. What's the point, I think I would be better off dead. Pope Patrick said that I won't go to Hell if my life ended now. I would be in Heaven or Irritum. Irritum doesn't sound too bad at all, probably better than a life of unfulfilled love and continuous daily torment. I would hate to grow old in an empty life of pretence and make believe. The alternative could be Irritum but it might just be Heaven, where, if I did manage to get there, I'm sure Mary would eventually join me. Maybe I could fall off the Howth cliff edge tomorrow or better still fall into the harbour at the same place where I fell in, all those years ago. I would definitely drown again, as I still can't swim. I better make sure this time that there is no one around to pull me out! But hold on, maybe all versions of me wouldn't drown, maybe I would end up in yet another universe. Maybe a happy universe, where I am still married to Mary and where John, Annette, Aidan, Luke, Ella and Josie are all part of my happy life. Is it worth the risk? I think it is, after all what have I to lose?

I decided to 'sleep on it'. Many decisions are best taken after sleeping on it. I turned off the light and tried to sleep. Although I lay awake for ages and ages, I must have eventually fallen asleep because I woke up with the sun shining into the room.

I was glad that 'I slept on it' last night'. Suddenly the world didn't seem so bad. As they say 'where there's life there's hope'. I knew what I had to do….. I had to find Mary, I had to befriend her and I had to somehow become part of her life again. I knew it wouldn't be easy and I knew it could take 'forever' but I am persistent and determined. I realised that life would never be perfect again, no children or grandchildren to complete our lives, but I knew that I could still be 'sort of' happy again.

Ok, there are a few major obstacles to me getting back with Mary again. I jumped out of bed and sitting at the desk, I grabbed a notepad and pen and decided to list some of the obstacles, in the order they occurred to me….

- Mary is already married with a husband and a grown-up son.
- How could I get to meet her, even if I found out where she lives, how could I approach her.
- Mary doesn't know me and I can't think of any good reasons why she would want to. I have nothing to offer her, no job, no home, no money, not even a name.
- She will no longer find me physically attractive, if she ever did, we are not sixteen anymore.
- I can't just follow along behind her, she would have me arrested as a stalker.

I thought that I would feel better once I listed the obstacles but I didn't. It only served to show how impossible my crazy dream was. I got dressed and went down for breakfast. I went for the full Irish this time, minus the sausage and the black and white puddings, of course.

After breakfast I visited the library and found, what looked like, the perfect book. It was a very short paperback entitled 'The Lions Community Concept'. I thumbed through it quickly, not too much jargon and concise enough to hopefully keep my attention. Back in my room I took the sheet, on which my list of obstacles to overcome was written, and put it in my desk drawer. For some stupid reason I turned the sheet over before I closed the drawer. Out of sight, out of mind?

I put on a warm sky-blue woollen sweater and a sky-blue baseball cap with 'Forman's Enterprises' emblazoned across the front.

Outside, I sat on the closest vacant garden bench, close enough to the main building to ensure I could still see the entrance lobby. I started to read the book from the beginning. It was a little awkward not knowing when exactly Mark might show up today, or if any of my other relatives might just show up, unannounced. I could definitely do with a new mobile phone, I kept looking back at the front door to see if anyone was looking for me.

I quickly became engrossed in the book...

The UK and the Republic of Ireland joined the European Communities, later called the European Union, in 1973. The Euro was introduced in 1999 but the UK kept the British Pound Sterling and the Republic of Ireland kept the Punt. For some time, there was much talk about either or both of them abandoning their currencies and joining the Euro but the political situation changed dramatically shortly afterwards, so the situation never arose. At many public meetings between the UK and the Republic of Ireland governments, at which all the main political groups from both sides of the Irish Sea and representatives from all religious groups were represented, some far-reaching decisions were taken.

It was announced that the whole of Ireland would be united and would in future be known as the Republic of All Ireland, RAI for short. The RAI would have an elected President and a Prime Minister. The new independent 'Irish Parliament' would sit in a purpose built complex in a town called Athlone, situated right in the centre of the island of Ireland. Politicians would be elected by proportional representation. All religions would be respected, tolerated and have equal status in the new country but no 'officers' of any religion could sit as a member of the Irish Parliament.

At the same time, it was announced that the UK, as it was then known as, would be dissolved as soon as the arrangements could be made.

Scotland would become the Republic of Scotland, with its own President and Prime Minister. Their parliament would sit in Edinburgh.

Wales would become the Republic of Wales, also with its own President and Prime Minister. Their parliament would sit in Cardiff.

England would become the 'Kingdom of England', KE for short. The Queen (or King) would be the head of state for England for as long as the majority of the people of England wanted it. As with the positions of President in the three republics, the Queen's role would be largely ceremonial. The English Government, under their own Prime Minister of England, would sit in the existing Houses of Parliament in Westminster but with its jurisdiction restricted to England only.

A new legal entity would be formed as soon as possible. It would be comprised of the KE, the RS, the RW and the RAI. It would have its own parliament and commission, more or less mirroring the then existing set up in the EU. This new community, which would be known as the **Lions Community**, would consist of members elected from all four member countries, again in much the same way as the members of the European Parliament were then currently elected.

A new assembly building was to be built in Birmingham, England to house the MLCPs. As soon as possible, but not later from two years from then, notice to leave the EU would be given by the countries of the LC. A new Lions Community Court of Justice would be formed and would sit on the Isle of Man. It was hoped that the divorce from the EU would be straightforward and friendly. Confidence was expressed that a free trade agreement would be quickly agreed between the LC and the EU, still allowing the LC to pursue its own trade agreements with the rest of the world. Both the British Pound Sterling and the Irish Punt would be abandoned and replaced by **The Pride**. There would be one hundred **Cubs** in one Pride.

I read the book from cover to cover, which covered only the discussion period, nothing had happened yet. I was intrigued. I wonder what happened next? I must find out more and the sooner the better if I am not to make a fool of myself in future conversations! I had just closed the book and placed it on the bench beside me, when Mark appeared and sat down. He picked up the book and looked at the cover.

"Well Bro, what do you think about the Lions Community?" he asked. "Is this much different to the world you and Mary lived in just a few short months ago?"

"Totally different Mark," I answered, "but did it all happen as planned and if so, what happened to the economies afterwards?"

"Conor, I will tell you more about it over a coffee and a cinnamon swirl," he answered and you can tell me about the differences, but first we have several more important issues to discuss."

On the wooden bench and far enough away for our conversation not to be overheard, we sat in the sunshine and sipped our black coffees and munched on our pastries. Mark explained that the Gardai wanted to talk to me about the counterfeit money and the forged bank cards. They also wanted to know exactly why I had 'spun all those yarns' about me being Ian Forman. They said that these were serious issues and they wanted my full cooperation. They threatened that I would be charged with wasting police time and possible misuse of public funds, if I failed to provide credible explanations. I had been invited to go to the Howth Garda station next Monday at ten o'clock, to be interviewed. Since I was not going to be arrested or charged with anything, I would not need legal representation but it was permitted, if I wanted it.

"Jesus Mark, how can I provide any credible explanations, there aren't any," I answered.

Mark re-assured me that he would pick me up and accompany me to the station. He said that the last thing we needed right now was legal representation. He stressed that I should not even attempt to explain anything. I should just keep answering that I must have been confused and that nobody knows yet what caused my confusion. I should tell them that I have no idea where the money or the bank cards came from, if I did, I would tell them. I should try to turn the problem back to them by asking them how their investigation to establish where I have been living for the past sixty-eight years, is proceeding. Whatever I do, I must stay calm and just keep acting helpful. I should 'emotionally' express my deep anxiety and my utter disappointment with the apparent lack of progress by the Gardai, how much longer can it take for God's sake? He said that I should then thank and praise them for all the effort they are making. Tell them that I have full confidence in them and that if I can help in any way, they only have to ask.

"With any luck Conor, if the interview goes according to plan, it will end up with the Gardai apologising to you rather than charging you with a crime. Try to get them to commit to re-doubling their efforts to find out all about your past and where you have been. Try to embarrass them, they will then start to feel incompetent. We both know that they will never succeed in finding out anything new about you, so hopefully we will never hear from them again," said Mark.

"Ok Mark, I will do my best but please stay with me at all times," I said. "But what else do you want to tell me?" I asked.

Mark gave me an update on the progress of my application for a Lions Community Passport. The forms I had earlier completed had been mailed to the passport office together with a copy of my 'long' birth certificate and the two 'witnessed' photographs. He managed to convince Sergeant Murphy, of Howth Garda station to sign the backs of the photos, stating that he knew me for several months. Everyone hoped that the passport office would accept my application, but we wouldn't know for sure for a few more weeks. We would have to wait until I had the passport before I could successfully apply for a new bank account or a driving license. Mark then presented me with a new bank debit card with Mark Forman embossed on it. He told me that I could use it for withdrawing cash from any 'hole in the wall' and also for small contactless payments. The passcode was the day, month and year of my birth, in reverse order.

Everything seemed to be getting sorted!

Before he left me, Mark told me that 'as I had suggested', he is trying to contact Professor Prieto. He had written to Professor Prieto's publisher, giving him his address, e-mail and phone number, asking the publisher to pass it on to the professor. He requested that the professor contact him confidentially to discuss a current true life 'Many Lives' experience he was keen to share with the professor. Mark said that he doubted he would ever hear from him but thought that it was worth a 'shot'.

"Then I won't 'hold my breath' Mark," I replied.

"Oh, it's not all bad news Conor," said Mark. "Our brother Patrick is flying over from Chicago, to meet you. I volunteered to pick him up tomorrow afternoon from Dublin Airport. He will be staying at the FFF, I'm sure you will meet up with him tomorrow night."

"I am looking forward to it already," I replied.

"Conor, if you are up for it, we can go to the live music session in Brian's Palace on Saturday night," said Mark. "I'm sure Patrick and the rest of the clan will also come along. I think you might enjoy it."

"So, what is the political situation in your universe Conor," asked Mark. You tell me all about your previous universe first and then I will tell you more about the Lions Community afterwards."

We spent a good couple of hours chatting. Mark listened politely as I told him what life was like in the UK but he was shocked that the North of Ireland was still part of the UK. I told him that my Universe never had a Pope Patrick to help bring the communities together. I 'cut it short' with Mark, I wanted to hear more about the LC. I learned that the LC was thriving and had a good trading arrangement with the EU and the rest of the world. 'Made in the LC' was the slogan everywhere. Each of the four countries in the LC had a healthy manufacturing industry and even had its own electric car assembly plant, using components imported from around the world. Mark said that he was really happy that the LC has complete control over the fishing rights around our coasts. Consequently, the fishing industry is really thriving while still maintaining fish stocks. Forman Enterprises employed over two hundred employees and exported fish throughout Europe and North America.

"Yes, the Lions Community has been good for all four countries and has maintained steady but consistent economic growth since it was formed," said Mark proudly.

Mark apologised that he wouldn't see me until tomorrow night but told me that brother Robert would pick me up at about noon tomorrow and entertain me for a few hours. Mark 'warned me' to be careful when I was talking to Robert. I must always be vigilant and always remember that I am Conor

As soon as Mark left, I returned to the library and read up some more on the Lions Community. I also used their computer desktop to look up

Forman Enterprises on the internet. I read that in addition to the fish business that it owned the FFF Hotel and the King Sitric fish restaurant in Howth. I resolved to spend all my spare time, from now on, reading in the library. Within a few days I thought that I would be knowledgeable enough to hold a sensible conversation with anybody. I was still not looking forward however to the upcoming meeting with the Gardai.

Chapter 16

I was sitting outside St John's, on my favourite bench when Robert's red/brown metallic BMW Seven Series pulled up on the driveway.

I opened the passenger door and slid onto the luxurious cream leather seat. Robert turned off the radio and looked at me. He asked me if I knew much about Howth. I said I knew a little but he should assume that I knew nothing. The automatic transmission was so smooth and the engine so quiet that I feared that pedestrians and cyclists wouldn't hear us coming. Robert was a brilliant tour guide. He not only seemed to know every road and significant building but he knew the history of everything as well. I thought that I knew a lot about Howth but soon realised that I knew practically nothing.

A quick coffee at the Summit Inn, then down the hill towards Sutton Cross, stopping on route to drop into the car park at Howth Golf Club, where we didn't linger. Robert told me that he and Mark were members of St Anne's Golf Club, neither of them liked 'negotiating' the many 'thrombosis hills' that were 'part and parcel' of Howth Golf Club. Although if you could physically endure the climbs, he said that the scenery was spectacular. Best golf course views in the world, he said. Robert was never one for understating anything! We turned right at Sutton Cross and headed off towards the village of Howth, approximately two miles away. Half a mile or so before we got to Howth he turned right and drove through the open huge black wrought iron gates which led up to Howth Castle. I knew exactly where we were going. Well, I thought I knew where we were going. What a transformation lay in front of me. The semi-dilapidated hotel that I had recently unsuccessfully tried to book into, only to find it had already closed down, looked spectacular. Although the name 'DEER PARK HOTEL' was still written above the entrance doors, it was a completely different hotel. It had been extended and 'spruced up'. The gym and indoor pool had not changed but the golf clubhouse had been greatly enlarged. Robert told me that the forty-five golf holes were reputed to be the best public golf holes in all of Ireland, maybe even the world! No exaggeration there then!

We sat up at the bar and Robert asked me what I would like. I noticed it was past noon so with 'the sun over the yardarm' I decided I would have a pint of Guinness. Robert ordered a pint of 'Neither'. The barman poured roughly half a pint of Guinness into each of the two 'straight' pint glasses. After the black liquid had almost settled, he completed pouring the Guinness into one of the glasses until it was full and then he set it aside to settle. He then filled up the other glass from a pump which had 'NFG' written boldly in large green Gaelic letters on it. It looked and poured exactly like 'regular' Guinness to me, perhaps it was just cooler. Robert was surprised when I asked him what he was drinking.

"I'm driving," he said, "got to be careful."

"What's NFG," I asked, "it looks just like Guinness."

"Haven't you seen it before Conor? It's zero alcohol Guinness."

"What does NFG stand for?" I asked.

"I don't know to be honest but most people assume it stands for Not Feckin' Guinness," replied Robert, "so everybody simply calls it 'Not'."

"Oh, I get it," I said, "you can have a pint of Guinness or a pint of 'Not'."

"Or a pint of 'Neither' if you want a 'half and half'" added Robert.

Suitably refreshed and re-educated, I followed Robert through the hotel and out the back to the tightly mown lawns. Robert told me that there were magnificent rhododendron gardens, probably the best in all Ireland, just a couple of minutes-walk further on, but suggested we take a look at them later. As we walked back to the car, he told me that he would love to buy the hotel but it would never be for sale. It was part of the Howth Castle Estate and completely out of reach for 'mere mortals' he said. I noticed five or six white VW minibuses parked outside the hotel with Howth Park & Ride emblazoned everywhere. That would explain why the car park was quite busy but with very few people in the hotel.

Back through the estate gates, turned right and a couple of minutes later we passed the DART railway station and The Bloody Stream lounge on our left-hand side. Robert turned left and slowly drove down the West Pier. We went right to the end, turned round and then drove back to 'Formans'. I felt very uneasy walking through the open yellow wooden gates. The premises were not much bigger than how I remembered it, I think they had absorbed only one of the adjoining premises on the right. Nothing much to see there really, I didn't recognise any of the maybe thirty or so employees and no one paid the slightest attention to me. Robert told me that the main factory, which housed the smokehouses was located in Finglas, just a few miles away, he said. No room to expand on the west pier!

We were just about finished the factory 'tour' when Robert's mobile rang. Marian told Robert that Patrick had just arrived by taxi and was waiting to see us. Back at the FFF Hotel and no sign of Patrick! He was obviously unpacking in his room while he waited for us. A few minutes later Patrick walked into the hotel lounge, chatting loudly to Marian as he came in sight. He walked straight over to me and almost squashed the life out of me with a big 'bear hug'.

"The taxi driver told me a great joke," he said.

I could see both Robert and Marian turn away, completely disinterested. I think I looked suitably interested!

"Paddy and Mick were on safari in Africa. They decided to venture a little on foot to explore the area, but went a little too far away from the

jeep and the driver/guide. Paddy looked behind him as they walked. He saw a huge male lion 'stalking' them. It was walking slowly but steadily closing in on them. They both stopped, frozen in fear. Paddy nervously looked down at his feet and saw a jagged stone, about the size of the palm of his hand. He bent down, picked up the stone and hurled it, with all his strength, at the lion. Bulls-eye.. it hit the lion right smack in the middle of its forehead. The lion staggered and dropped to the ground. Great shot said Mick, as he slapped Paddy on the back. Just then the lion stood up again and started to shake his head from side to side. Christ, we better run Mick, shouted Paddy, I think we made him angry. No Paddy, you better run. It wasn't me who threw the feckin' stone."

Patrick and I both laughed heartily at the joke, Patrick more so than me. Robert and Marian just smiled. They were 'embarrassed' looking smiles. Had they heard the joke before, I wondered?

"How was your trip over?" asked Robert."

"Jesus, you guys do really need to lighten up," said Patrick. "Do either of you ever laugh?"

"How long are you staying with us Patrick?" asked Marian.

"Jesus, I've only just got here and already you are trying to get rid of me," answered Patrick. "Conor, do you realise what you are 'getting into' here?"

I think Robert felt that he had 'done his duty', as he made an excuse and left me with Marian and Patrick. Marian quickly apologised and left us saying that she had lots of work to do. I felt nervous when left alone with Patrick. I wondered what I would talk about. I needn't have worried because Patrick could still 'talk for Ireland'. Thankfully he didn't ask me much about myself or where I had been living, instead I learned all about his wife Susan, their son Packy and their daughter Sarah. Within an hour or so I heard all about how well their grandchildren were doing at school and how great they all were at music and sport, American style. My sister Fiona and her husband Gearoid joined Patrick and I for a very late lunch at an exclusive fish restaurant at the top of the East Pier in Howth. Mark arrived unexpectedly, just a few minutes after we sat down. I had eaten several times before at the King Sitric, it was so difficult to act as if I had never been in the place. I went for a whole black sole with boiled potatoes and green beans. I enjoyed chatting with my siblings, I learned that Fiona was not a school teacher in this universe but was instead involved in the family business. She took great satisfaction in telling me that, as the company Financial Director, it was really her and not Robert who really called the shots. Gearoid didn't say too much over lunch, he was as quiet as I remembered him. He didn't work for the Gardai, he was the head of security for the company. Fiona told me all about their student children Emmet and Siofra. As I understood it, they were both pursuing almost the same career paths as they were in my world, how strange is that, I thought!

I was grateful that Mark was with us because he quickly changed the subject any time I was faced with an awkward question. I was beginning to think that maybe I could pull this act off. Mark dropped me back to St John's and congratulated me on my 'performance' during lunch.

I spent the next day, Saturday, in the library reading about Irish history and Irish current affairs. I also quickly glanced through a large volume about WW1 and an even bigger one about WW2. The Germans lost both times again!

Mark and I arrived at the FFF hotel sometime after 7:30pm. When we came to the reserved table in the function room, Robert and his wife Vinny were already into their first drink but Marian had not yet arrived. Robert, Vinny and I passed the time engaging in some small talk. Just for something to say, I asked Robert why the function room was called 'Brian's Palace'. He explained that Marian had a 'thing' for royalty, especially old Irish Royalty. Marian named it Brian's Palace after the last High King of Ireland, Brian Boru.

"I'm sure you have heard of him. You know the guy who defeated the Vikings at the Battle of Clontarf in 1014. Even though Brian Boru was killed in the battle, he lives on as a legend. Marian thinks he is the greatest hero that Ireland has ever had. Although Brian himself, his son and his grandson were killed, along with about ten thousand other soldiers, he won the battle and the power of the Vikings in Ireland never recovered," explained Robert.

"So why didn't she call it Boru's Palace, then everyone would know where the name came from?" I asked.

"Marian said that she doesn't even know if Brian Boru ever had a palace or a castle when he lived, but that he does now, thanks to her. She's more than a little disappointed that people just call it 'The Pally'. Make sure you always call it Brian's Palace when you are with her," added Robert.

"Thanks for the tip, I'll try to remember that," I smiled.

It must have been after nine o'clock before the band came on stage. As they were setting up, I took a good look around at the audience. People were seated at every table but there were still a few free places here and there. Everyone seemed to have a drink of some sort in front of them. Good mixture of ages, from twenties to sixties it looked like. I was surprised that quite a few were smoking and although there was extraction over each table there was a strange unfamiliar odour in the air. When I mentioned that I was surprised that smoking was permitted inside the room, Vinny explained that it was not tobacco being smoked but Marijuana. I tried not to act too surprised but I wanted to know more! Over the course of the evening I gradually learned that it was legal to smoke Marijuana in Ireland but it could only be purchased from a small number of Government licensed shops. Its manufacture in Ireland was restricted to just one licensed supplier. The Irish Government had apparently decided that it was better, for safety reasons, to control the product quality and at the same time to let the country benefit from its taxation. Prices were deliberately kept 'reasonable' to dissuade organised crime from becoming involved, there was apparently no incentive to do so. I presume it worked because all the 'roll-ups' looked to be the same and they were all packaged in identical cartons.

The band were finally ready to go, a Carlo Emerald tribute band. It was a trio named Blue Lips from Amsterdam. Robert told me that, like Caro herself, they 'hailed' from Holland. I guess that the band name was referencing that old sing-along song *Tulips from Amsterdam*. The female lead singer could only have been in her twenties, she 'looked the part', even though her bright royal blue lipstick was a little 'over the top'. The guitarist and drummer couldn't be much older but they were pretty good. Young 'blue lips' herself turned out to be a really good singer and performer. If I closed my eyes, I could swear it was Caro herself singing. Early on, I wondered whether she was miming but soon realised that she was just very good. She went through most of Caro's songs and they were nearly all well known to me. She started off with perhaps Caro's biggest hit *That Man*, and it was very well rehearsed. During the first song Marian joined us at the table. Songs such as *One Day* and *Doctor Wanna Do* followed by many more, one after the other with no more than, what seemed like, a couple of seconds between them. The noise level in the room, especially near the stage, made conversation at our table almost impossible but it didn't stop Patrick cracking jokes all the time, which since none of us could hear them, he was the only one who laughed at them.

The first session was really enjoyable, as they say 'the house was rockin'. The interval just seemed to come too soon. When they left the stage, Marian called the band over to our table. Now I realised why there were three spare chairs at the table. Marian wanted to get to know the band, I guessed she was thinking about booking them again. Griet, as the singer called herself was a very pretty girl close up, even with that stupid lipstick. She couldn't have been more than five feet tall but her dark complexion, long black hair and effervescent confidence, gave her plenty of 'stage presence'. She introduced the drummer as her brother Geoff, he could have been her older twin. Both Geoff and Griet spoke excellent English and were 'easy' to talk to. The guitarist was a tall, brooding, angry looking thirty something year old. He couldn't or wouldn't speak English and he looked away from the table as the rest of us talked. He made it obvious that he was totally disinterested in us. He acted like he didn't want to be there at all! He kept interrupting us, jumping in and speaking quite loudly in Dutch, mainly to Griet. It became clear to me that Leo was Griet's boyfriend and a very jealous one at that. Leo didn't know that I understood and spoke Dutch quite well but I never pretended to follow what he and Griet were saying. Geoff soon became embarrassed to be there but tried to smile anyway. Leo went 'on and on' about how he hated performing in this 'dump', in front of drunken and 'spaced out' geriatric imbeciles. As Leo became more and more 'worked up', his comments, all in Dutch, became even worse. He criticised Griet for her 'crap' performance and told her that the only reason that we were pretending to be enjoying her performance was because all we wanted to do was to go to bed with her. He suggested that he could see that even Vinny hated her because she could see that Robert was only interested in her. If my sister Marian had understood what he said about her, I'm sure she would have slapped him in the face. I sat there in shock during the ranting and raving. I suppose it was fortuitous that Patrick, Robert or Mark didn't understood a word of it and didn't even try to interrupt.

Eventually the band went back on stage and resumed their act. Although I'm sure they sounded as good as before, I just couldn't bring myself to sit there and listen to them. I excused myself, explaining that I wasn't feeling that well, which was true anyway.

I returned to the table just before the performance ended and awaited my opportunity. Patrick, Robert, Vinny, Marian and Mark were having a great time. Both Robert and Mark were smoking and seemed especially elated. I turned down their invitation to join them for a smoke. When Griet finished singing and the band started to dismantle and pack away their equipment, I walked up on stage and spoke to Griet in my best Dutch.

"Griet, I really liked your performance. Your singing was great and I'm not saying it for the reason your angry boyfriend suggested. I think the rest of my family also enjoyed the show for what it was, good entertainment. But if you want to ever perform here again, you will need to ditch that verbally abusive boyfriend of yours," I said. "If you ever accept an invitation from Marian to come back here again, with that so-called boyfriend of yours still part of your band, I will tell Marian and anyone else who will listen, all about Leo's interval comments."

Griet took a step back from me. I could see the shock on her face. She was truly 'dumb-struck'. Although he couldn't have heard my comments, Leo suddenly appeared at Griet's side and said in an angry tone in Dutch:

"For Christ's sake Griet, will you ever leave that sad old pervert alone."

Griet turned around in horror to face him as I took a step closer to him, so I could whisper, again in my best Dutch:

"Thank you for playing here for the last time ever Leo, your guitar playing was excellent."

The blood seemed to drain from Leo's face as it immediately dawned on him that I had understood everything he had said earlier.

"Thank you," he said to me in perfect English.

He nodded to me, then turned around and returned to packing up his equipment in stunned silence. I thanked Griet again and left the stage, feeling really proud of myself. I never heard from Blue Lips from Amsterdam again, since that night.

Later that night Marian told me that she had invited Blue Lips to play there again the following Saturday but Griet told her that the band had a prior booking. Griet promised that she would e-mail Marian with details of any free Saturdays available, but I doubt if any e-mail ever arrived.

So it was that the way was clear for my good friend Danny and his wife Ali to accept Marian's invitation to play at the 'Pally' the following Saturday. 'TED' were booked for the following three Saturdays on the strength of their web-site which, at my suggestion, Marian finally relented to look at. It probably also helped that I told Marian that I had heard Danny play and how good he was.

The following Saturday we took our places around the same table. Mark and Marian came a little earlier this time so we had time for a little small talk before Danny and Ali were ready to play. Robert was already on his first roll-up even before 'TED' started to play. Vinny didn't appear happy that Robert had already started on the roll-ups.

I was so pleased with myself that 'TED' went down so well in the room. Everyone seemed to be singing along with 'Ali', she 'brought the house down' when she sang a number of Amy Winehouse's songs in her own style. Danny's backing support was perfect. They played lots of songs that I knew quite well, but also some brilliant songs that I had never heard before. The crowd kept calling for a song called *Please Come Back to Me*, which TED eventually played. I later learned that the song was by an Irish folk group called the Liffey River Warblers or LRW for short. It turned out that most of the songs, which I didn't recognise that night, were by the two girl and two boy group, LRW, who wrote all of their own songs. All of the new songs were from LRW's latest album called *Get Me Out of Here*, I decided that I simply must learn how to play every song on that album, they were that infectious.

During the interval, Danny and Ali joined us our table and everyone got on so well. Who knows, perhaps helped with the abundance of roll-ups. Danny quietly asked me if I would join them after the break, to play and sing the two songs I had written. He told me that he had purchased a brand-new Martin acoustic guitar and had restrung it with my favourite strings. It was on its own stand, up on the stage. How could I refuse?

I was really nervous standing on the stage with the guitar strap draped around my neck and shoulder. Danny told me that it was already tuned so we dived straight into the Eagles' *Lying Eyes*. Danny had introduced it as a song which I had written and I actually felt bad about not denying it. When I had finished, it seemed like all of the audience got to their feet and applauded for ages, none of them had heard the song before and several of them asked us to perform it again. I noticed Patrick, Robert, Vinny, Mark and Marian were also on their feet calling for an encore. I don't think I ever felt better than this after singing a song before. As I thanked everyone, I still felt a bit of a fraud however. When the applause died down, without saying anything, Danny 'launched' into the other Eagles song, *Peaceful Easy Feeling*. Ali's keyboard playing, Danny's Fender electric guitar and my borrowed Martin guitar all seemed to 'come together' for the song. The crowd were on their feet from the first few bars of the 'Intro' and stayed standing until we finished the 'Outro'. Except for Danny, Ali and I, no one had heard the song before and the reception it got was amazing. I was a hero and yes also a fraud, but I liked it a lot. Mark caught my eye and winked at me.

When I had finished, I ignored the 'clamouring' for an encore and instead went back to my table. Sitting there smiling, I felt like a celebrity. People all around us came over to our table to congratulate me on the songs. When had I written them? Did I have any other songs?

Danny and Ali finished off their set to great applause. What a success, I felt just great! The crowd stood up once more calling for my two songs to be performed again to finish off the gig. If anything, the songs went down even better the second time around as the audience were now already a little familiar with them. When we finally finished singing and playing, Danny told me that the Martin guitar was a present from him to me, partly as a thank you for helping his band get the gig at the 'Pally' but mostly for allowing them to perform the two brilliant songs with me. The only condition was that I had to agree to play with them each time they were booked at the Pally. I was so humbled with the gesture that for a moment I felt like refusing Danny's gift. After all, the songs were not mine! Sense prevailed in the end and I accepted the gift. How good was that, I thought! If only my wife Mary had been there it would have been absolutely perfect. Mark booked a taxi to take me back to St John's, but before I was 'whisked' off, he whispered to me that Professor Prieto's agent had been in touch with him to tell him that the professor was intrigued and wanted to meet me as soon as possible. I didn't sleep very well that night.

Chapter 17

Patrick was due to return home to Chicago the following Saturday, so Mark had arranged for all my brothers plus Peter's son Alan to go on a pub crawl in Howth, on the Friday night. I always got on well with Alan, well at least I did with the Alan I knew previously. He stood about six foot three, was well built and had a wicked sense of humour. I wondered what the Alan, who I was about to meet, would be like.

But before all that, I had to attend an interview in the Garda station on Monday. As he promised, Mark collected me from St John's and stayed with me throughout the interview, which lasted no more than an hour. It was a lot more formal than I expected but the process went almost exactly as Mark had said it would. Superintendent O'Malley tried hard to adopt a serious demeanour but he still came across as a helpful friend, rather than an investigating officer. The Gardai obviously had no previous experience of dealing with someone like me and struggled to make progress. As prompted by Mark, I kept repeating that I had no idea where the bogus bank cards and counterfeit money had come from and I had no clue why I had earlier tried to 'pass myself off' as Ian Forman. I told them that my memory of my life as Conor Forman was totally blank. I said that I was desperate for their help and asked them when did they think they would succeed in finding out more about my whereabouts and my life from the time I was a baby, until now. They 'lied' that they were 'making progress' but they had nothing 'concrete' to report yet. At the end of the interview I was told that the Gardai would not be taking any further action on the bank cards or the cash as no persons or no organisations had suffered any losses. I agreed that they could permanently destroy the cards and the cash, to prevent any attempted future misuse. I kept waiting to be asked about my mobile phone but thankfully they seemed to have completely forgotten about it. They said that they were still not 'comfortable' with confirming my identity but had 'gone along' with Sergeant Murphy verifying my passport photos because not to do so, would be unfair on me. They were however, leaving the investigation open until further notice in case new evidence emerges. I thanked them for their excellent work so far and told them that I looked forward to hearing from them again soon.

Mark 'slapped me on the back' as we arrived back at St John's. He called Peter and told him how the interview had gone and asked him to let the rest of the family know.

"So, do you want to meet Professor Prieto, Conor?" asked Mark suddenly, as we sat in the garden.

I asked Mark what would be the point in such a meeting as I was now fully resigned to living the rest of my life as Conor Forman. Mark said that it would be interesting and fascinating to see if the professor could come up with anything and so what it he did, we didn't have to do anything about it anyway.

"Are you not curious to find out more?" he asked. "If it was me, I would be fascinated and would do anything to find out more."

I told Mark that I wasn't really that bothered as I didn't believe the professor could get anywhere anyway, but that if Mark wanted me to meet him, that I would go along with it. I left the decision in Mark's hands and he seemed pleased with that.

The Friday night of the pub crawl arrived. We started off in the nearest pub, the Top House. Mark took charge. He collected fifty Pride from each of us and promptly handed it to Alan. He told Alan that as the youngest and tallest, he was in charge of ordering and paying for all the booze. Luckily, Mark told me that we were going to visit all the pubs within walking distance so I knew that I had to 'pace' myself. I started with a pint of Guinness in the Top House and was given less than fifteen minutes to 'down it' before Mark 'ushered' us out and on to the next venue, The Cock Tavern. A pint of 'Neither' later and we were off down the steps to the third venue, the 'Abbey Tavern', where Mark decided that we would have time for two or three drinks. A pint of 'Not' and another pint of Guinness later and off we walked down Abbey Street and into the next pub, O'Connell's. I was grateful that Barbara's husband Graham was not behind the bar as I hadn't spoken to him since that night when he told me that Ian Forman was buried in the Abbey Graveyard. Mark seemed to relax more because he didn't put a limit on the number of pints he 'permitted' us to drink there. I sensibly stuck to alternating between Guinness, Neither and Not. Not sure if my 'drinking buddies' were controlling their intake, but the conversation got louder and more jovial. Lots of jokes being told, especially by Patrick. By now we had attracted quite a few 'hanger-ons', who Alan kept buying drinks for, from our communal pot, but we didn't care, we were all having a great time, laughing and joking all the time. The more we drank the louder we got and the more we laughed. Eventually Mark decided that it was time to move on, so we drank up and left. Mark had already instructed us to tell our 'hanger-ons' that we were going home, but few of them believed us. Three or four of them followed us to the next pub. We had another two or three drinks in the Waterside Lounge, before we doubled back on ourselves and walked up Careys Steps. Just one quick drink in the Lighthouse Bar and then across the road to the Top Shop. By now I had lost track of my drinking and I didn't care. I just let Alan decide to order whatever he wanted for me and I could feel myself getting 'tipsy'. It was a good feeling. Not sure how long we stayed there before Mark moved us on down the hill, toward the harbour. We staggered rather than walked. Mark and I held each other up but Patrick and Alan spent the few minutes playfully trying to knock each other over. By the time we entered

Findlater's Lounge I was 'well on'. I insisted that Alan order me a 'Not', but I doubt if he heeded me. Mark eventually announced that it was time to visit our final pub for the night. The Bloody Steam had not existed when I grew up in Howth. It is situated at the top of the West Pier, in a prime location, right beside the DART railway-station. We noisily stumbled down the steps, each of us holding the other up and none of us talking any sense, and entered the bar. I heard the wall clock chime for twelve o'clock as we entered. The bar was still half-full, mostly young couples sitting enjoying cocktails at tables close to the bar counter. We stood together propping up the bar and continuing to drink, but perhaps a little more slowly now. Sitting on a bar stool in the far corner, next to Patrick, was a little middle-aged man who was wearing a huge brown leather cowboy hat. We must have had at least a couple of pints during which time the 'cowboy' had barely taken a few sips from his Guinness. He just sat there, with both of his elbows resting on the dark wooden bar counter, staring straight at his Guinness. He clearly wanted to be left alone but that was never going to deter Patrick from trying to 'cheer him up'. Patrick moved a little closer to him and tried to attract the man's attention.

"I'm Patrick Forman," he slurred. "I used to live and work here in Howth, but now I live in Chicago. I'm flying back tomorrow. I flew here especially to 'touch base' with my brother."

Patrick expected to get a reaction from the stranger but all the cowboy did was lift his two elbows off the counter and move his gaze from his Guinness to Patrick's smiling face. He then looked back at his Guinness, without saying anything. Patrick looked at me and shrugged his shoulders.

"My brother is three years older than me," continued Patrick, trying to pique the cowboy's interest.

"Guess how long it had been since I had last seen my brother Conor here?"

Still no response!

"C'mon, have a guess, bet you can't guess," said Patrick.

"How would I know?" answered the cowboy, clearly irritated.

"Just guess, go on have a guess!" insisted Patrick.

"A week," he answered.

"No, have a proper guess, go on."

Patrick was clearly annoying the cowboy and both Mark and Alan were smiling and smirking at each other, enjoying the spectacle.

"A century," answered the cowboy.

Patrick laughed out loud and told the cowboy that he was getting closer. He then told him that he hadn't ever seen me until just a few days ago. Eventually Patrick gave up and decided to ask the cowboy about himself, he thought that perhaps he was sad and lonely, maybe he just wanted to be listened to, rather than spoken to.

"Ok, I've told you who I am and why I'm here," slurred Patrick. "Do you mind telling me what brought you here. Yeah, why don't you tell me what you are doing here?"

The cowboy sat up straight on his stool and looked straight at Patrick.

"Oh, so you would like me to tell you what I'm doing here, would you?" asked the cowboy

"Yes, I would," answered Patrick, not noticing the angry tone of the cowboy's question.

"Well, I'll tell you what I'm doing here, I'll tell you exactly what I'm doing here," he said.

"I'm minding my own feckin' business, that's what I'm doing and that's what you should be doing!" he shouted as he returned to staring at his Guinness.

Patrick turned around to us, and shrugged his shoulders again. Mark and Alan burst out laughing and I couldn't help but join in. After an awkward moment or two, Patrick joined in the laughter. He then however quickly drained his pint and 'announced' that he needed his bed, he had a long flight tomorrow, no not tomorrow, today! Outside the pub we all hugged each other and Alan told me that I would have to come over to his house for dinner sometime. Peter, Robert, Alan and Mark jumped into the first taxi in the rank which was parked right outside the pub. Mark was so drunk he didn't even think about how I would get back to St John's but Patrick said that he had twin beds in his room at the FFF Hotel and suggested that I stay there for the night. We had just started the fifteen to twenty-minute walk back to the hotel when Patrick had the bright idea that we could use one of the free 'golf buggies' to get us back to the hotel. There were lots of these strange small vehicles parked in the car park beside the railway station and Patrick unzipped the clear plastic side panel of the closest one and slid onto the seat. As I walked around to get in the other side, I saw him push a button and the buggy 'took off'.

"Race you home!" he shouted at me, and laughed at the top of his voice.

I quickly jumped into the next buggy, found the button which had 'FFF Hotel' marked on it and pushed it. The headlights automatically came on and I headed off in pursuit. Funny sensation, gliding silently along the road in my electric buggy. No steering wheel, no accelerator and no brake. No way to control the speed but I seemed to be gaining slightly on his buggy, perhaps because I weighed a little less. I caught up with him a hundred yards or so from the hotel but my buggy just 'tucked in' behind his. I guess they're programmed to not pass each other. The buggies came to a slow halt just outside the hotel front door. We got out of our buggies, laughing noisily. I watched Patrick lean back into the buggy and push a button. I saw his buggy leave and so I then pushed the button marked 'Home', on the dashboard of my buggy and watched in wonder as it 'took off', seemingly chasing after Patrick's buggy. We fell into our beds without another word being spoken.

I awoke with a terrible hangover and just lay there with my head throbbing and my stomach churning. I had no idea where I was or how I had got there. I slid out of bed and opened the curtains. I saw the other unmade single bed and suddenly remembered where I was and how I got there.

I showered and came down the stairs to meet the world. The lounge was closed and I decided not to go into the restaurant, the staff was already clearing the tables. The receptionist, Joan, smiled at me and told me that Patrick had just headed across the road to 'Starbucks'. I joined Patrick and ordered a large black americano and a blueberry muffin. First time I used this strange currency 'Pride', the cashier must have thought that I thought that I had been 'short changed' as I stared at the strange coins. Patrick was just finishing off his coffee as I sat down beside him. I don't suppose I actually looked any better than he did! He told me that his taxi was due to pick him up from the hotel in about half an hour but he had already packed his case, so he was ready to go. He chatted about his family as we sat there. He didn't once ask me anything about mine. What a strange situation, I kept expecting him to ask me about my past life, but nothing. As we both walked back to the hotel, he told me that he really enjoyed last night and couldn't wait to bring his whole family over to meet me. He then joked that although he had only met me a couple of days ago, he felt as though he knew me all his life! I waited in reception as he went to his room to get his bags. Marian joined me in reception and asked me what the hell I was doing in the hotel. I explained that I had 'crashed out' there, last night. She immediately offered to call St John's to explain why I didn't get 'home' last night. She said that she didn't want me reported as a missing person.

"So how are you feeling this morning Conor?" she asked. "I hope you feel better than you look. How did you get home last night?"

I told her that we travelled in a couple of strange, self-driving buggies and she explained that they are supplied by the Howth Chamber of Commerce, to reduce the car congestion in the village. Most visitors now park their cars at Deer Park and take the free minibus to the Dart Station and hop on a free buggy to take them anywhere they want to go to in Howth, for no charge. Each restaurant and pub, in the village, pays a small monthly charge for the use of a pre-programmed 'button', installed on the dashboard.

"You must have pushed the 'FFF' button," said Marian.

I told her that I was feeling 'ok' and confirmed that I had pushed the correct button. When I told her that I had indeed felt better on a several occasions, she laughed and said:

"Well you 'fared' much better than Robert then, 'cause he broke his arm."

Patrick then re-appeared and Marian told us that Robert had fallen over and broken his arm after he got out of the taxi last night. I was a little surprised that Marian found it all a little amusing! Patrick's taxi arrived and we waved him off. I grabbed my jacket from my room and went for a long walk, up towards the 'Cliff Walk'. I had almost forgotten how stunning the views were up there. I walked back to St John's, entered my room and collapsed down on my bed. I must have dozed off for an hour or so before being awakened by a knock on the door. Mark stood there a little the worse for wear but still smiling. We walked to the Summit Inn and had a light snack, no fish and chips on my stomach!

"Did you hear what happened to Robert last night," laughed Mark.

I told Mark that Marian had told Patrick and I about Robert breaking his arm

"Yeah, I saw it happening but we didn't realise his arm was broken as the rest of us drove off in the taxi," replied Mark. "What a pain that is," he sighed. "I guess I will have to find a new golfing partner for my regular Tuesday morning eighteen holes of relaxation."

"Where do you play?" I asked.

"Robert and I are both members at St Anne's Golf Club, perhaps you know it?"

I thought for a while before I replied. I admitted to him that I had played there many times before with Mary's dad Frank and had even played there once with my wife Mary, who I think beat me that day.

"Have you a golf handicap?" he asked.

"I used to play off a fourteen handicap, but I doubt I could play to that standard now," I answered hesitantly.

"Would you like to play with me next Tuesday?" he asked enthusiastically. "You could use Robert's golf clubs and electric trolley, as I don't think he will be needing them for quite a while."

I 'jumped' at the chance and even when I reminded Mark that I didn't have golf shoes or even suitable clothing to wear, he told me he would sort everything out. Just leave it to him he 'winked'. He told me that I needed to be standing in the hotel reception Tuesday morning at seven thirty am, we needed to get on the first tee before the 'ladies' arrived. He told me not to forget to pre-book my early morning call.

Chapter 18

Mark was 'as good as his word' so when he picked me up from St John's, he told me that he already had Robert's golf clubs and electric trolley in his car. Mark's sports car was not very suitable for carrying golf clubs but he didn't seem to mind having both sets of clubs on the back seat and the two trolleys in the boot. During the twenty minute or so drive to St Anne's Golf Club, Mark asked me if I had played St Anne's before and I repeated that I played there quite a few times with Frank, who is Mary's dad, and that I had also played there once with Mary, who beat me that day. Mark asked me about Mary's golf handicap and what the name of our golf club was and if we played on any other courses. It was great to be able to talk freely to Mark, without the risk of him thinking I was insane.

In the car park, I tried on Robert's golf shoes but, as expected, size nine were too big for me. Mark told me not to worry, we could buy a new pair from the Proshop. I picked out a new pair of 'Nike' white golf shoes, a cream jumper and a set of 'Galvin Green' gore-tex waterproofs. Mark insisted on the waterproofs even though there was no chance of rain that day. Mark paid for everything with his credit card, I just didn't yet feel comfortable enough to use his debit card. Before we changed shoes, Mark asked me to follow him up the stairs where, in the hallway, just outside the lounge he showed me the 'honours boards'. He wanted to point out that he and Robert had won last years 'Foursomes Knockout' competition. He asked me if I knew any of the other winners' names shown on the boards. It didn't take me long to find Mary's dad's name, I knew where to look. Frank Mooney had won the Senior Singles Knockout many years ago. I pointed out the name to Mark, who appeared shocked by my revelation.

"But Conor, I used to 'sort of' know him. I don't think I ever spoke to him but I saw him several times in the lounge and also on the golf course. From memory he used to play doubles matches with his son, whose name I can't remember but I do remember that he was a really good golfer," said Mark.

"That was probably his son Paul, he used to play off a three or four handicap," I replied.

Mark just nodded and headed back down the stairs. I followed him into the gent's locker room, where Mark told me that we should play a stableford competition. To make it interesting he 'winked' and proposed that we should play for 'doubles or quits' on the money I owed him for the clothes and shoes. He suggested that we play off our full handicaps, so he gave me two shots.

It soon became clear that Mark was taking the 'friendly' competition very seriously. After about an hour of friendly but competitive golf, we caught up on the group in front, I think it was on about the fifth hole. Mark said he knew the four members and also knew that there was no way they would ever 'call us through'. Fortunately, there was a wooden bench beside every tee, so from then on, we sat and waited until the group in front were 'well gone' before we tee'd off. Surreal situation, Mark only wanted to talk about the golf game and how he wasn't playing as well as he normally does, no discussion about our past lives. The conversation seemed more natural on the putting greens because we could discuss the line of the putt and how much uphill or downhill it was. By the time we reached the first par three on the back nine, I think Mark might have been one or two points ahead of me but since he had the only score card, I wasn't sure. The four dreadfully slow players had just played their balls onto the green when the three ladies behind, finally caught up with us and walked over to the bench we were sitting on. Mark stood up to let them sit down and wished them good morning. I also stood up but then almost fell over. It was Mary! No doubt about it. She looked exactly the same with her usual broad smile and the same youthful appearance. Why should I be surprised that in this universe she also looked more than ten years younger than her age and, if anything, appeared to be even better looking. My turn to be dumbstruck! My mouth was dry, I couldn't even say hello. I just kept staring at Mary, I didn't even acknowledge her two companions. I'm not sure if Mark noticed my shocked demeanour on seeing Mary. Should I say something? I think Mark must have noticed my unease because he quickly ushered me to the next tee to prepare to tee off, telling me it was my 'honour'.

"Conor, we can't keep these ladies waiting," Mark said out loud to me, as I half-stumbled to the tee.

"No hurry," replied the tall thin lady. "Take your time, Hannibal crossed the Alps quicker than those four in front of you can play eighteen holes. Enjoy your game, we're not in a hurry."

The rest of my golf round was a 'nightmare'. I just couldn't see the ball properly, never mind hit it the correct distance or in the right direction. I doubt if I managed to score a single stableford point from then on. Mark also lost focus. I could see that he realised something was wrong with me, but he never said anything. I made sure that we kept close to the group in front and I think that the ladies ensured that they didn't get close to us again. When the game finished, Mark and I shook hands rather formally and he told me that he had scored a 'miserable' thirty points and that I had managed a 'creditable' nineteen points. He told me to forget about the bet, saying that he knew what had happened to me. We changed our shoes in the men's locker room and placed our equipment back into Mark's car.

"Now for the main event," said Mark, as he led me up the spiral staircase and into the restaurant/bar.

Without asking me he ordered a plate of ham and cheese sandwiches and two bowls of cream of mushroom soup. Mark asked for a pint of

Guinness and I had a pint of 'Neither'. We sat at a table for four, next to the large window overlooking the last green. The drinks were going down extremely well as we awaited our lunch. I was really nervous. I kept looking at the door, waiting for Mary to appear. If she appears, should I say something to her? I wanted to, but what should I say? How would Mark react?

The soup and sandwiches arrived. Mark dived right in and I tried to do the same. I couldn't taste anything, even though I was starving by now.

The ladies all walked in together and walked up to the bar. I couldn't believe it when they carried their drinks, looked like gin and tonics, towards us and placed them on the adjoining table. It looked like they wanted to talk to us, Christ what do I do now? Mary looked over at Mark.

"It's Mark Forman, isn't it?"

"Yes, it is indeed," he responded, "and I think you are Mary. You're a member here, aren't you?"

Mary nodded and then Mark introduced me as his brother Conor. The tall lady introduced herself as Brenda, no second name I noticed. The shortest of the three, Jenny, who seemed to be a little younger than her two playing partners, walked over and shook hands with us. Mary took a step towards me with her hand outstretched. I thought I would faint as I limply shook hands with her.

"Hi, I'm Mary Kenny," she said, with a hint of a smile, "but aren't you the guy who once thought he was married to me? At least that's what the Gardai told my sister Ann."

I couldn't even manage a one-word reply. Mark saw that I was struggling and took charge.

"Mary, we're sorry we held you up today," he interrupted. "Hope it didn't spoil your round."

"Hope we didn't put you off too much," interrupted Jenny. "We all noticed that your brother was 'having a nightmare' out there."

Mary had still not let go of my hand, she wanted me to answer her. Mark came to my rescue again.

"Conor went through a bad patch a little while ago Mary, where his memory went haywire. It's all been sorted now though, thank God, but the doctor has advised us not to talk too much about those difficult times. Would you mind Mary?"

Mary suddenly let go of my hand and my arm fell limply to my side. I still didn't know what to say, I couldn't speak anyway.

"Of course, of course, I'm sorry to be so forward," said Mary, "I understand."

I knew of course that she could not possibly understand, how could she?

We finished our lunch at about the same time as the ladies finished their drinks so we all went back to the car park together. I watched Brenda get into the driver side of a white Range Rover and Jenny slowly got into the passenger side. Mary seemed to be 'hanging around' a little but eventually got into a pretty old but recently polished, black Ford Focus. I think she waved to me just before closing the door but maybe it was actually to her two playing companions. On the drive back to St John's, Mark explained that when I told him about Frank Mooney, he immediately knew that Frank's daughter Mary was a member of the golf club. He didn't expect to see Mary there today but admitted that he was intrigued to see what might happen if Mary and I bumped into one another. He apologised for not warning me in advance.

"I really think that the sooner we meet up with Professor Prieto the better," he said. "This could be the story of the century," he added.

I just nodded in reply.

As we pulled into the car park at St John's, Mark said he really enjoyed playing golf with me and asked me if I was 'up for it' the following week. I apologised for 'falling apart' and said that I looked forward to giving him a better contest next week.

So started our regular golf matches. As the weeks passed, I became much more relaxed, but try as I might, I still couldn't manage to beat Mark. I think that sheer determination somehow wins out every time. We were slowly becoming very good friends as well as even closer brothers and we talked openly about our lives. Mark now fully accepted that I was the 'returned Ian' and he confirmed that Professor Prieto had expressed an interest in meeting me for an informal chat. Mark suggested to the professor that he book into the Deer Park Hotel but asked him to keep his visit, plus our upcoming meeting, strictly confidential between him and Mark. Mark suggested that it would be best if we keep the upcoming discussion private, stressing that no one else in the family needed to know about it. It would only cause confusion in the family as everyone had now accepted me as Conor and hopefully, I would soon have my new passport. I told Mark that I fully understood and that as far as I was concerned, I am Conor! Mark said that he hoped the professor would fly over from Heathrow in the next week or so, but that he would let me know as soon as the arrangements were finalised.

I'm not sure, but I began to wonder if Mark deliberately picked the tee time just in front of Mary and her two lady friends. We met the three ladies each week and we usually sat at adjoining tables. Was it just wishful thinking or was Mary actually trying to get to know me? Difficult to believe it, especially since I was 'forbidden' from telling her anything about the 'real me' or the fact that we were married for over forty years and had two children and four grandchildren.

Despite the imposed restrictions, eventually Mary and I became more relaxed when chatting to each other. The conversations, always about Mary and her family, flowed. After four or five weeks we usually ended up with the five of us sitting at the same table, although the ladies never once ordered lunch. They just had a drink with us afterwards. Mark chatted to both Brenda and Jenny most of the time and they seemed to enjoy our company and conversation. I know I shouldn't have been thinking like this but I hoped that Robert's broken arm would take years to heal, I was happy once more with my life, I didn't want anything to change it.

Mary was keen to tell me all about herself. She seemed to be very curious but she must have respected Mark's wishes as she didn't ask me anything about my past. The only questions I had to answer were about whether I enjoyed playing golf at St. Anne's and whether I liked the members. I replied that I still only knew Mark and the three ladies and I liked all of them. I resisted the impulse to say that I liked one of the members a lot, in fact I loved one of them! One personality trait of Mary's remained unchanged, both Marys were very good listeners and they always seemed to be interested in what others had to say, later remembering every detail. On one occasion, when Mark and I were on the first tee, once more waiting for Hannibal's Army to take their second shots, Brenda and Mary walked up to us. Brenda explained that Jenny couldn't make it that day and suggested that we wouldn't have to 'hang around' all day, if we joined up. I have to say that it was quite different to the last game of golf I had played with Mary. Brenda had decided that it would be a match, the boys versus the girls, for the drinks afterwards. I'd never seen Mary stay so focused, that is until we had just a few holes to play and we stood alongside each other, in the middle of the fairway. Mark was 'miles ahead' in the right rough and Brenda was just ahead of us, just off the fairway on the left. Mary and I hit two good shots and stood there waiting for Brenda to play. 'Out of the blue' Mary started telling me all about her marriage to Joe and how he came to be in a wheelchair. She didn't stop talking until we walked off the last green, dropping her voice whenever either Mark or Brenda were near. She explained that her son Jonjo was a talented guitarist who used to play in one of the top Irish bands, back in the nineties. Her husband Joe often brought Mary to listen to the band, they particularly enjoyed listening to Jonjo sing ballads. One night, Jonjo's glamorous wife Sandra went along to one of Jonjo's gigs with four or five of her girlfriends, on a 'ladies' night out'. Mary and her husband Joe were also there in the audience, but on the other side of the hall. They could see that there was a group of 'boisterous' men sitting at the table beside Sandra and her friends. One of the men pulled his chair over alongside Sandra's and they appeared to be 'let's say' getting on very well. Joe knew exactly how jealous Jonjo could be, so between songs, he walked over to Sandra and started talking to her about Jonjo's performance so far. I guess Joe just wanted the other man to know that Sandra's husband was on stage! Anyway, all to no avail, as Sandra and her 'admirer' seemed to get even louder and became even more 'familiar' with each other. When the break came, we could see that Jonjo was really 'pissed off'. He almost threw his guitar onto its stand and quickly made his way off the stage and towards the table where Sandra was still 'flirting' openly with her new 'best friend'. Jonjo asked the guy to stand up, and when he did so, without warning, Jonjo punched him right in the face. The poor man did not know what hit him. He fell backwards knocking all the drinking glasses off the table and knocking one of Sandra's lady-friends onto the floor. She hit the floor with a sickening thud, which seemed to echo round the hall. Mary's husband, Joe, jumped up immediately and ran over to try to separate the two fighters. It's not clear exactly what happened then, but soon Joe was lying prone on the floor. He lay there unconscious for some time before the ambulance arrived. He had suffered a massive stroke, and was permanently paralysed from the waist down. His speech has only partially recovered. The police enquiry that followed was totally bizarre. All the witnesses confirmed that Jonjo had started the fight but, in the confusion, no one could be sure if Joe had been hit by either Jonjo or the other man. The police charged Jonjo with assault, but concluded that Joe's injury was a terrible accident. Jonjo ended up being sacked from the band and his wife Sandra left him immediately and divorced him shortly afterwards. He went back to live with his parents. Mary explained that she believes Jonjo still thinks that it was him who punched his daddy that night, causing his collapse and his stroke. He felt obliged to help his mammy look after his daddy and help run the shop. He had no other job or anywhere else to live anyway, so for a while it suited him. As the months and years passed however, Jonjo became more and more sullen and moody. He has no friends, no interest in anything, not even the rugby internationals. He never goes out and is probably clinically depressed. Mary then surprised me as we walked side by side towards the car park.

"Yes, he's depressed, perhaps I am a little depressed also. No going out anymore, no fun, no laughter. Just day after day looking after Joe as best I can, whilst trying hard not to resent it. We haven't been on holiday since that terrible night, not even a day out," confided Mary. "If I still wasn't in love with him, I would have left him years ago."

"Well at least you have your golf and your golf friends," I replied.

I didn't know how to react to her sad story. Why did she feel the need to tell me all about her depressed life anyway? Was she hinting at something?

On the way 'home' in the car I told Mark all about Mary's situation. He surprised me by suggesting that we invite Mary, Brenda and Jenny to join us at the Pally some Saturday night.

"Hey, I have an idea," he said. "You know that Patrick and his family are coming over again to visit us next month. This time he is bringing his wife Susan and their two children Packy and Sarah over here, he says mainly for them to meet you. Their seven grandchildren are also coming. Why don't we have a family night out at the Pally with all of us, minus the kids of course," enthused Mark. "We could ask the three lady golfers to join us, maybe cheer Mary up a little. What do you think?"

I was as nervous, apprehensive and excited as a fourteen-year-old boy who would soon be going on a date with the girl of his dreams.

Chapter 19

The first time I met Professor Carlos Prieto was a very enlightening experience. Mark and I picked him up from Terminal Two at Dublin airport. The Aer Lingus flight from London Heathrow had landed bang on time at 9:30am. We had no problem recognising him in the Arrivals Hall, the 'Face Time' call from the evening before, had seen to that. Both Mark and I had done a little internet research on Carlos, as he later said he wanted to be called, so the drive from Dublin Airport was not at all awkward. Mark thanked him for coming over to meet us and told him that he would personally take care of all his expenses. The room at the Deer Park Hotel was already paid for and he would reimburse him for the flight later that day. Carlos replied that the opportunity to meet me would be payment enough, he didn't need to, or want to be reimbursed.

When he had first walked through the arrivals gate, I thought that Carlos Prieto looked a little older than the sixty-seven years I knew him to be. He was of average height, maybe a little taller than me, and of average build. His 'swarthy' skin, thick grey hair, bushy grey moustache and dark brown eyes were striking. He was dressed casually in a blue shirt with black slacks and shoes. He carried a short blue rain jacket over one arm and a 'hand luggage' sized black leather bag in the other hand.

During the thirty or so minutes it took to drive to Deer Park, as instructed by Mark, I kept quiet and let Carlos and Mark chat away in the front of Mark's car. Mark had, quite clearly, briefed Carlos about my background and why we had asked to meet him. I sat 'like a mouse' in the back seat, listening to Mark answer all of Carlos' questions about me. Carlos avoided all questions put to him by Mark, saying that he would tell us all about himself when we arrived at the hotel. He told us that since his flight back to Heathrow was at 6:15am the following morning that he would book a taxi to drop him back to Dublin Airport.

Carlos was clearly impressed when we pulled into the Deer Park complex. He said that he wished now that he had booked in for a few days and had brought his golf clubs with him. He checked in, but his room was not yet ready so we made our way to the lounge and sat down at a small round table, in a quiet corner.

"Ok Gentlemen, before I start to tell you all about me, would you mind explaining more fully, why you invited me to meet you?" asked Carlos.

Mark told Carlos that we had both read his book 'The Many Lives Interpretation' and that we both thought he might be able to help us 'get to the bottom' of whatever it was that might be 'playing' with my memory.

"Conor, I know that I have heard much about your state of mind but would you mind summarising everything so far," asked Carlos. "I would like to hear it 'straight from the horse's mouth.'"

Over the following half an hour or so, I went over everything that had happened to me since I 'fell asleep' on that bench. Neither Carlos nor Mark interrupted my story, letting me speak without interruption but I noticed that Carlos took notes throughout.

When I had finished, Carlos referred to his notes and then repeated my story, almost word for word. I confirmed that Carlos had got my story correct and I asked him what his first thoughts were. He said that he would now try to convince both of us that he had some experience of similar situations and that at first glance it looked possible that I had indeed 'crossed over' from a parallel universe. He clarified this by saying that thinking this is one thing but proving it is another matter.

"Ok, gentlemen, rather than you two continuously firing random questions at me, I think it would be best if I give you a short background on me," said Carlos. "You have already told me that you have both read my book, thank you, but we all know it's better to chat face to face."

Mark asked him to 'hold on a minute' until he could order a pot of coffee and some scones. When Mark returned and took his seat, Carlos took a deep breath and having first looked at Mark, he seemed to talk directly to me.

"My full name is Carlos Emilio Prieto. I am a retired Chief Coroner of St. Pancras Coroners Court in London, where I thoroughly enjoyed working for many years. I guess you could say that I was married to my job until I retired some seven years ago. I am a contented confirmed Batchelor and I live alone in a comfortable detached house in Enfield, just outside London. I am happy with my own company, which is 'just as well' because not many people seek out the company of a retired Coroner, especially an old and grumpy one.

My primary purpose for coming and why I dropped everything to get here as soon as I could is to warn you that Conor could be in some danger."

Carlos' English was excellent and his South American accent added a strange air of foreboding to his warning.

"For you to appreciate and heed my warning seriously, I need to go back in time and tell you why I have this fanatical interest in 'cases' like Conor's and to try to convince you that I know what I am talking about."

He paused for dramatic affect...

"I was born on December 1st, 1949 in the city of Medellin in Columbia, South America. My family were poor peasant farmers, but poor only until the growing of cocaine became possible for my dad, under the 'protection' of the 'infamous', Pablo Escobar. By coincidence, I happened to be born on the same date and in the same district of the city as Pablo. We were in the same class in school and although you wouldn't call us friends, we knew each other quite well. In our class was also someone who was a personal friend of Pablo's. Emilio Aguirra's friendship with Pablo continued beyond his schooldays and he became a prominent member of Pablo Escobar's Medellin drug cartel. You have both probably heard of Pablo, may even have seen some documentaries about him. He controlled the cartel which was the main source of cocaine smuggled into the USA from the nineteen seventies onwards. He and his gang were ruthless gangsters, responsible for thousands of kidnappings and murders. He succeeded in corrupting many judges, politicians and policemen in Columbia. Anyone who opposed him was simply 'eliminated' and he was 'untouchable' for many years. He became extremely rich with a safe house, which was a 'mansion' on a private island. In today's terms he would be a multi billionaire and he was used to getting anything he wanted. I suspect that my family became fairly wealthy because of Pablo's 'empire' but my dad made sure that I did not get involved. I was put through medical school and after some years I worked as a pathologist in the city of Medellin, which is the second city of Columbia. I had an ambition to become a Coroner because I wanted to know, not only how someone had died but where and why they had met their, mostly violent and gruesome, death. I took a few years leave of absence and studied law, eventually becoming a qualified solicitor. My dad helped me get some law experience and I suspect he 'pulled some strings' to get me appointed first as an assistant Coroner and later a senior Coroner, in Medellin. At the time, serious crime was common place with gangland murders happening daily. Anyway, getting back to the point, one day I was presented with the body of Pablo's friend and our former classmate, Emilio Aguirra. It did not take me long to establish that he had been shot five times, including once in the head which proved fatal. It was suspected that the killing was the action of the Cali Cartel, the main rival of the Medellin Cartel, at the time."

"Sorry guys," I interrupted, "but I am bursting and can't hold it any longer. Would you mind waiting for me professor?"

When I returned Carlos resumed his story. I thought that he seemed a little annoyed that I had stopped him in mid-stream, but he was polite enough to not say anything.

"Ok, to continue," he said. "With Emilio still lying 'on the slab' in the local morgue, a man calling himself Emilio Aguirra walked into his house, shocking his wife and child. He looked and sounded like Emilio and did not know what all the fuss was about. He did not know anything about the shooting and took up his life as before. Pablo himself had no doubt that it was Emilio, back from the dead. Word spread quickly and some were saying that the Medellin Cartel must have the 'blessing of God', so had to be doing God's work. Emilio soon became a local hero and, during the following few days, he became a powerful recruitment tool for the Medellin Cartel. But a few days later I was presented with the body of this 'back from the dead' Emilio Aguirra. This time however his head had been 'hacked off'. It came to me in a separate sealed box. The Cali Cartel made it known that it was their work and that they wanted to make sure they 'got it right' this time. My investigation was very thorough and I involved as many 'experts' as I could. Although DNA analysis would not become available for another five or six years, from all other measurements available to us, we concluded that the two bodies were brothers and from witness accounts probably identical twins. This was the official statement published. The problem was that I personally knew that Emilio definitely did not even have a brother, let alone an identical twin. With help from Pablo's influential 'friends', I carried out an independent investigation. We searched through all the records, spoke to both of Emilio's grieving and heart-broken parents, who confirmed that Emilio was their only child. With Pablo's 'blessing' however, the 'authorities' confirmed that the second Emilio was an identical twin. No other explanation was 'believable'. I was told to keep my investigation 'quiet' and not to ever speak about the incident again. Pablo saw to it that Emilio's parents were well looked after in return for their silence about the matter. Some months later however, I made the fatal mistake of mentioning my investigation findings to my little sister Maria. She could not keep her mouth shut and, despite my warnings, she openly spoke about the miracle of the 'resurrection' of Emilio Aguirra. A couple of weeks later my sister Maria 'disappeared'. We searched 'high and low' for her for months. The police and even my parents finally abandoned their search when they indirectly received 'word' from the Cali Cartel that everyone should stop looking for her. They said that she would never be found and would never be able to come back from the dead!"

"What a shocking incident Carlos! How did you ever recover from this tragedy?" asked Mark.

Carlos just 'hung his head' and stayed silent. No doubt with horrible painful visions flooding through his brain.

"So, what were the official findings about Emilio Aguirra then?" I asked.

"That's the problem, there were none," replied Carlos. "We all learned to just forget about it all. It was as if nothing had ever happened."

"So, what's all this to do with me, Carlos?" I asked. "What are you implying?"

"This incident and several other incidents, two of which I will soon tell you about, convinced me that indeed some people do appear to come back from the dead! In my experience it only happens after a sudden, usually violent, death. It must be extremely rare however and I am trying to find a link between the incidents I am already aware about, in an effort to find any other possible plausible explanations," explained Carlos.

"But why is my life in danger?" I asked. "Who would want to physically harm me? and why? I thought that Pablo Escobar was long dead."

"Yes, he is. He escaped from gaol in 1991, the year that over twenty-five thousand violent deaths were recorded in Columbia. The Columbian police caught up with him about a year later and he and his bodyguard were shot dead while trying to escape by running over rooftops. He was mourned by thousands and thousands of people and his successors are still very active today," replied Carlos.

"But to answer your question Mr Forman, I think you already believe that you are not really Conor but rather the 'returned from the dead' Ian Forman. Mark has already confided this fact to me but can you imagine the public's reaction if you go around telling everyone that you have returned from the dead. Sure, most people will just laugh at you but some may think that you are claiming to be the next Jesus Christ, or worse still, a few disturbed individuals might think that you are really a devil. They could try to harm you 'for the glory of God," replied Carlos in a very serious tone.

"So, what do we do then Carlos?" I asked. "What's the point of your visit? I think you are suggesting that I continue to live as Conor Forman. Why are you here?"

"Yes, it would be safer for you to live as Conor but don't you want to try to prove that you really are Ian?" replied Carlos.

"How could we go about proving it Carlos?" asked Mark, "and what if we did prove it? What do we do then?"

The Professor paused and took a sip of his cold coffee before continuing....

"I suggest that you seek permission to exhume the body of Ian. I don't think anyone will object to this, they will be as keen as you, perhaps even keener, to get to the bottom of this. I think you already suspect that you will find that, you Conor, and the long dead child will appear to be identical twins. The sooner you establish this one hundred percent, the better. It would silence any weirdos that might believe that you are Ian, returned from the dead. Everybody will 'know' that since Ian is still buried in the ground, that you must be Conor.

"But this would only help to prove that this Ian is really Conor," said Mark. "It won't do anything to prove that he is Ian!"

The Professor thought for a minute or so before answering:

"As I see it gentlemen, we have two separate scenarios to confirm. Firstly, it would be 'nice' if we could find enough evidence to confirm that you really are 'another' Ian Forman, who has somehow returned from another life, body and soul from another universe. And secondly to 'prove' that you are not actually the 'original' Ian Forman. In my opinion it is essential that we all understand that when Ian unfortunately drowned that he didn't 'simply' switch over to a new identity in another universe. No, he didn't physically cross over, rather he 'emerged' and began a new life as 'another Ian' in another universe. The original Ian is still dead and buried, still being missed by his nearest and dearest," said Carlos.

"Ok, so proving that the original Ian, as you call him, is still dead, should be easy," said Mark, "but how do you prove that this man beside us here is 'another Ian', who has returned from another universe?"

"Ok, we won't waste time on checking out the original Ian," replied Carlos. "Instead, we should probe and explore everything that this Ian, let's call him Mr F to avoid confusion, can remember about his life in the universe where he has lived since the original Ian was drowned. I want to know everything about Mr F, such as where he lived and when, who he lived with, where he went on holidays, who his friends were, all about his family, what memorable experiences he enjoyed and suffered, all about his work and career, what films and music he enjoyed, what the politics were like, any major tragedies that occurred, what cars he drove, what sports did he enjoy, who won the football world cups plus anything else he can remember that we could possibly check up on."

"Look, if we all go along with this investigation, we need to think of three Ians. The original Ian, who we will hopefully soon confirm is still buried and has not risen from the grave like Jesus Christ, secondly the Ian who his family now accept as their long lost brother Conor, and this Ian here who we three think is another Ian who came from another universe. Would you mind if I just call you Mr F from now on?"

Carlos looked straight at me and said that if I agreed to work with him, he would document and record everything I could tell him about myself. He said that he would then try to follow up on everything I said, he would visit all the places, check all the facts and locate all the people. He would do his best to confirm the validity of my memories.

"But that could take an eternity and cost a fortune," I said. "Who will pay for all your time and travel expenses?"

"Don't worry about that Mr F" replied Carlos. "It won't cost you anything. I would be more than happy to spend as long as it takes, whatever the cost. It's my life's ambition to prove this theory."

"Then what do we do when you have completed your investigation professor?" asked Mark.

"We do whatever Mr F wants to do with the information," replied Carlos, "but I suggest that, if Mr F agrees, we could write a book together but defer its publication until both of us have passed away. Perhaps we could become famous when we are both dead, he smiled."

"But what's in this for you Carlos?" I asked. "How can we trust you?"

Carlos explained that he had inherited more than enough to live on from the, 'probably' ill-gotten, gains of his dad and that he had no heirs. He didn't need or desire any more money. He said that before we begin, he would sign documents agreeing that all written and recorded information coming from our investigation would be my sole property. He would really enjoy the process of the investigation, he didn't care if the outcome was never made public but that he would do everything it takes to try to prove the theory, for his own personal satisfaction.

"But why this fanatical interest Carlos and how did you end up living in England?" asked Mark.

"Good questions Mark, but bear with me for a few more minutes as I explain how I came to be obsessed with investigating the causes of death. Shortly after my sister disappeared my dad decided that I was in grave personal danger. He had a friend check out possible solutions and so I was 'sent' to England. I enrolled at the University of Buckingham, which was, and still is, a renowned private university not far from London. My English was already quite good and I had no trouble getting my law degree in just two years. I lived in the student accommodation in Buckingham Town and immersed myself in my studies and in furthering my English language skills. The university and the town were absolutely ideal for me, a good proportion of the students were mature and many were from countries all over the world. I fitted right in, without even being noticed. From Buckingham I moved to Cambridge where I read Medical Sciences for a further two years. After I graduated 'yet again', without any real expectation of success, I applied for a job in a London Coroners Court. I was amazed when I was offered the job. My employer even agreed to 'manage' the tricky question of a working visa, I think they claimed they needed my 'unique' knowledge of the Spanish language. Anyway, I got the position, for once without my dad's help, as least I don't think he was involved! I started the job already with a lot of experience, and over the years I gained an excellent reputation for being able to quickly get to the bottom of many unusual or unclear and difficult cases. So much so that I was occasionally 'seconded' by the armed forces to help them sort out their 'difficult to solve' cases. One such case involved the death of a soldier on duty some years ago in Afghanistan. I cannot mention his name or even the date, I had to sign the Official Secrets Act before being permitted to work with the army. This poor individual had stepped on a landmine and been blown to bits."

"Did they ask for your help with identification?" asked Mark?

"No, not at all, well not really. The remains of the soldier were gathered up and were brought back to base and 'normal' procedures commenced. However, the very next day a soldier who identified himself as the very same 'blown up' soldier casually, walked into the base and reported for duty. You can imagine the consternation this caused but the commander just had to accept that the blown-up soldier must be someone else, there must have been a mix up with identification. The 'new soldier' was welcomed back and took up his duties. Unfortunately, the 'new soldier' was shot dead when out on patrol the very next day. They now had two dead soldiers both of whom were thought to be 'soldier X'.

Eventually, I was called upon to get to the bottom of the dilemma. I quickly established that no other soldiers were unaccounted for, no servicemen were missing! It took DNA evidence to establish that the two soldiers were identical twins but since 'soldier X' didn't have a twin, let alone one who was in the same regiment as him, this was not possible. With some difficulty, I secretly checked the fingerprints of both corpses and found them to be identical. Since I knew that even identical twins don't have identical fingerprints, I knew that they could not be identical twins. No, incredible as it might seem, both corpses must be the same person. I decided to keep this secret to myself, the situation was complicated enough without me 'throwing another spanner in the works'. The commander quickly thanked me for my work and sent me home, with strict instructions never to talk about the case."

"So, what happened in the end?" asked Mark.

"I did what I was told to do, I went home and kept my mouth shut. I don't know what happened next but I later heard that the 'shot soldier X' returned home and was buried with full military honours. I never heard anything more about the 'blown up soldier X', and I never got any more 'contracts' from the armed forces," said Carlos.

"What an intriguing story, Carlos. How have you kept it to yourself until now?" I asked.

"Actually, it was easy to keep quiet about it. What could I say anyway?" exclaimed Carlos.

"The next case I want to tell you about is even more relevant to the case of Mr F. I promise that I won't bore you with too many details. When my dad died, I inherited a significant sum of money. A few months later I retired. I wanted to 'work' full time on my hobby of seeking out cases of people reportedly returning from the dead. I wanted to find plausible explanations. I've lost track of the number of cases I have investigated. I am prepared to travel anywhere in the world and social media has made my hobby much easier. Anyway, I have to say that nearly every other case I investigated came down to mistaken identity, more often than not, siblings. Then I heard about the 'Ballad of Bindi Walker'. Through social media, I came to hear about this Australian folk song that had been written by a local singer-songwriter, about the strange case of his ten-year old sister. The song had been written about twenty years earlier so his sister Bindi must have been about thirty years old, when I heard about it. The song told the story of how his sister had gone swimming with some of her friends on her way home from school in a small town called Baralaba in Queensland, Australia. She had been attacked by a large crocodile and all of her friends saw the crocodile go into its 'death roll' and disappear beneath the water with the lifeless body of Bindi in its huge jaws. Bindi's friends raised the alarm and the whole community tried to track down the crocodile but no trace of Bindi or any of her clothing were ever found. As darkness fell, the search was abandoned for the night, with the intention of resuming at first light. Bindi's family were shocked but overjoyed, when later that night, Bindi casually walked into her home in Woorabinda. She claimed that she knew nothing about any crocodile and that when she had finished swimming, she returned to the river bank. All of her friends had gone and she spent a long time calling out for them, but no one answered her frantic calls. As it was already dark, she became frightened but was calm and mature enough to walk home."

Carlos then explained how he had searched the internet and discovered that Bindi's brother Darren, the songwriter, had died suddenly a few years earlier. Through a contact of a contact however, Carlos eventually tracked down Bindi. She was living with her husband and two young children in a small indigenous 'settlement' called Woorabinda. She agreed to speak to Carlos but only if she was paid for her time. Carlos then explained how he spent over twenty-four hours flying to Brisbane and then another hour or so flying from Brisbane to Rockhampton. As had been arranged, Carlos was picked up from the airport by a village elder, who seemed overjoyed to be hired for the day. It took several hours to get to Woorabinda and Carlos said that he was totally exhausted and jet lagged when he finally got to Bindi's home. Although very excited about meeting Bindi, he didn't know how he could stay awake long enough to talk to her. Fortunately, Bindi, who Carlos said was a strikingly beautiful woman, and her family made him very welcome and even offered to allow him to stay with them until the next morning. Carlos explained that this was the first time that he had actually managed to talk to someone who had reportedly come back from the dead. His discussion with Bindi however did not get him much further. She was very open and friendly but she really didn't know what all the fuss was about. She went swimming, she got out of the water, everyone was already gone, so she walked home in the dark.

Next morning, Carlos rose early and after a delicious traditional Aboriginal breakfast, some other village folk came to Bindi's home. Bindi introduced all five of them by name and said that they were the 'friends' who had 'abandoned her' when she straight went swimming. The three women and two men all looked to be about the same age as Bindi and they all wanted to talk at the same time. Carlos explained who he was and why he had come all the way from London to talk to them. As they excitedly recounted the story about the crocodile, it crossed Carlos' mind that he was being 'entertained', maybe just for money. They all told the identical story, it seemed to Carlos that the story was perhaps too neat and well prepared, especially after twenty or so years. However, he took notes and wrote down all their names, taking the time to listen attentively and asking them details like which of them actually ran for help and who returned to lead the search, and who eventually called off the search that night. All five of her friends swore that they clearly saw the crocodile 'take' Bindi, three of them were still in the water when the attack happened. The two boys were already on the bank and looked on helplessly when they heard the commotion. The two best 'runners', one of the boys, together with one of the girls ran for help while the other three kept vigil on the bank. When help arrived more than half an hour later, there was no sign of either Bindi or the crocodile. When they saw Bindi walking and talking the next day they thought they were seeing a ghost. The story went through the community like 'wild fire' but no 'formal' investigation took place. After all, what was there to investigate? Probably because no adults witnessed the event, the story was not taken seriously. It was put down to children's hysteria especially given Bindi's assertion that nothing had happened. If it wasn't for Bindi's brother Darren writing that ballad, the story would probably have died. Carlos thought that the five witnesses really welcomed the opportunity to tell the story again and he was convinced that they all believed that they 'saw what they said they saw'.

By the time Carlos had explored all possible sources of evidence, it was already too late to catch the flight back from Rockhampton but Bindi and her patient husband put him up for another night. Carlos lay in bed that night thinking about how welcome he had been made by the villagers but he still couldn't make up his mind about what, if anything, had happened to Bindi. He needed to leave very early the next morning so, before he closed his eyes, he prepared envelopes containing very generous sums of money for each of the people who had spoken to him. Bindi had not told him how much she expected to be paid for her time and did not tell him the cost of two night's bed and breakfast, not to mention the delicious home-made meals. He really got to know Bindi's family and he could see that although they hadn't got a lot, they were willing to share what little they did have, with him. He put fifty brand-new Australian fifty-dollar notes in Bindi's envelope and wished he could be there to see her face when she would open it, after he had left. Twenty-five hundred dollars wouldn't change their lives but he was sure it would be put to good use. Certainly, better use than he could put it to. Carlos said that he felt really pleased with himself. So much so that he got out of bed and increased the cash in all the other envelopes from fifty dollars to one hundred dollars. He slept very soundly that night, he felt a little like Santa Claus.

Early next morning, Carlos could hear the commotion before he was even dressed. It seemed like half the village had arrived to see him off. The driver was standing by his 'clapped out' silver Toyota with both of the front doors wide open, in a vain effort to cool the inside. It crossed Carlos's mind that perhaps everyone wanted to be financially rewarded for 'helping him' and he again had doubts about the 'crocodile story'. Was it all just a 'yarn' for his benefit, in a concerted attempt to 'squeeze' money from this silly old naïve stranger. With some misgivings, he handed out the envelopes, keeping Bindi's one until last. Whatever their motives, he enjoyed his visit to Woorabinda and the opportunity to spend time with Bindi, her family and her friends.

As he threw his bag into the back seat of the car, he was surrounded by all the people holding their envelopes high in the air. The envelopes had been opened before he even left. Despite Carlos' protestations, all of his money was handed back to him. They all said that he had already made them feel 'believed' and 'whole' again. They were very grateful for his generosity but accepting money for telling the simple truth would not sit well with their consciences. Bindi returned the envelope with tears in her eyes. It was obvious that she was 'in two minds'. She could really help her family with all that extra money but she just couldn't take money for talking to a friend. Carlos' attempt to at least 'pay his way' for the meals and accommodation was respectfully declined. Carlos said that he left the village deeply 'moved'. He had made some real genuine friends! He left promising to return one day but knowing full well that he never would. He also understood that none of the villagers, not even Bindi herself, thought that he would return either."

"What a delightful, heart-warming tale Carlos," said Mark. "Why wouldn't you return some day? I think I would if I was you."

"So, what did you actually conclude Carlos?" I asked. "Did Bindi really come back from the dead, or was it just hysteria?"

"I don't know. I am in two minds about it. Some days I am convinced the children saw what they said they saw, then on other days I'm not so sure," answered Carlos slowly. "One thing I am certain of however is that all of the witnesses are convinced, not one of them accepted any money for speaking to me and they were all very happy when I told them that I believed them."

"What about your driver, did he accept payment for ferrying you to and from the airport?" asked Mark.

"Of course, he did. He witnessed all the others returning the money and took the opportunity to add a little to the previously agreed fare, saying that I changed the 'contract' by returning a day later than planned. I thought about it for a while, then smiled and thanked him for his services. Before I closed the car door, I mentioned that I admired his 'enterprise'. It restored my faith in the 'real world'," smirked Carlos.

By the time Carlos had finished his 'unbelievable' stories I was a firm believer in the Multi-Verse. I think Mark was already convinced even before meeting Carlos. We all quickly agreed that it would be interesting to work together to try to prove the theory. Mark told Carlos that he wouldn't hear of him having to pay his own way, and I saw them quietly come to some agreement before Carlos left. Carlos said that he needed a few weeks to get everything together for his investigation but would return on the car ferry with all his equipment. Since he intended staying in Deer Park, he would bring his golf clubs with him and Mark suggested that we could perhaps all play a few rounds of golf together. Carlos said that he would book in initially for one week and 'see how it goes'. Carlos refused Mark's offer to buy him dinner, he apologised and said that he was more tired than hungry. He said that he wanted to have an early night in readiness for the early start next morning. As we parted, Carlos asked me to allow Mark to try to get a charger for my i-Phone, saying that any photos on it would be very helpful.

Mark dropped me back to St John's and joined me for dinner there, only then did I realise that we had only eaten sandwiches throughout the day, yes plate after plate of assorted sandwiches. Although it was very late in the evening, we enjoyed our delicious bowls of 'Irish Stew' followed by apple tart with 'gallons' of custard poured over it. Afterwards, while he waited, I went to my room and collected my i-Phone and handed it, somewhat reluctantly, to Mark. He knew that I wasn't too happy about handing it over so he promised to look after it, with his life. I purposely didn't give Mark the password to open the phone and was pleased that he didn't ask for it.

Chapter 20

I really enjoyed doing my 'little set' with Danny and Ali, every Saturday night. They even persuaded me to join in and support some of their other songs. I began to feel like I was 'fitting in' and contributing something. I really loved singing with Ali and playing along to my now favourite song, *Please Come Back to Me*.

After our next round of golf, Mark and I sat in the clubhouse bar, awaiting the arrival of 'our' group of ladies. Professor Prieto was due to arrive back in Howth the following week and Mark had still not managed to get his friend to build a suitable charger for my mobile phone but he said he was confident that he would have it ready soon. By now I couldn't wait to get my phone back and to spend all of my spare time 'reliving' my past life. Mark told me that the Gardai had suddenly put a hold on the issue of my new passport. Our brother Peter had told Mark that it wouldn't be issued until Ian's body had been exhumed and that DNA evidence was obtained to confirm who exactly was buried in the grave. Peter was now trying to arrange the exhumation and the later re-burial, which he expected would be very soon.

"It's as though they overheard the professor asking us to have it done," said Mark. "What a stroke of good luck!"

We stopped talking when we saw the three ladies order their G&Ts and join us at our table. Mark told them all about the planned music evening and asked them if they would like to be his guest at The Pally the following Saturday week. Brenda and Jenny 'jumped' at the chance and immediately said yes. Mary didn't say anything at first, she was definitely hesitant. Finally, she said that although she would like to go, she wasn't sure if her husband Joe and son Jonjo would be happy for her to go.

"Oh, for Christ's sake Mary, how old are you now?" exclaimed Brenda. "Just tell them that you are going out with us to celebrate Jenny's birthday or something."

"But my birthday isn't until next October," 'piped up' Jenny.

"Who cares about the details Jenny, they won't know that, will they?"

"Yeah, but I don't fancy driving at night and I haven't been in a taxi for decades," said Mary. "In fact, I haven't been out at night for what seems like decades," she added.

Mary seemed to be looking for excuses but Brenda then offered to pick up both her and Jenny, if Mark would be good enough to sort out a taxi for them to share home.

Mary nodded slowly, under pressure. I think she felt that she had been bullied into saying yes. Mark told them to get there for about seven pm and that they would be at a table with him, his brother Robert and Robert's wife Vinny, plus of course, Conor. He said that 'hundreds' of other

Forman family members would be there, maybe one or two of them would share their table also.

"I think you will really get a kick out of my 'American' brother Patrick," laughed Mark, "and you might be surprised with a song or two, from Conor here."

The American invasion of Ireland took place on the following Sunday. They all looked tired from the direct flight from Chicago. I found it very awkward talking to people I knew well but had to pretend I was meeting for the first time. Patrick helped by being his usual effervescent self. He introduced me to his wife Susan, who I had met 'millions' of times before and knew quite well. Next came his son 'Packy', who I also knew well but shook hands 'formally' with him. Standing beside 'Packy' was a woman I hadn't met before, his wife, Janine. I felt more relaxed meeting her, no pretence needed. I could see Patricks daughter, Sarah, standing impatiently in line, waiting to be introduced to me. Another surreal moment as she hugged me, as only an American can. It had been a few years since I had seen Sarah but she didn't seem to have 'aged' a bit. Her husband, Dave, was a giant of a man who really was a stranger to me. His massive hand 'engulfed' mine as he gently took hold of it and wouldn't let go for several seconds. Packy and Sarah then introduced all the grandchildren. I had only seen photos of them so it was easy to 'meet them for the first time'.

Over the next few days, I spent lots of time walking around Howth with my grand-nieces and grand-nephews and enjoying the odd pint of Neither, with Packy, Sarah and their better-halves. Mark convinced Patrick to join us for our round of golf on Tuesday. I don't know where Patrick's golf clubs came from but they looked new to me. As usual, Mark won the golf game and Patrick and I finished tied in second place. The three ladies joined us as usual in the clubhouse and, as expected, Patrick kept them entertained the whole time we chatted. Mark asked Patrick if he and Susan would join us at our table on Saturday night.

"You betcha," replied Patrick with a smile, "I'm looking forward to hearing Conor sing those two famous songs of his."

That Saturday night, I arrived early to our reserved table, probably a good hour before TED was due on stage. I took the opportunity to tune up my guitar with the 'snark' before anyone else showed up. Five or ten minutes later Danny and Ali walked in and immediately started setting up. Ali seemed very relaxed as she unpacked and set up her keyboard. As always, she was very friendly and as animated as ever, continually brushing back her long dark hair off her forehead. I once thought about asking her why she wouldn't tie it back but thought that might be seen as 'getting too familiar'. Ali always had her lime-green trouser suit on, I guess it was her 'stage outfit'. Although she looked very nice, and 'fronted' the band she was clearly not trying to attract attention to herself, maybe she just wanted to be the 'background' support for Danny, who clearly loved the attention. After Danny had tuned up his electric guitar and his mandolin, which I hadn't seen before, I called Danny and Ali together and asked them if they knew the music to Elton John's, *Daniel* and also to the Bellamy Brothers' *Arms of Mary*. They both nodded but said that they hadn't played them for years. I told them that I wanted to sing both of these songs during the second half of the show tonight, so without delay, the three of us played through both of the new songs several times. Both Danny and Ali were proper musicians and soon were proficient. I knew both songs quite well, we decided on the most suitable key to play each song and we were all set to go. The trick is to decide on how best to get 'into' and 'out of' the songs in time. I then left Danny and Ali on stage to finish their final sound checks and went to the hotel lounge where I drank a large Diet Coke. I was unbelievably nervous.

It must have been around 7:20pm or so when I returned to the Pally. Robert, Vinny, Patrick and Susan were already seated at our table and the hall was starting to fill up. No sign of Mary, Jenny or Brenda, I wasn't surprised! I sat down for a minute but then stood up and walked around the tables, shaking hands with everyone that I was already supposed to know and asking to be introduced to relations which I also knew but wasn't supposed to know. What a farce, but I was getting better at it. Seemed like every relation I knew was there, what a turnout! I was particularly happy to see my sister Fiona and her husband Gearoid seated at the same table with her twin brother Mark and his youthful, tall, blond girlfriend, whose name I couldn't pronounce. Peter was also at the table, seated with his son, my 'drinking partner' Alan and Alan's wife Brenda. Peter's daughter Barbara sat alongside her husband Graham at the end of the table. For some reason Barbara didn't acknowledge me!

"Mark, I thought you were going to sit at our table tonight," I said and then immediately regretted it.

"Sorry Conor, but I thought it best to let you talk to your three lady friends without me around," he replied.

Patrick's 'kids' Packy and Sarah and their partners were seated together on another table with my sister Marian and my deceased sister Jean's daughters Gina, Marian and Louise. Everyone seemed to be 'primed' and ready to have a good time.

By the time I arrived back at my table, Mary, Brenda and Jenny had walked in and Robert was busy introducing them to his wife Vinny and Patrick's wife Susan. When we all sat down, I found myself seated between Susan and Mary. She didn't have to sit beside me, why did she? Thankfully we had Patrick right opposite us on the round table, so no one else had to make conversation. Patrick joked and laughed right up until the time TED came on stage. The band launched into their usual first set, which again 'went down a bomb'. It didn't take long for everyone in the hall to join in by singing along, some even standing up and trying to dance between the tables. I was starting to feel nervous about getting up to sing, so much so that I 'stuck' to only drinking pints of 'Not'. Everyone else at my table was 'knocking back' the booze and no one was paying for anything, Patrick was 'running a tab'. I noticed that Mary was 'pacing herself', sipping slowly on her gin and tonic. About halfway through the first session Danny stopped playing and announced that the time had now arrived for his guest singer/songwriter, his friend Conor Forman, to take the stage. Luckily my nerves disappeared once I launched into *Peaceful Easy Feeling* and immediately followed up with *Lying Eyes*. Danny and Ali were brilliant and this time Ali joined in by singing each chorus with me. Although I had sung these two songs so many times now, I still got a 'great kick' every time the crowd applauded loudly. During the songs I frequently looked over and saw Mary listening intently but she seemed to only 'gently' applaud after each song. When I finished my 'set' and started to leave the stage, Danny announced that I would be singing another couple of better-known songs, after the interval.

Back at the table, I was pleased with the reaction I got from everyone seated. Mary asked me where the songs came from, she said that she "quite liked" them but had never heard them before. Brenda and Jenny both asked me if I would sing the two songs again in the second half but I told them that I had a couple of little surprises planned. Not much casual conversation possible while the band were playing, many 'budding singers' were singing along, so the noise level was too high. I noticed that although quite a few people were smoking joints, no one at our table joined in. I suspect Robert was heeding Vinny's warnings and Patrick and Susan didn't seem interested, perhaps it was not 'the done thing' in Chicago. During the interval I paid a visit to the 'boy's room' where I had a real friendly chat with Alan.

I was back at my table just before the band was ready to re-start. The crowd were getting louder and louder, most of the time I couldn't hear Ali's voice, she was 'drowned out', by the unpaid and obviously unrehearsed 'backing singers'. I was having second thoughts about taking the stage again. I knew that most of the crowd would know the words to both *Daniel* and *Arms of Mary* but I had changed the lyrics in an attempt to 'reach the hearts' of some of the people present. The last thing I wanted was for the crowd to start singing the correct lyrics.

The time for my second set was fast approaching and I had to take a large 'gulp' from my first pint of Guinness to try to overcome my nerves and to get some moisture back in my dry mouth. Eventually Danny called me up on stage. I prayed that my nerves would disappear once I started singing!

I pulled the leather guitar strap over my head and moved closer to the microphone. I decided I needed to properly introduce the first song if it was to 'work'.

"Good evening ladies and gentlemen, and welcome to the Pally, sorry

Marian, welcome to Brian's Palace. Most of you know that there are a fair number of Formans in the room tonight, including my American brother Patrick and his family, who have come all the way from Chicago. It's understandable that Patrick is extremely proud to call himself American, after all, he has lived there since he emigrated when aged just twenty. Yes, he may have an American passport but I know that, in his heart, he still carries fond memories of Ireland. When I heard that his extended family were coming 'home' I decided to try to 'capture in song' the moment when Patrick emigrated. I heard many times from different people that Patrick was his mammy's favourite and that she was heartbroken when he left home. I have changed some of the lyrics to Elton John's song *Daniel* to try to portray what I imagine that moment would have been like. Can I please ask you to bear with me and let me indulge in this by asking you not to join in with the singing, none of you know the words, no one has heard it before, not even Danny and Ali."

My announcement had the desired effect. The crowd fell completely silent. Christ, I hope I don't bore them too much!

"I have called it *Song to Patrick* and I hope Elton doesn't sue me if he ever gets to hear about this."

I counted down .... one, two, three, four and started the 'Intro'. Danny and Ali got it 'spot on'. I closed my eyes to help me concentrate and started singing:

Patrick is leaving tonight on a plane
We can see the red tail lights, headin' for the USA
Oh, an' mam can see Patrick waving goodbye
She said it looks like Patrick, must be the tears in her eyes.

He heard the states were pretty, though he'd never been
Now he says it's a great place, the best he's ever seen
Oh, an' he should know, he's lived long enough
Oh, you've done well Patrick, you've achieved so much.

Patrick my brother, you are younger than me
Do you still feel the pain, missing Louis, Ian and Jean
Blue eyes still shine and they smile all the time
Patrick family star, shining bright in my eye...

Instrumental

Patrick is leaving tonight on a plane
We can see the red tail lights, headin' for the USA
Oh, an' mam can see Patrick waving goodbye
She said it looks like Patrick, must be the tears in her eyes.

Still visit Howth, forever in your blood
Climb aboard a fishing boat, I'm sure you would if you could
Drink with old friends, oft you'd more than enough
Bet you miss it Patrick, think you miss it so much.

Even better life, with Sarah, Packy and Sue
Lots of great new friends, yes and grandchildren too
Happiest times now, it's clear to be seen
Yes, you've made it Patrick, a real American dream.

Patrick my brother, you are younger than me
Do you still feel the pain, missing Louis, Ian and Jean
Blue eyes still shine and they smile all the time
Patrick you're a star, shining bright in my eye ...

Patrick is leaving tonight on a plane
We can see the red tail lights, headin' for the USA
Is that really Patrick waving goodbye?
Mam says it looks like Patrick, must be the tears in her eyes.

'I'm sure it is my Patrick, but could be the tears in my eyes"

I finished the song with tears in my eyes. I couldn't believe how emotional I felt. The audience applauded politely, I guess the song didn't mean that much to many of them.

I put down my guitar and told the audience that I would be back in ten or fifteen minutes to sing one more song. They didn't seem that bothered, had I made a mistake in singing that song in public? Perhaps I should have saved it for a smaller family gathering. Rather than going back to my table I went straight out the door and out to the car park, I needed some air. I needed to wipe the tears from my eyes and get my composure back. I couldn't have been there for more than a minute when Barbara, Marian and Fiona arrived and stood around me. I could see the tears in Marian's eyes as they all put their arms around me. Mark and Sarah then arrived and we all had a long tearful 'group hug'.

"That was really beautiful Conor," said Fiona, "could you send me the words."

Rather than help me regain my composure, I was actually trembling with emotion. What no one there knew, except maybe Mark, was that I was actually there when Patrick emigrated, I can still remember how upset our mammy really was.

After ten or fifteen minutes, Fiona suggested that we go back inside or people will start to think something was wrong. I visited the 'boys room' to splash cold water over my face and eventually went back inside and sat back down at my table. All eyes were on me but thankfully there was no sign of any emotion.

I had just taken another 'slurp' out of my pint of Guinness or Neither or Not or whatever it was that Robert had probably got for me, when Danny called me back up on stage to sing my second song. Should I go ahead with it, I wondered? Would it come across as stupid, why did I want to sing these lyrics anyway? As I strode to the stage, I still wasn't sure if I would sing my version of *Arms of Mary* or just sing *Lying Eyes* again. I know that the audience still seemed to react really well to *Lying Eyes*.

Danny made the decision for me by announcing:

"Ladies and gentlemen, Conor will now sing a song and I think that many of you will know the tune very well. It's the Bellamy Brothers, *Arms of Mary*. Can I however, ask that you don't join in because Conor says that he has changed the lyrics. Ali and I have no idea what's coming but we hope it doesn't have everyone crying like the last one.

Danny started the intro and I started strumming. I hoped I could get through this!

Fun night here at the Pally, sing along with Dan and Ali
Oh, but I'd rather be, lying in the arms of Mary
Our innocence of childhood, it blossomed into true love
Oh, how I wish I could be, lying in the arms of Mary.

Mary was the girl I married happy times ago
Been together since our very first date
Took some time till we learned what we had to know
But we knew how to give .... not just take.

But now I'm just sad and lonely, I've lost my one and only
How can I ever be, lying in the arms of Mary.

Mary is the girl I lost not so long ago
I woke to find she had another mate
Is all hope gone, our past she doesn't seem to know
She's now living in a world that is fake, woah.

Fun night here at the Pally, still singing with Dan and Ali
Though I know I can't again be, lying in the arms of Mary
She's right before me but she doesn't see me.
Still livin' in a world that is fake.

She's livin' in a world that is fake, oh, oh, oh.

Danny and Ali completed the outro on their own. I just stood there with the guitar draped over my shoulder. I took a bow as the audience politely applauded. I wondered whether the applause was simply to spare my embarrassment. Apart from one person, no one else in the audience could have any idea what the song was about. I thought that I shouldn't have gone through with it, but how else could I have got the message across to Mary. But had I got the message across to Mary? Strangely I didn't feel emotional at all as I sat back down beside her. Mary looked 'puzzled' as she looked at me, no smile or hint that she knew what I was singing about. I looked over at Mark and he gave me 'the thumbs up'. I knew that he understood what I was trying to do. When TED had just finished their rendition of 'Fields of Athenry' and the hall was hushed, Patrick suddenly stood up and 'announced' to those seated at our table:

"Conor, that was the nicest thing anyone has ever done for me, thank you."

He then came around the table and asked me to stand up so he could give me a 'man hug'.

I really appreciated Patrick's words but was thankful that he showed no signs of emotion. My mind was still on that abomination of a song about Mary that I 'murdered'. Did Mary think I was a 'head-case'?

Some twenty minutes or so before TED were due to finish, I could hear Jenny asking Mark if he could sort out their taxi. Minutes later and with the band still in full flow, Brenda, Jenny and Mary stood up and shook hands with everyone at the table, their taxi had arrived and they said they had to leave. Mark walked out with them to 'see them off'. I thought about doing the same but I felt too embarrassed about my stupid behaviour so I just waved goodbye and remained 'glued' to my chair.

What a 'balls up', I thought. What do I say to Mary the next time we meet? Will there ever be a next time?

When TED announced that they would now finish with that old 'Planxty' favourite *Cliffs of Dooneen*, I stood up and told everyone that I wasn't feeling that great and needed to go to bed. I thanked everyone and said I would see them tomorrow. I walked out without looking back. I hailed down a passing taxi and 'escaped' to my familiar new home, St John's. Minutes later I was lying on my bed. I lay there all night in my 'party' clothes, I couldn't be bothered putting on my pyjamas. Eventually I slipped off my shoes and drifted in and out of sleep all night. What a fool I had made of myself!

Chapter 21

Mark called me to say that Professor Prieto would be flying in on Saturday evening. He would make his own way to Deer Park and would like to meet both of us for breakfast there at about 9:30am on Sunday. He asked us to arrive ready to play golf.

During breakfast, Carlos outlined his plan. In a quiet corner of the breakfast room, he explained that it would probably not be possible to prove conclusively that I was actually Ian, who has come back from another dimension, but if we approach the task in a systematic way, we should be able to arrive at this conclusion, beyond a reasonable doubt.

He said that he had rented a small meeting room at the hotel for the complete week and he proposed that we meet every evening from say 6:00pm till late. During each session he wanted me to tell him everything I could remember about my past life. He said that, if I was happy with it, that he would use his old video camera to record everything that was said at our meetings and that he would leave the camera running all of the time. No editing would take place, all the sessions would be recorded live. He said that it was essential that Mark be present at each session, if he couldn't be there the session would be postponed. Carlos said that, during the sessions, he would interrupt me regularly to make sure what I said was crystal clear. When all the information had been gathered, he would task Mark with trying to verify everything I said about my family and my life in Howth and Dublin. He himself volunteered to travel 'wherever' and talk to 'who-ever' to verify my past experiences outside of Ireland. He expected that it would take all week to complete the facts gathering process but that there was no time constraint, it will take as long as it takes.

We all agreed that we would only discuss my experiences when all three of us were present and then only when the camera was rolling. The first session would start that evening at 6:00pm.

While we were still eating our 'full Irish' breakfast it started to rain very heavily and we agreed to wait in the lounge until the rain eased off. A couple of hours later and we were still waiting! Carlos asked if we had any questions about him or his proposed process. He asked if we had any other suggestions. I took the opportunity to try to get my curiosity satisfied before our process started.

"Carlos, you earlier explained how you became interested with the 'parallel universe' phenomenon but are you also interested in investigating other reported paranormal activities such as ghost stories, demonic possession or poltergeists", I asked. "Do you believe in ghosts?"

Carlos took a few minutes to reply before saying that he would prefer to talk about these issues when we had finished our investigation. He wanted to try to keep focussed on the task at hand.

Carlos then asked if he could be excused as he wanted to prepare for the first session. He left Mark and I rather abruptly, he seemed distracted. We all agreed to meet again at reception at 6:00pm. Mark dropped me off at St John's, saying that he would collect me later.

When we met again at 6:00pm, Carlos was 'beaming' from ear to ear. It was clear that he was 'on a mission'. He led us to his booked meeting room. A plain oak chair was positioned at one end of a small oak boardroom table with just another couple of chairs on either side of the table. To the side of the end chair stood an easel on which was displayed today's Irish Independent newspaper, open on the front page. A small video camera, a Canon FS100 was positioned in the middle of the table, facing the end chair. Carlos asked me to sit on the end chair and to face the camera.

He leaned over and turned on his camera. He then moved over beside me and introduced himself to camera and asked Mark to do the same. With Mark and Carlos back in their seats and with his notebook and pen at the ready, Carlos asked me if I was ready to begin. He said that to enable the process to proceed smoothly that he had prepared a series of questions. I was to assume that he knew absolutely nothing about me, to act as if this was the first time we had ever met. I nodded and he cleared his throat to ask the first question.

"What is your full name and when and where were you born?"

"I'm Ian Raymond Forman, I was born in Dublin in January, 1949," I replied.

"Who are, or were, your parents and tell us a little about them?" he asked

"My Daddy was Peter Forman and my mammy was Georgina Florence Hughes, but she was always called 'Flo'. My daddy owned a successful fish business in Howth which employed about twenty people, including his brother James and his sister Annie. From time to time my brothers Peter, Louis and Robert also worked in the business. My daddy was killed in a car accident in 1980 and my mother died some years ago, when she was in her eighties," I replied.

"Are you married Mr F, do you have you children?"

"Yes, after I graduated, I married my childhood sweetheart Mary Mooney, on July 13th, 1973 and we emigrated to Canada a couple of weeks later. We have two children, John who was born in Canada in 1974 and Annette who was born in Belgium in 1976," I answered.

"So where do you all live now?"

"We lived in several different towns in Ontario, Canada, for a total of about two years and then I was offered a job in Belgium where we lived for almost ten years," I answered.

"So where do you live now Mr F?"

"Mary and I live in Buckingham, England. Annette, her husband Phil and their three young children Luke, Ella and Josie, live just ten minutes-drive away. Our son John lives with his son Aidan in north London."

"So, what are you doing in Howth Ian?"

"Mary and I drove over to attend my brother Peter's seventieth birthday party, wished we hadn't now."

"What is your brother's name Mr F? Where does he live? Does he have children?" he asked.

"My oldest brother Peter is almost two years older than me. He moved from Portmarnock to an apartment nearby, a few years after his wife Claire died from cancer. They have four children, Gavin, who now lives in Australia, plus Alan, Paul and Barbara, who all live in Dublin."

"What are the names of your other siblings Mr. F, you can tell us more about them later on?"

"I was one of nine children. Six boys, Peter, Louis, Patrick, Robert, Mark and me. There were just three girls, Jean, Marian and Fiona."

"That's some family Mr. F, so there were nine children in total," he said.

"Yes, that's right, but sadly only six are still with us," I replied. "Sadly, Jean, Louis and Robert have already passed away."

Carlos slid several blank pages in front of me and, handing me a black ball point pen, he asked me to write down as many details as I could remember about my family. I wrote my home address, the phone numbers and e-mail addresses for Mary and I, plus addresses and contact details for John and Annette. I surprisingly remembered the home addresses of Peter, and Fiona but not their e-mail addresses or phone numbers. When I had written down as much as I could remember at the time, I handed the pages back to him.

"Thanks Mr. F, that's brilliant," he smiled.

He then promptly handed the pages back to me and asked me to read the details out loud to the camera, a ritual that continued throughout the questioning process.

"Ok Mr. F, could you tell me about your school days?"

I looked straight at the camera and began again.

"I enjoyed going to school at the Howth National School, where I played on the school Gaelic and Hurling team, winning several medals. I was reasonably good academically and at fourteen years of age, followed my older brother Peter, to St Paul's College, Raheny. It would be fair to say that I did not enjoy my two years at St Paul's College and spent most of my time trying to dodge homework and avoiding the many, mandatory regular religious gatherings. Despite my lack of interest, at age sixteen, I did quite well in the 'Intermediate Certificate' and my older brother Peter did well in his final 'Leaving Certificate' in the same year. My younger brother Louis decided that college life was not for him, so he joined my daddy and uncle James, in the family business.

By age fifteen I was already interested in girls, at the expense of almost everything else, and by sixteen I had already met Mary. From my first dance with Mary, at Oulton Tennis Club in the summer of 1965, I couldn't think of anyone or anything else, and we have been inseparable ever since, well that is until I recently fell asleep on a park bench on Howth promenade. I left St Paul's College in the middle of the next term, I remember I was a little disillusioned with school life but mainly I wanted to earn money, so I could go out with Mary. My decision to give up school also led to my younger brother Patrick leaving at the same time. Patrick still 'half-jokingly' blames me for influencing him to give up on education, but deep down he knows it eventually led to him having a really happy family life and career in Chicago.

I was lucky enough to soon find a job as a trainee draughtsman, where my English boss at 'Smith & Pearsons' in Dublin, Mr Waterhouse, first encouraged me and eventually persuaded me to go to evening school to complete the 'Leaving Certificate'. Since I already had all the necessary books, I studied hard each evening and sat the exam the following year, so both Mary and I passed the 'Leaving Certificate' in the same year. Looking back at it now, this was the perfect solution for me, I had enough money to keep Mary entertained and still finish my secondary school without losing any time."

I could see that Mark was getting bored with my narrative.

"How am I doing Carlos?" I asked, while looking directly at Mark.

"You're doing just fine, Mr. F. I think you are going at just the right pace, with just enough detail to allow us to probe further where we need to, at a later stage," replied Carlos.

"Ok, where was I, oh yes, Mary and I had both just got our Leaving Certificates. I decided to go back to full time education and enrolled on an engineering degree course at Bolton Street College in Dublin.

So, it was with mixed emotions that I 'knuckled down', oh if only I had, to the so-called hard work of studying for exams again. I was, once more, a little 'schoolboy'.

It's strange but leaving paid work made me feel like a boy again, instead of a grown-up. Mixing with lots of teenagers, rather than 'responsible' grown-ups, brought out the fun-loving, partying, gambling and of course drinking side of my personality. My parents supported me and my 'working' older brothers all helped me out financially throughout my study years.

Mary had found a really good office job in Dublin City and was taking home enough money for us to have fun every weekend. This was the start of a 'share and share alike' relationship with Mary, which continues throughout our lives, well until now that is. We honestly had no concept of 'his and hers' and although it was never discussed, I guess we both just assumed that we would each live (for free) in our own homes and that Mary would help finance our nights out during my many years of study.

Looking back at it even now, I think both of us may have realised that these could turn out to be some of the best years of our lives. I actually enjoyed studying and learning, I don't ever remember being stressed about exams and Mary loved her job and 'independence'. We had enough money to do what we wanted to, we didn't have to bother with saving for the future and Mary was able to keep up with the latest fashions. We were on friendly terms with all of our close relations and we had lots of 'fun-loving' friends. Yes, if you are rich enough, there is a lot to be said for being a full-time permanent student. I was still however very 'big-headed' and felt I was the 'envy' of most of my male friends. I was 'going steady' with, not just one of, but 'the' most beautiful girl I had ever met, who, despite being extremely popular with all my male friends, did not consider herself to be 'all that attractive'!

I thought life was great and couldn't possibly get better!

During the last couple of years at Engineering College, I became best friends with a classmate, Joe O'Connor. It wasn't long before Mary and I met up with Joe and his girlfriend Marie. The four of us went out together most weekends. Mary and Marie both had 'office jobs' and Joe and I earned a little bit of cash from odd jobs and from summer work. We made enough to be able to go to the local disco each weekend and to go to the cinema every so often. I'm afraid, however, that much of Joe's and my spare cash went on boozing, but despite this, we both managed to pass our final exams, qualifying as mechanical engineers in July 1973. The four of us had already romanticised many times about what we would do once we graduated and now, we had the opportunity. Since my younger brother Patrick had emigrated to the USA a year earlier, I convinced everyone that we should first try for the USA. Over a few beers one evening, we agreed that we would make appointments to visit the American Embassy, followed by the Canadian Embassy and finally the Australian Embassy, all on the same day."

I paused to 'catch my breath'.

"So did the four of you emigrate to the USA together Mr F?"

"Well no, without pre-arranged jobs, the USA wouldn't have us so we went for our second choice, which was Canada. We first flew to New York where we stayed overnight before we flew on to Toronto. Thinking back on it, we were so unprepared for our adventure. We had nowhere to stay, none of us had jobs and we had absolutely no contacts there. We booked into a hotel for a couple of nights, bought a local paper and spent the time looking for an apartment to rent. We spent the first four weeks in a cheap two-bedroom apartment in a suburb of Toronto, with Joe and I trying to find work. Luckily both Mary and Marie found office work within a few days and they 'kept' Joe and I."

"So how long did it take you to find work Mr. F?" asked Carlos.

"Within a few weeks, Joe and I found work at a company called Daal Specialties, which made seatbelts for motor cars. Joe's position was at their factory in Collingwood and mine was at their other factory in Windsor, Ontario."

"Was that the last you saw of Joe and Marie?" asked Mark.

Carlos looked over at Mark to remind him that he asked the questions. I ignored the distraction.

"From memory it was a good four to five-hour drive from Windsor to Collingwood but we kept in touch by phone. Mary however, became very homesick and to be honest I wasn't much help, too focused on my work," I replied.

"So how long did you stay in Canada for?"

"In total we lived in Canada for about two years. Just under one year in Windsor, which ended when the company closed down immediately after most of the office staff joined a Trade Union and demanded a large increase in pay. I was lucky enough to be offered a choice of jobs with the company. I spent a couple of weeks at their huge new facility in Macon, Georgia, USA, assisting with the transfer and set up of the production assembly lines from Windsor. At the end of the assignment I was offered a job in Macon, a permanent job of Production Line Supervisor, with a great salary increase. I was also offered an alternative job of a supervisor's role at their factory in Collingwood, Ontario. The Collingwood job involved running the metal stamping department, which pressed the metal brackets used in the manufacture of the thousands of seat belts they produced. Unfortunately, by this time Joe had already left the company for a better job in Toronto, so it would be like another fresh start wherever we went. Mary was by this time quite lonely and was not at all happy with the thought of a move to Georgia. Perhaps I shouldn't have told her that the rattle snakes could be kept out of the back garden by sinking a chain link garden fence deep into the ground!

Shouldn't have told her that my potential future boss in Georgia, Mike, had promised to show me how to safely kill a rattlesnake with a garden spade. I stupidly thought this would ease Mary's concerns about living in Macon!

No surprise then that we soon moved to Collingwood, unbelievably straight into Joe and Marie's old apartment, which had been vacant for a few weeks. Although we soon made friends and I was enjoying my new role, Mary was still not really settled. Our son John arrived a few months later, heightening Mary's sense of isolation. A visit from Mary's parents Frank and Jo, brought some temporary relief for Mary. They stayed in a local hotel and helped Mary settle into her new role as a mother.

"So how long did Mary's parents stay with you?"

"Frank and Jo stayed for a few weeks and helped us greatly. I got to know them very well and Frank became a great friend, not just a 'Father-In-Law'. When they left us to go home to Dublin, I think Mary felt even more isolated. It did not help that everywhere was covered in several feet of snow. We could not walk anywhere and Mary had to wait until I came home from work before we could all go out shopping. I had the mandatory snow tyres fitted to our red Ford Cougar, so at least we could all go to the Mall for our 'evenings out', which really just involved grocery shopping.

I gradually realised however, that I needed to change our circumstances if we were going to make Canada our home.

Six months later we moved on. This time, back down to the Toronto area, where we could once more meet up regularly with Joe and Marie. We lived in Port Credit, which is part of Mississauga, just outside Toronto. I took a job as an Industrial Engineer in a factory which made hospital furniture. Things really were on the up again, I enjoyed my work, Mary was very contented, spending lots of time with John. We met up with Joe and Marie most weekends."

I paused to see if I was holding Mark's attention before continuing ....

"Our now settled life was soon to come to a sudden end again though. After just four or five months working at Dominion Metalware, I arrived home one night to be told by Mary that I was to call a phone number in New York. Mary explained that she had taken a call from the Personnel Manager of Allied Chemical Corp., the owner of Daal Specialties. He explained that he was calling from their HQ in New York, to speak to me about a vacancy for the Industrial Engineering Manager of their brand-new factory, which had just opened in Ieper, Belgium. I had not heard from anyone in Daal Specialties since I had left months earlier, but I had, for some reason, left a forwarding phone number.

I returned the phone call and listened with great interest to what Mr Wild had to say.

Mary did not take much convincing as she was excited to be going 'almost' home. So it was, that we decided to 'up sticks' again and move to another foreign country. The official job offer arrived within a few days and I handed in my two-weeks-notice.

Our friends next door, in the apartment block, John and Sue, were surprised and genuinely seemed sad, when we told them about our planned move to Belgium. They were only recently married and were just a couple of years older than us. I can't remember what they did for a living but they seemed to 'not want' for anything and were great fun to be with. I imagine now that they could have turned out to be close friends had we not left. They invited us to their apartment for dinner, a day or two before we were due to leave Canada. I think Mary really liked the way they treated our baby son John with such great tenderness and affection. They did not have any children at the time, but Mary and I believed that it would not be long before they did! Wonder how they are now?

After dinner Sue asked us more about what we would be doing in Belgium. I could hardly 'keep a straight face', when she asked me whether Belgium was in Northern Ireland or in the Republic of Ireland. She explained that she looked but could not find it on a map of Ireland, which she had looked at in the local library. I had heard that many people in North America were 'insular' but I remember being shocked but unsure whether she was joking or not. When I saw that she was waiting for my answer, I asked Sue if she had ever heard of Brussels, at which point she exclaimed:

"Oh yes, I have. Is Belgium in Brussels?"

I tried my best to 'keep a straight face'.

"Sorry to interrupt again Mr. F, so what was living in Belgium like?" asked Carlos. "How did you both get on with the language, was it French or Dutch?"

Before I could answer, Mark stood up and said that he needed a break. He suggested that we all go to the lounge and have a drink before we continue. Carlos didn't look happy with Mark's suggestion but when I stood up to follow Mark, he looked at his watch and decided to call an end to our first session. He switched off the camera and put it in its case. We all drank a couple of pints of Guinness each, courtesy of Mark. We were careful not to continue our discussion about my life, instead talking about the weather. We agreed that golf wouldn't be on the agenda for a couple of days, at least. Mark's offer to drop in on Carlos next morning was politely declined. He said that he wanted to go over everything recorded so far on the camera and needed some time to prepare for the next session tomorrow evening.

Chapter 22

It was raining heavily again the next morning. Mark called me to say that Carlos called him and asked to be left alone until our next arranged meeting at 6:00pm. He told me that he had an important business meeting he had to attend that morning but that he had succeeded in charging up my phone and would drop it, plus the new charger up to me, in the next few minutes. I met Mark in the car park outside St John's. I was really excited! Mark's meeting must have been very important because when he rolled down the car window, he quickly handed me my phone and new charger and apologised that he couldn't stay. He said he would call back at about 5:00pm in order to get a glimpse of my photos before our meeting with Carlos that evening.

Back in my room, I lay on my bed and turned on my mobile phone. I was apprehensive, what if my password didn't work in this universe? I need not have worried. It was fully charged and I got straight into 'Photos'. I spent hours going through all my albums, over and over again. This evidence will surely dispel any possible doubt over my claim to be Ian! I had lots of images of Mary, our family, my friends and our thousands of holiday snaps, all dated and timed. I was elated, I felt like cheering out loud. I finally pulled up the photo of the headstone showing there was nothing wrong with my memory. My name was not inscribed on it, Daddy had died when he was fifty-six and my brothers Louis and Robert had both died on May 12th, seven years apart, when they were both only fifty-five years of age. I turned off my phone and placed it on the bedside table. What should I do now? I lay there and closed my eyes, trying to concentrate. Random thoughts and questions filled my brain. Is it really possible that anyone, except Mark and Carlos, will believe that I am Ian Forman, back from another dimension? No, of course they won't. Who in their right mind would believe this, everyone knows that photos can easily be faked! Much easier to believe that some photos have been faked than the stupid alternative of accepting that I have crossed over from another dimension! Ok, maybe Carlos can come up with strong and compelling additional evidence, but what then? Most people will still believe it's all faked evidence and that we are all conmen. What will Robert think if I show him that photo of the gravestone with his name on it? Robert is the one person I know, who will never believe that I am back from another dimension. What about my new life as Conor? Can I really tell Mary that she is married to me as well as to her current husband? What about my other brothers and sisters, what will they believe? They have only just now begun to accept me as Conor, and I am beginning to accept it myself, life could be ok for Conor! What are my best chances for getting to know Mary better? I think she will likely shun Conor if he tells her that he is really a different version of her previous husband Ian, in another dimension! She's hardly going to leave her current husband to be with a deluded stupid conman.

I jumped off the bed and took a shower. I turned on the TV and watched an old episode of the western series Bonanza. I knew that I needed to clear my brain, but I couldn't. What should I do now? Now that I really know who I am, does anyone else need to know? I know that I am sane, I don't need any more proof. Why continue with this Carlos study? Who will benefit from proving I came from a parallel universe? I know it's true, so 'sod' everyone else! If I don't think I will gain anything from the study, should I just ask Carlos to push off and leave me alone? I think Carlos is doing this for his own satisfaction anyway, I know it's not really for my benefit! Also, can I really trust him not to tell anyone if he believes he has all the evidence he needs? Maybe he will just publish my story in an attempt to become famous. The more I think about it, the more I believe that my best option is to live out the rest of my life as Conor, I haven't given up on getting back with Mary yet, I shouldn't risk 'cocking it up'. I need to make sure that I get that new passport in Conor's name.

As the afternoon went by, despite thinking of nothing else, I was no further in knowing what to do for the best! Some moments I was sure I should forget about helping Carlos establish the truth, *beyond reasonable doubt* but at other times I was certain I should get on with just living as Conor. Mark arrived a few minutes after five pm, primed and ready to go through the photos with me. He asked how I had got on with the photos. I lied that I thought that we should respect Carlos' wishes and suggested that we should all three go through the photos together. I could see that Mark was a little 'taken aback' but when I told him that I hadn't even looked at the photos myself yet, he nodded and invited me for a drink at the hotel before our planned session with Carlos.

We arrived at the Deer Park Hotel with plenty of time to spare and I really enjoyed my pint of Guinness with Mark. Knowing what Carlos was like, we didn't want to be either early or late so we knocked on the meeting room door a few seconds before 6:00pm. Carlos was already in position and seemed keen to re-start. After a very brief welcome he indicated that he wanted me to sit down in the same chair. I noticed that the newspaper on the easel had been replaced with today's Irish Independent. Carlos must have thought that this would be 'back up' if anyone questioned the date shown on his video.

"Ok Mr. F, you were about to tell us about your life after you left Canada," said Carlos.

"Carlos before we re-start, Conor here has something to tell you and more importantly, to show us," announced Mark, triumphantly.

I told Carlos about the phone and the charger, that my password worked and that I had access to lots of photos. I looked at Mark and thanked him again for the phone and apologised for not letting him see the photos yet. I then told them that I had already looked at all of the photos and that I had seen everything I needed to see.

"That's brilliant Mr. F," exclaimed Carlos. "Is it too soon for me to start calling you Ian?"

"Look if you both don't mind, before we start again, I want to go over the purpose of this investigation. I'm not sure what it is we are trying to achieve and what we would do with the results anyway," I said.

"Are you having second thoughts about this Mr F?" asked Carlos. "Look, if you are not entirely happy with all this we can stop right now and you have my word, as an honourable man, that I won't breathe a word about our discussions to anyone."

"Carlos, I am not questioning your integrity and I know I can depend on Mark but after spending the last several hours looking at the photos on my phone, I know for sure who I am," I replied. "You have already opened my mind to the existence of other universes so I am now certain that I am a returned Ian, I don't need any more proof."

"Ok, I understand what you are saying, but do you really think that your photo evidence would be enough to convince a serious 'doubter'?" asked Carlos.

"Probably not Carlos, but with all due respect, why would I want to convince anyone else anyway? From now on, I want to live out the rest of my life as Conor and, to be honest, I am quite happy to do so. I have been welcomed by my brothers and sisters and I might have an opportunity to get to know Mary all over again. Why rock the boat? Anyway, although I now know that nothing can help me re-unite with my children and grandchildren, I still have the memories and now I also have the photos," I replied.

"Mr F, you don't need to 'rock the boat', as you call it, I agree that even if we could prove that you are a returned Ian, that you must still pretend to be Conor for as long as you can," replied Carlos. "But what would you do if something unexpected happened, where would you be then?"

"Thanks for your, I'm sure, genuine concern Carlos, but if I continue to pretend to be Conor from now on, what could possibly go wrong?" I asked.

"Perhaps you are right Mr F, and I don't blame you for adopting a selfish attitude. You have certainly been 'through enough' and deserve to live out the rest of your life in peace," said Carlos.

I looked at Mark and he nodded in agreement. He reminded me that everybody has now accepted me as Conor and as soon as I get my passport and driving license that I have nothing more to worry about. He promised that he would take my 'secret' to his grave.

"Yeah, thanks Mark, but would you be tempted to divulge my secret if and when you yourself come back from the dead," I laughed.

Carlos didn't laugh, he didn't even smile, he didn't get my humour. I was again reminded that this was a very serious life's mission for him, not just a bit of fun.

"Carlos, why have you accused me of being selfish? I asked. "This is my life and nobody else's. I am not a curiosity to be observed and studied, I am a living and breathing person."

I could see that I had hurt Carlos with my comments. He stared straight at me for several seconds. I knew that he was thinking carefully about how to respond, I almost regretted that I had been so blunt, but I needed to get my feelings across.

"Yes, you are right again Mr F, perhaps it's not fair of me to expect you to think of others," whispered Carlos in a defeatist tone.

How can this strange man make me feel guilty for not helping him? What was he 'going on' about?

"Ok Carlos, I think I get it now," I said. "You want me to help you gather enough evidence so you can make it all public and become famous. You don't really give a shit about me! Do you Carlos?"

Mark stood up suddenly and said that we should take a short break and suggested that we all three have a drink down in the bar. Carlos and I stood up together, avoiding eye contact. Mark didn't ask us, he just ordered three pints of Guinness and 'ushered' us to a small round table, in the far corner of the bar.

"Well I thought that went really well lads," said Mark. "It's a shame you didn't have your camera rolling Carlos, it would have made hilarious viewing when all this is over and done with."

Carlos and I made eye contact and smiled at each other. I apologised for my unwarranted outbreak as I tried to reassure him that I trusted him. He told me that he thought he understood me and that he took no offence. He said that he probably owed me a fuller explanation for wanting to prove his theory. He explained that I represented a unique opportunity for a thorough investigation, none of his previous cases presented this opportunity and he doubted he would ever get a better chance. To his knowledge, no one else was stupid enough to try to attempt to pursue an investigation into this phenomenon, so if he didn't do it, then it just wouldn't get done. He felt he owed it to those other unfortunate individuals who might have 'transitioned' as I had done. He explained that it was impossible to believe that the only people it happened to, were the few that he was fortunate enough to have previously met, dead and alive. He said that there must be hundreds, if not thousands of others. I was very, very lucky to have the 'missing' Conor as a 'believable' explanation for my sudden re-appearance. If he hadn't written his book and if Mark had not read it and if Conor had not 'propped up', he doubts I would ever have been released from a mental institution. I should be grateful that it worked out so well for me, otherwise it would only have been a matter of time before I would have gone insane anyway. If, however, he and I could eventually 'prove' the theory and make all the evidence available, it could change everything. Perhaps it could lead to many other unfortunate souls being believed and being helped to recover their sanity. Not everybody would be happy however, he said that many religious leaders might see it as a threat to their belief that when your body dies that only your spirit lives on. Some sceptics might even suggest that Jesus returned from the dead three days later from another universe. The revelation would also raise lots of legal issues, like what rights would the 'returned individual' have, what about those 'last will and testaments', could the 'returned individual' take back everything that had been left to his successors? He wondered whether everyone who died suddenly of unnatural causes might re-appear minutes, hours, days or even years later, in some other universe. Did Hitler wake up in another universe and cause havoc again? Would this finally lead to the abolition of capital punishment? Carlos explained that he believed that he 'owed' the world an explanation and would like to trigger a review of the relevant legislation to accommodate the theory. He repeated again however that he would understand if I didn't want to co-operate but that he was now more determined than ever to realise his life's ambition. He would just have to find someone else like me, however long it took.

I was beginning to understand Carlos much better. I now properly realised that he was fanatical and passionate in his quest but I nevertheless believed him when he said that he would respect my wishes. I knew that if I decided to co-operate fully with him it would mean approving his plan to publish all the evidence. Was I ready for that? Definitely not while I was still alive, I didn't want to be the focus of intense media, religious and Government attention, I wanted a simple normal 'rest of my life', as Conor. But what harm could it do if he waited until I had passed away? I need to think about it before I decide. No, I don't want to show him, or Mark for that matter, any of my photos, at least not at the moment.

"Carlos, thank you for providing that explanation, I do see the benefits of completing the investigation, but it won't benefit me, will it? I asked.

"Perhaps you can't see any personal benefits for yourself right now Mr F, but you might later get some satisfaction from knowing how much good you might achieve after you have passed away," said Carlos.

"Ok granted, perhaps I might," I replied, "but it could only be published after I am no longer here. What would happen if you die before me?" I asked.

"I've thought of that Ian, sorry Mr F," he replied. "We would need to prepare everything. We could draw up the necessary legally binding agreements between the three of us and ultimately authorise Mark to deal with it all, should I 'pass on' before you."

I nodded to show that I thought this 'sounded good' but I asked for a little more time to think it all through. I promised to give my final answer the following evening. Carlos said that he was very happy to wait and that he would accept my decision as 'final'.

"I'm still a little confused though Carlos," I said. "How will your visits to England, Belgium and Canada and meeting my former friends prove that I knew them in another universe? Wouldn't it instead indicate that I really am Conor and that I have been living there all these years?" I asked.

"It will depend on how I 'handle' all of the meetings I manage to arrange with them," he replied. "To recognise them I could do with copies of any available photos you have. I need to verify that they are who you say they are, but most importantly, I will need them to confirm that they have never met you and have never heard of you. The final step might be for you and I to return there and perhaps walk into some of the clubs and pubs you remember and see how many people you recognise there and whether anyone there recognises you. But we can't do that until you get your passport."

I thanked Carlos for his explanation and was pleased when Mark asked if he could join us to visit all my 'old' clubs and pubs in Canada, Belgium and England. I 'kind of' looked forward to it!

We broke up on friendly terms and Mark dropped me back to St John's. Nothing else was discussed during the journey, Mark said that he would pick me up at 5:45pm the next day.

Chapter 23

The three of us met up at 6:00pm the next evening, and every other evening for the rest of the week. I had decided to tell Carlos everything and to show him all of my photos. We decided to forget about playing golf together, Carlos said that he needed the whole day to prepare for each evening session.

I was much better prepared for this now and each evening I brought with me the notes I had prepared earlier whilst alone, in my room. I wanted to make sure I got everything correct!

Carlos was extremely happy to hear that I agreed to continue. He suggested that we look at the photos after I had finished 'doing my piece' to his camera.

"Mr F, rather than have you recount episodes of your life in chronological order, I suggest we 'mix it up a little', are you ok with that?" he asked.

When I responded that this would be fine, he asked me to tell him everything I could remember about the very first time I left Ireland to visit another country. I only had to think for a moment or two, before replying, I could remember every detail as if it happened only yesterday.

I excitedly related about the time my daddy brought me to see the 'big' horse race, the Prix De L'Arc De Triomphe in Paris, France. It was only Daddy, his business friend and me. I could still remember his friend's name to be Kevin Doyle. Mammy and Daddy regularly went horse racing in Ireland at that time and I occasionally went with them. The big race took place in October, I had already turned sixteen and as a reward for doing well in my college examination, the Intermediate Certificate, Daddy surprised me by telling me he was taking me to Paris. I was so excited at the thought of it all that I failed to notice how upset some of my brothers and sisters were that I had been 'singled out' for such a treat. My younger brother Patrick still talks today about him being told to 'go play in the sandpit' as the taxi arrived take us to Dublin airport. We flew early morning to Paris, on a day package, and were transported by coach straight to Longchamp racecourse. I spent the day in a dream. I had been bought a new suit and given a small amount of money to bet on the 'French Tote'. I thought I was the king of Paris that day, and I will forever treasure the photo I have (sorry had) of my daddy and me standing beside the parade ring, beaming in the bright sunshine. I'm afraid, we all backed the Irish horse Meadow Court in the big race, which was won by the favourite Sea Bird, who I still rank as the best horse I have ever seen race. We were supposed to take the coach back to the airport immediately after the big race but my daddy and his friend decided we would 'risk it' by staying for the next race, in which the Irish horse Red Slipper was a 'long odds chance'. The three of us put all the money we had left on Red Slipper and we were jumping and cheering when it won. We had to wait some time to collect our winnings, by which time our coach had left and we were stranded. My daddy organised a taxi and the driver 'drove like a madman' to get us to the airport on time. I remember going up one-way streets and driving on footpaths, with lots of other drivers honking their horns at us and our driver shaking his fist and shouting at them through his window. We got there 'in the nick of time' but my daddy said later that it cost him all of his winnings. It was a one-off unforgettable experience I shared with my daddy.

Carlos interrupted my story telling, by raising his right hand.

"What year did you say that was Mr F?" he asked.

"Let me think. I know that I was already sixteen and was already going out with Mary. I remember that she was really impressed when I told her about my trip to Paris, so it must have been 1965," I replied.

"You don't happen to have any photos of the trip downloaded on your phone," asked Carlos.

"Afraid not," I replied, "and my framed photo of my daddy and I that day, must now be in a parallel universe."

Carlos picked up his mobile and pushed some buttons.

"Spot on," he exclaimed, "Sea Bird won the Prix De L'Arc in 1965."

"You mentioned that Mary was impressed about your Paris trip Mr F, what do you remember about your wedding day?" he asked. "Was Mark there?"

"Yes of course he was, do you want to see the photos now?" I replied.

"Well I don't remember being there," said Mark, "and it's not something I would forget. I would love to see the photos right now."

"Patience Mark, said Carlos. "Let's hear about the wedding day before we look at the photos."

I hadn't related any details of our marriage for over forty years, I took my time…

"Mary and I got married in St Gabriel's Church in Clontarf, Dublin. It was Friday July 13th. Yes Friday 13th, neither of us were superstitious. We didn't settle on the wedding date until I had completed my final college exams and felt comfortable enough to book everything. By that time there wasn't a suitable hotel available for Saturday 14th, they were all already booked up. We had no trouble getting our preferred hotel, the Crofton Airport Hotel for Friday 13th. We decided to book a live band as we planned on having over one hundred guests, courtesy of Mary's daddy Frank. We knew quite a few local bands and we had a particular favourite, I can't remember the name now. The band was unfortunately already engaged for that night but they recommended another band, which we had never heard play, we had never even heard of them. We were reassured however that they were very good and were also a little less expensive. On the morning of the wedding Mary phoned me in a panic! Her mammy, Josephine, had just taken a call from the band we had booked, their lead singer had woken up with a very sore throat and couldn't sing that evening. Mary told me that her mammy was 'screaming' that she knew something would go wrong, why did we have to get married on Friday 13th! Mary told me that her mammy hung up on the caller, she couldn't listen any more. I called the band manager. He apologised and confirmed what the problem was but he said he wouldn't let us down. He explained that he had already 'called in some favours' and had succeeded in getting another band to change their schedule and replace our band. I laughed when he told me that our band was going to be replaced by the very band that we tried to book in the first place. The band manager said that the 'replacement band' usually charge more but that they would only charge the agreed amount. What a result! Friday the 13th and all! I called Mary and she was 'over the moon' with the news but she later told me that her mammy was still convinced that the panic she felt that morning was because it was Friday 13th. The church service went well, Mary's sister Ann was her bridesmaid and my brother Peter was my best man. The sun shone brilliantly during the taking of the usual photos and Mary looked happy and radiant in every photo. The reception that night was a brilliant party, against my advice, Mary's daddy decided to pay for a 'free bar' for the whole duration. Ok, a few people got a bit 'merry' but everyone let their hair down and seemed to enjoy themselves. At one point I remember seeing my sister Jean doing a very lively jive with Mary's brother Derek. They were getting more and more energetic until finally they both ended up 'in a heap' in the middle of the dance floor. The band stopped playing for a minute or so, while Jean and Derek got back to their feet, trying but failing to hide their embarrassment. Everyone, except Mary's mammy went into hysterics with laughter. Later in the evening, I needed to pay a visit to the Gents. When I entered, I saw my brother Louis sitting on the floor, propped up between two of the porcelain wash basins. His knees were pulled up under his chin, his eyes were partially open and he had a permanent smile on his face. He told me that this was the best party he had ever been to. Louis resisted all my efforts to get him to stand up to re-join the party, so in the end I just left him sitting there, still smiling and still thanking me. Somebody must have later come to his rescue because he wasn't there when I returned an hour or so later.

Mary and I were enjoying the party so much they we may have been among the last to leave. Lying in our bed that night in the bridal suite, I mentioned to Mary that her mother was totally wrong. Friday the 13th was a great day to get married. Mary replied, in a jokey manner that there was still plenty of time for things to go wrong. Minutes later, I swear I could hear someone knocking on the outside of the bedroom window. I always knew that Mary's brother Paul would try to play a trick on us, so I jumped out of bed and pulled back the curtains. I fully expected to see Paul standing there grinning but instead I could see car lights moving along the road, seven floors below. I jumped back into bed and we both laughed out loud for ages. Certainly, a day never to be forgotten Carlos, and lots of our friends and relations later told us that our band was the best they had ever heard playing live."

"But you can't remember the band's name Mr F?" asked Carlos.

"No, I am afraid not," I replied.

"Can we see the wedding photos now Conor, I can't wait any longer?" asked Mark.

We all stood up and huddled around my mobile phone as I opened up the wedding album photos. Mark almost collapsed when he saw himself standing there in his smart bright blue suit beside his twin sister Fiona, both beaming. Carlos asked me to name each person in each photo and there must have been close to one hundred of them in total. Mark could hardly speak, he just kept nodding to confirm the identities. He mentioned that Mary looked exactly like a younger version of Mary Kenny.

Mark insisted that we go through each photo several times. He kept saying that he knows that he wasn't at the wedding, but now, here he was, looking at photo after photo of, not only him, but of his parents, brothers, sisters, aunts and uncles.

"Jesus Conor, I now really appreciate what you are going through," exclaimed Mark.

"Mark, can you confirm that Mr F has correctly identified everyone?" asked Carlos.

"Well I certainly recognise all my family, but I don't recognise the groom, replied Mark.

"No, of course you don't Mark," said Carlos. "In our universe your brother Ian had been dead about twelve years before this photo of him was taken. He had died Mark, years before you were born!"

"Jesus guys, this is getting unreal," said Mark. "I know that I said I believed in all this crazy stuff, but looking at photos of myself at a wedding I know I wasn't at, standing next to an older brother who I know wasn't alive at the time, is just….is just, well, .. mind boggling. It has just made it all so real for me and I'm not sure I can handle it."

Carlos decided that we needed a break, so we all retired to the bar. We sat there sipping our drinks, no one spoke. Mark sat on one end of the couch, staring straight at me. Eventually Carlos brought the session to an end, suggesting that we adjourn until the next evening. I agreed that I would next talk about my life in Belgium and England.

Mark picked me up at the usual time next evening and we drove in eerie silence to Carlos' hotel.

"Ok, Mr F, you can begin whenever you wish but I suggest we wait until you have finished speaking, before we look at any more of your album photos," said Carlos.

I related as much as I could remember about my ten years in Belgium. I told them that I started work as an Industrial Engineer at the company's factory in Ieper, Belgium. Klippan, which was part of Allied Chemical Corporation, had factories in eight different European countries, but the factory in Belgium was the largest. I was one of five industrial engineers in the department, two locals and three Irish nationals, Brendan, Tom and me. We became very friendly with Brendan and his wife Gabriel. At its peak the factory had over eleven hundred employees and made seat belts for almost every type of car. It was high volume production with lots of automation, at one point we were manufacturing twenty-two thousand seat belts daily. Mary and I rented an apartment in a town called Roeselare, about a half hour's drive away, north of Ieper. Brendan and Gabriel took an apartment in the same building as us, so Brendan and I regularly car-shared. I think Mary was very happy with her life at this time. She had Gabriel for company and appreciated her help with our son John. At over six foot five and very 'Irish looking' with his fair complexion and full head of ginger hair, Brendan stood out from others. His great sense of humour kept us entertained on the many nights out we had together. Gabriel became great friends with Mary, they were of similar age and shared the same interests. Gabriel is quite a bit taller than Mary but her short blond hair and similar fashion sense, made them look like sisters, rather than just friends. Our daughter Annette was born in the 'Moeder Huis' in Roeselare. The apartment was, by then, a little too crowded for the four of us, so we rented a really nice new house in a village called 'Vlamertinge', which is just a few miles south of Ieper. Work was great and our home life was full of excitement. Mary was brilliant at making friends with many of our neighbours and we still met up with Brendan and Gabriel on a regular basis.

"Mr F, do you still remember your addresses in Roeselare and Vlamertinge and are you still in touch with Brendan and Gabriel?" asked Carlos.

"Yes, we are still in touch with Gabriel and their three children but unfortunately Brendan died at a very young age, many years ago."

"Mr F, when you have finished telling us about your life in Belgium, could I ask you to write down the names and addresses of everyone you can remember there?" asked Carlos.

I resumed my story. I explained that after almost six years working at the factory in Ieper that I became bored with the job. Most of the investment had been made, the new product line had been introduced and my work now was mostly routine.

I accepted a new job in a town called Leuven, or Louvain as it is called in English. We moved to a beautiful, but rather dark, rented house in a small village called Rotselaar-Heikant. By this time Brendan was working at the Klippan HQ, which was also in Leuven and he and Gabriel were renting a house nearby. We continued meeting regularly and shared some great times. My job as Group Industrial Engineering Manager for Donaldson, meant I had to travel regularly to their factories in France, Germany and England. John and Annette went to the local primary school and although they always spoke English to Mary and I, they usually spoke Dutch to each other. Surely, we were now finally settled down, life and work were great and, as usual, Mary wasted no time in getting to know our neighbours. We had lots of new friends, most of them were parents of children who played with John and Annette. We started a volleyball club which drew all of us even closer together. Our 'group' occasionally went on holidays together and partied regularly.

"Mr F, do you remember any of the names of people in your social group?" asked Carlos.

"Yes, of course I do. We are still in touch with many of them and I have photos of some of them," I replied.

Carlos handed me more blank paper and the ballpoint pen again. I wrote down all I could remember. We enjoyed lots of good times with Ann and Leo, Geoffrey and Griet, Jan and Jacinta plus many more couples whose names I recalled and jotted down.

"So why did you desert this seemingly idyllic lifestyle Conor?" asked Mark.

"Donaldson decided to expand their factory in Hull, England and I accepted the position of Plant Manager," I replied.

"But what about your children Conor, what about leaving all their friends and the fact that their first language was, by then, Dutch," asked Mark.

I explained that it was a difficult decision to make, especially after almost four years in the community and having just two months earlier purchased the house, which we had been renting, but it was a golden opportunity which might never be repeated and that we just couldn't turn it down.

"So how did your children adapt to life in England Conor?" asked Mark. "Did they need much support?"

"We were lucky enough to quickly sell our house in Belgium and so had the deposit for a small bungalow in Beverley, which is close to Kingston-Upon-Hull. John and Annette went to the local school in Beverley and they seemed to have no trouble settling into their new surroundings. For whatever reason, Annette put Belgium 'behind her' but John retained his interest in Dutch, which continues to this day," I answered.

"What was life like for your family in Beverley Mr F?" asked Carlos.

I decided to keep it brief this time and explained that, once again, Mary quickly made friends with our neighbours but that we have since lost touch with all of them and that I couldn't even remember their names. Work was exciting but our home life was more mundane than it had been in Belgium.

"So how long did you stay there Mr F?" asked Carlos. "Why did you move to Buckingham?"

"We lived in Beverley for almost four years and the company went from strength to strength. After a few years however, I started to clash with my new boss, who was based in Belgium. I was openly sceptical about the direction I was receiving and I made no attempt to conceal my dissatisfaction," I replied.

"Did you leave or were you pushed Conor?" asked Mark.

"Well, eventually I did find another job," I replied. "I was asked to leave and I did so, as they say, by mutual consent! When I later related to my Father-In-Law how I came to lose my job, he said he knew exactly how it ended:"

"Ian, the simple truth is that you must have been talking when you should have been listening!"

"Did you then move to Buckingham, where you still live Mr F?" asked Carlos.

I told them about how I accepted a job in a then small engineering company called 'Broadways Stampings' and shortly afterwards I was promoted to the position of Managing Director.

Carlos suddenly interrupted me:

"Mr F, at this stage you don't need to tell us all about the company, we can get to that later," he said, rather impatiently. "Could you just write down the dates you worked at the company and the names of all of the people you can still remember."

When I silently completed this assigned task, I handed the paper back to Carlos.

"Mr F, while you are at it could you please write down the names of your current neighbours and the contact details of some of your closest friends?" added Carlos.

I referred to my notes and then wrote down the addresses for Barney and Jill, Richard and Ada, Graham and Tracey, Richard and Joyce, John and Sue and several more friends with whom we regularly meet.

"When did you retire from Broadways Mr F?" asked Carlos.

"I didn't retire from Broadways," I replied. "After a very fruitful and enjoyable twelve years there, I was head hunted and eventually accepted the position of Managing Director of a small engineering company in Witney, Oxfordshire."

"But Conor, I thought that you still live in Buckingham," said Mark.

"Yes, we do, but Witney is less than an hour's drive away, not worth uprooting everybody again!"

Carlos slid more blank paper and the pen over to me and said:

"Mr F, can I ask you to do the same again? Please write down the details of the people you worked with."

It took me a little while to jot down the details.

I told them all about my twelve-year career with DEL Equipment in Witney. Really enjoyable time, initially reporting to Ken and then a couple of years later to Michael. Michael ran the businesses in Canada and the USA and I took care of business in England. Michael and I met three or four times a year, mostly to go through business ideas on some of the best golf courses in England, Ireland, Canada and the USA.

"So where do you play golf now?" asked Carlos. "Are you a member there?"

"Mary and I recently joined Silverstone Golf Club, near Buckingham. Previously we were members of Whittlebury Golf Club for many years," I replied.

I was again asked to write down the names of our golfing friends at both Silverstone and Whittlebury. Without being asked, I also gave the names of our friends in our 'local pub' with all the addresses I could recall.

"So why did you leave DEL Conor?" asked Mark. "Why did you 'pack it in?"

I explained that Michael, as planned, sold his independent family business to a large Finnish multinational engineering company. Part of the deal was that I 'signed on' for five more years. This led to me accepting a much broader role in the global business. I travelled regularly and worked in their factories in countries like China, Sweden, Denmark and Poland. Although the experience was brilliant and the role extremely rewarding and fulfilling, I knew that I couldn't keep going forever so I decided to retire at sixty-four years of age. I wanted to spend more time with family and friends.

"You must have then struggled to keep yourself busy Conor," said Mark.

"No, not at all," I replied. "Quite the opposite in fact. When I retired, I took guitar lessons and now play almost every day, I play more golf in all kinds of weather, Mary and I go on several holidays each year and most satisfying of all, Mary and I spend lots of time with our grandchildren."

Another clean sheet of paper was provided and, as requested, I wrote down where my grandchildren went to school.

On the final evening Carlos summed up what we needed to do for the next few weeks while he was back in England.

Carlos asked me to give Mark a tour of the places in Ireland, which I had told them about, and to try to 'accidentally' bump into as many of the people I said that I knew in my teens and early twenties. He asked Mark to make notes about all of the encounters and to make sure that we included visits to my secondary school, all places where I said I worked during my student days, the engineering college I said I graduated from, Mary's parent's house, the church where we were married, the hotel where the wedding reception was held, my friends names and where they lived, Mary's brothers and sister and anyplace or anybody I thought might add credence to 'my story'. If possible, Mark was to 'secretly' take photos as we went along and we would later compare these photos with the dated historical photos already on my i-Phone. We were to take care not to raise suspicions but we needed to confirm if all of the places and people, I said I knew, still existed and that they were accurate. Of vital importance was to confirm that none of the people we met, had ever heard of me or actually recognised me. Confirm that there is no written or verbal evidence that I ever attended any of the schools and that there was no record of the wedding ceremony or the wedding reception.

Carlos told us that he planned to visit as many of the places and meet as many of the people I spoke about in England. He asked Mark to take a photo of Carlos and I standing beside each other and to e-mail it to his phone. He intended showing the photo to anyone who showed interest and to ask them if they recognised me. He said he would definitely visit the golf clubs, my former places of work, the pubs Mary and I went to and the football club we were season ticket holders of. He would try to chat to as many people as possible to confirm their identities and that they had never heard of me. I e-mailed Carlos lots of relevant photos of my friends, making sure I was not in any of these photos. Carlos said that he would visit our son's and our daughter's houses and take photos, again to compare with my i-Phone photos. I told him that the best pubs to visit would be The Wheatsheaf in Maids Morton and The Bull and Butcher in Akeley, where on a Sunday afternoon he might see Paul play his right-handed guitar using his left hand. Paul had reversed the strings so he could play it upside down. Carlos said that he would visit the Bull and Butcher because it is a little detail like that, which could be compelling evidence. I suggested to Carlos that he should try to buy our friends Tracey and Graham a drink in the Wheatsheaf. I suggested that Graham would first taste a drop of the latest real ale before ordering a pint of it and that Tracey would order a medium Pinot Grigio with 'just' one block of ice! Carlos said he would check this out and would take as many photos of places and people as he dared. He said that at a later date he thought it would be a good idea for me to accompany him to all the same places to support his evidence. We agreed that later, after I had obtained my passport that all three of us would repeat the process in Belgium and Canada and maybe even Sweden.

Carlos said that he thought he needed maybe three weeks in England and would contact Mark before he returned. He asked me to prepare, while he was away, as detailed a description of my past universe as I could. He said that he was already aware of my accounts of the different religious and political differences and that I seemed to know some songs which nobody else had ever heard of but he wondered if there were any notable scientific or medical breakthroughs in my universe which hadn't yet been discovered in his universe.

"Don't tell me anything now Mr F, take some time and write down every breakthrough you can think of," he said. "Don't worry about whether the breakthroughs were also made in our world Mr F, I will check everything out when I get back from my travels."

He added that it could be very useful, maybe even very profitable, if I wrote down the names of all the pop songs that I could remember. He asked Mark to check out all of the songs and related artists on the internet and if he found out they didn't exist he wanted him to record me playing them on my guitar.

"Who knows," he smiled, "maybe Mr F, you will become rich and famous as the writer of lots of hit records!"

With Carlos seemingly in jovial mood, I decided to ask him again about ghosts and poltergeists, did he believe in them? He explained that he did consider investigating some of the more well known and most often reported spirit phenomena but that he thought he would have more success concentrating on the, more easily verified, Many Lives Interpretation. He admitted that he believed that the evidence for poltergeists is really compelling but that he has no idea what they might be. He said that it was possible, maybe even likely, that there are other invisible entities all around us but as to what they are and why they throw things around, he has no idea as they don't communicate with us. With regard to ghosts, he has already concluded that some people do see them but since communication with them has never been possible, he doesn't want to waste any time trying to find plausible explanations. He said that he noted one similarity with his field of study because all the ghosts he has ever heard of, are supposedly spirits of people who met untimely and grisly ends. He pointed out however some major differences because it seems that ghosts don't age, don't change clothes, don't eat, don't drink, don't see us, don't speak, don't laugh, don't cry, don't move from their place of 'haunting' but they can walk through walls which perhaps didn't exist in their lifetime. They never stop to read any written messages we leave them and haven't yet left us any written messages, except, of course, in Hollywood movies.

"In short Mr F, they are boring entities who, for some unknown reason, are condemned to repeating some boring activity forever, whether we are there to observe their presence or not," said Carlos. "Maybe even after the world has ceased to be."

"But you must have some theory about these ghosts Carlos?" I asked.

"Well, I once wondered if they are 'essences' of real people who died 'before their time' in their universe and whose spirit managed to come back from the other dimension but whose body failed to re-appear," he replied. "But since I've no way to investigate this, it will always be conjecture."

We said goodnight to Carlos, who said he needed some sleep before his early flight to Heathrow next morning.

Mark told me that he wouldn't be able to meet me next day but that he would pick me up at the usual time on Tuesday morning for our usual game of golf.

Chapter 24

I spent all day Monday 'working' on the instructions left by Carlos. I opened the blank notebook, which Carlos had given me, and I listed dozens of songs I knew some of the chords and most of the lyrics of. I covered a diverse range of artists starting with 'household' names like Frank Sinatra and Elvis Presley, gradually adding acts from the seventies, eighties, nineties and concluding with the present day. I thought that the list would provide Mark with plenty of material for internet search. In the afternoon I played some of the songs on my guitar, I couldn't believe how many chords and lyrics I could still remember. I later took a stroll in the gardens and even ventured outside and had a couple of pints of Harp larger in the Summit Inn. I was exhausted by the time I got into bed but I just couldn't sleep.

I couldn't stop thinking about what I would say when I meet Mary at golf tomorrow. Why did I sing that stupid song *Arms of Mary*. I can't 'balls it up' this time, it might be my last chance. I need to have a plan, yes, I definitely need a plan and also a 'plan B' in case plan A doesn't go as well as I dared dream about. Mike Tyson's response to a question from a 'pushy' boxing reporter immediately came to mind.

Reporter: *"I hear your opponent has a clever plan for defending your left hook. How do you respond?"*

Mike Tyson: *"Everyone has a plan until they get punched in the face."*

No, I didn't expect that Mary would punch me in the face, but she might be capable of plunging a proverbial dagger through my heart.

Early next morning, Mark and I pulled into the car park at St Anne's Golf Links. His mobile phone rang just as he switched off the engine. He got out of the car to take the call. He was back within seconds and told me that he had a problem to deal with. He explained that he needed to go straight back to work for an 'emergency' meeting. He didn't know how long it would take, did I want to go back with him or did I want to play some holes on my own? I quickly changed into my golf shoes and took my clubs and golf trolley out of his car. Mark rolled down his window and handed me a 'wad' of bank notes.

"Best if you take a taxi home Conor," said Mark. "I'm not sure when, or even if, I will get back."

"Ok, don't worry about me," I replied hastily. "I'll be fine."

I paid my green fee and explained to the golf professional, Dave, that I was on my own as Mark had to leave suddenly.

"I'm afraid you are going to be behind the four 'snails' again Conor, do you want me to ask the three ladies behind you if you could join them? Otherwise you will be 'hanging around' all day."

Thirty minutes or so later I teed off and walked over to the ladies' tee. Mary, Jenny and Brenda had immediately said it would be ok for me to join them but I couldn't help thinking that I was intruding on their 'women's talk'.

By about the third hole I was starting to relax. No, I wasn't imagining it, Mary was definitely trying to include me in their conversation and soon it was Brenda walking alongside Jenny and Mary walking alongside me. Mary was again talking about her home life. All was definitely not well for her at home. The breeze was starting to pick up and the sky quickly clouded over. Without warning the 'heavens opened' and the rain started to pour down. As the ladies quickly 'donned' their 'wet gear', I realised that I had left mine on the back seat of Mark's car. I didn't even have an umbrella. We all tried to play on through the rain but it was becoming very difficult. Mary offered me her umbrella because she had her waterproofs on, but I was already soaked through, so no point. I certainly wasn't going to be the first one to quit so I drudged on, getting wetter and wetter by the minute. After nine holes we were back near the clubhouse and I must have looked a 'sorry sight'. I think Brenda knew what was going on and probably felt sorry for me. She suggested that we all pack it in for the day, it wasn't worth getting pneumonia over a game of golf, she said. It was still raining when we arrived back at the car park but I had nowhere to put my clubs. I accepted Mary's offer and put my clubs and trolley into her car boot, placing them carefully on top of her's. Only then did it occur to me that I had left my shoes in Mark's boot. I had to keep my soaking-wet golf shoes on, so I would not be allowed to go up to the club lounge. Shit, I said to myself, what an idiot! I really am losing the plot! I explained my predicament to Mary and asked her if she would mind calling me a taxi while I took my clubs back out of her boot. She looked directly at me for a few seconds and then said:

"Conor, why don't I drop you back home, the sooner you get out of those wet clothes, the better. I have nothing else planned for the rest of the day and it's not a hundred miles away, is it. Where do you live anyway?"

"Christ Mary, it's a long way out of your way, are you sure?" I said in surprise. "It's no problem to get a taxi, honestly."

"Would you prefer to get a taxi?" asked Mary.

"No, of course not," I replied, "but I thought you would like to have a chat with your lady friends up in the bar."

"To be honest Conor, I prefer chatting to you," smiled Mary.

Mary told Brenda and Jenny what she was planning to do. I saw them shaking hands and then she came back to her car. She changed out of her golf shoes and removing her waterproofs she threw them onto the floor between the driver seat and the back seat of her car. Off we drove towards

Howth. She drove slowly, she clearly wasn't in a hurry.

"Conor, what was that song all about," asked Mary, after just a couple of minutes driving.

"It was about what I imagined it was like when my brother Patrick left for America, aged just twenty," I replied.

I daren't presume she was asking about *Arms of Mary*.

"No, not that one Conor," she interrupted. "The other one, the one about Mary."

'What do you think it was about Mary? I asked.

"I'm going to sound ridiculous now Conor, and I might be deluded, but I think you were trying to get a message to me," she answered.

"How do you mean Mary?" I was now playing 'hard to get'.

"Conor, I know what's going on. Since you first 'arrived on the scene' I have been 'googling' parallel universes and the theory about the multiverse. I can't say I understand any of it but I think that you believe that you were once married to me. But not here, rather in a parallel universe," explained Mary.

This was going to be easier to talk about, than I first thought.

"Mary, not so much once married to you, I still might be," I replied. "Unless I died on that park bench on Howth promenade. However, unfortunately Mary, we are obviously not married in this universe that I now find myself in."

"Why do you say unfortunately, Conor?" asked Mary.

Was she mocking me? I wondered.

During the drive to Howth we chatted openly and freely. As we came to Sutton Cross she suddenly turned left and parked outside Quinn's Supermarket. She asked me to wait in the car while she picked up something she needed. She was gone just a couple of minutes but the cold started to penetrate my bones, I needed to get out of these damp clothes as quickly as possible. Back in the car Mary continued where she left off, she wanted to know everything about my former life with, who she called, her 'other self'. It took me a little while to fully 'take in' that she was taking it all quite seriously, as the more I told her, the more she wanted to know. When she asked me if the 'other Mary' was prettier and more desirable than her, I told her that, if she wanted, I would show her a photo of Mary Forman when we got to the support centre.

Mary carried my golf trolley and I carried my golf clubs to my private room. She did not appear to be at all nervous, unlike me. She suggested that I get out of my wet clothes and take a shower.

When I had finished showering, I dried myself and put on my white bathrobe which, luckily, was always hanging on the back of the bathroom door. I hadn't thought about taking a change of clothes into the bathroom with me, hopefully Mary wouldn't 'read anything into' me coming out of the bathroom in a bathrobe. When I came out, I saw that Mary had taken her shoes and her, probably damp, golf jumper off. She was propped up on my single bed, with her head resting on my two pillows. She was smoking one of those 'government issue' marijuana 'joints' and seemed extremely relaxed. She had, what I can only describe as, a mischievous smile on her face.

"Conor, I really like your room, how long do you plan to stay here?" she asked. "It must be costing a fortune."

I replied that I wasn't sure how long more I would be in St John's but since I wasn't receiving any treatment, that I didn't think it would be for much longer. I explained that I was 'at the mercy' of my family, they made my decisions for me.

"Can I see that photo of my prettier 'other self' then Conor?" she asked.

I took my i-Phone from my bedside drawer and opened it up. Didn't take long to find that photo of Mary and I, posing in our hotel room in the Marine Hotel. I leaned over to show Mary the photo. She slid over on the blue and yellow duvet, inviting me to lie beside her to look at the photo. She was genuinely shocked at what she saw.

"That's me!" she exclaimed. "How can it be?"

I showed her more of the photos in my phone, but I was a bit surprised, disappointed even, when she showed little interest in my children or grandchildren. Mary lit up another 'joint' and, asking me to put my phone down, she asked me to lie beside her, for a 'smoke'. She wanted to know all about my life with 'her other much luckier self', as she now called 'my Mary'.

"Conor, I don't mind telling you that my home life is total 'crap'. Joe is paralysed from the waist down and is too depressed to go out anywhere. If it wasn't for my friends at the golf club, I would go mad," confessed Mary. "Have you and my 'other self' been anywhere 'exotic' Conor? I imagine that you have both been on lots of golf holidays."

"I suppose we have Mary, we both enjoyed golf, maybe still do somewhere else," I replied.

As we both lay there on the single bed, puffing away on our 'legal joints', I told Mary about some of the places I had visited with her 'other self'. Don't know if the marijuana was helping but Mary seemed to be 'living' the experiences I was telling her about. I think she most enjoyed hearing about the three weeks we spent, with eight other couples, on a golf trip to Capetown. We golfed every other day and did the other normal 'tourist things' the other days. I think I saw tears in her eyes as I spoke about our emotional trip to Robin's Island and about standing in Nelson Mandela's tiny cell. I 'lightened it up' by telling her about how our friend Mike was frightened as I stood up in the cable-car as we ascended Table Mountain. He had to close his eyes and 'cling on' to his wife Joy.

Our two-week golf trip to Argentina with three other couples took some time to relate. She wanted to hear all about our visit to Eva Peron's grave, our horse riding at a gaucho ranch, our internal flight from Buenos Aires to Mendoza to visit several 'Malbec' vineyards, where we ate and drank far too much. She wasn't surprised when I told her that Mary quickly got out of breath when we got out of the bus to walk over to the border with Peru. She had to get back in the bus to sit down, it is difficult to breathe when you are half way up the Andes!

I thought about which event to talk about next. At the rate I was speaking it would take forever. She wouldn't let me skip over any details. She listened about our golf trip to Thailand, together with our elephant ride and about how Mary and our three other lady golfing companions jumped up on stage to sing *Rolling Down the River* with the resident female singer, at a rather seedy night club in Pattaya. I suppose I always took these trips 'for granted' but as I was relating all of these experiences, I think I appreciated them even more than the first time around. Trips to Brisbane and Sydney; walking on the Great Wall Of China; a Mediterranean Cruise which took in Venice and Dubrovnik; a river cruise which started from Budapest and took in Vienna; visiting Niagara Falls with Mary's parents; golf holidays in Spain, Portugal and Tenerife; becoming completely overwhelmed again each time I strolled amongst the seemingly countless white gravestones in the first world war cemetery outside Ieper. Mary interrupted me in order to light up the other two 'joints'. She commented on how I seemed to be enjoying the 'joint' so much.

"Conor, have you never taken any drugs before?" she asked. "I can't believe this is your first ever time."

"No, I've never tried any type of drugs before," I honestly replied.

I awoke to the sound of the pump from the power shower. Shortly after the shower stopped, Mary walked out of my bathroom draped only in a large white bath towel. She lay down on the single bed next to me.

"Do you want me to continue telling you about the many places Mary and I visited, or are you bored with it all?" I asked.

"Conor, I don't just want to hear all about them, I want to live them!" she replied. She continued ... "I'm not so sure about riding an elephant in Thailand or horse riding on a gaucho ranch in Argentina but I want to experience everything else that you have already done with my 'other self'. I want to immerse myself in the sights, sounds and smells of walking through the old market place in Jerusalem; I can't wait to peer over Niagara Falls; stroll on the Great Wall of China; cruise up the Danube; climb the Eiffel Tower; lie back in a gondola in Venice; play golf in Thailand, Spain, Tenerife and Portugal; sip Malbec in Mendoza; visit Eva Perone's grave in Buenos Aires; watch the New Year's Eve fireworks over Sydney Harbour Bridge; hike down Table Mountain; pay homage to the great man as I stand in the middle of Nelson Mandela's cell; walk down

Hollywood Boulevard. Conor, I want to do everything else you told me about and everything else you haven't yet told me about. When can we leave?"

"Conor, did you have any holidays booked for this year, would you prefer us to go somewhere new?" she added excitedly.

"Well, yes we had," I replied quietly. "We booked a three-week river cruise on the Mekong River. First flying to Singapore, then to Ho Chi Min City, or Saigon as you probably know it. We would have called in on, and walked through lots of small villages and finish up in Angor Wat before flying home from Siem Reap."

"Oh my God Conor, let's do it now," gleamed Mary. "Do you want me to book it up?"

Mary took me completely by surprise! When she came out of my bath room I thought she would talk about feelings of guilt and tell me that she could never see me again. Far from it, she had already planned some new adventures with me.

"But Mary you are married to Joe, who I think completely depends on you," I said.

"Depressed Joe and his ruffian son can both 'shag off'. I've had enough of both of them! It's time I started to live my own life. I only wish you had come along years ago. But at least, finally, you are here now."

Mary was clearly excited. She went on to explain that as she stood under the shower, she figured it all out. She would divorce Joe, sell their house plus the business and simply take off. Hopefully never have to see or talk to either Joe or Jonjo again.

"But Joe will never agree to a divorce Mary, he depends on you."

I was trying to calm down Mary, she clearly hadn't thought things through!

"Oh, he will agree to a divorce all right, especially after I tell him what I have been doing all afternoon and how much I am looking forward to our next get-together," she smiled.

"Jesus Mary, he might kill you rather than divorce you," I whispered.

"Conor, are you 'up for this or not', it sounds like you are having second thoughts. I'm already sixty-seven, yes I may be reasonably fit but for how many more years will we be physically fit to travel around the world, I have no time left to fart around."

Mary was becoming more and more animated.

I got up from the bed and started to pace around the room, trying to organise my thoughts as quickly as I could. I noticed that Mary was a little more subdued now.

"Conor, if you are worried about the money, I can more than 'pay my way'. I reckon I will end up with close to four hundred thousand Pride when the divorce is finalised. I don't care if we 'blow it all', I want to live before I die," she enthused.

I sat back down on the edge of the bed and looked directly at Mary. She seemed to be 'high' on something. Was this all just the result of the marijuana, I wondered. I didn't think so though, she seemed too lucid and she had a plan. Where's Mike Tyson when you need him?

"Conor, was this just a 'one afternoon fling' for you? I really thought that you wanted to be with me, you certainly gave that impression. Even Jenny and Brenda commented on your persistent 'interest' in me. Did I read your motives all wrong?" asked Mary.

"No, you didn't read me wrong Mary. I very much want to spend the rest of my life with you. It's just I wasn't expecting it to develop this suddenly. I was fully expecting to have to, as they say, woo you. In truth, I didn't think I would even succeed. I couldn't see what I had to offer! Mary I'm not worried about the money, I'm told I will soon receive a large monthly allowance from my daddy's will. Between us, I suppose we could afford to have a holiday for the rest of our lives," I said slowly.

"Great, let me get the ball rolling," said Mary, as she jumped up and dressed herself in just a couple of seconds. "I can't wait to see Joe's face when I give him the good news," she giggled.

Mary left me in a hurry. Could she really get divorced and sell everything in just two or three months as she said? Why was I feeling 'rushed' and pressurised? Hadn't I succeeded beyond my wildest dreams in getting Mary back. Why wasn't I jumping up and down with joy!

Mary not only left me in a hurry, she also left me in turmoil. Who was this woman? This is not how 'my Mary' would behave. She almost frightened me. Yes, she did frighten me but she also excited me. Maybe I can sort-of understand her excitement, she really believed she would be starting a new life with a new adoring partner, but what about me? I would be embarking on a new venture with someone who looks like Mary but she's not 'my Mary'. She is a married woman, who I have just met, and I have no idea what she is really like. Someone who was prepared to quickly 'drop' her needy husband, at the first opportunity. 'My Mary' just wouldn't do this! Why can't she be like 'my Mary'? Why do I feel I would be cheating on 'my Mary' if I started a new life with this new Mary? I feel sorry for Joe, perhaps he needs her more than I do.

I was still lying on my tossed bed, happy but confused, when a good half an hour later, there was a knock on my room door. Mary stood there with her arms straight down by her side. I could see she was distressed, had probably been crying. She came in and sat down on the side of my bed, her eyes avoided mine, she kept looking down at the floor. She started to cry again, I could see her shoulders shake. I was never much good in situations like this, I knew the proper thing to do would be to sit down beside her and put my arm around her shoulders but I was always awkward when alone in the presence of a woman crying. I walked into the bathroom and returned with a glass of tap water. She was now standing up and was drying her tears in a damp tissue.

"Conor, please forgive me," she sobbed. "I have made a terrible mistake. I never should have come to your room today. I'm really sorry that I led you astray, I think that 'joint' turned my head. This can't happen again Conor, I'm feeling far too guilty and very unhappy."

"But you bought the 'joints' Mary," I blurted out. "You must have had this in mind all along."

What a stupid thing to say, I thought. I really was good at speaking before thinking, I'm great at making a bad situation even worse!

My response really shook Mary. She immediately went on the defensive. She apologised for her behaviour and said that she hoped I wasn't angry with her. She explained that this could never happen again, that her priority was to look after her loving husband Joe, for the rest of her life. She didn't think that she would ever forgive herself and that if Joe or Jonjo ever heard about it, her world would be ruined, her life would be ruined, and her reason for living would cease to exist. She said that we could never meet again and added that she was going to give up golf so we didn't bump into each other again. She asked me if I could 'keep our secret' and half-smiled when I re-assured her that I could and I would. She promised that she would never ever talk to anyone about me, I didn't need to worry about that. I told her that it wasn't necessary for her to give up golf, she needed to continue to meet her friends. I said that I wasn't 'that bothered' about golf and promised not to play at St Anne's Golf Club again. Mary bowed her head to silently thank me and turned away to leave.

"Mary you needn't have apologised to me for your behaviour," I said. "I enjoy every minute I spend with you, just chatting over a cup of coffee would make me happy, that's all I need. But I'm sure you are right, you can do without even more 'grief'. I understand and appreciate your loyalty Mary, I'm really sorry that I put you in this position. I promise not to pester you again."

Mary didn't look back as she walked out the door and out of my life. She didn't respond, without looking back she raised her right hand in the air and waved. She didn't even bother to close the door behind her.

I closed the door and sat down on the edge of my bed and stared straight ahead. I resisted the temptation to watch her drive away, just too final! What now I thought? I've cocked up again, Christ there is no hope for me! I was surprised however that I didn't feel totally devastated, I should be, after all I had just been rejected and condemned to live the rest of my life without Mary. So why did I feel better now than I did when Mary was all excited and talking about leaving Joe and holidaying with me? Maybe I felt that I was 'let off the hook'? Was I having second thoughts about Mary number two anyway? Was I relieved? I drank down the full glass of water, which Mary had ignored, in one gulp. I don't know why, I wasn't thirsty. Perhaps I saw it as 'drawing a line' under this agonising experience. Mary had shunned the glass of water, just as she was going to shun me. I needed to get some fresh air quickly, I felt sick. Was I feeling the effects of the 'joints' or was I just sick at the thought of the dull and lonely life ahead of me?

    Out in the garden I sat on my favourite bench and closed my eyes. I tried to think it all through, what was today all about? Was it just a 'one off' few hours of drug induced madness? I liked Mary number two, I really liked her. She was just like my Mary, she wasn't prepared to abandon Joe, he needed her and she wouldn't let him down. I loved her for that, I loved her for being like my Mary. I now knew for sure that I wanted to be with her more than ever, but felt even less confident I ever would be. I need a new plan and this time I can't rush it. I will probably fail but it won't be for the want of trying. Sympathetic as I am to Joe and Jonjo, my only chance is to be totally selfish. At least I now know that she is interested in foreign holidays, maybe I do have something to offer after all, but is that enough? I realised that a future with Mary number two would not be all 'peaches and cream', some people would get hurt and I know that Mary is a sensitive loving person, I think she would forever regret hurting Joe. Could a future together be truly fulfilling? What happens when one of us is no longer fit enough to travel to exotic places, would we still be happy just sitting on the sofa watching TV together? Am I being selfish by wanting to be happy again? So, what if I am being selfish? Why should I put Joe's happiness ahead of mine anyway? Ok, maybe I can 'get over' upsetting Joe and Jonjo, but what about Mary's happiness? Hadn't she said that she loved Joe and wanted to take care of him! Hadn't she said that she was very unhappy and regretted spending the afternoon with me! Hadn't she said she never wanted to see me again! Wasn't she crying openly and feeling very miserable! What should I do? I don't want to make Mary's life sad. I want her to be happy. But I don't believe her, I don't believe that she is happy at all, I think that she is just being loyal and is now confused and doesn't want to 'rock the boat'. I want to be happy but I know that I would only be happy if Mary is also happy. I made up my mind! I decided to do nothing for now as I thought that if I 'pushed it', I could lose her forever. I have to be patient, I will 'step aside' for as long as I can and just hope that love will find a way.

Chapter 25

I wasn't hungry next morning, I needed some quiet time alone, time to think. I skipped breakfast and took a walk down to the Bailey Lighthouse. I went through everything over and over again and each time I came up with the same answer, difficult as it will be, I have to leave Mary alone and hope against hope that we 'accidentally' bump into each other again. How will I tell Mark that I don't want to play golf at St Anne's again? Maybe I'll 'buy some time' by telling him that I twisted my ankle and hope I don't forget to keep limping. I decided to try it now, I would try to walk back to St John's, limping all the way. I practised grimacing as my left foot touched the ground. I think I could pull it off, at least for this week anyway.

As I went through the open gate, I spotted Mark's car in the parking lot. I exaggerated my limping in case he was looking. As I entered the building, Mark was leaning over the reception desk. He turned to meet me.

"Ok Bro, do you want any help getting your things together?" he asked calmly.

"What do you mean?" I asked, in surprise.

Mark didn't reply but instead guided me back to my room, I unlocked the door and we both entered. I forgot to limp! My bed had already been stripped. Mark explained that he had earlier received a phone call asking him to come and collect me. When he got to St John's, the manager explained that there was clear evidence that I, or someone I was with, had been smoking marijuana in my room and that this meant immediate expulsion, with no appeal and no prospect of returning.

"Bro, I don't mind if you bring women back here, it's your life and you are free to do what you want but why did you have to break the rules by allowing the smoking of 'pot' in your room? You knew what would happen, why did you do it here?" asked Mark.

"What makes you think I invited a woman to my room Mark, who told you that?" I asked. "Was someone spying on me?"

"Conor you were seen arriving with her, she was seen leaving several hours later, only to return shortly after and then almost immediately dash out again and speed off in her car. She passed someone at the front door and he said that she appeared very upset and was crying. She didn't answer when he asked if she was ok, he even considered calling the Gardai but instead decided to just inform the manager," said Mark.

I couldn't speak for several seconds, I just looked at Mark, open mouthed.

"Look Conor, I have spoken to the manager here. He says that he doesn't want to know any more, he will only take it further if the woman later makes a formal complaint, will she make a complaint Conor?" asked

Mark.

I decided that the only thing to do now was to tell Mark all about Mary and what had happened. I told him everything, well almost everything, leaving out only the personal sensitive parts. When I had finished, Mark didn't seem happy that I had told Mary about my parallel universe and said that I definitely shouldn't have shown her the photos. He said that he was now worried about meeting her at the golf club again. He suggested that she just played along with me so I would tell her everything and that he thought that she might now sell my 'fantastic' story to the media, he added that she's probably talking to an agent right now.

I reassured Mark that I was sure that Mary wouldn't tell anyone. What Mark didn't know was that I knew, full well, why Mary would want to keep our liaison a secret.

We drove away from St John's in silence. Mark pulled up outside the FFF Hotel and got out of the car without saying a word, he didn't try to hide his anger. I followed him inside to be greeted with a friendly smile from my sister Marian. Marian was proud to be in charge of the hotel and showed it. She threw her arms around me and welcomed me. She said that she was really happy that I had decided to leave St John's and that I could stay in her hotel for as long as I liked. She explained that she had already prepared her best room for me. It had a double bed, an ensuite bathroom with both a full-sized bath and a shower, a writing desk and plenty of wardrobe space. She said that it will now be much more convenient for me to play my music there on Saturday nights.

"Well, the double bed might come in handy Conor some time," said Mark. "Thanks Marian, for all your help, sorry we couldn't give you more notice but when I met Conor this morning, he just said that he had had enough of the restrictive rules and regulations at St John's and had to get away immediately."

I nodded sheepishly, and thanked Mark for 'everything' and then thanked Marian for her amazing hospitality.

Mark left me without saying when we would meet again. As he left, I apologised to him for causing so much trouble and said that I looked forward to seeing him again soon. I expected him to talk about his plans for checking out everything which had been suggested by Carlos. It was obvious that he was really angry with me, I guessed mainly because I shared so many of 'our' secrets with Mary, perhaps he felt that I had somehow betrayed him! The truth was that I just didn't know 'this Mark' well enough to know how long he might be angry with me but I knew that I really needed him now, more than ever. Through my stupid selfishness I had already lost Mary and now it looked like I had lost the confidence of the one friend I could rely on, the only person I could properly confide in. Here I go again, making a mess of every opportunity I'm given, why can't I see it coming and stop myself? Hopefully he will 'come around' before

Carlos returns from England.

Marian sat with me for lunch and we chatted about how well the hotel was doing. I evaded all questions relating to my past, I just kept changing the subject and turned the conversation back to her and her family. She eventually 'got the message' and suddenly said:

"Conor, are you going to witness the exhumation of Ian's body tomorrow?"

I told Marian that I was unaware that the exhumation was planned for tomorrow but since I hadn't been told about it, let alone been invited to be present, that I would give it a miss.

The exhumation took place at first light on Thursday morning. The parish priest of the Church of The Assumption in Howth, was present throughout the exercise. Father McCracken had never been involved in anything like this before and he was very uneasy. Peter and Fiona were there to represent the family. Sergeant Murphy was on hand to dissuade any 'nosey' bystanders, but in the event, there was no one else around. The secret had either been very well kept or perhaps no one could be bothered to get up so early and stand in light, persistent drizzle, in a graveyard.

The dirty white coffin was still fully intact but the undertaker had anyway come prepared with a larger black sealable plastic box, into which they carefully placed Ian's tiny white coffin. The other disturbed coffins were replaced neatly back in the grave. The specialist 'crew' knew their job well. They had all the necessary expertise and equipment to ensure as little disruption as possible. The earth was shovelled quickly back on top of the other coffins, not too much ceremony with this process. The grave was then covered with a white plastic 'tent'. The black box containing Ian's white coffin was carried up the crumbling steps and taken away by a waiting funeral hearse. A few interested people had gathered during the few hours the process had taken, but Sergeant Murphy had placed a police barrier around the cemetery gates and several feet away from the boundary wall. No onlookers could get close enough to view the process or to take photographs. The Forman family had arranged and paid for twenty-four-hour private guards at the graveside. The family grave would be guarded until Ian's body could be reburied. Ian's second funeral was already planned for exactly one week later, at 2:00pm in the afternoon.

The North Dublin City Coroner went about his duties in the professional manner expected of him. He had already been briefed that, unusually, he was not charged with establishing the cause of death of the male child. Doctor Malloy was thankful that all he had to do was extract enough tissue from the child, who had died over fifty years earlier, to enable a 'definitive' DNA analysis to be performed. The process did not take long and later that day Ian's remains were on their way to Jennings Undertakers in Fairview, Dublin. Peter and Fiona took care of the funeral arrangements. Robert had suggested that it be a 'quiet affair' but both Mark and Fiona reminded everyone that they had not even been born when Ian's first funeral took place. When Peter and Marian agreed with Mark and Fiona, Robert finally relented and Peter later met with Father McCracken to finalise the funeral arrangements.

The tissue samples were subjected to thorough analysis and as a precaution, were sent for a separate analysis at a second laboratory. Per the Gardai instructions, the data was scrutinised at the two separate locations and was compared with the DNA of Peter and with whom they believed was his twin brother, Conor. The results were conclusive. The deceased child was Peter's brother and was an identical twin of Conor Forman.

No one was surprised and the Gardai gave the formal 'green light' for Conor to be issued with his official 'Lion's Community' passport.

I know it was stupid, but it felt like I had been born again. Ian was 'officially' dead, or so they said, and so I was 'officially declared' to be Conor.

I realised I would have to go to Ian's funeral, well my funeral really, and since I can't 'handle' funerals at the best of times, I didn't know how I would cope at my own!

The church service was arranged for the following Wednesday evening at 6:30pm. I had spent the week, mostly alone, walking around Howth and just being miserable. I still awaited my passport after which I could open a bank account and receive the very generous monthly allowance I had been promised. I dreaded my funeral but the whole family planned to be there, even Patrick and his family were flying over from Chicago. Of course, I had to attend. I had not seen or heard from Mark since that fateful day and I had no idea how Carlos was getting on, I wondered if Mark had been in contact with him. I wondered if Mark had told Carlos about my behaviour at St John's, maybe they had decided to forget about me but when I thought about it, I knew that there was no way Carlos would miss this opportunity, with or without Mark's help.

I sat alone in my room, looking at the clock. At just after 6.00pm I dressed for the church service, I wasn't hungry at all, I was shaking and had never been so nervous as this. I sat back down on the chair and stared out, through the net curtains, at the people and traffic busying themselves on Main Street. I didn't feel like waiting in hotel reception but Marian knocked on my door and shouted that everyone was waiting for me. Everyone was gathered in the lounge and it seemed to me like they all turned to stare at me as I entered. My brother Patrick was already 'in full flow', talking and laughing non-stop as he sipped from his pint of Guinness. I headed towards him and tried to strike up a conversation.

"My God Patrick you've started early," I said nervously.

"Well Conor, I wasn't the first to start drinking, because you know what they say, the early bird gets the worm but the second mouse gets the cheese," he said loudly and smiled. The whole family walked 'en-masse' the few hundred yards to the church, which was already full of worshippers, well maybe not worshippers, more like inquisitive neighbours. There were three benches at the front reserved for Ian's family and I was seated at the end of the row, no more than a few yards from the new gleaming shiny white coffin, which was standing on a trolley with several colourful wreaths carefully arranged on the closed and sealed lid. I tried to keep calm inside but I wasn't sure if I could manage it, I tried to clear my head of the image of a decayed and decomposed body of the twelve-year-old Ian screaming to be let out of the coffin. I almost screamed out-loud in harmony with the pitiful child, but I was distracted when the funeral service began. I needed to get out of here right now!

In my mind I started to play the front nine holes at Silverstone golf course. I imagined playing with Mary and we both hit 'cracking' drives straight down the middle of the fairway of the first hole. I visualised every shot we each took in turn, I even made sure to hit a bad shot into the water hazard on the third hole and then I lost my ball in the long grass on the right of the fourth hole. It had to be realistic, so I made sure we didn't take "more than the allowed" five minutes looking, without success, for my imaginary golf ball. Unlike me, Mary was playing very well and was four stableford points in the lead. I needed to win the next hole but just as I was lining up my par putt on the fifth hole, Mark elbowed me in the ribs. The service had finished and I hadn't heard a single word. Not for the first time, I had managed my emotions at a funeral by playing an imaginary round of golf. What a wonderful coping skill I possess, I thought. Hope I can repeat the exercise tomorrow in the graveyard, I have to keep my emotions in check!

As we streamed out of the Church, it was still bright. I could see tears in the eyes of several people, some of whom I had never seen before but thankfully no one was actually crying. One or two people did shake hands with me but I avoided all eye contact even as they repeated the usual 'sorry for your trouble'. Everybody now accepted that I was Ian's twin and was expected to be feeling sad but they had no idea about the complex and troublesome thoughts whizzing around my head. Ian wasn't my twin, he was me! Mark seemed to be my friend again. He invited me to join all the family members in the Palace Lounge for a 'bit of a spread' after the church service.

"Mark, I really don't feel very well," I started. "I suddenly feel exhausted and I don't think that I could eat or drink anything without throwing up. Neither am I in the mood for standing around chatting and listening to everyone reminiscing about how friendly and nice Ian was and shaking their heads from side to side as they commented on the injustices of life and how it was a shame that such an angel like Ian had his life cut short, so tragically."

Mark looked at me very sympathetically and said that he understood perfectly and would make my apologies to everyone. I promised Mark that I would join everyone later on, if I felt any better, but I didn't want anybody to come to my room to offer sympathy or support, I just needed to be alone.

Up in my room, I threw off my shoes and 'plonked' face down on the bed. How will I ever get through the burial service tomorrow? Should I make my excuses in the morning by saying that I am not well and just stay in bed? No, I must face my demons! I will play a virtual round of golf at Woburn Golf Club. Perhaps Mary and I will play with our friends Barney and Jill, on the Duchess Course. I tried to convince myself that I was actually looking forward to it but I couldn't. I dreaded it! I slept very uneasily, waking up every few minutes throughout the endless night. I was thirsty, hungry, weak, exhausted and depressed. Not only all of these, I was also a fraud.

Chapter 26

I awoke the next morning to the sound of laughter outside my room. I pulled back the curtains and looked out of the room window, it was already light. There were two angry cars fighting over the one remaining parking space opposite. Considering the large number of parked cars, I was surprised that there was hardly anybody moving around, where was everybody? I showered and dressed but didn't put on my black suit yet. I sat alone in the corner of the breakfast room and devoured my almost-full Irish breakfast. I felt much better after eating, so donned some warmer clothes and ambled down Abbey Street past the Abbey Tavern and the high graveyard retaining wall, to the promenade. I didn't feel like talking to anybody so, whenever someone appeared in front of me, I crossed to the other side of the road. The sun was shining with just a few wispy white clouds overhead with a gentle warm breeze from the south-west. It was the typical kind of day when a happy contented fool would say 'it's a great day to be alive', but I was instead thinking that it was a very bad day for a burial, especially my own. I walked slowly all the way down the East Pier, on the lower level and upon reaching the lighthouse I scrambled up the steep granite steps and gazed over at Irelands Eye. I tried to imagine what life would have been like for the monks who once prayed to their God in the now dilapidated church ruin, all those centuries ago. Did they feel happy with their spartan lives, or were they just 'content' to suffer in this life in the hope that their penance would bring them everlasting happiness in the next life?

I looked over across the harbour to the West Pier where I could see lots of people working, busily going about their daily tasks. I wondered if any of them were thinking about the 'next life' as they struggled to eke out an existence in this one, I doubt it. I walked back along the top level of the East Pier, didn't bump into a sinner. Back on the promenade I headed towards the West Pier, always being careful not to accidentally get too close to anybody, I didn't want conversation. Part way down the West Pier, I peered through the open gates of the family fish business which still had the huge red letters shaped in a crescent, not quite framing the Howth Stone arch. 'Peter Forman and Sons Limited' had been started by my grandad Peter and his sons were my daddy Peter and my uncle James. All three of them now long since departed but their names still lived on, above the thriving business premises that was such a major influence on my character and on my way of life. I must have dwelt too long gazing and reminiscing but I hurried on when I saw that Nicky had stopped working and had started to walk in my direction. I waved, then turned my back on him and continued on my journey of distraction. I climbed up the wide steps at the end of the West Pier and watched the three anglers concentrate on their so-called pleasurable task of trying to catch an unwary shiny wriggling mackerel on their hooks. I thought that in all my years of watching this boring and lonely pastime, that I never actually saw anyone catch a fish there. Perhaps catching a fish is not really the end goal, perhaps standing there, oblivious to everything else, is their way of bringing some calm into their otherwise hectic lives. I never did 'get' angling, probably because I had spent many hours on trawlers catching hundreds of fish at a time. I considered fishing to be just another job and certainly not a pleasurable pastime.

Walking back up the West Pier, I stayed as far away as possible from the open yellow gates of Peter Forman & Sons Ltd and found myself pausing on the quayside alongside the concrete steps, from which I had fallen, all those years ago. Don't know why, but I descended halfway down the steps and sat down on a damp step with both of my legs dangling over the water. This time, there wasn't a boat tied up alongside and the water was calm and clear. I was transfixed looking at the small fish fry darting first in one direction and then another. Time seemed to stand still and I felt at peace. I must have been there several minutes trying to pluck up the courage to lean forward and gently slide into the cold, welcoming sea water. If I moved slowly, feet and legs first, I could do it without even making a ripple and no one would be there to see me, let alone rescue me. I knew I wouldn't scream, and although I still couldn't swim, I knew I was focussed enough not to splash about struggling. This could be the perfect answer to my miserable existence, I would be right back where I started from. No more fruitless chasing after Mary and causing her grief and no more pretending to be my twin brother, Conor. My life was just too complicated and was without purpose or direction, I wanted out and now might be a great time to move on. Perhaps I could be laid to rest alongside myself in that white coffin! I edged a little closer to the edge of the step but stopped when I heard a loud voice above me…

"Hey, is that you Ian, are you ok?"

I slid back and started to get to my feet, shit I missed my chance! I didn't answer straight away but stood up and ascended the steps only to come face to face with Paddy and Jamie.

"Hi there, yes I'm fine thank you, I was just resting after my long walk," I replied.

"Do you remember us Ian? I'm Paddy and this is my son Jamie. Did you ever find your stolen car? We didn't hear anything more so we assumed that it must have been found."

"No unfortunately it just disappeared," I answered truthfully. "But luckily the insurance company covered it," I lied.

Jesus, how am I going to get out of this, I thought. They obviously hadn't heard about the emergence of Conor or maybe they just didn't link him to me. I asked them where they were headed and made my excuses when they said they were headed down to the end of the pier.

"It's great to see you both again, wished I could stop and chat but I'm running late," I said.

Paddy and Jamie 'got the message' and continued on their way, oblivious to the fact that they had just saved my life. I really didn't know whether I should thank them or punch them in the face! I continued to walk, a little more briskly now, up the hill and past the family home which was now my brother Peter's house and then up the 'back road' past Grace O'Malley Road and down the slope, until I was back on Church Street. Back in the hotel and the reception area was a flurry of activity. Several people were standing around talking, I guessed waiting for the bar to open in about five minutes, twelve noon. I bent my head down, looking at the carpet, as I silently walked straight past everyone. I lay on my bed for more than an hour, how was I going to get through the day? In the bathroom, I splashed water all over my face and brushed my teeth furiously before dressing formally in my white shirt, black tie, black socks, and brand-new black suit. I slipped on my shiny new black shoes and didn't mind at all when they 'pinched' a bit, the pain might keep my mind off things. I was sitting on the edge of my bed, feeling each second slowly tick by, when abruptly there was a knock on my door. I let Patrick in, he was quite sombre, no joking today, thank God.

We walked together the couple of hundred yards to the church. Thankfully the weather was still holding up, no sign of rain and the light breeze was even warmer than earlier. The Church was already half-full when we joined the rest of the family. I had noticed Danny Boyd and his wife Alison sitting and fidgeting about half way up the Church, how thoughtful of them to come along I thought, I must remember to thank them afterwards. After a short service, lasting no more than ten or fifteen minutes, the tiny new white coffin was lifted onto the stretcher to be carried to its final resting place about ten-minutes-walk away. Peter, Patrick, Robert and Mark took turns with the carrying, I don't know why I wasn't invited to take part, perhaps it had all been decided, in my absence, the night before. As I walked slowly behind the coffin, in step with my sisters Marian and Fiona, for some stupid non-sensical reason, that song by the Hollies, *He Ain't Heavy He's My Brother*, started to play around and around in my head. So far so good I thought, I was succeeding at staying detached from it all! At the graveside Father McCracken led a decade of the rosary and recited the usual 'ashes to ashes' speech, which I never quite got the purpose off, perhaps it was designed to make people cry and then feel better afterwards. The hundred or so people hung around for just a few minutes after the coffin was lowered into the grave. I don't know what was going on in my mind, I didn't feel I was even there. I just couldn't accept that it was really me that was inside that coffin, I tried to drum out the deafening sound of those shovelfuls of clay hitting the wooden coffin lid. The burial service was surreal, no one was crying, no one was shaking hands with bereaved family members and no one looked even the slightest bit sad. As we left the cemetery, I walked alongside Robert as most of us made our way to the Waterside Lounge.

"Well you managed to control your emotions very well Conor, considering you believe that was your twin, who you were saying your final goodbye to," said Robert.

Robert's comments took me by surprise, why did he say 'considering you believe'?

"Thanks Robert, it wasn't easy but it's such an unusual freaky situation," I replied.

"Oh, really Conor! With your acting ability, I fully expected you to be in floods of tears and un-ashamedly seeking everyone's sympathy," said Robert, in an unconcealed cynical tone.

I was completely 'taken aback' by Robert's comments and was stuck for words. As we walked through the open doors of the lounge, I saw him head straight for the bar so I moved away from him. I tried to forget about him as I headed over to Danny and Alison.

"Thanks for coming along today you two, I didn't expect you to be able to make it here but I really appreciate you coming," I said.

I'm sure I looked totally dis-interested in Danny's reply as I really wasn't listening. I just couldn't get Robert's remarks out of my head. The sandwiches had now arrived and most of the men were drinking Guinness and talking about football, horse racing or golf. Many of the ladies were sipping lukewarm tea from delicate decorated china cups and nibbling on iced cup-cakes, all of them being so nice and polite to each other. I didn't feel like conversation, which is just as well because it seemed like nobody wanted to talk to me anyway. Without saying goodbye to anyone, I slipped out the door and escaped before it all got too noisy and everyone got stupid drunk. I had to get away! I walked quickly at first, I didn't want to risk anyone seeing me and trying to entice me back. What was Robert hinting at?

Back at the funeral reception the drinks were flying and someone had decided to start singing sad songs. Lots of the men joined in but the ladies just smiled on in embarrassed encouragement. No one was in a hurry to leave. Peter noticed Robert sitting alone at the end of the bar, sipping his Guinness.

"Hey Robert, have you seen Conor? I haven't seen him around for ages," asked Peter.

"Who, oh Conor, yes I saw him sneaking out, with his tail between his legs, just after we arrived," replied Robert.

"Christ, I hope he's ok, did he seem ok to you today Robert?" asked Peter.

"Well to be honest, he seemed a little agitated with me, after I made some 'telling' remarks to him, on the walk down here, earlier," replied Robert.

"Oh Robert, what did you say to him? You know how vulnerable he is," said Peter.

"Vulnerable my arse!" replied Robert. "He's about as vulnerable as a fox in an unguarded henhouse."

"Robert, what has 'gotten into you', you don't have to like him, but for the sake of the family, you should try to make him feel welcome as you earlier promised me that you would," exclaimed Peter.

"That was before," replied Robert.

"Before what?" asked Peter.

"Before I knew the truth," said Robert very slowly.

Robert picked up his half-full glass of Guinness and carefully slid off his barstool. He gestured to Peter to follow him. Peter was intrigued and quickly followed Robert to a free table for two, in the far corner of the lounge.

"Peter, before we start you have to promise me that you won't ever breathe a word of what I am about to tell you to anyone else and if someone comes near us, I will change the subject straight away. Do you understand and swear?" demanded Robert.

"Jasus Robert, are you drunk or something?" exclaimed Peter.

"Do you swear Peter?" insisted Robert.

"Ok, ok, don't panic Robert, I swear," said Peter. "But this better be good as it's keeping me away from some serious drinking."

Robert proceeded to un-burden his secret. He reminded Peter that he had engaged a private detective to try to track down where his brother Conor had been hiding for all those missing years. Where both the Irish Gardai and the English Police had failed, his private detective had succeeded. Robert waited a minute or two, to ensure that he had Peter's full attention before he continued his story. He asked Peter if he could remember their mammy's so-called best friend Kitty Muhearn, she may have been a distant cousin, who came to live with them during the last few weeks of Mammy's pregnancy with Ian. It was said that Kitty came to help Mammy cope, following her earlier difficult pregnancy with you, Peter. Peter said that he couldn't remember that at all, but it wasn't that surprising because he was less than two years old at the time and even their sister Jean was still a toddler.

"Look Robert, what the feck has Kitty Mulhearn got to do with anything?" asked Peter impatiently.

Robert gave Peter a 'filthy look' and continued ...

"After the twins, yes twins Peter, were born at home, apparently without any help from a doctor or midwife, Kitty returned to Dundalk, with a new baby in tow. Unknown to anyone, bar her husband Frank, our mammy and daddy and of course herself, Kitty had recently lost her own baby in the very late stages of pregnancy. Within hours of returning home she claimed that her baby had been born at her home in Dundalk, something which her husband obviously backed her up on. This deception would have been much easier to pull off in those days when the presence of a doctor or a midwife was not always the norm. The male child was registered as having been born on January 15th, 1949 and he was soon christened Francis, after his 'daddy'. Don't ask me why Mammy arranged for that other birth certificate for Conor Forman to be registered. Perhaps she felt guilty and our daddy made some deal with a 'doctor' afterwards, no one will ever know. Anyway, Ian's twin brother is actually still alive and he's named Francis Mulhearn. Francis is living in a care home in Dundalk, where he is suffering badly with dementia. Now I think of it, perhaps Mammy arranged that bogus birth certificate to throw anyone, who got suspicious, 'off the scent'. Maybe Mammy had earlier mentioned she was having twins to some of her friends, who knows?

Robert abruptly stopped talking when he spotted Mark, out of the corner of his eye, approach their table.

"Hey, why are you both so serious over here?" asked Mark as he slapped Peter on the back. "What the hell are you two talking about anyway?"

"Robert is telling me a fascinating story Mark, why don't you grab a stool and join us," said Peter.

"Ah, sure I'm almost finished now anyway," said Robert quickly. "Mark, why don't you get us both a pint and we'll join you at the bar in a couple of minutes."

After Mark left them, Robert gave Peter a very stern look and reminded him that he had agreed to keep everything secret.

"Oh, for Christ's sake Robert, Mark will have to be told sooner or later," said Peter.

"Perhaps," replied Robert, "but let me decide when and how to break the news. You must see that Mark and this cunning money grabbing imposter Conor are as 'thick as thieves'. I have no idea why they meet this English ex coroner in secret, but I'll bet they won't be discussing anything innocent. Anyone can see they are 'up to something'."

"But Robert you only have circumstantial evidence about this guy called Francis Mulhearn," said Mark. "Just because he was born on the same day as Ian and there was a connection between Kitty and Mammy doesn't prove that Francis is actually Ian's twin. Also, what about the DNA evidence which proved that Conor is our brother and also Ian's identical twin? You can't fake DNA evidence Robert!"

"Peter, that's what that crook Conor was banking on," replied Robert. "I don't know how he did it but I'm sure that this bastard found out all about Francis Mulhearn and must have paid him a visit in the care home. It would have been easy to get some DNA from an old man suffering from dementia, but the clever part was figuring out how to substitute the stolen DNA for his own. He's bloody clever, I'll give him that Peter. If it wasn't for my private detective, he would have got away with it."

"But how certain are you that Francis is Ian's twin?" asked Peter. "How can you be so sure?"

"Because my brilliant and thorough detective also got DNA from Francis, without raising any suspicions, and I have personally had it checked out," answered Robert. Believe me Peter, there is no mistake, Francis Mulhearn is our missing brother. This guy calling himself Conor is nothing but a lying cheat, who is trying to con us out of money."

"Jesus Robert, what a con-artist, I hate him, I must admit it, he had me fooled. What do we do now? Are you going to confront him directly? I'll bet you are looking forward to it," smirked Peter.

"Well, that's the dilemma Peter," replied Robert. "You see this guy who calls himself Conor obviously knows about Francis and to be honest I don't think it makes sense for the whole family to know about Francis. If I confront Conor and 'back him into a corner', I think he would threaten to tell everyone about Francis and I don't think that would serve any good purpose. It could cause a lot of heartache if Conor told everyone all about what our mammy did and of course it would also make Francis our responsibility. We don't really want another brother in the family, certainly not a helpless penniless dementia-suffering old man."

"So, what do we do? We can't simply do absolutely nothing Robert," said Peter.

"No, we can't, but we need a plan. Let me pick the place and time. Perhaps I can persuade this evil man to simply disappear. I would rather pay him off and have him go away than allow him to bring Francis into the picture," said Robert.

"Ok, I will keep my mouth shut and leave it to you but what about Francis, does he have any family? asked Peter.

"No, he never married and his only other sibling, a younger sister, who was a 'true' Mulhearn, died from a heart attack some years ago," replied Robert. "When Francis dies, which will hopefully be very soon, all evidence will die with him. Everyone thinks he has no living relatives so his body will be cremated along with any incriminating DNA evidence."

"So, will you wait until then Robert?" asked Peter.

"I'm not sure Peter, let's keep the secret to ourselves and see what this criminal old fart, who calls himself Conor, does next," answered Robert, with a wink to Peter. "Perhaps, after Francis has been safely cremated, we'll find a way to get a proper DNA sample from this feckin' Conor 'fella'," smiled Robert.

"Christ Robert, how long can we keep this to ourselves?" asked Peter. "I don't think I will be able to look him straight in the eye from now on."

Chapter 27

When I eventually got back to the FFF Hotel, the receptionist Joan called to me.

"Conor, your brother Mark called earlier," said Joan. "He asked if you could be ready by 8:30am tomorrow morning and if you could pack a case for a couple of nights stay away. He said you were to call him back if you couldn't make it, otherwise he will see you for breakfast in the morning."

I didn't call back. I went straight to my room and packed my new soft black rucksack, I didn't know where we were going but assumed it would be to places, I had said that I knew. I was pleased that Mark was communicating with me again and looked forward to our mystery short vacation. I didn't sleep that well and was up from about 6:00am. I decided to wait for Mark to arrive so we could have breakfast together and was starving when I finally saw his car pull into the carpark at about 9:00am.

"Sorry I'm late bro', are you ready because we need to get going now," shouted Mark out of the window of his car.

"But what about breakfast?" I protested.

"Oh, I grabbed something before I left home," he replied. "I'll be fine, so let's get going before the traffic builds up too much."

I walked quickly into the breakfast room, poured myself a large glass of orange juice, which I downed in one gulp. I quickly cut two bread rolls in two and stuffed some chunks of cheddar cheese in one roll and loads of sliced Limerick ham in the other, I didn't bother with butter, no time. I ate the cheese roll on the way to my room to collect my rucksack but was still munching on my 'workman's' ham roll, when I slid in beside Mark. We took off at speed, I first thought that something must be wrong but later realised that Mark was just in a hurry. A first he didn't give me any clues as to where we were going, all he told me was that we had a lot to do before Carlos arrived back on Monday afternoon, I confirmed that I had packed enough clothes for two nights, the Friday and Saturday night. He explained that he needed to get back early Sunday afternoon as he had some business to attend to.

"Ok Conor, you told us that you have driven to the Galway Races before and you said you stayed in the Galway Bay Hotel so please be my Satnav."

I had no trouble directing Mark, I even suggested that we stop off at the horse racecourse at Naas on the way. We visited several golf courses including Athenry, Galway Bay and Galway before eventually arriving at the Galway Bay Hotel. At each location I showed Mark photos of Mary and I, with our friends Pete and Liz, from my phone gallery, and in each case, he got me to pose in the same position while he took photos. On the Friday night, Mark and I sang along to the brilliant live Irish music in

O'Connor's pub in Salthill. My dated photos really made it easy for me to relive my earlier visit with Mary, Liz and Pete. On Saturday morning we drove to Lahinch Golf Course, then to Waterville before finally finishing up at the Old Head Golf Course, near Kinsale. I told Mark about playing golf there with a group of eight players including Mary and my American ex-boss Michael. One of the tee boxes required us to descend some steep steps down the cliff side until we were almost in the Atlantic Ocean, where I overheard Michael's caddy advise him...

"Ok Michael, that's the Atlantic Ocean on your left and that's Ireland on your right, just hit Ireland!"

As I expected, Michael tried to bite off a little too much of the corner and we saw his ball splash into the expectant choppy ocean. Another lesson learned but quickly forgotten, I'm sure.

Mark's phone was filling up with clear evidence that I had been to all the places, I had said I had been, and that Mary was with me every time. We found a bed and breakfast just outside Cork City for the Saturday night and 'crashed out' from exhaustion. Early Sunday morning and off we were again to Dublin. We stopped off outside St. Gabriel's church in Clontarf, where I posed for a photo in the exact same spot as the photo I had of Mary and I being covered in confetti on our wedding day. I could have shown Mark lots of more places but Mark said that we had enough evidence to get us started. I felt elated as Mark dropped me back to the FFF. He apologised for having to rush off, not even time for a quick drink he said, but he told me that he was very satisfied with what we had 'discovered' over the last few days. He said he would pick me up at about noon on Monday, Carlos was expecting us at the Deer Park Hotel at about 12:30pm.

I stood to wave goodbye to Mark, I really felt brilliant, I now definitely had at least one true believer. I knew that I hadn't gone mad but despite the evidence, the truth just didn't seem believable, even to me.

As I walked through reception Joan called me over and handed me a small parcel, which was wrapped in brown paper and secured with what seemed like a whole roll of Sellotape. Joan said that it had arrived by post just after we left on Friday. I borrowed her scissors and carefully 'broke into' the parcel. I didn't know what it was, it looked like a giant type of glove or some sort of mitten. There was definitely only one in the parcel, blue on one side and pink on the other. I had no idea what it was or where it came from. I looked at Joan for help and she smiled widely at me.

"Don't you know what it is Conor," she laughed. "God, I haven't received one of those since I was a teenager, haven't even seen one for years and years."

"What the hell is it Joan?" I asked.

"It's a *Friendship Mitten*, Conor," she replied. "You have a secret admirer Conor, some lady who wants to get to know you better."

"Some lady?" I asked.

"Yes, pink for the lady and blue for the gentleman," she smiled. "Why don't you check it out on their website Conor."

Up in the privacy of my room I took a better look at the mitten. I discovered that there was something stuffed inside it, covered in Bubblewrap. My hands were shaking as I tore away the wrapping to unveil a mobile phone, complete with a charger. There was a white sticker attached to the screen on which was hand-written: *4 digits, my birthday, which you say you know, but backwards, M.*

I sat on the edge of my bed, staring at the phone. What was this all about? I would like to believe that M must be for Mary, but do I dare get my hopes up? I don't think I could 'handle' another disappointment.

What was this all about, why all the cloak and dagger? What's the cryptic message all about? In a flash it came to be, in truth it didn't need Sherlock Holmes to figure it out.

I turned on the i-Phone and when it asked for the password, I typed in 0906 (the sixth of September backwards). An error message followed so I tried 9060, I was in!

I immediately saw that there was one unread message so I clicked on it.... it was quite long.

Hi Conor, I was so sorry to learn that I may have caused you to be thrown out of your home. I called to St John's a couple of days after our last meeting and the receptionist told me, in confidence, that you had been asked to leave. She had no idea why and couldn't or wouldn't say, where you went. She made no effort to help me, she couldn't care less. Fortunately, as I was leaving, the doorman, who seemed to think he knew me, actually winked at me and suggested that I should try the FFF Hotel. One phone call later and Joan confirmed that you were staying there. I hope you don't mind me 'tracking you down' like this Conor, I hope you weren't hoping to avoid me! Conor, I really hope that you can find it in your heart to forgive me for my behaviour. I know I 'led you on' and then when I felt guilty for what happened, I blamed you for everything. The truth is Conor that I enjoy your company and am still hoping that we could still enjoy spending some time together, perhaps not in the frantic passionate way we started off, but I would love to get to know you better. If you are interested in meeting up again, please text me back with YES. Alternatively, if you have had enough of me and don't wish to hear from me or to ever meet up with me again please text me back with NO THANKS. Either way Conor, I would like to hear from you but please don't phone, text only please, it's vital I keep this private. Either way you can keep the phone Conor, as a thank you for 'spicing up' my previously boring life, even if it was only for a short while.

Mary

I went into my bathroom and splashed cold water all over my face but the tears kept re-appearing in my eyes. I don't remember ever feeling so excited or elated. I thought of the saying 'you don't know what you've got till it's gone' but I could now replace this with 'but it's even sweeter when you get back what you thought you had lost.'

I went back down to Reception and turned on the hotel desktop computer. Joan couldn't stop smiling as she scribbled the computer password for me on a scrap of paper and wished me good luck with my new adventure. I googled 'Friendship Mitten' and couldn't stop smiling to myself as I learned that the term first came into use more than twenty years ago. In a few short years the sending of 'Friendship Mittens' replaced the Valentines Card industry because the intended message was less open to misinterpretation. The mitten is designed to allow a right hand from one person and the left hand from another person to fit snugly inside. The intention is to signify that the sender was interested in 'getting to know' the recipient, it was not necessarily an invitation for starting a romantic relationship, at least not straight away. There were several colours now commonly in use….A pink/blue mitten was between a girl and a boy, sky blue was used for a boy/boy exchange and shocking pink was for a girl/girl exchange, snow white for a platonic exchange and fire engine red could be used to either reject an unwelcome advance or to end a relationship, which was going nowhere. Unlike sending a Valentines Card, to be effective the sender had to provide the recipient with his or her contact details. The unwritten rule was however, that if the advance was not accepted, that the recipient had to keep the gift private between the two of them. Statistics showed that the overwhelming profile of users were teenagers and people in their early twenties but there was an upward trend for use among older adults who had lost a partner.

I returned to my room and replied to Mary.

Hi Mary,
   YES, YES, YES
   I only got your gift and welcome message a few minutes ago, as I have been out exploring the countryside for the last few days with my brother Mark. I was surprised and excited to hear from you, I really thought that I had messed things up and that I wouldn't hear from you again. Please forgive me for my appalling and selfish behaviour Mary but yes, I would very much like to meet up with you again, but this time I understand that it's all about FRIENDSHIP. When you are next on your own please listen to that old Beatles song 'I Wanna Hold Your Hand', John Lennon has already said it for me.

Take Care,
Conor

A good hour passed and still no reply, I must have caught her at a bad moment. Just when I resigned myself to being shunned again, she replied.

Thanks for replying Conor, I'm so glad you want to meet up again. Conor, nobody else knows about us and I need to keep it that way, if you don't mind. I can only communicate on this, my second mobile, which I will always have on silent, I will check it every few hours or so, hence the delay in responding. I need to go to Quinn's Supermarket at Sutton Cross this Thursday and will be alone. Could we meet at say 2:30pm in the nearby coffee shop on the corner, I think it's called Insomnia, or something like that. I hope you can make it. In the meantime, why don't you listen to the song 'Patience' by 'Take That'.

Mary
XXX

I didn't have to listen to the song, I knew the lyrics so well already. My God, life is just fantastic, I hadn't allowed myself to dare dream that I would be involved in a secret romantic liaison with my new Mary. Having to keep it all a secret just made it all so much more exciting, even at my age. I wondered what would 'my Mary' think if she knew I was planning to meet 'my new Mary' but somehow, I convinced myself that she wouldn't mind at all. I typed out my answer to Mary....

I'll be there and, by the way, thank you for the mitten.
Conor
XXXX

I found it almost impossible to sleep that night. I spent hours thinking through different scenarios for how our new relationship might develop, am I premature in calling it a relationship? One thing for sure, I will let Mary drive everything, at least she is not shy in coming forward. She even picked a meeting place which I could get to by public bus. I understood why she wanted to keep our meeting secret, she has no idea where it might go, but is she planning to meet me in secret forever or just until she is 'sure' about me. There I go again, trying to run before I can walk! I assume she will also expect me to keep our meeting a secret, how will I manage to do this with Mark as my almost constant companion and with Carlos back on the scene tomorrow. Anyway, it's not till Thursday and tomorrow's only Monday, I will figure something out.

Chapter 28

Mark and I were seated in Carlos' hotel room as he told us that his trip to England had provided lots of photos. He then listened as Mark told him all about our trip to the places that had been selected for us to visit in Ireland. I didn't think that Carlos was very impressed with what we had to say, even when Mark showed him the photos we had taken.

"Gentlemen, thanks for taking the time to do all that," said Carlos. I think the wedding photo could be useful."

Carlos picked up his i-Pad.

"Mr F, I have some photos I want to show you, would you bear with me a minute or so, until I hook up my i-Pad to the TV?"

He didn't expect an answer, so neither of us replied.

"Mr F, I would like you to comment as I show you each photo. Tell me as much as you can about the places and the people you see in each photo. Let's see if we have time to go through the hundred or so photos that I have selected from my collection, which I think are relevant."

The large TV screen came to life and the first photo filled the screen.

"That's Buckingham Town Centre, with the Old Gaol in the foreground," I said immediately.

Prompted by Carlos, I briefed him about Buckingham, its shops, parks, market place, restaurants and pubs.

"That looks very like our house but our windows are brown not white as shown in the photo and I don't have all those shrubs out front, our driveway is mostly block paved," I commented on the second photo.

"Do you recognise the people in the photo Mr F?"

"I don't know the man and lady on the left but that is my neighbour Joyce on the right."

Carlos referred to a small notebook he opened up and read from.

"Mr F, that is indeed the house you claim to be yours. Yes, that is Joyce and the couple beside her are Mr and Mrs Davis, who have lived at that address for the last six years or so."

Before I could respond the next photo lit up the screen.

"That looks very like our daughter Annette's house in Old Stratford but I don't recognise the people standing outside her front door," I said hesitantly.

"Mr F, that is the house you said your daughter, her husband and their children live in but it is, in fact, occupied by the Windsor family," said Carlos. "They have lived there for more than three years and they claim that they don't know anyone called Annette Webster."

We were next shown a photo of the front of the house where our son John lives with his family. Carlos told me that there is a young family named Kipling living there. Again, they had never heard of John or anyone in his family.

"Mr F, the next photo is a group photo, can you tell me where it has been taken and how many of the people you recognise, starting from the left?"

"It's on the terrace of Whittlebury Golf Club," I immediately replied. "It is overlooking the ninth green on the yellow course. Let me take a look at the faces... ok starting from the left you have: Jim, Lilian, Ken, Barbara, Kevin, Gill, Phil, Tracey, Jim, Carole, Barney, Jill, John, Sue, Mark, Ali, Barrie, Ron, Pete and Chris," I answered. "I'm afraid I don't recognise the three people on the extreme right."

Carlos asked me to tell him a little bit about all of the people I recognised during which time he constantly referred to his notes. He confirmed that I correctly identified everybody but I was not accurate about all of the details about them. He told me that he established that neither Mary nor I had ever been members of the golf club and that none of the people recognised me from the photo he showed them of me, which he had on his phone. He next showed photos of all of the 'honours boards' which were displayed on the club house wall. Not one of the boards indicated that Mary or I had ever won any golf competitions at Whittlebury. I raised my hand to ask Carlos to stop for a moment, at which point I pulled up photos from the gallery on my mobile phone. We counted out our victories, Mary had won a total of seven competitions and had recorded a 'hole in one' on the seventh hole on the 'blue course'. I had only won six and we shared one together, the mixed knockout. The photos from Carlos indicated different winners in the years we had actually won, many of the people I knew and I remembered three or four of them were the people we had actually beaten in the competition finals. Carlos was very pleased with himself and reminded me to make sure that I saved my photos to a separate device.

Carlos continued to go through his collection with much the same results until I noticed he had switched venues.

"That's Rodney, the club professional, sitting behind the counter in the Proshop of Silverstone Golf Club," I answered slowly. "I think that's Sue he is serving."

"Correct Mr F, but you are not a member there and neither of them recognised you from the photo," said Carlos.

"That's some of my friends standing outside the front door of the Wheatsheaf pub in Maids Moreton," I said. "My God you have been busy!"

"Who do you know Mr F?"

"I know all of them: that's Graham and Tracey, Andy and Helen, Steve and Geeta, Brad and Jo, Richard and Joyce and that's 'Wacky' on the right," I answered.

Carlos confirmed that I correctly identified everyone and that most of the details I knew about each of them was correct. He said that not one of them recognised me. He then abruptly turned off the TV and disconnected his i-Pad.

"This is all looking very promising, very promising indeed," said Carlos. "But I've just made a big mistake Mr F, I forgot to use my video camera to record and date your reactions as you looked at the photos."

"Well Carlos, just start your camera now and we will look at the photos again," said Mark. "Conor can comment again as he looks at them, what difference will it make?"

"It would make all the difference, Mark," replied Carlos. "Any person would be able to see that Mr F had seen the photos already, they could easily see that his reactions were rehearsed."

Carlos explained that everything he records on his camera needs to be 'live', he said that he has lots of other photos to go through, so the situation could be partially recovered. He then said that we should now definitely make use of Polygraph Tests later.

"Can you explain more about these Polygraph Tests?" I asked. "How do they work and are they reliable?"

"Very good questions Mr F," replied Carlos. "It's true that some people can fool a Polygraph Test or lie detector test as it is usually called, especially if they are hardened criminals or 'professional liars' but they work very well for 'normal' people. We'll have to wait and see how you get on Mr F, but I am very hopeful that we will find the tests useful."

Carlos said that he hadn't brought his equipment with him this time but would bring it with him the next time he returns, that is, if I agreed to undergo the tests. He explained that he would ask me to reply either 'YES' or 'NO' to a series of, what he called 'Relevant' and 'Non-Relevant' questions, related to what I had just been talking about. His equipment would monitor my stress levels or nervousness while answering the questions and from the graphs produced by his equipment, Carlos will be able to determine if I was telling the truth or was lying. He said that we would need to remind him to record everything live.

"The equipment will make a trace of your stress levels Mr F, which should be higher if and when you are lying," replied Carlos. "During the questioning, it will continuously monitor your blood pressure, your pulse rate, your breathing and your galvanic skin response."

"What the feck is galvanic skin response, when it's at home?" I asked.

"It's a measure of how much you are sweating, which should be higher if you are lying," replied Carlos.

"How can we be sure that you know what you are doing Carlos?" asked Mark, "have you done anything like this before?"

"Yes, I have Mark, but you are right to ask," replied Carlos. "If you look up the 'English Polygraph Association' website, EPA.com, you can read about some of the work I have done. Yes, I do know what I'm doing."

"Ok, so if I pass all the Polygraph Tests, will that be enough solid evidence to convince everyone that everything I have said is true?" I asked.

"Maybe, maybe not," replied Carlos. "I suspect that there will be a few events in your life, which you will not be able to remember well enough, maybe you pushed some of them into the back of your mind. If this proves to be the case, I would like to use hypnosis to help you remember. There may have been one or more traumatic events which you have subconsciously filed away into your brain archives, maybe some more details about the occasion when you almost, or perhaps, did drown!"

"To be honest Carlos, I'm a bit nervous about hypnosis," I said. "You hear about people who remain in a hypnotic state forever and I have also read that some 'practitioners' may even 'plant' ideas into their patients' brains while they are under hypnosis."

"I suppose you are now going to tell us Carlos, that you are a member of the 'World Hypnosis Association'" said Mark, somewhat sarcastically.

"Not quite Mark, but I am a 'fellow' of the 'English Hypnotherapy Association'" replied Carlos. "Again, you can check me out, if you want, on the web."

Carlos put my mind at ease by informing me that he would ask Mark to be present at any hypnosis sessions and that everything would be on video for me to look at later. If I didn't like something I said under hypnosis, I could have that part of the recording permanently deleted, provided it wasn't misleading. However, he suggested I might also find it interesting, maybe even amusing, to look back at the recordings.

"Ok, so the interrogation is complete, the lie detectors have done their 'bit' and you have both had a good laugh at me under a hypnotic trance, is that it then?"

"Maybe, maybe not," replied Carlos with a broad smile. "If you feel that you are 'up to it', the last part of the programme could involve you undergoing a medically controlled test where you take a 'so called' truth serum."

"Jaysus, don't tell me you are qualified to do that as well," interrupted Mark.

"Now, don't be ridiculous Mark," replied Carlos. "But I have already taken the liberty to ask a former colleague of mine in England, a Doctor Franks, if he would be prepared to administer it. Assuming you agree Mr F, we would have to travel over to his laboratory in Birmingham, England, but we could do this later when we go over to check out more of your past experiences.

"Christ you have thought about everything, haven't you," I commented. "What does the test involve exactly Carlos?"

Carlos explained, in a very serious tone, that Doctor Franks had suggested that, if I was willing and if everyone agreed, that he could inject me with a small dose of 'sodium thiopental'. This would be done under strict laboratory conditions and he would have no problem with the use of a video recorder, in fact he would insist on it. Carlos mentioned that I would probably not remember anything I said while under the influence of the drug, so it was vital that everything was recorded. Again, if I didn't like the video, I could have part or all of it, permanently deleted.

"Does it work Carlos and can I be sure it will have no lasting negative affect?" I asked.

"Here, I need to be honest with you," replied Carlos. "I have never been involved with this before, but Doctor Franks is a renowned expert and I am one hundred percent confident in his integrity and his confidentiality."

Carlos explained that he had already researched the process on the web and Doctor Franks had assured him that he had discussed the process with two separate consultants who both confirmed the appropriate dosage.

"We could get another doctor involved, if you wish, but the fewer people involved the better, I think," said Carlos. "Why don't you and Mark familiarise yourself with sodium thiopental, there's lots of information on the web. But I suggest that we wait until everything else has been explored before we decide on whether to use the truth serum or not, we don't have to decide now," added Carlos.

"But does it work and are there any negative side effects?" I asked again.

"It's not really clear exactly how it works but I understand that, with the right dose, it induces a feeling of a very pleasant state, like half way between being asleep and awake, where you just couldn't be bothered telling a lie. Apparently, you just feel great and just want to answer all questions truthfully, you, sort of, feel compelled to 'help' your 'friend' the doctor."

"And side effects?" I interrupted again.

"No, there are no recorded adverse effects, with the correct dosage," replied Carlos, "but when you check it out you will see that the drug can and has been used in the past, for lethal injections."

"Mother of God!" I exclaimed. "I don't think I want anything to do with this."

"Well, like I said earlier, we don't have to decide about that at the moment," replied Carlos. "But you don't have to undergo the test, if you don't want to. It's up to you," he smiled.

Before we broke up that day, Carlos summarised what he thought we had achieved and again apologised for his 'cock up' with forgetting to use his video camera to get my first immediate reactions. He said that we should finish going through the rest of his 'English' photos tomorrow so he could plan his next excursion in search of further evidence. He asked me to think about what we should talk about next day. He wanted to know as much as possible about the time we spent in Belgium, France, Germany, Holland and Sweden plus any other of the cities, towns and villages we spent enough time in to be recognised by the people there. He asked me to go through my photos that night and be prepared to suggest workplaces, schools, houses, pubs, restaurants and most importantly as many people as I could remember, who were featured in my collection of photos. I reminded Carlos that Mary and I had lived in Canada for two years and then Belgium for a further ten years, so had hundreds and hundreds of photos. I also reminded him that I had also worked on assignments in Poland, Denmark, Switzerland, Italy and Spain.

"What about my holiday snaps Carlos, do you also want to visit golf courses in Portugal and Turkey and elsewhere? This could take forever," I exclaimed.

"Let's not rule out anything for now Mr F, let's see how it goes tomorrow," replied Carlos. "We are not short of time, are we?"

I spent many hours that evening going through my photos and making notes. When I finished my task, it was past midnight and I realised that there was no way we could go through everything in just one day, but that wasn't my problem.

Mark picked me up next morning and appeared to be very anxious. When I asked him what the problem was, he said that we would discuss it when we were with Carlos. What the hell was the problem now? I thought that it must be serious, Mark just wouldn't engage in any conversation whatsoever. I was becoming more and more nervous, what had suddenly gone wrong? Did he perhaps find out about my plan to meet Mary on Thursday? No, he couldn't have, but I decided that I had better tell both him and Carlos about my upcoming liaison with Mary, I didn't want either of them to hear it from someone else.

Carlos was already prepared for us when we entered his room. His camera was primed and ready to go. After the welcoming handshaking, Mark said that he had something very important to tell us and asked Carlos to switch off his camera.

"When I left here yesterday, I unmuted my mobile phone and noticed that I had a message from my brother Peter asking me to call in on him, at his home, as soon as I could," said Mark gravely.

Mark went on to explain that Peter had asked him there to tell him something in the strictest confidence. Mark had to swear that he would never divulge what he was about to hear, to anybody, no matter what the circumstances. Peter then told Mark that he couldn't bear to see Mark making a fool of himself by getting so involved with 'that fraudster' who calls himself Conor, he wanted to advise him to 'back off' before it got any further.

"Peter told me that Robert has concrete proof that Conor is not who he says he is," said Mark.

Mark looked straight at me...

"Robert told Peter that, although he has no idea how you did it, that you must have somehow substituted your DNA samples, by switching it somehow, because there is no way you are Conor," said Mark, almost accusingly.

"Did Peter say what Robert intended to do next?" asked Carlos.

"Well, I asked Peter that very same question and he replied that Robert didn't tell him but said that when the time was right, he would 'make his move' and bring all of his fraudulent theft and pretence come crashing down," replied Mark.

"Peter only told me so I wouldn't get too 'taken-in' by all of this so-called Conor's bullshit," he added.

"And what do you think Mark, do you think I am a fraud and a thief?" I asked.

"No, of course not Conor, I've already seen more than enough evidence already," replied Mark. "I know that many of my friends and probably all of my relations think that I am a little gullible, but I'm not that gullible."

"Thanks for that Mark," I replied, "but remember *I never said I was Conor*."

"That's it, Mr F!" exclaimed Carlos. "That's exactly it! We already know that you are not Conor, and we already know that you haven't switched DNA samples, but how and why is Robert so certain that you are not Conor?"

"Hold on there, maybe Robert is just very suspicious but knows that he can't prove anything. Perhaps he asked Peter to do some 'digging' and ask some questions in the hope that he will flush Conor out of hiding," suggested Mark.

"That's a good possibility," I said. "Robert has not yet really 'embraced me', he always seems suspicious of me, especially so at Ian's funeral."

"I think you are spot on, Conor," said Mark. "I think Robert is using Peter to put doubt in my mind, in the hope that I will accuse you. I think Robert loaded the gun, Peter has 'cocked it' and Robert is now expecting me to fire the bullet."

"But what if Robert really is convinced that you are not Conor," asked Carlos. "What would make him so sure of his facts and why does he think that you have somehow switched your DNA samples?"

"I think there is only one way he could be so sure," said Mark. "I know he hired a private detective, so maybe he has found who he thinks is the real Conor."

"But then this mystery guy must have given Robert some of his DNA, which Robert has since had checked," I added.

Carlos, Mark and I discussed what this latest revelation changes and how we should respond. We couldn't figure out why Robert, if he did have enough evidence, wouldn't just tell everybody now and get rid of me straight away. Either he didn't really have the evidence he claimed he had, or there is some other reason why he is 'biding his time'. We concluded that we should assume that Robert had found the real Conor Forman because after all, there is a birth certificate for Conor Forman and we all already knew that I definitely wasn't Conor. We agreed that we should do nothing for now, except maybe expedite Carlos's evidence gathering and hope that Peter would 'tip off' Mark when Robert was about to drop his bombshell. Carlos suggested that before Robert decides to go public that we would have to 'bring him in' on our secret study, if I still wanted to live the rest of my life as Conor. Carlos suggested that, when that time comes, we may need to let Robert get more DNA from me and then when he checks it out, he will have to make up his mind about whether I am then one of triplets or accept that I am really *the* Ian, returned from another universe. We all agreed that we need to have all of our evidence ready before Robert is ready to make his move, but we had no idea how long we had. Carlos interrupted our discussion then, by suggesting that we get back to what we were there for. We spent the rest of the day going through my list of names and places and sharing lots of photos, this time all done while Carlos's camera was rolling. Mark informed us that he hadn't yet had the opportunity to go through my list of songs but that he would 'get on it' tomorrow. When we had finished for the day, Carlos said that he would prefer to make plans for his trip to the continent and would leave the next morning. I thought about it for a while but decided against telling Mark or Carlos about my upcoming meeting with Mary, just not the right time!

Carlos said he would be as quick as he could, but needed to make a thorough investigation. He told us that he hoped to be back with us in about three weeks.

"Don't underestimate Robert," said Mark as we parted. "He is very resourceful and he is also a bit unpredictable."

Chapter 29

Jonjo didn't even try to smile back at the bent-over old couple, who had called in to cash their pension cheques. Why couldn't someone show them how to do it 'on line'? Why did they have to bother him when all he wanted was to be left alone? They always called him by his first name but he could never remember their names until he looked at the cheques, and as soon as they left his shop, and the sooner the better, he quickly forgot their names again. He hated working in Raheny Post Office, he hated every second, of every minute, of every hour, of every day. He knew that he had to do it, but nobody said that he had to like it, so he didn't bother to try. What difference would it make, nobody called in to chat to him anyway. No, they called in to get something from him, he was helping them, it's them that need to be grateful, not him! He couldn't care less if they lived or died, in fact if they died it would be less trouble for him. His mammy, the 'lovely' Mary, God bless her, kept on and on at him, day after day, to try harder to be 'nice' to their customers but what does she know? She can be as nice as she likes but he would continue to 'be himself' and if the customers don't like it, well, they can sod off somewhere else. Instead, his annoying stupid customers kept coming back, no matter how he treated them. He wondered if he was to tell the most annoying of them to 'feck off', would they finally get the hint. His daddy Joe, was in the upstairs lounge, sitting and dribbling, in his wheelchair, watching a repeat of last year's All-Ireland Gaelic Football match between Dublin and Mayo. Jonjo couldn't help smiling to himself when he thought that his daddy probably thought the game was being broadcast live, he never seemed to want to watch anything else these days. Would Daddy do his best to silently cheer when Dublin wins the game again, and again by just one point?

Jonjo unhappily shared the shop duties with his mammy, he opened up every morning and she took over after she made lunch for Daddy. He had just about 'got used to' having to work all day every Tuesday when his mammy went off to play boring golf with her boring friends, but for the last few weeks he also had to work all day Thursday. Why had she suddenly decided to now play golf twice every week? She just took him for granted, she just assumed he wouldn't mind the extra hours and she didn't bother to ask, probably because she knew what his answer would be. She didn't care how he felt about being prevented from working out in his home gym, no, it didn't matter to her, she only cared about herself. She was now starting to remind him of his ex-wife, that bitch, Sandra. His mammy didn't appreciate the effort he had made nor the money he had spent on converting the garage into a gym and in having his own private suite built above it. He even had his own entrance so he didn't have to disturb them as he came and went, but in truth he never went out anyway, except to give his dilapidated old Ford Focus its weekly run to the off-license in nearby Fairview. His regime forced him to limit his drinking, the only alcohol he ever allowed himself were cans of Guinness and Black Bush Whiskey. A daily 'dose' of two cans of Guinness and a large whisky over one block of ice definitely wasn't overdoing it. In fact, it probably did him good, the Guinness gave him strength and the whiskey thinned his blood, preventing him from ever having a stroke, like his daddy had. Some Saturday nights as he sat in his suite, picking out old tunes on his mandolin, he was tempted to have a second whiskey but he knew how to control his desires, he would never submit to temptation like that bitch of a wife he was so lucky to finally get rid of. But he still kicked himself every day for waiting until she filed for divorce, why wasn't he quicker and get in first? He should have done it straight away and not allow bitch to pretend to be the injured party. He had heard that some of his so-called former friends had thought that he over-reacted that night but it was bitch who started it all. If it wasn't for her 'carrying on' with that idiot drunk, life would have been so different. She had spoiled it all, she had cocked up his life and he would never forgive her, not ever. He didn't blame 'that man' for 'trying it on' with bitch that night, any normal red-blooded man would have acted the way he did to bitch's flirting open invitation. Jonjo's only regret about that night was that he didn't just hit his wife straight away, it wasn't that feckin' man's fault, it was bitch's fault. Wouldn't it have been justice if it was her that had suffered that stroke instead of his daddy. Even if he had had to serve some time for hitting her, it would have been worth it, he would have been out of gaol by now but she would still be an invalid, dribbling and grunting all day, every day. She would no longer be able to throw herself at every man in a pair of trousers that showed her any attention, oh why hadn't he just done it?

He had to admit that his mammy had 'stuck by him' afterwards though, ok maybe it was because she needed help with the shop but she had never accused him of causing Daddy's stroke, although he knew that she thought it. It was his mammy who insisted that he take those stupid ridiculous anger-management classes. What a total complete waste of time they were, he thought, but his mammy kept telling him that he was so much nicer now and that he also seemed much happier. What a load of crap! Yes, it may be true that he has never outwardly lost his temper since that fateful night but that didn't mean he didn't feel the anger. He just didn't have the 'opportunity' to 'lose it'. He knew his anger with bitch hadn't gone anywhere, it was all still inside him, festering away, waiting for the right moment to be let loose. The best thing he had ever done was to have bitch's face printed on the cover of his punch bag. He practised every day, sometimes using just left jabs, other times a few left/right combination-punches, such satisfaction! It was a shame however, that no matter how hard or how often he hit her, she just kept smiling. Try as he might he couldn't knock the smile off her face and he couldn't even leave a bruise. It was perhaps fortunate that his daddy wasn't capable of coming into his gym and that his mammy wouldn't dare. He wished now that he had a photo of bitch with a bruised face to stick on his punch bag, but no such luck.

In the early days he used to take great pleasure in keeping track of what bitch was doing and he had warned off every new man that she tried to become friendly with. He was so proud of himself for never actually having to physically harm any of her potential suitors, a few thinly veiled threats always worked. He took great pleasure in knowing how threatening he could sound, he knew that he was brilliant at appearing to be mentally unhinged, who wouldn't be frightened of a violent madman? One who was already suspected of causing his daddy to have a stroke! On at least two occasions the Gardai had spoken to him but it was always his word against bitch's 'frightened mouse'. On those couple of occasions, he turned on the charm for the always dis-interested, incompetent Gardai. "No Sir, of course I didn't mean him any harm." He thought he was a pretty good actor and he knew full well that the Gardai will have told Sandra that unless he actually did become violent, there was really nothing they could do. He had lost count of the number of her pursued potential boyfriends he had got rid of, he was invincible, and he knew it. At least he thought he was, but the clever bitch eventually met some ageing Australian divorcee and she tricked him into taking her with him to Australia. He still managed to keep track of her whereabouts and he had heard that, of course, she had soon afterwards dumped her grandfather boyfriend. He knew that she was still living in Australia, in a seaside resort called Pacific Paradise, about an hour north of Brisbane. It pissed him off that he didn't know whether she had a new boyfriend or not but no matter, he knew what fate awaited her. It would not always be paradise for her, he'd see to that. He had thought about 'bumping her off' before she emigrated to Australia but he knew that he would end up with a long prison sentence and that his mammy and daddy still needed him. He had even thought of killing all three of them together and then taking his own life but, however useless his parents were, they didn't deserve that fate. No, he would bide his time and wait till Mammy and Daddy died and then he will live out his dream and travel to Pacific Paradise. He had two worries however, the first was that his mammy and daddy would outlive him, hence the controlled drinking, and the second was that bitch's next gullible lover would get there ahead of him, when he eventually realises how much of a bitch she really is.

Jonjo's pleasurable thoughts were suddenly interrupted when he heard a heavy thud on the floor above him. He dropped everything and sprang up the stairs, two at a time. His dad was lying on the floor, motionless. The crowd at Croke Park were going wild as Dublin took the lead again, so Jonjo quickly turned off the TV and returning to his daddy, he bent down to check if he was still breathing. Thank God yes, he was still breathing but his eyes were closed and his face was badly contorted. Jonjo had seen it all before, he knew his daddy was having another stroke. He quickly went downstairs, locked up the shop and called an ambulance. He knew his mammy had some 'special tablets' hidden away somewhere in case this happened again. While he waited for the ambulance to arrive, he searched everywhere for the feckin' tablets, eventually finding them in his mammy's bedside drawer, under her mobile phone. He forced one tablet into his daddy's mouth and thought he had better then call his mammy. Oh shit, her phone was still in the drawer, she forgot to take her mobile phone with her, what a bloody stupid woman, the one time I need her and she cannot be contacted. The ambulance quickly arrived and the slow-motion paramedics took his daddy off to Beaumont Hospital. He refused the offer of accompanying his daddy in the ambulance, he explained that he needed to get hold of his mammy first. He had a brainwave, he phoned the golf club Proshop and spoke to the dumb kid on reception, who told him that he didn't think his mammy was there today but he thought that, her usual playing partners, Jenny and Brenda were out there somewhere. Jonjo cut him off and jumped into his car, the golf club was only ten to fifteen-minutes-drive away. That idiot in the Proshop still hadn't a clue but Jonjo thought he knew what time they would have tee'd off at and where they would be, on the course, by now. Ignoring the idiot, he leaned over the counter and grabbed the keys for one of the electric buggies. It didn't take him long to catch up with Jenny and Brenda, who were wandering down a deserted fairway. Even before he had caught up on them, he could see that his mammy wasn't with them. How stupid of him to forget to look for her car in the car park. He pulled up beside Brenda who looked very surprised to see him. Brenda and Jenny had seen Jonjo once or twice over the years but he seldom, if ever, spoke to them, in fact, he seemed to go out of his way to shun them. Jenny walked over to join Brenda, just as Jonjo arrived, she immediately thought that something must have happened to Mary.

"What's up, has something happened to Mary?" asked Brenda.

"Where the feck is she? I thought she was with you?" said Jonjo.

"No, this is Thursday, she only plays golf with us on Tuesdays," replied Jenny. "What's wrong, Jonjo? You look very upset."

"I know it's feckin Thursday, so where is my mammy then?" said Jonjo impatiently. "It's my daddy Joe, he's been taken off in an ambulance, I think he's had another stroke."

"She's probably at her piano lessons in Howth," replied Brenda. "Why don't you call her on her mobile?"

"Piano lessons!" exclaimed Jonjo. "Where the feck does she go for piano lessons?"

"Didn't she tell you? she has taken up playing the piano again, I think it's in the lounge of the FFF Hotel in Howth," replied Brenda. "Why don't you just call her, Jonjo? she will want to know about Joe straight away."

"Don't you think I feckin' know that," shouted Jonjo. "That's why I'm here. The stupid woman forgot to take her mobile phone with her, she left it at home."

"No, she didn't forget her phone Jonjo," responded Jenny, "I spoke to her just before we tee'd off this morning."

Jonjo did his best to look calm but the ladies could see that he was totally confused. Eventually Jonjo politely thanked them for their help and started to drive away in his buggy.

"Jonjo, let's know how Joe is, as soon as you know something," shouted Brenda after him.

Jonjo heard Brenda call him but he ignored her. Back in the golf club car park, Jonjo parked his buggy and taking his mobile out of his pocket, he dialled his mammy's number. After just a few rings, Mary answered him. He thought that she seemed to be flustered even before he told her what had happened to Daddy, what the feck was she 'up to' anyway?

Jonjo told his mammy that Daddy was on his way to Beaumont Hospital and that it didn't look 'too good'. He could hear the sense of panic in her voice as she exclaimed that she should have been there when it happened. He heard her shout 'oh, it's my fault, oh it's my fault'. Jonjo resisted the temptation to ask where the hell she was, he just agreed with her that they should make their own way to the hospital and he would meet her there. Jonjo hung up and then 'threw' the buggy key back onto the counter of the Proshop. What the hell was going on? On the way to the hospital he took a detour back home, he had to investigate that mobile phone, which was hidden in his mammy's bedside table drawer. Up in her bedroom, he turned on the new mobile, he had no trouble with the password, his geriatric Mammy used the same password for everything, probably because she could only remember one password!

He was shocked at what he read, his mammy was having a feckin' affair! He was disgusted, what the hell was she doing at her age? He read about her several secret rendezvous with someone named Conor, who the hell is Conor? I'll feckin' kill him, I don't care who he is. He had to sit down, as he read on. Christ they were drinking and playing music together, and God knows what else, and all behind his poor daddy's back. They even had a plan to soon spend seven days golfing together in Tenerife! His conniving bitch of a mother had hatched a plan to tell his daddy that she was going away for a few days with Brenda and Jenny. What a two-faced bitch, Christ has she no shame? What pissed him off even more was that she had 'taken for granted' that he would take care of both his daddy and the shop, while she was away. Jesus, all women are the bloody same, he thought. If you can't even trust your feckin' pensioner mammy, who can you trust? She's worse that that bitch Sandra. He carefully closed down the mobile phone and replaced it back exactly where it was.

As he drove to the hospital his brain was working overtime. Why was everybody trying to cock up his life? Why can't people be more like him, he would never do anything like that. It's women, it's all women, they only think about themselves. Selfish bitches, every one of them. By the time he reached the hospital he already had formulated a plan, and a simple one at that. He was proud of himself to have already worked out the two brilliant options.

Option number one, he spoke out loud to himself: If his poor daddy failed to recover from this, it was all his mammy's fault and only her fault. She would pay dearly for her deception, but it would have to be subtle. He would wait a few weeks, maybe even a few months after the funeral, before she met her fate in some blameless terrible accident. After a suitable length of 'mourning', he would then sell off the Post Office and use the proceeds to take a one-way flight to Australia and live out his 'dying' wish. He was relishing the thought of meeting Sandra again, this time for the very last time.

Option number two, he again spoke out loud to himself: 'If his daddy recovered, and he wasn't sure now if he wanted him to or not, it could be a long dragged-out affair. He guessed that his daddy would then probably need twenty-four-hour care, for God knows how long. His poor daddy would need his 'adoring' wife to take care of him, Jonjo wouldn't want to take this on alone. Shit, he hated the thoughts of it but he would then need help from his cheating, lying feckin' mother. But his daddy probably couldn't live for much longer anyway. With any luck, hopefully sooner rather than later, his 'loving tender' mother could look forward to some, as yet undefined, terrible accident. Getting rid of that imbecile Conor would be easy, he didn't even need to hurt him and his mammy would never get to know why her new 'lover' had abandoned her, in her hour of greatest need. He knew that a few 'chosen' words from him and Conor would see that he had better 'cut his losses' and still live. He would make it a condition that Conor would not be able to say anything to his mammy, he would have to swear to ignore all her calls and messages, that is only if he valued his life, of course. He actually chuckled at the thought of his then rejected mother not only feeling guilty for causing his poor daddy such pain, but also desperately sad and depressed about losing the new love of her life, and never knowing why. Let's see how she likes joining my DMC, my 'depressed members club', he thought.

Jonjo had cheered himself up by the time he was walking from the hospital car park. He knew that he couldn't let his mammy know that he knew all about her dark secret. He had to play cool and see what happens, he had plenty of time. As he headed towards the hospital ward, he saw his mammy outside in the corridor. Her crocodile tears were pathetic!

"What kept you son, I thought you would be here ages ago?" she blurted out.

What's with the 'son' bit, he thought to himself. He couldn't even remember when she last called him her son.

"Sorry I had to interrupt your golf game Mammy," apologised Jonjo, with not even a hint of sarcasm. "Were you playing well at the time?"

Chapter 30

We had just finished playing *Brown Eyed Girl* together, when Mary's mobile phone rang. The blood seemed to drain from her face in an instant, I'd never seen such a sudden and frightening reaction. Her face went white, she slumped over and leaned to one side, I thought that she was about to fall off the piano stool. I dropped my guitar onto the stage and ran over to her, just managing to catch her before she hit the stage floor. I knew something dreadful had happened! As I listened to her conversation on her phone, I had a good idea what the problem was.

"That was my son Jonjo on the phone," she blurted out, "Joe has had a bad turn and is on his way to hospital, I need to get there straight away. Oh Jesus, what have I done! It's all my fault, I should never have left him this morning."

"What's happened Mary, can I help?" I asked, but I already knew the answer.

"It's my fault, God did that to me because I have been lying to Joe!" she sobbed. "If something bad happens to him I will never forgive myself, I wasn't there when he needed me most."

Mary left in a panic, she didn't look back, didn't say or even wave goodbye.

"I text you later," I shouted after her, "I hope he'll be ok."

I picked up my guitar and made my way up the stairs to my room. I didn't know how I felt. I was very worried about Mary's state of mind. If Joe has had another stroke, he could be even more disabled and possibly need full time care, that would be the end of Mary and I! I figured that the best that could happen is that Joe eventually makes a full recovery and gets back to where he was before. What would happen then, I wondered? Mary is such a caring and devoted person she would still feel very guilty and forever blame herself for 'poor' Joe's stroke. Ok, she might feel that she 'got away' with her selfish neglect, but she would never take another risk like that. So, no matter how it turns out for Joe, I realised that Mary and I, as a couple, are finished! From now on, Mary will be fanatical about taking care of Joe, I simply won't figure in her thoughts again. I couldn't help myself, I was starting to hate Joe and I didn't like myself very much for that. Once again, I felt completely helpless, the situation was completely out of my control. Over the past few weeks, I thought I had 'played my cards' really well with Mary. I hadn't rushed things and she made it easy for me to really get to know and like her. She was becoming more and more like 'my Mary' every day. I still didn't allow myself however, to believe that she had any feelings for me, I just hoped that this would come with time. My goal was to get her to just like me enough to want to spend time with me, but this dream had just 'gone out the window'. I lay down on my bed and tried hard to think if there was any way I could turn this mess around, but I kept 'hitting a brick wall'. Some problems just don't have any good solution and this was definitely one of those problems.

The previous few weeks had been wonderful. I didn't know how she managed it but Mary had found the time to spend lots of time with me. We had a 'get to know you better' chat over coffee at Insomnia on Wednesdays, I guess she told Joe that her weekly shopping was just taking a little longer than it used to. She didn't 'lead me on' in any way, she always insisted that she would never leave Joe but that she thought she could balance her life and spend some of her spare time with me. Mary surprised me however, with her comment when she stated *"what Joe doesn't know, won't hurt him"*.

Over coffee, on that first Wednesday, I asked Mary if she still played piano. I told her that ever since we first started going out together as teenagers, I used to love sitting in her parents living room, listening to her playing many of the classics by the great composers. I didn't know anything about classical music but I soon got to know and appreciate all those rich tunes, even if I didn't know what they were called and couldn't tell Mozart from Beethoven or Bach. I had never heard anyone playing music like that before and now, here I was, listening to Mary play with such enthusiasm, just for me. She was not only the most beautiful girl I had ever set eyes upon, she was also the most talented. Best of all, she was my girlfriend. As we sipped our second black coffee in Insomnia on that first occasion, Mary told me that unfortunately she no longer had a piano in her home and since neither Joe or Jonjo showed any interest in her hobby that she just didn't bother. I told Mary that 'her other self' had purchased a second hand piano when we first arrived in Belgium years ago and that it had 'followed us around' ever since. I explained that 'my Mary' played for at least an hour almost every day and that she enjoyed every minute of it.

Before we finished that second coffee, we had 'hatched a cunning plan' together. I asked her if she would like to 'have a go' on the piano, on the stage at the FFF hotel. Mary 'jumped at it' and said that she would tell Joe that she was going to play golf the next day. She said that she was confident that Jonjo wouldn't mind taking care of the shop when she was out. My mind was a whirl as I walked Mary to her car, which was parked in the supermarket car park. We said goodbye with a 'sneaky peck on the cheek' and I was really pleased that Mary didn't seem in the least bit worried if someone she knew might see the pair of us together. As soon as her car disappeared out of sight, I quickly went into the adjoining Apple shop. Just minutes later I walked out of the shop with a brand-new iPad Pro. I knew just what to do, I had set this up before, at our home in the England. Back at the FFF hotel, I downloaded the App for piano music,

Music Notes. I had done this already for 'my Mary' several years earlier and it only took me a few minutes to download some of the great tunes, which I remembered, 'my Mary' had played all those years ago. I also downloaded some of her favourite tunes, which she often played at home in Buckingham, including many of Adele's hits and the one that she had just started to practise, Queen's *Bohemian Rhapsody*.

Mary was a little shy and a little 'rusty' when she played on stage in the deserted Pally, deserted that is except for me, that first Thursday, but by the following week she was 'well into it' and encouraged me to join in with my guitar. We had again found something which we both really enjoyed and each day I downloaded a few extra tunes. Mary told me that she had told Joe that she had started to play golf on Thursdays in addition to the regular Tuesdays and she giggled with excitement at the thought of 'sneaking behind Joe's back'. I had already stopped playing golf at St Anne's and now only played occasionally at Deer Park with Mark.

I couldn't believe my luck when Mary agreed that she would come with me on a short holiday to the sunshine Spanish island of Tenerife for a week of fun with a few rounds of golf at Los Americas golf course, thrown in. We agreed to go for just seven days this time and that I would reserve the flights and the Mediterranean Palace Hotel in Las Americas. I had all the arrangements sorted by the following day and had sent Mary the confirmation by text. As agreed, Mary would pay her costs direct and would tell Joe and Jonjo that she is going on a golf break to Tenerife with Brenda and Jenny. She planned to tell Joe that Brenda and Jenny are going to share but she will have a separate room for herself. She told me that she wasn't going to tell either Brenda or Jenny about her secret plans, saying that they didn't need to know. Mary giggled every time we spoke about our holiday, which was now booked to start on my birthday, just weeks away. Mary and I were acting like teenagers in the first flushes of love as we exchanged texts several times each day, we were actually going away for the first time ever, together. She said that Jonjo wouldn't mind taking care of both Joe and the shop, she thought he would feel proud to be depended upon. When I asked Mary if she was worried if Joe or Jonjo might discover our plan, she replied that since neither Joe nor Jonjo ever bump into Brenda or Jenny, they will never get to know. To be safe however, she said that she would wait until after Christmas before letting them know about the planned trip. We were really excited and we enjoyed texting each other several times each day. I told her all about the many brilliant restaurants and music bars which I planned to take her to in Tenerife. I didn't mention it to Mary, I mustn't rush things again, but it crossed my mind that if we can get away with this, we can get away with lots of other holidays in the future. God, my life here, in this universe, has taken a turn for the better!

Mark had done a lot of work on the list of songs I gave him to check out and we had serious discussions about what to do next. The list of 'unknown' songs from my universe contained about 15 new 'hit songs' which I knew in full and another ten or so, which I knew parts of. We would need to form a band and see if we could turn them into hits all over again, which I would pretend to have written. I know that Danny and Alison would love to get involved, perhaps with a couple of new band members, but all that would be for later. But what would I do when I exhausted all the songs I knew already, my so-called prolific song writing talent would soon 'dry up' and I had absolutely no clue how to write even one original tune. But all the songs, which I already knew, are really good so maybe we could manage to 'live off' them. For this to work, I knew that it is now absolutely essential that I continue to live here as Conor. Although I wonder what will happen with Robert? Carlos is right, we need to bring him in on our secret before he blows it by exposing my pretence to be Conor. But if he knows I'm not Conor, why would he want to do this? Carlos had said that there must be a very good reason why Robert was still staying quiet, and I thought that he must be right, because we hadn't heard any more about Robert's 'newly-found Conor', since Peter 'tipped off' Mark, several weeks ago. The good news is that Carlos had been in touch several times with Mark and reported that he was making excellent progress in his travels around Europe. He was doing so well, he planned to stay there for another week or so, to complete the job. With nothing negative seemingly forthcoming from Robert, Carlos thought that perhaps we have more time than we first thought. Anyway, all my plans had now been blown away again, by that call from Jonjo. I didn't care about making music with Danny and Ali, I didn't care about anything. I didn't even care about Robert and his plan to expose me. He can do whatever he likes, I don't care as he can't make things any worse than they already now are.

Before I got around to contacting her, Mary sent me a text that evening. She explained that Joe had indeed suffered another stroke and it didn't look too good. It was too early to tell, but it looked like he would probably survive but he could lose even more mobility and he still hadn't managed to speak yet. She shouldn't have left Joe alone that day, it was her fault but it will never happen again. Joe didn't deserve this, but if as expected, he survives, she will from now on, fully devote herself to his care. It looked like this could be a twenty-four-hour job for the foreseeable future, but she would 'stick by him' for as long as he needed her. She apologised and said that she hopes I can understand but that she won't be able to continue with our music sessions any more. She also asked me to cancel my booking to Tenerife and promised to reimburse me for any money I lose.

I went up to my room and lay down on my bed. I was totally devastated. What a bloody awful turn of events, just when things had picked up, I get knocked down again. What's the point? I tried to convince myself that I felt really sorry for Joe, what a bleak boring miserable future he had ahead of him, my misery is nothing compared to his! I knew that I should, but I just couldn't sympathise with Joe. I knew I shouldn't think like this, but I couldn't stop myself, I have to admit that I am hoping that he won't pull through. Wouldn't it be better and more humane if Joe would simply 'slip away', in a painless and peaceful way. Not only better for Joe but also for Mary and I. I hated myself for thinking like this but if Joe would just die now, it would solve so many problems for my future with Mary. All obstacles removed 'at a stroke' or should I say 'by a stroke'. Mary wouldn't have to have a messy divorce from Joe, she wouldn't have to sell the business, unless she wanted to, of course, and I would be happy to become Jonjo's step-father. Oh, I shouldn't allow myself to think like this.

Chapter 31

That text from Mary really upset me, I couldn't see a way back from it. Next morning, I called Mark and told him that I didn't feel very well and just wanted to be on my own for a few days. Although he said that he understood, within half an hour, Mark caught up with me at the hotel. I decided it would be better if I told Mark everything, this 'cloak and dagger' was driving me insane. Mark appeared to be sympathetic and explained that since Carlos was not due back until late next week, I could 'take as long as I like' and call him when I was ready to resume my life again, as Conor. I had a miserable weekend. I didn't hear from Mary and although it was difficult, I resisted the temptation to text her.

Mark phoned me late on Monday night and he seemed worried. He told me that Peter had just called him and told him 'confidentially' that Robert was now ready to 'get rid of that lying thieving fraud, who calls himself Conor'. Mark told me that Robert intended finding some pretext to meet up with me to try to secretly get some of my DNA, which he said would prove conclusively that I wasn't his brother Conor. Robert was hopeful that the DNA would finally establish my real identity as he thought that I would probably be on some police force's criminal data base.

"So what Mark, let Robert do his worst," I responded flippantly. "We both believe that Robert already knows that I'm not actually Conor, but he will get a shock when he discovers that I really am his full brother and that I'm also Ian's identical twin!"

"Yes, I know that Conor, but we don't want any of this to happen until Carlos gets back from Europe, so can you please avoid meeting up with either Robert or even Peter, for the next few days. I will contact Carlos and let him know what is going on, added Mark."

"Ok Mark, I promise I won't make any arrangement to meet either Robert or Peter and if either of them 'accidentally' bump into me, I will make some excuse and slope off," I replied.

Mary was racked with guilt and she was devastated that Joe was not making much progress recovering from his second stroke. She visited Joe early each morning and stayed by his side, until late each night. Mary hardly spoke to Jonjo, since the Thursday when Joe had been hospitalised. She was really grateful that Jonjo had taken over the running of the Post Office full-time, but he didn't encourage conversation with her, not ever. Mary didn't care about the Post Office, all she wanted was for Joe to begin to show signs of getting better. The consultant said that he was confident that Joe was not in any immediate danger but that he would need to stay in hospital for several weeks and then would need months of support when he went home. On the first Monday night after Joe was taken to hospital,

Mary asked Jonjo if it would be alright if she joined her friends for her usual game of golf the next morning and afterwards go straight from the golf to the hospital to visit Joe. Mary knew that this could be the last time she could meet Brenda and Jenny for several weeks, maybe even months because once Joe was allowed home, she wouldn't leave his side again.

"Mother, I don't care where you are planning to go or who you are planning to meet or what you plan to do when you get there," replied Jonjo. "As far as I'm concerned you can even go to play piano all day with 'Jack the Ripper' if you like."

Mary loaded her golf clubs into her car early Tuesday morning. There was still a slight frost on the ground but for a December day, she thought that this was as good as it gets. She hadn't slept very well, she still felt a little guilty about looking forward to playing golf with Brenda and Jenny, while Joe was lying on his back in a hospital bed, in a bleak public ward. She thought back to how abruptly and cynically Jonjo had answered her the night before but he was clearly still very upset about his dad. No, Jonjo just couldn't possibly know anything about her playing the piano, could he? She had been ultra-careful about keeping her secret and now that it was all over, neither Joe nor Jonjo would ever get to know about it. Having that second mobile had been a stroke of genius, no, she was sure that Jonjo had just mentioned the piano at random, just to unload his anger with everything. Jonjo just couldn't have found out anything about her secret meetings with Conor because if he did know, he would have let her know in no uncertain terms. As she drove to St Anne's Golf Club, she tried to remember the words Jonjo greeted her with when she first arrived at the hospital on that fateful previous Thursday. She couldn't remember his exact words when they met at the hospital, but she thought he mentioned something about hoping that she wasn't playing golf too well. Not something he would ever care about and certainly not at a time when his dad might be dying in intensive care. No, she knew that she was becoming paranoid, Jonjo was just being his usual cynical and grumpy self.

Brenda and Jenny were already in the changing room when Mary arrived, so she quickly changed her shoes and walked with them to the first tee. Brenda asked Mary how Joe was getting on and Jenny wanted to know all the minute details. Mary was pleased that her friends showed genuine interest in Joe's health, it hadn't occurred to her to ask Brenda and Jenny, when and how they had heard about Joe but she thought how true it was that 'bad news travels fast'. When they all three stood next to each other on the fourth tee, Brenda suddenly said:

"Well Mary, at least it was great to see that Jonjo is still looking very fit and healthy, it's been years since we last saw him. Is he ok now Mary? He seemed very upset when we saw him here last Thursday."

Mary stopped moving, she was in shock. She listened in horror as

Brenda and Jenny recounted everything that had happened that Thursday.

"Jonjo came here looking for you Mary, he was in a panic," said Brenda. "He told us what had happened to Joe. He told us that he couldn't contact you because he thought that you had left your mobile phone behind, in the house. We were surprised when Jonjo said that he didn't know about your piano lessons at the FFF hotel, I hope we haven't 'given the game away', Mary. Fortunately, we were able to tell Jonjo that you definitely had your mobile phone with you, so he hurried off to call you. I'm glad we could be of some help to him Mary, he looked distraught."

Mary needed to sit down on the nearby wooden bench and think. She was feeling sick to her stomach, what should she do now? What could she do? What was Jonjo planning? He clearly knew much more than he pretended. Mary asked her friends if she could take a minute to make a phone call, she stood up and took several steps away. She turned on her mobile phone, she knew she had to warn Conor immediately. She guessed that Jonjo must have come across her 'secret' phone in her bedside drawer. She worried about what he might do next, Jonjo was so unpredictable, there was no telling what he might do. Shit, she said out-loud when she realised that she didn't have Conor's number in her phone, in her panic, she had temporarily forgotten that it was only 'plumbed' into her second mobile phone. Without thinking she dialled the Post Office land-line, she had no idea what she would say when Jonjo answered. She let the phone ring and ring, maybe Jonjo was serving a customer. She suggested to Brenda and Jenny that they should carry on without her, she told them that there was an issue at home that she needed to attend to. She waited until her friends had disappeared out of earshot and tried the Post Office number again, it kept on ringing, Jonjo must have forgotten to switch on the answer phone. She sat back down on the bench and tried to think straight, but her heart seemed to beat even faster, she couldn't stop it racing. She closed her eyes and tried to be rational, should she try Jonjo's mobile phone? Without thinking about it any longer, she scrolled down to Jonjo's number and dialled, it went straight to answer phone. She hung up in panic. She dialled again and this time left a message for him to call her back. She was still in a state of panic when she got back to the Post Office, which was locked up and deserted. She saw the 'Closed Today' sign on the front door. She let herself in and quickly ran to retrieve her other mobile phone from her bedroom. She had to call Conor now, she knew he could be in danger, Jonjo was 'on a mission' so she couldn't risk just texting Conor, she had to speak to him. The phone wasn't where she had left it, where could she have put it? A thorough search of her bedroom failed to find it, she had a brainwave, she would call her missing phone using the Post Office land-line! She picked up the phone and hesitated, shit, she couldn't even remember the number. She continued her search until finally she checked Jonjo's room and then his gym. She was at first shocked and then disgusted when she saw his punchbag, Christ he really must be sick! Yes, he's sick in the head, bitter, twisted and very dangerous. There was no alternative, she jumped back into her car and headed off to Howth and the FFF Hotel. She prayed that she would get there on time. As she drove, she figured out that Jonjo must have found her phone and then discovered her password. She assumed that he must have taken her phone, oh Christ, what will he do?

I had long finished breakfast and had freshened myself up. I decided that the weather was excellent for a stroll around the Hill of Howth, not a breath of wind and the temperature was a few pleasant degrees above freezing. I thought that the Cliff Walk was just what I needed to get all the negative thoughts out of my head. Although Mary still hadn't contacted me, I felt confident that, in time, she would. As soon as things settle down with Joe, I felt that she will get in touch. At least I tried to convince myself of that, I had to believe that! I approached the hotel front desk but even before I got there Joan smiled at me and shouted over …

"Hi Conor, anything exciting planned for today, any piano lessons scheduled?"

"Morning Joan, no, not today, I'm going to take advantage of the very clement weather and take a walk around the Cliff Walk and maybe have lunch at the Summit Inn," I replied. "Can I have a copy of 'The Independent' Joan? I like to read it over lunch," I asked.

"Oh, sorry Conor, I just gave my last copy of 'The Independent' to that gentleman sitting just over there, he's waiting for his friend to arrive," she replied apologetically. "How about The Times, would that do?"

I glanced over and saw a rather large rough-looking middle-aged man sitting on the settee next the window. He was 'pasted' into a slightly worn black studded leather jacket. His scruffy black beenie was almost pulled down completely over his eyes. He immediately stood up, God, he was a big menacing guy, handed me his newspaper and walked out through the front door. He never said a word and didn't even nod when I thanked him.

"What a strange guy Joan, how long has he been sitting there, have you ever seen him here before?" I asked.

Joan told me that he had been sitting there for almost an hour, without hardly looking up from his newspaper. She said that he wasn't a resident and he never mentioned who he was waiting for. She said that he just grunted a refusal when she offered him a cup of tea.

I buttoned up my jacket and tucked my newspaper under my left arm as I turned left on Nashville Road and within a few minutes, I turned right on Balscadden Road. The view of Howth Harbour with all its pleasure boats was, as always, breath-taking. The sky-blue water and the magnificent brown-green island of Ireland's Eye, was stretched out before me. Life could be very good here in Howth. I was getting to know all of my brothers and sisters plus their children and grandchildren all over again and I knew that as soon as Robert finds out that I am not a lying cheat, he might even become my best friend. I felt I already knew Peter, Mark and Marian quite well, but Fiona, who seemed so nice, was only a child when Mary and I emigrated to Canada. I could now look forward to spending more time with everyone and getting to really know them even better. Wish though, that I could have just one more chat with my dead brother Louis over a pint and have lunch just once more with my dead sister Jean! I wondered if Carlos could help with that stupid impossible wish!

I wouldn't allow myself to become depressed about Mary, I hung on to the belief that we would soon be together again, "it's just a question of time," I said out-loud to myself.

I had now arrived at the impressive yellow walls of the 'stretched-out' Balscadden House. It was perched on the edge of the cliff on the left with just enough room for a footpath wide enough for only one person. Each time you met someone coming the other way, you had to step onto the very narrow winding road to let them pass. As I had done many times before, I stopped and stood back to read the plaque which was fixed to the eight-foot-high solid wall. The house and gardens were certainly secluded, impossible to see over the wall, privacy was important for those 'hiding' behind the impenetrable façade. The words on the plaque, which must have been erected by the Irish tourist board proclaimed:

W. B. YEATES
POET
LIVED HERE 1880 -1883

I had seen the plaque many times but had never thought much about it before. Yes, I knew of William Butler Yeats, but I knew nothing about him. I didn't 'get' his poetry but thousands, perhaps even millions of other people admired both the man and his poetry. Perhaps it was because I had to learn some of his poems off by heart, for school exams that I didn't like them. I took my old i-Phone from my pocket and 'googled' him. I have to admit I still couldn't get excited by his words, they must be 'above me'. He certainly had an interesting life though. I hadn't realised that he 'dabbled' in the occult and had even attended several seances. I continued to read through some of his quotes, as I strolled slowly along the path which led to the start of the Cliff Walk. When I read his next quote, it took me aback:

"There is another world, but it is in this one."

I searched but couldn't find the context in which the quote was made. What was William trying to say to us? The uncertainty about the workings of the smallest particles in nature hadn't even been dreamed of back then and neither had the concept of parallel universes. Was William, or Bill or Billy or whatever his friends called him, maybe onto something? Had his interest in the occult led him to think about reality and the possibility of 'other realities'? No way of knowing but an intriguing thought, none the less. I turned off my i-Phone and opened up the 'secret' mobile, which Mary had given me, and checked to see if she had sent me any new messages, no, not a sausage! Disappointed, but not surprised, I turned off the phone and started to walk a little more quickly. Oh, right now I wish I was a poet as only a poet could think of words beautiful enough to do justice to the inspiring views in front of me. I was now several hundred yards along the narrow, rocky and slippery Cliff Walk. There were signs everywhere, warning about the steep drop and I was fully aware that quite a few people had slipped to their deaths over the years, either accidentally or by their own hand, who knows? I loved the surroundings but I had a healthy respect for the terrain and always made sure not to walk too close to the crumbling edge. I turned around the 'head' and noticed a person leaning back against the edge of the bank. From the distance I thought that it looked like the man from the hotel lobby. When I got closer, I knew it was him and for some unknown reason my heart skipped a beat but at least I knew that he couldn't have been following me, as he had got there before me. As I came alongside, he turned to meet me and stood up straight, looking straight at me. He still had his jacket zipped up and his hat seemed to be pulled down even further over his eyes. I couldn't help notice that his grizzly face hadn't seen a razor for several days.

"Good morning," I said, with a strange sense of foreboding. "Thank you for the newspaper."

"Are you Conor?" he asked gruffly.

"Who wants to know?" I answered.

"I'm Jonjo. I'm Mary's son. I believe you know her," he responded in a friendly tone.

"Pleased to meet you," I said, as I held out my hand.

He took my hand and seemed to take pleasure as I winced from the pain of his deliberate vice-like grip. He then let go of my hand and apologised for "perhaps squeezing it too hard."

"Sorry Conor," he apologised, "sometimes I just forget my own strength. Do you mind if I walk along with you for a while? I think we need to have a friendly discussion."

"It's a free country Jonjo, I couldn't stop you walking alongside me, even if I wanted to, which I don't. But what do you want to talk about?" I responded.

"Conor, my mother Mary has told me all about how friendly you believe that she and you have become. You probably already know that my dad has been taken to hospital and my mammy is completely heartbroken. She felt so bad, that as my dad lay in his hospital bed, she confessed to him. She told us all about you. She was crying as she made it clear that there was nothing between you two, she just selfishly took the opportunity to have some fun wasting your time and money. She asked for our forgiveness and said that she will never make the same mistake again. She said that she won't even bother to say goodbye to you. Mammy even told us about your booked holiday to Tenerife but she said that she would never have gone through with it, she said that she wouldn't have shown up at the airport. Conor, don't get me wrong, I do love my mammy but since dad had his first accident all those years ago, she hasn't been all right in the head. Some of her friends have even commented quietly to me that 'she's not the full shillin'."

Shit… was I in big trouble or what! It didn't help that I was standing on the edge of a path that had a more than fifty-foot drop into the open sea. The fact that I couldn't swim was not a problem as I would be dead before I hit the water. I looked ahead of and behind me…. not a soul in sight. I had better 'buy time', I thought.

"Why are you here Jonjo, what do you want from me?" I asked, in as friendly a manner as I could.

"Conor, I don't know you, but you seem like a nice man," he started. "I'm sorry that my mother tricked you into showing her affection but it's not the first time that she has done this to gullible old men. I'm afraid that I have had to keep an eye on her Conor, which is why I am here today. I have had to give some helpful advice to at least another three 'lonely hearts', over the last few years. Fortunately, all of them saw sense before any damage was done. My dad never got to find out about the others," he added.

"Tell you what Jonjo," I stuttered, "why don't we walk up to the Summit Inn and have a friendly chat about it all, over a pint or two?"

"Conor, what are your intentions? My dad needs my mammy now, more than ever. She doesn't need any distractions like some silly old man who thinks he is wanted and needed. In truth Conor, I like you and just don't like to see you being made a fool of," said Jonjo.

"Jonjo, are you now offering me some friendly advice?" I stupidly asked.

At last I could see a man in the distance walking toward us. He was walking a large black dog, probably a Labrador, on a tight lead. He was perhaps just five-minutes-walk away. I suddenly felt a little safer. Jonjo suddenly went quiet, he seemed to relax a little.

"Jonjo, you must see that your mother hasn't had much of a life so far. Are you that surprised that she wants to start enjoying herself a little?" I asked.

"Surprised? No, I'm not surprised at all," he replied. "As I already said, you're not the first 'sucker' she has tried to 'rope' and I'm sure you won't be the last. I have had to 'warn off' countless other delusional men before, some much younger and better looking than you, before. Some of them even had hair on their head! But she has always 'seen sense' in the end though, before my dad got to learn about them."

"Jonjo, I know what you are trying to do and I know why. But it's not going to work. I know that your mother is not how you are portraying her. Jonjo, your mother is not deluded and neither is she mentally disturbed. She is mature and sane enough to know what she wants," I said matter-of-factly. "If she wants to spend some time with me, I will be very happy to oblige but I won't force myself on her, against her wishes."

He went very quiet. He continued to walk along beside me for several minutes, without saying a word. The man and his dog then passed us by, with a cheery "good afternoon" but neither Jonjo nor I answered back, we just nodded in his direction. A few minutes later Jonjo stopped walking and looked straight at me. I stopped to meet his stare.

"Conor, you don't understand," he said, in a threatening tone. "I can't just stand by and let you 'fool around' with my mammy! I won't allow you to feck up my life, I won't, I won't."

"Jonjo, your mother says that you have done a pretty good job of fecking up your own life. In fact, not just your own life but also her life and your dad's life, into the bargain," I responded.

I didn't see it coming. Jonjo pointed out to sea and when I turned to see what he was pointing at, I felt his two huge hands flat on my back, between my shoulder blades. I hadn't the strength to resist, I was walking straight over the edge of the cliff. I tried to grab his jacket but he brushed my hand away like swatting a wasp. I tried to scream but my mouth was dry. I could feel myself falling and falling. I think I got hold of some long grass or weeds but I kept on falling……

Chapter 32

I was slowly becoming aware. I was lying in bed and my back ached constantly, whether I moved or not. I could hear two people talking quietly, but I kept my eyes closed. I had absolutely no idea where I was, but I hoped to glean some information from the conversation continuing beside me. The man and woman seemed to be oblivious to my existence, but they gave no hint as to where I might be.

I could smell someone's toothpaste breath just above my face. I slowly opened my eyes but the face above me was very blurred. I quickly closed my eyes again and lay there motionless.

"Are you awake Mr Forman, can you hear me?" said a very gentle soft female voice."

"Sort of," I answered. "I think so, but my eyes are a little blurry."

"Well, don't try to open them just yet," she said. "Let me get you some eye drops."

I could feel the mist being sprayed onto the outside of my top eyelids. I waited a minute or so and then tried to open my eyes again. After a few blinks, my vision started to clear.

"Welcome back, Mr Forman, do you know where you are?" she asked.

I looked at the face of the friendly voice, she smiled at me encouragingly. I looked at the name of the badge pinned to the lapel of her outfit.... Nurse Green.

"Yes, I do," I replied. "I'm in hospital."

"Do you know which hospital, Mr Forman?" she asked. "Do you know where you are?"

"Well, I presume it's Beaumont Hospital but I'm not sure," I answered.

"Do you know your full name and what today's date is?" asked Nurse Green.

"Yes, of course I do," I answered. "I'm Conor Forman and I think today's date is December 14th."

"Do you know the year Mr Forman?"

"Yes, it's 2017. But only for another couple of weeks," I answered.

"Ok Mr Forman, let me get the doctor to have a word with you, I'll be back in a few moments," she said.

I lay back in bed and tried to remember how I ended up in Beaumont Hospital. I remembered falling, and falling forever, seemingly in slow motion, whilst trying to cling onto anything I could grab hold of. This was no accident! In a rage, Jonjo had deliberately pushed me off the cliff. I must have had a very soft landing because I didn't feel like I had any broken limbs. Maybe Jonjo had second thoughts and pulled me back up, after I had been knocked unconscious! I cannot remember anything after that feeling of falling and falling. I knew that there were several needles stuck in my arm and that the bed was beginning to feel more and more uncomfortable. I looked out the window to my left and saw that there was a wind up, the leafless branches were swaying wildly to an erratic rhythm. The doctor soon arrived and introduced himself as Doctor Brain. What a great name for a medical doctor, I thought. He bent down over me and checked my eye movements with his narrow beam torch.

"Remarkable, remarkable," he said very slowly.

"What did you say your first name is, Mr Forman?" he asked.

"I'm Conor, Conor Forman," I replied.

"And the current date Mr Forman?"

"Well, I'm not sure how long I've been lying here," I replied. "I know that the accident happened on December 14th so it might be the 15th, or even the 16th, I suppose."

"Remarkable, remarkable," he repeated. "What exactly happened on the 14th, what can you remember?" he asked.

"Doctor, someone deliberately pushed me off the cliff in Howth, it couldn't have been an accident. One moment I was walking along, chatting to Jonjo and the next minute I could feel him pushing me over the edge of the cliff. I've no idea who rescued me, maybe it was actually Jonjo himself."

"And who exactly is Jonjo, Mr Forman?"

"Jonjo is Mary's grown up son. Together they run the Post Office in Raheny. Christ, Jonjo knows about us Doctor, I think that Mary might be in danger, would you be able to get in touch with her quickly, before it's too late?"

"Where's Raheny, Mr Forman?" asked Doctor Brain.

Jesus, how can the doctor not know where Raheny is, what planet has he been on, I thought!

"Raheny is an area of Dublin, it's only a few miles from here," I replied. "Doctor, would you mind calling the Post Office and ask Mary to drop in to see me as soon as she can? Tell her that she may be in danger."

"Mary who, Mr Forman, what's her surname?" asked the doctor.

"Her married name is Kenny," I replied. "She's married to Joe but he probably won't be there at the moment as he is in hospital, having recently suffered a stroke. Christ, he's actually a patient here in this hospital doctor. Christ, Mary is probably here right now, she spends most of her free time sitting by his bedside, keeping vigil. Don't bother calling the Post Office just yet doctor, I'm sure you will find Mary is already in this hospital somewhere."

Doctor Brain assured me that I was not in any danger but that I needed to get some rest. He told me that I had nothing to worry about now, it's just that I was a little confused after being unconscious for such a long time.

What was the stupid doctor on about? I thought, but it didn't matter, he left the room immediately, leaving me alone with Nurse Green. I assumed that he went off to see if he could locate Mary.

Nurse Green sat silently in the visitor's chair by my bedside. I tried to engage her in conversation but she didn't answer, she just smiled back at me. I couldn't sleep now, how could I sleep at a time like this?

After a wait of about fifteen or twenty silent and anxious minutes, Doctor Brain walked back into my room, with Mary walking right behind him.

"Oh, thank God you are here Mary," I exclaimed. "How is Joe today, is he feeling any better?"

Mary looked at me with a puzzled expression. She ignored my question about Joe, instead she asked me how I was feeling. I told her that I was feeling ok, considering what happened. Mary asked me to explain everything I could remember about what happened. I told her that she might want Doctor Brain and Nurse Green to leave the room for a few minutes, because what I needed to say was very sensitive and very private. Mary insisted that she didn't mind the doctor and nurse being present, she said that it would be better if they stayed to hear what I had to say. I checked that Mary really meant what she said before I spoke about the incident.

"Mary, Jonjo knows all about us, I don't know how he found out, but he even knows that we were planning to go on holiday together to Tenerife," I began.

I went on to relate what had happened on the Cliff Walk that day and that Jonjo deliberately pushed me off the cliff. I warned Mary to be careful around Jonjo, I told her that he was capable of anything. I was surprised that Mary didn't seem in the least bit concerned about what I told her about her son, maybe Jonjo had already confessed?

"Mary, has Jonjo already told you all about what happened?" I asked. "If he said it was an accident, he is lying Mary. Don't trust him and whatever you do, please don't allow him to come here to visit me. Promise me that Mary, don't let him in here and be very careful yourself."

"Don't worry Ian, I won't let him in here, I promise," she replied tenderly.

"You've changed your hair Mary, it's like it used to be," I said.

Jesus, was I hearing things, had Mary just called me Ian?

Just then the door opened wide and Nurse Green walked in, followed by my daughter Annette and my son John. It was my turn to look bewildered! What the hell was going on? Where was I? Who was I?

Annette stared straight at me with tears in her eyes and exclaimed...

"Is Dad ok now, Mum?"

"Are you ok Dad?" asked John. "Do you need anything?"

"He appears fine Annette, but he is very confused. He thinks his first name is Conor rather than Ian and he thinks that he was pushed off a cliff by someone called Jonjo, but he seems to know me ok," explained Mary.

My mind couldn't focus. Of course, I knew who Annette and John were and I suddenly realised that this was not Mary Kenny in front of me. It was my wife Mary, it was my Mary, yes, my Mary. I couldn't help myself, I screamed out her name at the top of my voice. Everyone was startled and Annette looked frightened. I wanted to jump up and hug them all but I was suddenly drained of all energy. Luckily, I calmed down enough to persuade Doctor Brain not to give me the sedative he was already preparing.

"Doctor Brain explained that you were very confused Dad but that hopefully this confusion might eventually pass," said John. "He asked us to leave the kids at home for now, will you be up for seeing them tomorrow morning? They are all dying to see you again."

I couldn't answer, I just started crying. I couldn't stop until Mary handed me a tissue and held my hand.

"Perhaps we better wait a day or two, Dad," said Annette.

"No, don't do that, I want to see them now, are they outside?" I asked.

Doctor Brain 'stepped in', suggesting that it would be better to wait until tomorrow, Friday, after they get home from school. I realised then that I hadn't lost any days, it was still Thursday, so why did Doctor Brain think it was remarkable that I knew the date?

Dad you've no idea how ill you've been for the last few months," said John. "You are not in Beaumont Hospital in Dublin, you are in the Red House Nursing Home, in Maids Moreton. Do you know where that is Dad?"

"Yes of course I do, it's only five-minutes-drive from our house in Buckingham, but how did I get here so quickly, I only fell off the cliff in Howth, this morning," I replied.

"You didn't fall off any cliff this morning Dad, you suffered a severe stroke when you and Mum were in Dublin for uncle Peter's 70th birthday party. You were taken to Beaumont Hospital, where you slipped into a coma. You didn't come out of the coma for eight days but when you did, you didn't regain full consciousness. Dad, you have been in, what's known as, a continuous vegetative state, since last April. None of us ever thought you would come back to us. You have been lying here in this room for months Dad. I don't believe in miracles, but I don't know what else to call this. I have never heard of anyone making a full recovery, like you appear to have, after such a long time being 'out of it'."

"But I haven't been lying here, 'out of it', all that time John," I whispered. "I have been elsewhere. But it's fantastic and completely overwhelming to be back with you all."

I was suddenly completely exhausted. I couldn't keep my eyes open and I could hardly speak. I heard Doctor Brain say that I desperately needed some rest and that everyone should leave. I didn't even have the energy to acknowledge everyone saying goodbye and promising to be back tomorrow. I was slowly losing consciousness.

When I awoke, it was pitch dark outside. No one had bothered to pull the white spotted sky-blue curtains. Had I imagined everything that had just happened? Fortunately, Nurse Green soon came back into my room and handed me my charged up mobile phone and told me that it was after 10pm. I was 'over the moon' and still a little surprised when she confirmed that, Mary, John and Annette would be back to visit me, with my grandchildren, tomorrow. I had never felt so happy in my life before! But what was the past several months all about? Did I simply have a very long nightmare that seemed to pass in real time? Could I really have been dreaming continuously for months on end and have dreamed up such diverse and rich characters as that? Did I actually enter a parallel universe, not just once but several times? Did I perhaps regain consciousness here at the Red House Care Home, just as 'my other me' died, slipping off the Cliff Walk? What a weird dream that was, but I don't want another one like it!

I opened up my i-Phone. I looked at my photos. Nothing surprising there, there were no photographs taken after I thought that I had 'fallen asleep' on that park bench on the promenade. Tears came to my eyes as I looked at the photo of the gravestone once more, my brother Robert was dead again!

I 'pulled up' google. There were no references to the Lions Community. There was no hotel called the FFF Hotel in Howth, the site was still just a derelict old hotel. Peter Forman and Sons Limited had indeed closed down years ago and there was no Support Centre on the Hill of Howth called St John's. There had never been a Saint Patrick, shit then Hell must still exist! The Phoenix Centre in Grangegorman, did exist however, but what shocked me was to find that one of the nurses employed there was a certain Danny Boyd. How did I dream up someone I never heard of, but who actually does exist? I typed in the 'River Liffey Warblers', I couldn't find any reference to them anywhere. I next tried their best-known song *Get Me Out of Here* but again I couldn't find any reference to it. I laid my phone beside me, on my bed, and silently sang the song from start to finish! How could I have learned to play and sing a brand-new song in my dream, one which apparently doesn't exist but which I knew the chords and lyrics of? I typed in 'The Many Lives Interpretation'. Yes, it's there, it's a recent book by Professor Carlos Prieto. I decided that I should try to clear my head by getting some sleep, so I turned off my phone. My head was buzzing. I was going to enjoy the rest of my life to the fullest, I resolved to spend as much time as possible in the company of Mary, John, Annette, Aidan, Luke, Ella and Josie. Just one thing I need to do however before I start the rest of my new life, first thing tomorrow morning, I will order a copy of 'The Many Lives

Interpretation', from Amazon. I want to see if I enjoy reading it the second time, as much as I did the first time! I can't wait to track down Carlos and have a friendly chat with him. I wonder what he will think, when I tell him all about my recent experiences?

It's so unbelievably great to be back with my family again but I also hope that Mary Kenny finds some joy and happiness, in the universe, in which I left her. I must ask Nurse Green if she knows where my other mobile phone is!

Acknowledgements

There are many people I wish to thank for helping me complete my first novel. Especially my...

Sisters Marian and Fiona.

Brothers Peter, Patrick and Mark.

Children Annette and John.

Nephews and nieces, who are mentioned in the novel.

Niece Roisin Mc Andrew and my grandnephew Colin Mc Andrew.

Close friends Bernard Aldous, Tracey Maw, David Balls and Andy Hall.

My heartfelt thanks to all of you, plus anyone else I have failed to mention, for proofreading my earlier drafts, discussing the story with me and providing valuable constructive criticism throughout the seemingly endless process.

Finally, I wish to thank my very patient wife Mary for her positive suggestions, enthusiasm, encouragement and support during the writing of the first draft and the many re-writes.

About the Author

Born and brought up in Howth, Co Dublin, Ian Forman married his childhood sweetheart Mary just a few days after graduating and, a few days later, they emigrated from Ireland in search of work and adventure. They first went to Canada and lived there for two years before moving to and living in Belgium for a further ten years. They have now settled in the market town of Buckingham, UK. They have two grown-up children and four grandchildren. This is his first novel.

You can follow Ian on Twitter @irformanAuthor or on Instagram #irformanAuthor.

You are welcome to join Ian's Facebook Group ... I Never Said I Was Conor-Waking Up In Howth, where you can ask questions and make comments about the book and the author.